Of Silver and Curses

A Lingering Fates Novel

Maddox Grey

The Lingering Fates Series

This is an interconnected standalone series, meaning each book will focus on a different couple but will be set within the same world.

Technically, they can be read in any order, but the recommended reading order is below.

Of Melodies and Maledictions (Prequel Novella)

Of Silver and Curses (Book 1: Scythe and Talon)

Published by Greymalkin Press
www.greymalkinpress.com

Dev & Line Editing by Proofs by Polly
Copy-editing and Proofreading by Rachels Top Edits
Cover Design by Subtle Touch Creations

Ebook ISBN - 978-1-963368-11-6
Paperback ISBN - 978-1-963368-12-3

Note From Author

Let's chat real quick about what to expect in this book. This is a fantasy novel that contains adult content and situations. If it was a movie, it would probably be rated "R" for violence, language, and sexual content.

Did you read that last sentence in the movie guy voice? Because I definitely did.

Seriously though, both of the main characters are morally grey and have zero qualms about killing people. Which they do. Often and brutally.

Also... quick little note on language. I am a strange, strange person, and I've lived a bit of an odd life. I was born and raised in California, but was mostly raised by my Canadian grandmother and was then unofficially adopted by an Irish family in my late teens. You might be wondering why I'm mentioning this, and the reason is that I have a bit of a magpie approach when it comes to the English language.

Sometimes I like the American English spelling... sometimes I'm really attached to that extra "u" and go for the non-American version. Variety is the spice of life y'all.

Bless the soul of my copy-editor because she just sighs heavily at the start of each manuscript and deals with my eccentricities. So if you're an American and looking at a word and thinking it's not spelt right... it is most likely the non-American version of the word.

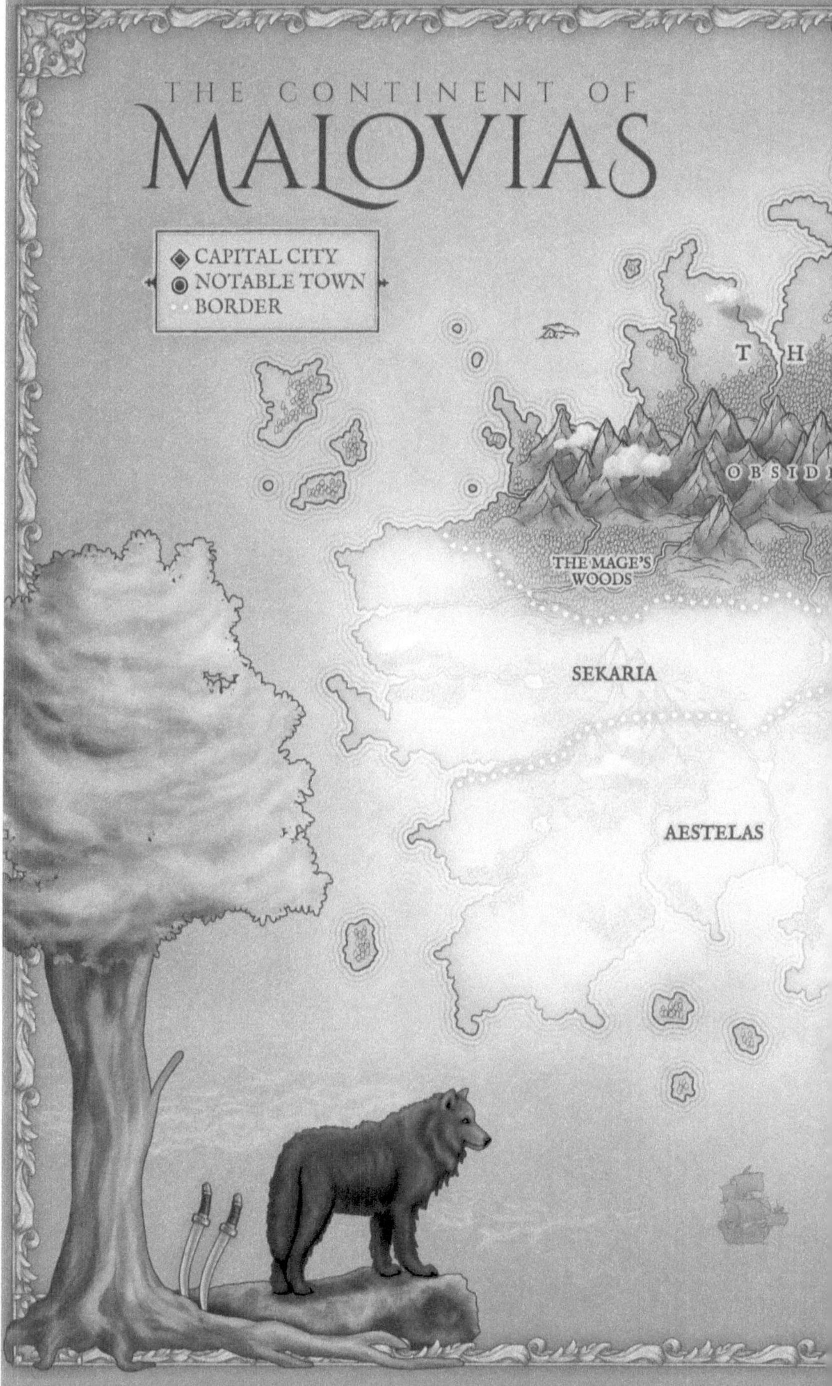

THE CONTINENT OF
MALOVIAS
CAPITAL CITY
NOTABLE TOWN
BORDER
T H
OBSIDI
THE MAGE'S
WOODS
SEKARIA
AESTELAS

WILDS
UNTAINS
THE WITCH'S WOODS
SOVARE
RENSWOOD
SHALEWOOD
NEIDELL
TENRESAN
MABRIA
ALBADRID
ELEOYN
KESDRIL
RIRITHA

This is for all my queer nonbinary folks.
You are fucking perfect.

PROLOGUE

~

Scythe

"WHAT IN ALL the hells is that?" the man screams as his ass hits the ground and he scrambles away. His less-than-graceful retreat cuts off when a body falls from the trees and lands directly behind him. Unfortunately in his haste, he couldn't stop in time, so he ends up halfway over his disemboweled friend. "Oh fuck!" He yanks his hand out of his friend's bloody mess of an abdomen and pales at the gore dripping off it.

"Her?" I stroke the feline's head when she bumps it against my waist. "Her name is Necos, and it's funny that you mention the hells." I point my scythe—still dripping with blood—at him. "Because she's what's commonly referred to as a devil cat."

In truth, she is an eastern mountain panther, but 'devil cat' has a nice ring to it, and considering her red eyes take on a bit of a glow at night, the name is apt. Necos purrs loudly as I reach under her chin to give her a good scratch.

"You're her! You're Scythe!" The raider pales even further. "I thought you were a myth!"

"Is that why you decided to trespass in my forest?" I twirl the weapon that gave me my nickname, sending flecks of blood flying. The man flinches as some of it lands on his cheek. "Clearly you're not from Eleoyn. Everyone there is well aware that the Witch of the Woods is flesh and blood, and they always come with far greater numbers than this." I glance around at the various body parts lying on the forest floor—some of them my work and others that of Necos and her pride. "Where are you from, friend?"

His tear-filled blue eyes watch in horror as one of the panthers leaps down from the trees to pick up an arm before disappearing back into the branches. "Ae-Ae-Aestelas." His voice shakes as he speaks.

"Interesting." I place the end of my scythe's long handle against the ground and lean on it like a staff. "You traveled all the way here from the opposite corner of the continent. Why?" I ask calmly. My little sister, Astria, refers to this tone as my "Scary Death Witch" voice. She isn't wrong. It tends to unnerve people when I speak as if we're discussing the weather while I'm covered in the blood and gore of their friends.

The forest can get lonely sometimes. I have to do something for entertainment.

"There's a rumor..." He presses his lips firmly together before shaking his head violently. "I don't know anything! Was just a hired guide, that's all. I swear!"

"Do you know why they call me the Witch of the Woods?" I start humming a tune, the low, dark sound carrying through the trees until it reverberates around us.

"What are you doing?" Panic flares on his face, and this time, he doesn't let the body of his dead friend stop him. He scuttles away, twisting to jump back to his feet, but immediately crashes down when the intestines he tore from the corpse trip him up.

I keep humming, and the silver tattoo of a serpent winding its way up my right arm starts to glow, as does the tattoo of a rearing buck with a full set of antlers on my left arm. Magic courses through and fills the air—dark and ominous.

Once upon a time, I used my magic for something other than death. Before the corruption, greed, and fear spread through the four kingdoms. Before my people left me here. The Last Guardian of the Wilds.

That is the other title the humans gave me. It is a lie. There is another to the west, but sooner or later, one of us will fall, and then I suppose the remaining one could truly bear the title.

Half a dozen dark, slithering forms slip from the trees. Their nearly ten-foot-long bodies easily glide over the roots, fallen branches, and rocks on the forest floor.

The raider screams and leaps to his feet, only to be knocked down by Necos as she slams into his back. As soon as he hits the ground, she nimbly jumps off him and into the branches above with the rest of the panthers. Glowing red eyes watch as the serpents close in.

I plant my foot on the man's chest after he flips onto his back. He struggles for a few seconds but freezes when the blade of my double-edged scythe kisses his throat, drawing a trickle of blood.

"Please," he pleads as one of the serpents slides over his chest and another flicks out its forked tongue next to his eye.

I stop humming, but the magic permeating the air remains. "Most people think a witch's tattoos correspond to specific abilities." The antlers of the buck on my left arm shimmer as I move my arm to show it off more. "They're wrong; our tattoos are a reflection of our soul and our bond to the forest. Always two animals—one prey and one predator because you cannot have one without the other."

He whimpers as the snake on his chest raises its head to stare at him over the scythe. Its yellow eyes shine brightly against its obsidian black scales.

"Sylan's asper," I tell him. "The song I hummed summoned them here. They're only found in this forest." One of the aspers winds its way up the scythe's handle and rests its triangular head on my arm. I smile at it. "Their venom is necrotic and also causes paralysis." I look away from the serpent to meet the man's terrified eyes. "In other words, you won't be able to move as your body slowly rots. Excruciating way to die."

"I'll tell you anything!" He squeezes his eyes shut as the asper smelling his cheek crawls over his face to coil on the other side, ready to strike.

A mild wave of disappointment flashes through me. Given that small amount of backbone he showed earlier, I thought he would've held out longer.

"How lovely." I lift my foot off his chest but keep the scythe at his throat. "Go on then."

"Call them off!" Trembles race through his body, and I have to pull my scythe away so I don't accidentally slice his neck open, then a hum slips from my lips, melodic and peaceful. One by one, all the aspers disperse back into the forest—except the one resting its head on my right arm. That one climbs further up until it moves around my shoulders and then back down my left arm.

"You were saying something about a rumor?" I drawl.

Slowly, he opens his eyes and peers around, his expression relaxing for a moment when he sees the aspers have left but quickly blanching upon spotting the remaining one on my arm. Necos leaps down from the trees and prowls towards me—ignoring the serpent—and a low rumble pours from her throat as she looks at the raider.

"I suggest you answer quickly," I say mildly. "My friend is hungry."

"The Eleoyn King has increased the reward!" he blurts. "It's nothing official yet. He's only offered it to the top tier of the mage hunters—the ones who have killed the most Obscuras."

A small amount of dread pools in my gut, not at the mention of the Obscuras—rebel mages—being killed in droves, but because I know what is required to claim the reward, which is cutting a safe path through my forest to the Wilds up north. It's the untamed land that no one from the four kingdoms has set foot in for the last few centuries, not since the Malovian War that ravaged the continent and resulted in the kingdoms being formed in the first place. The Eleoyn King doesn't want to visit the Wilds for its beauty—he desires the vast resources it contains.

Before all trade stopped between the northern part of the continent above the Obsidian Mountains and the four kingdoms, there was a steady supply of gems and other minerals that the mages require for most of their casting. Not to mention all the nobles who love to cover themselves in shiny jewels.

When it became clear that the four kingdoms were on a downward trajectory though, the denizens of the Wilds—mostly werewolf packs, dryads, and nymphs—pulled back and chose to isolate themselves instead. They'd had enough of war and wanted no further part of the madness the rest of the continent was wading into.

The rulers of the various kingdoms did not take this news well, but it is no easy feat to get to the Wilds. Before they can even attempt to traverse the Obsidian Mountains, they have to get through me or my fellow guardian to the west. I don't know why he feels compelled to be a guardian, but the witches swore an oath to protect our forest and those who dwell beyond the Obsidian Mountains. My kin might have abandoned that purpose, but I will not.

"So the king increased the reward—and what? You lot thought you could just cut a trail through *my* forest?" I cock my head. "No one has walked into these woods and out again in over a century. What exactly made you think you were special?"

"Why do you even care about guarding this place? We all saw the witches set sail for Arandia twelve years ago, which means they left you behind," he counters in a voice that barely trembles. I'm marginally impressed that he managed to dig down deep to find his balls again. "Why do you still fight when you know your death and the conquering of the Wilds is inevitable? You shouldn't be here anymore."

The fear still present in his eyes betrays the bravado he's trying to pull off.

"Oh? Do you—a human—presume to tell me where I should be?" I let out a low chuckle. "These are *my* woods. Even if you thought I was a myth, you must have known something prowled this forest. Otherwise, the four kingdoms would have marched through it long ago to pollute the Wilds with their greed as they have their own lands."

"I don't have anything else to tell you." The raider's gaze flicks quickly between me, the serpent, and the panther. "Everyone knows the Eleoyn King is desperate to get through these woods, so if one of us can create a safe trail, surely he'll reward us for our efforts! That's all this was! I've caused you no harm!"

Tension bleeds through the air for several moments as I ponder him. "Very well." I move away from him and wave a hand at a break in the trees leading away from here. "If you truly haven't harmed me, then you can leave."

He quickly gets to his feet and takes a few steps towards the path to freedom before freezing. "Is . . . is this a trick?"

I smile. "That depends."

"On what?" he asks shakily.

"I am the forest." I raise the asper to my face and nuzzle its nose with my own. "And the forest is me." My silver eyes fall on the raider. "If you've harmed the forest, *then you've harmed me.*"

His hands fall to a pouch attached to his belt.

"That's what I thought." I shake my head as if I'm disappointed, when, really, I've known all along how this was going to play out. Perhaps Astria is right and I do spend too much time with the panthers, but I can't help but play with my food before I eat it.

Granted, I won't be eating the hunter, but my forest is always hungry.

The raider spins on his heels and bolts, only to let out a cry as a root from a large oak tree rips from the earth to trip him. In an instant, Necos lands on his back, pinning him to the earth as I stroll forward.

"You and your men raided a den of Tremarcian bears while their mother was out. The teeth of the cubs are in your pouch. I can still feel their anguish and fear." I slam my scythe into his leg and cherish the sound of his screams. "The forest will claim what it is owed."

The asper slides down my arm and onto the ground beside the man as he alternates between sobbing and cursing. This is exactly why I hate the raiders. At least the mage hunters can be a challenge for me. The raiders just pillage my lands and then get all hysterical when I pull their bodies apart piece by piece or let some of the beasties chew on their flesh. They don't even have the decency to make me earn their screams of terror.

Pathetic. I could be enjoying a late-afternoon nap right now.

I pull my blade free and watch as he tries to drag himself away, only to cry out as the asper strikes him. Summoning the last of his strength, the raider lunges to his feet and takes off as fast as he can deeper into the woods.

I debate telling him he's going the wrong way, but why bother? It's not like he'd ever reach the border of the land I claim as mine. And he wouldn't make it far even if he weren't practically dragging his wounded leg behind him. He's got a mile at most, then his body will give out as the venom courses through his blood and rots him from the inside out.

Necos lets out an annoyed chuffing sound as we watch the raider.

"Don't be like that," I chide her. "Your pride has plenty to eat. It's not my fault you're fussy about meat and don't like things killed by the asper. Ingesting their venom won't hurt you at all."

The panther gives me a baleful look before turning around and heading back to her pack, then I watch as the asper glides into the forest. At least the serpents aren't fussy.

I look up through the forest canopy to the bright summer sky. The hunt didn't take nearly as long as I hoped, nor was it all that satisfying. I know the myths that surround me, that I can feel anyone who sets foot in my woods and am aware of every step and trespass they commit in my domain. It isn't true though. Not exactly. I can feel anything within roughly a mile radius, but the mage hunters have ways of disguising their presences. They are, after all, mages themselves. The only difference between them and the Obscuras is that their magic is sanctioned by the king.

This had to be at least the tenth group of raiders to plunder my forest as they tried to find a way to the Wilds. They aren't a danger to me—I kill them with laughable ease—but they have a tendency to slaughter the young and innocent denizens of my home, and that annoys me.

I just want to fight someone who can take a stab to the chest and try to hack my head off in retaliation. Is that really so much to ask for?

The scent of blood must have roused the jackals from their den despite it still being daytime because a symphony of barks and cackles sound throughout the trees. At least *they* aren't picky eaters.

With some reluctance, I turn to the north and start walking. Three taps to the ring on my right pinky finger, and the scythe vanishes. Mage magic is good for some things. If only there were some way to magically fix things between me and my sister. We'd been in the middle of an argument when I sensed the intruders and seized the opportunity to get away.

I was hoping I could work out my aggression on them, but that wasn't the case, and now, without the raiders distracting me, all the frustration and anger I felt earlier comes rushing back in. I love my sister more than anything, but I don't know how to talk to her anymore. These past few months, it feels like everything I say is wrong and just furthers this divide between us.

I glance down at my clothes. Blood and what I think might be a bit of brain matter are splattered across my light green top, courtesy of Necos grabbing one of the raiders, hauling him up a tree, and then dropping him onto a boulder below. My dark brown pants aren't in much better shape. I'm also soaked in sweat thanks to the hot summer day.

Instead of turning towards home, I head in the opposite direction towards a nearby stream. I'll clean up and maybe use this time to figure out what to say to Astria, hopefully something that won't result in us fighting again. Plus, I further rationalize, this will give her some time to cool off, and I'll be less frustrated when I return as well.

This is a good plan, I assure myself. We'll both be in a better state of mind, and we'll be able to have a rational conversation like two adults.

"IF YOU'RE SO eager to die, I can just slit your throat here!" I pull my favorite dagger from the sheath on my thigh and point it at the blonde-haired young woman before me. Between the weapon and the fact that my words are barely more than a snarl, she should be trembling. Just last month, a mage hunter decked out in full armor and sporting a ridiculously large broadsword pissed himself at the sight of me.

The difference between that man and my younger sister is that she has a spine. I would know—I raised her to have one.

Really regretting that now.

"If you're so eager to be dramatic, I can build a stage for you here," Astria snaps back. "Necos and the rest of the panthers can be your audience!"

Necos cracks open one bright green eye before closing it again, then lets out a low, grumbling noise that very clearly says she is not happy about our argument ruining her nap.

I inhale deeply and try to calm down a little. Up until the last few months, my sister and I had never argued once. I'd fought with everyone else in my family, but she and I are always on the same team—until that damn human showed up and stole her heart.

"Astria," I say evenly. "You know it's not safe beyond these woods." I fling my hand out and point south. "Mage hunters are crawling all over the Eleoyn Kingdom, and the borders are shut down to the other three—not that they're any safer. I can protect you here, but not out there."

Some of the fire dampens in Astria's cornflower blue eyes, but the determination remains. "There's more to life than safety, Cece."

My heart clenches at hearing the nickname she gave me when she was a toddler and couldn't pronounce my full name. Nobody but her ever calls me that, and hardly anyone refers to me by my real name anymore. I am Scythe to most of the people who cross my path.

My sister is all I have left. I've sacrificed so much for her because she is my everything, but I am *not* her everything, and that simple fact has been bleeding me dry the last few months. Ever since she started talking about leaving the woods.

Leaving me.

"Look." I take another deep, calming breath. I can do this. I can be reasonable. "I understand that first loves can be exciting, and Ravyn is a sweet girl, but she's human—you're a witch. It's not nearly as dangerous for her to go gallivanting about Eleoyn."

Astria lets out a scornful laugh. "I may be born of witches, but I have no magic, and look at me." She gestures at her face before holding up her arms. "Not a lot of witches with blonde hair and blue eyes. Not to mention the lack of tattoos. People look at me and don't think witch—they think human."

She isn't wrong. With my lilac hair and silver eyes that match the silver of the tattoos winding their way around my body, there is no mistaking me for anything but a witch. We don't get our tattoos until our twenty-first birthdays, but our eyes are always silver and our hair is always some shade of blue, green, or purple. My parents knew what Astria was the second she opened her newborn eyes and revealed them to be blue.

I think they are beautiful, whereas my parents thought they were shameful, and they never let her forget it.

"You're still witchkin," I argue. "Your blood still runs far darker than that of a human. The fact that you have no magic will not make a difference to the mage hunter who cuts off your damn head!" My silver tattoos flash brightly as the hold on my temper starts to fray.

"Talon will keep us safe." Astria raises her chin. "They're a good fighter—as good with their daggers as you are with your scythe and good with a sword as well."

I scoff. "Trust me. Talon's mediocre with their sword at best."

A wry grin spreads across her face, one I haven't seen in quite some time thanks to all the tension between us. "Really? Is that why you haven't bedded anyone since them? If Talon is so mediocre, I would think you'd be eager to wipe the memory of their *sword.*"

Once again, my mind helpfully conjures up the image of Ravyn's older sibling, Talon, and how it felt to have their hands on me. We shared one night of passion . . . which ended with our blades at each other's throats.

I haven't seen them since that night nine months ago. They— along with Ravyn—belong to a troupe of traveling performers who are currently camped in the town on the edge of my forest. Much to my annoyance, the troupe has been lingering in the area for far longer than these types of performers tend to. Especially considering how small Shalewood is. It's not like they're making much money there, so I don't know why they haven't left yet.

It's inconvenient for a lot of reasons. It's meant Ravyn has been able to court my sister these past few months, and I haven't been able to go to Shalewood without the risk of running into Talon. So I've just stayed in my forest . . . brooding. It isn't that I don't love my home—I have no intention of ever leaving it—but I do have needs, and my fingers can only get me so far.

Usually I disguise my witchier characteristics and go have some fun with someone in town for a few hours, but I haven't been able to do that because I can't get Talon's *sword* out of my mind.

That's a lie. The sex was amazing, definitely the best fuck I've ever had in my life, but it's the hours we spent together before they pinned me against a tree that haunt me. Dancing around the bonfire and trading wry jokes back and forth.

Talon made me feel alive in a way that nobody else has, and fates damn it all, they did fuck like a god. That definitely didn't hurt.

"Thinking about that *mediocre sword*?" Astria gives me a knowing look, that impish grin still splashed across her face.

"You're hilarious." I glare at her. "Perhaps we should build *you* a stage so you can practice your jokes. Necos was amused, I'm sure."

The panther's tail twitches, but other than that, she continues to ignore us.

"Perhaps that's what I'll do with the troupe," Astria says lightly. "Everyone has to pull their weight, so I'll have to do something to earn my place with them."

"You would." I nod. "If you were going—which you're not."

"And how are you going to keep me here?" she asks softly. "Because you'll have to chain me down to keep me from Ravyn. I love her."

"You barely know her!" I throw my hands up in the air. Necos officially gives up on her nap and leaps to her feet, stalking off on silent, angry paws into the dark forest. "This passion between you two will fade! Then you'll be alone in a land full of people who want you dead!"

"No, they want *you* dead!" Astria's blue eyes light up again with frustration and rage. I hate that this is how she looks at me now, but I don't know how to stop it. "You're the Last Guardian! The Witch of the Woods! It's you who hunts down the raiders and mage hunters who set foot in this forest." She shakes her head. "And you know nothing of love."

I clench my teeth. "You are twenty-two years old. I've seen two centuries come and go. I'm well aware of how fleeting love is. You are young and naive, and I won't have you put your life in jeopardy over some damn human girl who whispered sweet nothings into your ear!"

"You know nothing," she repeats harshly. "Vaeril walked away from you like it was barely a hardship! Your own fucking mate! If anything, he seemed eager!"

I flinch as she strikes at the old wound. Vaeril and I were mated for nearly a century. She's right. He left me like it was nothing. Like *I* was nothing.

"And all you have now are one-night stands with strangers who don't even know who you are!" She laughs, the sound striking me once more. "You're a liar, *Scythe*."

I open my mouth to say something I'll probably regret but click it shut when I feel it—the presence of two beings heading straight towards us.

Speaking of one-night stands . . .

"You told them where we live?" I suck in a breath. Astria has always gone to see Ravyn in town; she's never brought her back here to our home.

"Ravyn is going to help me pack." My sister swallows. "Talon offered to help as well."

A pained sound slips from my lips before I can claw it back. This is really happening. I'm losing her. Gods, how my parents and mate would laugh at me now. I gave up everything for Astria, and she is walking away from me.

The betrayal cuts deep.

"Cece—" she starts.

"Don't." I take a step back. "Enjoy your life, Astria. For your sake, I hope your faith in Talon's ability to keep you and Ravyn safe isn't misplaced, because if you get into trouble out there, I won't come to save you."

She calls after me, but I ignore her as I make my way up the winding stairs that lead to my home. I start humming halfway up, and the stairs fold behind me until they lie flat against the tree trunk, preventing Astria from following after me. Or Talon from coming to see me. The asshole would probably gloat about how my life is crumbling.

When I reach the top of the stairs, I pad around on the wrap-around porch and sit down, my feet dangling over the edge. Necos appears within minutes and stretches out next to me. Soon, all the panthers make their way over and choose a spot to settle near me, offering their silent support as tears stream down my cheeks.

We watch as a dark-haired young woman enters the clearing and wraps her arms around my sobbing sister. Together, the two of them make their way up to Astria's home, which is in a tree several over from mine. My gaze pulls away from them to the second person who enters the clearing.

I'm far enough up that I can't see them clearly, but I'm still painfully aware of what they look like because they haunt my dreams almost every night. Chiseled cheekbones, strong jawline, and captivating eyes. Silver earrings that dangle from their right ear, declaring their nonbinary nature, and the multiple daggers they keep strapped to them at all times.

Sometimes, in my dreams, I'm slowly pulling those daggers off them and setting them aside. More often than not, they're pushing one against my throat.

Not sure what it says about me that I'm turned on either way.

But those are just dreams. They're not real. I know without a doubt that Talon is looking up at me—with hatred. They are a cursed werewolf, and it was the witches who cursed their bloodline.

It doesn't take my sister long to pack. Given that she is signing up for a nomadic lifestyle, it isn't like she can take much with her. She hesitates for a moment and looks over her shoulder up towards my house, but then Ravyn slips her hand into hers and the two of them walk off into the woods without a backwards glance.

Talon stares up into the trees for a long moment before turning and trailing after the girls.

And suddenly, for the first time in my entire life, I am alone.

CHAPTER ONE

~

Talon

ONE YEAR Later

"I DON'T BELIEVE I know you."

I turn slightly from where I casually stand in front of the ice sculpture of a swan—only rich people would pay for such a thing in late summer—to face the man who spoke.

"It's a masquerade." My lips curl up into a charming but slightly mischievous grin. "Aren't we all mysteries to each other this evening?" I brush two fingers against the silver stylized jackal mask that covers my upper face. A crown made of the same silver with gold woven through it rests on my head, my black hair that is usually tousled is styled neatly this evening. I don't just look good —I appear as something infinitely more useful.

I look rich and like I *belong* here. It truly is amazing how far the proper attire and confidence can get you.

The man laughs, his gaudy gold wolf mask catching the light. "A wit to match your mask. If the old gods were still around, do you think they would take kindly to you borrowing their appearance?"

"Perhaps I *stole* both the mask and the crown," I say slyly. "It was said Azdall preferred to be impressed by their followers rather than worshiped like the rest of the gods."

I don't consider myself a follower of the fae gods, but if I were, Azdall would be the one I would choose to devote myself to. A nonbinary god of thieves? How could I not? Of course, I'd still rob them blind and probably steal their heart. I am quite good at my trade.

Maybe not the stealing of hearts lately, but I'm sure I'll figure out that mess sooner or later.

"Ah, Aurora, thank you, my dear," the wolf-masked man says in greeting as a woman wearing a gold mask stylized with roses that only covers her eyes hands him a glass of wine. Her golden blonde hair goes perfectly with the light blue dress that clings to her every curve, leaving little to the imagination. Gold jewelry adorns her neck, wrists, and fingers. I'm fairly certain there are even gold flecks in the pink gloss on her full lips.

The goddess of love made flesh.

Or at least that's what she's clearly going for. Erdite was known for dressing simply and letting her beauty speak for itself. She wasn't one to drown herself in jewels. At least according to the stories. The gods had been absent from these lands for quite some time.

"Who's your friend?" she purrs. Blue eyes almost the same shade as her dress peer out from the mask to study me, a knowing smile playing across her lips.

Too bad her eyes are the wrong shade of blue. Not that it matters. Those eyes had been a lie. Such a cunning little liar though.

"A mystery." The man laughs. "Perhaps we should just call them Azdall for the evening."

I tip my head in acknowledgment, that easy, charming grin still on my face.

"Well, our mysterious friend . . ." The woman sips her own wine before tilting her head in a way that elongates her neck and draws my eye down to where she is doing an impressive job of pushing her chest forward. The man certainly seems to think so based on how glued his eyes are to her cleavage. "Are you enjoying our party?"

"I am enjoying myself." A waiter with a plain black mask walks by, and I swipe a glass of wine from his tray. "And if you are the hosts responsible for this delightful party, then you have my thanks and gratitude for saving me from a dull evening."

"A dull evening in Albadrid?" The man chuckles, his eyes flicking away from the woman and back to me. "Then you are doing it wrong. This city is full of all sorts of delights." He turns and nips at the woman's neck, and she lets out a husky laugh, but her eyes are on me.

My tongue darts out to lick a drop of wine off my glass, and I'm rewarded with a flush of color across her cheeks. If the man—who I know to be her husband—notices, he probably attributes it to the way he's tracing his hand across her hip.

"Perhaps I can show our would-be Azdall around?" Aurora offers. "Show him all the fun he's missing out on so he comes to more of our parties."

A brief flicker of irritation runs through me at being referred to as *he*. The man likely only used *them* because he's going along with the whole Azdall bit, but his wife doesn't bother, even though she's seen me outside of this mask and knows the earrings dangling from my right ear aren't just for show.

Then again, I guess I shouldn't expect much consideration from nobles. Even one who has chosen to dress like a goddess who regularly switched between she and they.

"Splendid idea!" the man exclaims. "Although you'll have to lose the mask for our usual events. This masquerade was my beautiful wife's idea—sprung it on me last week, and our poor staff had to scramble to update the invites. Apparently, the prince is holding one soon, so they must be all the rage."

"Please. It's not like the staff had anything better to do." She laughs. "They'd just laze around otherwise. Honestly, I think we overpay them."

My smile gets a bit of an edge to it, but neither notice as I extend an elbow to the woman. "I would be honored if you would show me around. Perhaps I've judged this city too harshly."

"Come." She loops her arm through mine. "Let me introduce you to my cousin."

"Wonderful! We could have a god marry into the family." The man chuckles as we walk away. For twenty minutes, I let the woman drag me around the room, weaving between elaborate ice sculptures as we walk across the marble floor that no doubt cost an obscene amount of money. My costume is a big hit amongst the other partygoers.

Technically, worship of the old gods is outlawed in the Eleoyn Kingdom, but it's common for the working folk to still have altars or little trinkets dedicated to their patron god despite the risks. If they're caught with such things though, they're fined—if they're lucky.

If they're not lucky . . . well, the Eleoyn citizens do love a good public execution.

But the rules are different for the wealthy. To them, someone coming dressed as Azdall is a novelty. A decade ago, I would have found it frustrating and vile. Now, I just find it amusing . . . and convenient, especially considering how things are going to play out tonight.

Because the wealthy do have a different set of rules and assumptions. While the younger me raged against them, the older me embraces it for one simple reason—once you understand how the wealthy operate, it becomes child's play to take advantage of the system.

If you are bold enough.

"And so I told her she was welcome to sit on it and find out for herself," I finish telling yet another salacious story. Aurora's cousin laughs loudly. It's more a shrilling sound than anything, and I'm thankful for the mask because I can't stop myself from wincing a little as it pierces my sensitive ears.

"Oh!" Aurora waves at someone across the room. "So sorry, Delilah, but I must introduce my companion to someone else."

"Will you come and see me later?" The strawberry-blonde woman blinks her hazel eyes at me. I'm fairly certain she's trying to flutter her eyelashes, but clearly it's something she should practice in the mirror because she's failing at it miserably.

"I will do my best."

She giggles as I gently grasp her hand and raise it to my mouth, brushing a kiss against the back of her knuckles.

The hand around my arm tightens as my hostess tugs me away in the direction she waved at, and I glance across the room to where her husband is well into his fifth glass of wine by my count. The tall, broad-shouldered man is gesturing wildly as he regals some story to the dozen other partygoers who have gathered around him.

Everyone here is wealthy, but not *marble floors and solid gold masks* wealthy. They all want a piece of him, which is why they hang on his every word and laugh at the perfect moments. My gaze cuts to a slender woman with fiery red hair in a crow mask and then to a dark-haired, enormous man wearing a silver fox mask.

Neither of them acknowledge me in any way, but they both meander through in my general direction. The tug on my arm grows more insistent as we duck out of the crowd and up a flight of steps. Servants swerve around us, their eyes cast to the floor as we go up another set of stairs, until the noise of the party dies down and Aurora pushes me against a wall, her lips on mine a second later.

She tastes of wine and a sweetness, likely from whatever gloss she applied to her lips. I part my mouth, letting her tongue slip in and teasing it with my own. She moans against me, fingers gripping my arm even tighter before she finally pulls back with a giggle.

"I didn't think you'd actually come!" At least it's a nicer laugh than her cousin's. Lighter and more lyrical.

"How could I deny a beauty such as you?" I grip her by the waist and flip us so she's against the wall, and her perfect body with its soft curves writhes underneath my grip as her eyes darken.

"To think I almost didn't stop at Sapphire today," she purrs. "I would have missed out on making your"—her hand drops to cup my cock through my pants—"acquaintance."

Revulsion flashes through me, and I want to rip her hand away, but I keep all that off my face. It's not the first time a noble has gotten grabby with me, and it's not like I'll allow it to go any further. Ravyn hates that I do this. She doesn't understand why I can't just slip in unnoticed.

It's not the same though. I can tolerate their hands on me because it'll make the look on their faces that much sweeter in the end.

"And such a tragedy that would have been." I grin and glide my right hand up her body to brush against the side of her breast.

She lets out a harsh, excited breath. I'd purposely teased her at the brothel earlier, leading her on enough to secure an invite to this party.

Just as she reaches to unbuckle my belt, something crashes in the stairwell. We both freeze, and she stares to where the sound came from like a rat who has been raiding the kitchen when the lanterns suddenly light up.

"Is your room up here, love?" I ask in a low, husky tone with just the right amount of urgency.

She wavers for a moment, dropping her hand away from my crotch as she thinks over the full ramifications of what she's doing. It's one thing to cheat on your husband in a brothel. It's quite another to meet a stranger in a brothel, invite them to a party, and then fuck them while your husband is two floors down.

My thumb glides over her nipple, the fabric of her dress thin enough that I can feel how hard it is, and she shivers beneath my touch. I lean forward and kiss her harshly, stealing her breath at the same moment my left hand drops to her ass and tugs her against me. She gasps into my mouth, and I swallow the sound.

Then I pull back to gaze into her eyes again. "Your room?" I repeat.

"Thi-thi-this way," she stammers, and I step back enough to let her guide me down the hall and around the corner. Only two rooms are in this hallway; dark mahogany doors at the very end and another set of doors to the left with a lighter wood, which is another unique trait of the rich—married couples typically keep separate bedrooms.

She quickly inserts her ring into the lock above the handle of the lighter-colored door, then a click sounds, and she opens it, pulling me in with her. Immediately, her lips are back on mine as she frantically explores my body with her hands.

"Show me your bed," I murmur. "I want you on it so I can feast on you. Would you like that, my pet?"

"Fuck." She quivers against me. "I'm so glad your favorite was occupied and I struck up the courage to talk to you. I never talk to any of the other members at Sapphire."

"How fortunate for me indeed," I tease as she leads me further into the bedroom. A massive four-poster bed sits against the wall to the left, and she practically leaps onto it. I have to bite my lip to keep from laughing at her enthusiasm . . . and her gullibility.

The gold mask goes flying a second later, revealing a stunning face, high cheekbones, and perfectly arched eyebrows. Everything about her face is captivating, including the makeup that has been expertly applied to play up her pretty features.

Just like when I met her the first time, she does absolutely nothing for me. She's so . . . boring. There's absolutely nothing unique about her. Pretty sure I would have to beg my dick to get hard. Maybe resort to bribery of some kind. Luckily, I don't have to worry about that right now.

"Hands above your head." I unbuckle my belt and slide it free. She whimpers as I crawl onto the bed and straddle her but does as I order, stretching her arms up. I lean down and kiss her collarbone, then trail kisses up her neck as I wrap the leather around her wrists and the wood slots of the headboard.

She hisses a little when I pull the knot tight and glances up at where I tied her to the bed.

"Don't go anywhere." I kiss her nose before rolling off the bed and heading towards the door.

"Wait, where are you going?" she calls after me in confusion.

I swing the door open and grin at the crow mask and fox mask that greet me. My two best friends, Mattias and Vesi. "Told you it'd be easy."

"It's pathetic how quickly they fall for your bullshit," Vesilia complains, shoving her crow mask on top of her head. "And these masks are ridiculous."

"You think so? I kind of like mine." Mattias tugs his fox mask off and admires it. "Made me feel dashing."

As usual, I get a little amusement at seeing them next to each other. Vesilia is pale-skinned with a sprinkling of freckles across her nose and cheeks. She looks sweet and wholesome, which is hilarious because she is anything but.

Meanwhile, Mattias towers over her with his broad build wrapped in light-brown skin. His curly brown hair would soften his appearance but he keeps it closely cropped to his skull, which only draws more attention to the jagged scar starting above his right eyebrow and cutting diagonally across his face all the way down to his jawline. The skin puckers in some areas where the cut was extra deep. Between his large build and roughed-up face, he looks like the far more intimidating one of the pair, but he's the type to catch a spider and release it outside whereas Vesilia would burn the house down.

I step back to let in my two best friends and shut the door behind them, then they follow me into the bedroom, where Aurora jerks on the bed. "What the fuck is going on?"

"Oh." I shrug. "We're robbing you."

She lets out an ear-piercing shriek, and I roll my eyes before strolling over to the bed and slapping my hand over her mouth.

"First of all, this room is soundproof. I activated the charm already, so nobody will hear you."

Her eyes dart to Vesilia and Mattias, who are already pillaging the jewelry boxes. The trick with jewelry is you don't want to take anything too unique because it will be harder to sell off. Nobody wants to get caught holding the stolen heart-shaped diamond necklace with hand-carved silver roses that's been passed down through six generations of some asshole noble's bloodline. That is a quick way to land yourself either on the gallows or in the darkest prison cell imaginable. But the everyday jewels? The sapphires and emeralds set in simple gold bands? Those are easy to sell off and almost impossible to trace.

"And second," I continue, "nobody is going to harm you in any way. Honestly, none of us have the slightest interest in you. We don't slum it with nobles; all of you are terrible in bed."

Vesilia laughs as she examines a gold ring, holding it up to the light of a nearby mage lantern.

"It's true," Mattias grunts out. "No creativity."

"I'm going to take my hand away. No more screaming." I lift my hand but stay on the bed, waiting to see how she'll react. Aurora eyes us all, an indignant rage stamped all over her pretty features, and then starts wailing again. Mattias winces and Vesilia just snorts and goes back to examining jewelry.

The screams die a second later when I press a silver dagger to her throat. "Perhaps I should amend my previous statement about no harm." A little bit of fear creeps into her eyes at the coldness in my tone. "Your life means *nothing* to me. The only reason I have no interest in killing you is because these sheets are satin and the blood will be impossible to get out, but that won't stop your prick of a husband from demanding the impossible from the staff and then punishing them when they fail."

"Could always carry her to the bathing chamber," Vesilia points out. "Cleanup would be easy."

"My friend makes a valid point." I turn the blade and tap the flat side against Aurora's neck. She does her best to sink into the bed away from me, but I see the glimmer of calculation in her eyes, so I get to my final point. "And just so you know, it's in your best interest not to breathe a word of this to anyone. We both know you can have all these jewels replaced within a week. Your husband spends far more money on the three mistresses he has on the side; he won't even notice the added expense."

Aurora doesn't even blink at the reveal. She knows where her husband spends his free time. Just like he knows she makes regular visits to the upscale brothel. Affairs aren't just common amongst the wealthy—they are expected.

There *are* still rules though, and one of them is to not fuck your spouse's political rival.

"I'm sure you're aware that businesses like Sapphire keep extensive records—who was with who and for how long. They keep the records private of course, but it's how they handle the monthly billing." I tilt my head, still adorned with the jackal mask. Aurora already knows what I look like because when she met me earlier today I hadn't been wearing it. My mask is controlled by magic, and I don't want to reveal that little tidbit because if she recognizes it as fae magic and not the work of a mage spell, she might be more inclined to report me regardless of what I threaten her with.

The fact that I'm not fae won't matter. The mage hunters will torture me until I tell them where I acquired the mask, and I'm too pretty to have my face fucked up like Mattias'.

"I might have gotten my hands on said billing." I boop her nose with the flat edge of the knife. "And you, my dear, have been very, very naughty."

"What are you talking about?" Her voice trembles as she speaks.

I grin wickedly. "Twice a week, you visit Sapphire and rent a room for five hours, but you only make use of the courtesans for *one* hour."

"Strange that your husband's main political rival has the same schedule," Mattias adds.

"Does make one wonder," Vesilia chimes in as she pulls an entire drawer out of a jewelry box and looks at it for a few seconds before dumping it into her bag.

"We don't—we aren't—" Aurora starts to hyperventilate as she stumbles over her words. "We were just talking!"

Mattias and Vesilia pause their raid of the jewelry to stare at the noblewoman on the bed. The one who dragged me—a person she's only known for a few hours—to her bedroom. Then the three of us burst out laughing.

"You should work on a better cover story while you lie there in case your dear husband ever starts to suspect something is amiss." My thumb holds a steady pressure against a glyph on the back of the blade's handle, and after an intentional mental command on my part, the dagger vanishes back into the tattoo on my palm.

Fae magic is nifty.

I roll off the bed and help myself to the jewelry on this side of the room.

She literally has an entire chest of drawers dedicated *just to bracelets*. This heist was a bit of a risk because Aurora's husband is on a first-name basis with several of the king's advisors, but only her ring can access her bedroom, and it only works if it's still on her finger—and only if that finger still has blood coursing through it. Vesilia literally pouted when I told her that after she suggested we just cut it off. Then she declared that I couldn't possibly charm a noblewoman enough to get an invite to a private party and that there was no way we could just enter through the front door. From that point, I hadn't been able to walk away from the challenge, and here we are.

I admire the sparkling jewels laid out before me, enough to feed me, my sister, and Astria for probably the rest of our lives. Granted, I won't be keeping all of this, but still, the risk is more than worth it.

Plus I'll be able to brag about this for years to come to Vesilia. That alone makes it worth it.

Fifteen minutes later, we're tying the bags beneath Vesilia's ridiculously puffy skirt. She's wearing tights underneath it and a harness over that, so we have plenty of hooks to secure things to. Her corset has thin gold chains with little trinkets attached that chime against each other while she walks to cover up the sounds of the jewelry knocking around.

Once we're satisfied everything is secure, Vesilia and Mattias head out. They'll leave first since they arrived together.

Aurora's bright blue eyes glare at me as I saunter over to the bed before I deactivate the spell on my belt, which ensured the knot would stay, and untie her wrists, slipping the belt back onto my pants. She waits on the bed, frozen, waiting to see what I'll do next. When I hold my hand out to her, she blinks, clearly not expecting it.

"Come on." I grab her wrist and pull her off the bed when she makes no move to take my hand. "It's time for us to head back downstairs."

She stares at me for a long moment, her eyes sparking with outrage. "You can't be serious."

"I'm craving another glass. As much as I hate to compliment anything about your husband, his taste in wine is quite good." I loop my arm around hers and drag her towards the door.

She plants her feet and refuses to move. "You seduced me under false pretenses, *robbed me*, and then blackmailed me into silence." I nod, and her eyes widen. "And now you expect me to just walk around the party with you?"

I give her the same panty-melting grin that got her attention at Sapphire. "Yes."

"Well, I refuse," she hisses. "I will not be humiliated any further."

"Technically, nobody knows about what happened but you, me, and my dear friends," I point out. "So it's not like you're *that* humiliated." I think about it. "Although, we are going to have quite a few laughs at your expense later."

"Fuck you. I will not—"

"You will," I cut her off. "Because while we were freeing you from the burden of having too much jewelry to choose from, we planted some of your lover's personal effects in your room. So you can try to blow my cover, but I don't have any of your jewelry on me and my friends are already gone. It'll be your word against mine, and something tells me your husband won't be in the best state of mind upon hearing that some of his rival's things—rather intimate things, I might add—are in your room. The one that only you have access to."

"We've been married for five years," she spits out, even as uncertainty flashes in her eyes. "He doesn't even know you. My husband will believe me when I tell him the truth."

I lean closer to her. "You willing to bet your life on that?"

She drops her gaze.

"That's what I thought." I continue towards the door, and this time, she follows. "Come along. I could use that drink, and I suspect you could too."

CHAPTER TWO

~

Talon

"Leaving so soon, Tal?" Vesilia calls out over the crowd gathered at Last Copper. It isn't the seediest tavern in Albadrid, but it definitely doesn't cater to the upper-class locals either. The trio who own and operate the place are Tovenian. It's rare for someone who belongs to our culture to settle down in one place, but it does happen, and when it does, they pretty much have a guaranteed customer base because every Tovenian troupe passing through the city will stop there. "Not going to partake in all the night has to offer?"

I grimace but hide it behind a lazy grin as I spin around to face the table I just vacated, where my friends and two very attractive women still sit. Can't remember their names for the life of me. Genevieve and Scarlette? Katra and Sil . . . fra? Is that even a name? I frown. How many drinks have I had?

"Just going out for some fresh air. It's a lovely night."

"It's not even midnight. You ain't got nowhere else to be." Vesi

30

drops her chin onto her hands propped up by her elbows. "And we've barely started drinking."

The dozen glasses on our table say otherwise, but I know what she's getting at. It's the same thing she always pokes and prods at, because while Vesi is one of my best friends . . . she is also the biggest pain in my ass.

Our troupe has been camped outside Albadrid for almost two months now. The coastal city enjoys coming to see us perform, and there are always well-paying gigs for those who choose to keep their trade on the legal side of things. For myself and a few others . . . well . . . there is no shortage of easy marks in the city.

Mattias and Vesilia have been my partners in crime since we started small cons as scrawny teenagers to the larger ones we pull off now. Which means they've spent the last decade witnessing what I do after every successful heist—slam back as many shots of cheap liquor as possible and then direct my trademark charm at anyone with a nice pair of tits and a warm cunt to bury my cock in. Occasionally multiple somebodies.

It's never particularly hard for me to find a bedmate for the evening. I'm well aware that my looks are an asset to take advantage of. I have a strong jaw, full mouth, and chiseled cheekbones, which I always show off by staying clean-shaven. Silver earrings dangle from my right ear, keying everyone aware of Tovenian culture in on my nonbinary nature. Recently, I cut my black hair from my shoulders to just below my ears because it's too damn hot for long hair this time of year. More than one woman has told me I have *devil eyes* while giving me a flirtatious smile.

Most Eleoyn women are used to brutish men who do little to woo them. They're already intrigued by my good looks, so by the time I start flirting with them, they're practically taking off their panties and throwing themselves at me. If I don't want to spend a night alone, I don't. Easy as breathing.

Yet . . . I haven't gotten laid *one fucking time* in nearly two years. Not since I pinned that damn witch against a tree and watched as she threw her head back and screamed my name to the night sky.

Every time I go out with the intention of getting her out of my system once and for all, my stomach churns as soon as I feel a pair of lips against mine that aren't hers. Any determination I have to just do it and get it over with fades when they smile in a way that is nothing like her lopsided smirk.

I don't know what this is—this all-consuming need—but I fucking hate it, and it's her fault.

"Don't tease them, Vesi," Mattias booms loud enough that the two young women sitting across from him wince. Once the large man gets a few drinks in him, he really only has one volume—headache-inducing. "They're still pining over that strawberry-blonde beauty from Shalewood."

I clench my jaw hard enough that a sharp pain shoots through my head, and I force myself to relax. No one but me knows the "strawberry-blonde beauty" I danced with was really a silver-eyed witch with lilac hair. I only saw through her charmed disguise for a few seconds, but the image is seared into my memory.

"How's Eliza doing these days?" I ask lazily. Three years ago, Mattias fell head over heels in love with the pretty brunette who owns a tavern in Neidell. She feels the same, but they're in a bit of a stalemate because he refuses to settle down and she refuses to live a nomadic life.

"Don't know, don't care." He shrugs.

Vesilia catches my eye from where she's sitting next to him, and we both grin. Despite what he says, we both know that if the two very attractive women sitting across from him started stripping right now, he wouldn't even be tempted to look. No one exists for him but Eliza.

They're both just too stubborn to do anything about it.

When Vesi and I break out in laughter, Mattias crosses his arms over his barrel chest. "At least I have somebody! How's your love life these days, Vesi? Pretty sure you managed to piss off *both* Kayla and Nicolai last week."

Vesi's laughter abruptly cuts off, and she glares at Mattias. "I was over them anyway."

"Sure you were," I retort with a chuckle. Vesi falls in and out of love so fast, it's hard to keep track, but she seemed to genuinely like those two and didn't give any impression of breaking it off with them, which means she did something to implode the relationship.

My own chuckles fade as I prepare myself for his ire next. Mattias picks up his glass and downs the rest of the ale before slamming it onto the table. The two women who joined our group look torn between bolting or staying around for the drama.

"Do you even know the name of the woman you're pining over, Tal?" Mattias squints at me.

Cerelia. The name slithers across my soul, consuming everything in its wake. I thought the name was a lie, just like everything else about her from that night, but when I told Astria that, she gave me a strange look and informed me that it is in fact her sister's name—her true name.

Not the moniker the world gave her. Scythe.

The chatter around us dies as the others from our troupe eavesdrop on our conversation, waiting to see what I will say. I'm well aware of the fact that my recent run of celibacy hasn't gone unnoticed. Pretty sure there are bets being placed on when I will break and that Vesi is in on them.

I only like being the center of attention on my own terms. The predator trapped under my skin is also not pleased about this turn of events. "I need to go check on my sister." A few people groan at my declaration, but I ignore them as I turn back towards the exit.

"Ah Tal!" Vesi yells. "Don't go yet! Help me put this big bastard in his place!"

Mattias grumbles something vaguely apologetic, but I'm already halfway to the tavern door. My hand slams into it, swinging it open, and I step out into the cool night air. Then I stalk down a few narrow pathways before stopping and leaning against a rough stone wall.

This madness needs to end. I need to figure out how to get her claws out of me. Maybe a trip to Tenresan is in order. The capital of Eleoyn is a dangerous place these days, especially for a cursed werewolf. The mage hunters would delight in slicing the flesh from my bones, but surely I can find *someone* there to finally get the damn witch out of my system.

Yes, that will work, and while I'm there, I can find a job to pull off. It's been a while since I pulled one on my own, and as much as I love working with my friends, sometimes a solo hunt is just what I need.

Thanks to the haul we got, courtesy of Aurora, I don't need the money, but the money is only a small part of why I do what I do. Mattias does it because it benefits the entire troupe and it's in his nature to care for everyone. Vesi does it because she thinks she can buy gifts—or maybe pass off stolen jewelry that she pretends she bought—to her lovers to make up for how shitty she often treats them.

I do it because I'm angry. Enraged at the world, where a bunch of made-up rules mean one person can have a room filled with priceless gems and stones while a child starves on the street halfway down the block. A kingdom where magic is outlawed—unless you serve the crown, in which case, you can use your magic to hunt down others and inflict all kinds of cruelty.

A society where my parents died protecting the woman they loved while those gathered had laughed.

Fuck it all. I hope the old gods come back one day and burn it all to the ground.

"Well, what do we have here?" a nasally voice says from my left. "Aren't you a pretty boy . . ."

"Not a boy." I sigh and turn my head to watch two people enter the narrow alleyway I ducked down. Both are a little taller than me, the left one a bit gangly and walking with a slight limp, while the right one is a beast of a man, even larger than Mattias. The lower half of their faces are covered by black fabric wrapped around their heads, but based on the worn leather vests they wear and the curved daggers at their sides, they're Ririthan raiders.

Not surprising. Albadrid is close to the border, and even though it's closed and heavily patrolled, the raiders have ways of slipping through.

"They're nonbinary, you git." The larger one smacks the back of his companion's head. "Told you about the whole earring thing with the Tovenians."

"The Eleoyns do it as well." I push off the wall so I can face them. "They don't wear as many earrings." I brush my finger up my right ear where several dangle on the lower part and silver bands run up the upper half. "But they use the same system."

"We thank you for the information, my pretty *friend*. We're still learning the customs around here," the nasally man responds with a rogue smile. "Now hand over everything you got in your pockets and that nice dagger on your thigh."

"This one?" I pull the blade free and hold it up like I'm examining it. "It's my third favorite one. Not entirely sure I feel inclined to give it up, although I do appreciate you respecting my choice of pronouns. Some Ririthans can be rather rude about it, and I don't actually enjoy cutting out tongues. It's messy, and they're hard to hold onto. Half the time, I end up dropping the damn thing and then the person chokes on it. Have you ever listened to someone die while choking on their own tongue?" I scrunch up my nose. "The sound is kind of grating."

Wariness creeps into both of their postures as they realize their easy mark isn't what they thought. They unsheathe their swords, the shorter style common in Riritha. They're just under two feet in length and double-edged on both sides. I'm not particularly good with a sword, definitely better than average, but half the time, I don't even carry it on me.

Broadswords are the more common style in Eleoyn, but I find

them cumbersome. I've fought against some talented sword fighters from Riritha . . . it's not fun. If they know what they're doing, they take advantage of the double-sided edges, and I still have a scar on my side to prove just how much damage that can do.

Luckily for me, these two are standing off-balance. Definitely not skilled fighters. Just assholes with swords.

Perfect. I've got some frustration to work off.

"Here you go." With a flick of my wrist, I fling the dagger to the ground, its blade sinking into the dirt exactly midway between me and them. "It's all yours . . . if you can get it."

The smaller man steps forward but is halted by his friend, who places a hand on his chest, eying me suspiciously. "You said that was your *third* favorite. Where are the other two?"

"Aren't you a clever would-be thief?" I wink, and his brows bunch together. Holding my hands up, I show them my palms and the two archaic symbols tattooed on them. One for life. One for death.

At least that's what my friend told me. I can't speak or read fae, so I had to take their word for it.

My thumbs push against the tattoos, and two black daggers blink into existence, their handles fitting perfectly in my palms. Instead of a blunt end, the handle of each dagger has a ring that my index finger slides through, allowing me to flip the blades easily from the inside of my palm to rest against the outside of my knuckles.

The two men stare at the short, curved blades that look like talons, the shiny black metal reflecting the dim light of the fae lanterns at either end of the alleyway. "Kruxtia's claws," the larger man sneers, instantly recognizing the weapons that the goddess of vengeance was famous for wielding. His hand drops from his friend's chest. "Only a fae could have given you those tattoos. And the fae don't work for money. Consider it beneath them. You fucking one? Thought the mage hunters killed off all the fae lovers here."

I shrug. "Missed one."

"Pity we won't get a bounty for turning in your bones like we do for the fae we manage to find." The smaller man takes a step towards me, his friend doing the same. The teeth dangling from their necklaces rattle with each footfall. The token was the first thing I looked for when I suspected them of being Ririthan. Like the mage hunters of Eleoyn, there are some from that kingdom who specialize in hunting down fae. Although there are few fae left these days.

The raider's insinuation that I am fucking a fae is incorrect. Ryllae is a friend. A good one. Which is why, as a favor to them, I do my best to kill every raider I come across. Especially ones who decorate themselves in the bones of the fae they have slaughtered.

The raiders close the distance between us, but there isn't room for them to spread out and flank me. The narrowness of the alleyway is to my advantage, not theirs. My daggers are meant for up-close fighting, whereas their swords require more space to wield.

I twist my body as the smaller man strikes at my ribs, the edge of his sword sliding close enough to slice through my shirt, a hair's breadth from my skin. With a practiced motion that is second nature at this point, I spin the blade in my right hand around to the outside of my knuckles and jab it forward, its point sinking into his eye.

He screams and jolts back. My other hand shoots forward, and I slice his throat open with the back edge of my other dagger. As the man lurches to the side, clutching at his throat, I can't help but feel vindicated. Ryllae and I argued for weeks over whether or not the daggers should have dual sharp edges. *They* were partial to the fae tradition of only the inside of the curve being sharp. Their argument being that if you need to be defensive, you could have the outside portion against your flesh and not worry about slicing yourself open.

As the man lies bleeding at my feet, desperately trying to keep his lifeblood from pouring out of his throat, I once again feel like I made the right call. Tradition be damned. Offensive fighting is more in my nature anyway.

The remaining raider blinks at his soon-to-be-dead friend and rage flashes in his dark eyes before he charges at me with a roar. I duck beneath the swing meant to take my head and slash across his stomach with both blades, crossing my arms swiftly.

Then I step back as the man staggers and his sword slips from his fingers. He clutches his stomach in a desperate attempt to keep his intestines from sliding out. Dispassion fills my eyes as I watch him drop to his knees and then topple over.

"Welcome to Eleoyn." I crouch next to him, dismissing my daggers, and rip the necklace of teeth from his neck. "Lovely chatting with you."

One last flash of hatred flares in his eyes before they dim and stare out into the world, unseeing. I swipe the necklace from the other man and continue on. Someone will find the bodies eventually and get them cleaned up.

There is no shortage of death in this kingdom.

***

"I'm back!" I call out as I stroll into the clearing of the woods outside of town. It's nothing like the forest Astria grew up in. More like someone dropped random clusters of trees onto a grassland and called it done. The troupe Ravyn and I belong to is fairly large, with almost a hundred people, most of whom are part of family units, but there are some singles mixed in like Mattias and Vesi.

We travel around Eleoyn, setting up outside cities for weeks or months at a time before moving on to the next one—an endless circuit around the kingdom.

Four wagons with tents extending out from the back of them are situated in this clearing. Mine, the girls', Mattias', and Vesi's.

The rest of the troupe has clumped in similar ways in the few trees available, giving everyone some privacy.

The larger tents we use for performances are set up in the meadow. Despite it being so late, I still hear cheers and clapping. Albadrid is always a good city for us and far less stressful than the capital or some of the other cities further inland that have a much more paranoid atmosphere.

There is a large noble population here, who enjoy the ocean views. Higher-ranking ones like Aurora and her husband never deign to leave the city walls to sit in a tent, but there are plenty of lower-ranking ones who love the novelty of it all.

And we like taking their money.

Neither my sister nor Astria rush out to greet me. I glance at the closed flaps of their tent. Ravyn always worries when I go out on a heist, and she's been extra worried about this one because of the brashness of it. I expected her to come storming out, eyes filled with relief even as her lips were pursed in annoyance at me for not coming home straight away.

Maybe somebody let it slip that I was at Last Copper celebrating after the heist and she's pissed off. Guilt nips at me. I should have come back here first.

"Ravyn? Astria?" I walk over to their tent and poke my head inside. A thin rug stretches across the ground, and I glance to the cushions set around a low table to my right before swinging my head to the clothes haphazardly piled in heaps to my left. No sign of either girl.

Maybe they're at one of the performances? They said they were taking the night off though. Unease slides through me for no rational reason, so I step inside and quickly head to the stairs at the back of the tent that lead up to the wagon, where their bed is located.

"If you're back here, please cover yourselves," I announce loudly. "I *really* don't want to get an eyeful of either of you again."

I hop up the stairs and rip back the curtains, but an empty

mattress greets me, the covers still cast to the side like the girls got up in a hurry. That unease blossoms into a cold panic as I spin and leap back down the stairs.

As I rush towards the front of the tent, I tell myself that my instincts are just on high alert because of the leftover thrill from the heist and then the fight in the alleyway. Ravyn and Astria are probably just watching some of their friends' performances over at the main tents. I'm worried about nothing, and Ravyn will laugh at me when I tell h—

My eyes latch on to the letter pinned to the side of the tent, right by the entrance. I walked right past it when I strode in.

I rip it off the thick canvas and read. The tendrils of dread that have been drifting through me since entering coalesce into a hand that grips my heart and squeezes.

A numbness spreads over me, shoving the panic and dread aside. It's like I'm walking through a dream as I move over to the table and sort through the various notes on it. Ravyn is a list maker, it's what she does when she feels overwhelmed, so her handwriting is everywhere. With a mechanical detachment, I place the note beside list after list, comparing the handwriting of each.

It all matches. The numbness spreads even more.

I stare at the note, feeling everything and nothing at once. Is this what the witch felt when her sister told her she was leaving?

No. I jerk my head in a harsh shake. Ravyn wouldn't do this to me. She would have told me, not slipped off into the night.

I'm out of the tent in a flash, sprinting towards where we keep the horses roped off. Most of them stand in the small patch of trees, and they snort in annoyance as I wind my way through the herd, counting off.

They're all here, but there are other ways to get a horse, and my sister has money of her own.

I duck under the rope fence and whistle, and a dark bay stallion trots out from a copse of trees. I don't bother to saddle him up, just swing onto his back, wrap my fingers around his dark mane, and click my tongue. Draco takes off at a ground-eating gallop towards the city.

Fae horses are far more clever than the average horse. Between Draco's empathic traits and the slight shifts in my weight, he knows exactly where to go.

The city guards yell at me as Draco races through the east gate, but the small fortune in gems I toss their way ensures they won't give chase.

Stable after stable, inn after inn, Draco and I dash all over the city, and the sun is rising by the time I return to camp in defeat. Nobody matching my sister's or Astria's appearances has purchased a horse or booked a room in any of the inns. It's possible they left on foot, but it would take weeks to walk anywhere, and it's dangerous to do so. I don't think my sister would do such a thing.

Then again, I never thought she would just leave me like this either. It's not like I wouldn't go with them if they wanted to travel apart from the troupe for a while. Everyone in the troupe is close, but we are also a bunch of independent fucks. It isn't uncommon for people to go out on their own for a while. Sometimes returning, sometimes not. As long as no one does anything to harm the troupe, nobody cares.

Loyalty is all that matters.

I slump onto one of the cushions in Ravyn and Astria's tent and stare at that damning note. It's my sister's handwriting. I'm sure of it.

Maybe what it says is true and she and Astria really have left. Maybe they'll return in a couple of months, bright smiles on their faces as they recount their adventures.

There is another truth though. It's what keeps me from accepting the words in my sister's handwriting.

She has never signed anything as "Rav" in her life.

CHAPTER THREE

~

Scythe

"You can't possibly be her." The fair-haired mage hunter laughs. "I mean . . . look at you."

"She looks tasty." Another mage hunter licks his lips. He's a big one, close to six and a half feet tall, with shoulders so broad, I bet he has to twist just to fit through doorways. "I call first dibs."

The rest of the mage hunters chuckle as their eyes trail down my body at all the skin I have on display. It's an impossibly hot and muggy summer day. A thunderstorm has been threatening to break all week, but so far, not a drop of water has fallen. Instead, the humidity has risen to an almost unbearable level and the air has a static charge to it.

So when I woke up this morning, I decided that I didn't actually want to die by wearing my usual long pants, shirt, and vest, which is why I am wearing loose-fitting pants that I cut off at the knees and skipped the shirt entirely, opting to wear only a breastband. The thick straps cross above my chest before going over my shoulder and attaching to the back of the stretchy black fabric.

As usual, my feet are bare. I only wear shoes when I go into one of the nearby towns, and I hate every second of it.

Between the outfit and my waist-length lilac hair that I twisted into two thick braids, I have to acknowledge that I don't look all that intimidating. But they're all going to be dead in a few minutes, so does it really matter?

"You're trespassing." My scythe appears in my right hand, the silver blade stretching horizontally out at a ninety-degree angle from the top of the dark wood handle before curving downward to end in a sharp point. In many ways, the weapon looks fragile. The handle is a branch I whittled down, and the blade is so thin that logic says it should snap at the slightest pressure, but my mage friend assured me that nothing in the world could break it, and twenty years after he placed it into my hand, it doesn't bear so much as a scratch.

The amused and leering looks slide off their faces as they stare at the scythe and back up a step.

"What kind of witch uses mage magic? Your magic must be weak if you have to rely on that weapon." The fair-haired mage's mouth twists into an arrogant smile. Based on the gold medallion clasped to his cloak, I assume he's the leader.

I lazily spin the scythe. "What type of mage hunts their own kind? Your conviction must be weak for you to follow the orders of a traitorous king."

"The Mage Council of Sekaria are the traitors." The smile is gone from his face in an instant, and he draws his sword, pointing it at me. Black flames dance along its silver edges. Mage fire. Great. That's going to sting. "We will never serve them."

"The Obscuras don't serve them either," I say lightly. "They are rebel mages who fight against the Council, and yet you hunt them down as well. Methinks you care less about what has become of the Mage Kingdom and more about the money and power that comes from getting on your knees for the Eleoyn King."

At once, the mage hunters draw their weapons, bristling at what I am insinuating, and I give them all a wolfish smile.

"We didn't come here to justify our allegiance," the leader growls.

"No." My smile sharpens. "You came here to die."

A few of the hunters shuffle uneasily, but most just sneer at me.

"While I had my doubts about your abilities—and still do, considering you're just one woman—I did come prepared." The leader laughs and waves a hand at the hunters gathered around him, who are all men. There are no female or nonbinary mage hunters to my knowledge despite gender having zero impact on power when it comes to mage magic. The Eleoyn King has prejudiced views on many things, so I suppose having a foolish understanding of gender shouldn't be that surprising. "Twenty of my finest mages. There must be others in this forest helping you. Once we've had our fun and leave your broken corpse behind, we'll hunt them down and burn a path through your precious forest."

My whirling scythe slows until it stops completely. Then I loosen my fingers around the staff as I hold it out to my side.

"You're right, I do have help, but it's not a who—it's a what." I bare my teeth at the hunters. "And you really shouldn't have threatened my forest."

I whirl as the two hunters lying in wait strike at my back. The lead mage lied; there aren't twenty mage hunters here—there are forty.

Outside of my forest, this could pose a problem. But here? I might as well be a fucking god.

A wordless song erupts from my throat, the melody harsh and fast, and roots rise from the earth to wrap around the hunters. The ones with mage fire start hacking their way free; the roots won't hold them for long. That's fine—I only need a moment.

It was sloppy of me to allow myself to get surrounded like this, but I was aching for a fight, so when I sensed the mages crossing the boundary into my forest, I ran to meet them head-on, not even waking Necos and the rest of the panthers from where they took a midday nap in a sunny clearing. Unfortunately, the mage hunters are getting better at crafting hiding spells, because I didn't detect the second half of the group until they were less than twenty feet from me.

The melody of my song changes, the harshness shifting to alluring and the urgent notes slowing to something powerful and ancient. Mist rises from the ground to hover in the air, thick and stagnant, and the mage hunters curse as they continue to cut themselves free from the roots.

For all my magic, even I can't see through the mist, but I don't need to. This close, I can sense where every single one of them are. Their charms may have become more effective over the years, but this is still my domain. They can't outpower me.

Now that I've called the mist up, my singing fades and morphs into a deep hum that bounces off the trees, making it impossible to pinpoint where it's coming from. The mages go silent other than the few still trying to get free of the roots. My tattoos react to the magic coursing through me and give off a faint glow, but the mist gobbles it up. The thrill of the hunt calls to me, and I give myself to it.

I close my eyes, magic flowing from the earth into my limbs and back out into the air. My body moves to the rhythm of the song I hum, and I glide forward, twirling as I slice my scythe through the air in front of me. The mage hunter doesn't even have time to scream before the sharp edge of the blade slices through his flesh like paper and his head topples to the ground.

One down. Thirty-nine to go.

"Somebody shut her the fuck up!" the leader bellows from somewhere in the mist.

I cut down another three mages before I hear it—the whistling sound of multiple blades cutting through the air from multiple directions. My arm snaps out, and I spin my scythe quickly until it's only a blur as I turn my body in a tight circle. Two blades get knocked aside, and I dodge the third but not the fourth.

Pain erupts from my shoulder, and a brief hiss interrupts my song. I stagger back but recover quickly, pulling the dagger free and holding it up close to my face so I can see it properly. The blade has a greenish sheen to it. A stinging sensation spreads from the wound, and I grimace. Poison spurred on by magic to make it faster acting.

Again, I adjust my song, asking the forest to help me purge the toxin and heal the wound while also keeping the mist up.

Silver flashes, and I barely jerk my scythe up in time to catch the sword barreling down on me. Gripping the rough wood staff with both hands, I catch the sword an inch away from my throat. My song instantly dies as I concentrate on staying alive. The mist will linger for a few minutes, but the pain shooting through my shoulder is almost unbearable; I barely made a dent in getting the poison out. The enormous man who called me "tasty" earlier looms over our crossed weapons, and I dig my feet in. He pushes harder, and a grunt slips from my lips as I double my efforts to keep his blade from slicing into my flesh.

"You smell just as delicious as you look, witch," he taunts, and I notice the gold bar piercing the septum of his nose. I missed that earlier. It probably enhances his sense of smell. Clever. Annoying, but still clever.

A tremble starts in my biceps and spreads. Even if I could spare the air to sing right now, there is no song that will make me stronger, and I have maybe ten seconds before he shoves the sword into my neck.

"That's nice," I hiss through clenched teeth. Fuck, this is going to hurt. I push up the blade end of my scythe, letting the other end dip, and his sword scratches along the staff as it travels downward, following the path of least resistance. He growls as it drops below my throat, and then he shoves harder, which is the part of my plan that I really hate. I drop my scythe away and can't hold back the scream as his sword bites into my shoulder.

He laughs as he slices downward before jerking his sword back to strike again. Adrenaline floods my system, and I block out the pain, then, in one smooth motion, I step back and flip my scythe so the blade is towards the ground before I arc it back up, putting all my strength and skill behind the maneuver. A pissed-off song spills from my lips as the blade slices through his groin and up his torso before finally exiting out of his shoulder in a spray of blood and gore.

I enjoy the surprised look on his face before his body falls into two gruesome halves as the song fades from my lips. Exhaustion washes over me, threatening to pull me under. As sharp as my blade is, it needs help to cut through a body like that. It's smarter to slice through the neck because there isn't nearly as much resistance, but that hunter really pissed me off.

Too much magic for one enemy. I can practically hear my father's chiding voice in my mind.

That temper of yours really is unfortunate, my mother would have added with a slight crease between her eyebrows, which was about as much emotion as she ever showed.

"Whatever," I mutter. "Worth it."

I hum again, that lulling song encouraging the mist to stay, then I weave in the notes to get my body to heal and purge the poison. I give myself thirty seconds to piece myself back together enough to finish this. I'll need more time to heal, but I just need to keep my body functional for now. Survival comes first.

No more fancy moves though. Maintaining the fog and keeping myself from passing out will take what's left of my magic. After this, I'll need to rest and maybe nap on the forest floor for a bit to replenish my reserves. Luckily—or maybe unluckily—I have a high pain tolerance. When you're a one-person army, you get used to fighting with broken bones.

A crack sounds to my left. The mage hunters are good at moving silently, but not as good as me and definitely not in my fucking forest.

I sprint forward, letting the magic of the forest guide me, and my scythe slices through two hunters before it clangs against steel resistance. Dark eyes full of hate meet mine, and I break apart from the hunter, mist swirling around us, hiding parts of our bodies before moving again. I hear others closing in on the sound, which means I need to end this so I can take care of them.

Unlike the broadswords most hunters use, this one has two shorter swords. I slide my hand farther down the handle of my scythe, and he eyes the movement before charging forward. My fingers brush the marking carved into the wood as I spin away from the hunter's attack. The dual-wielding mage pivots gracefully on his feet, black flames dancing down both swords as he swings them towards my legs from opposite directions, knowing I'll never be able to block both with only one weapon.

His swords slam into curved silver, and he blinks at the *two* scythes with smaller handles that I now wield in each hand.

"Surprise." I give him a feral smile before lunging back and pulling my weapons away from his. He stumbles forward at the sudden lack of resistance, and I slice a blade across his throat. Hot blood spurts onto my face, and I lean back until I'm almost parallel with the ground as another sword cuts the air above me.

I whirl upright and slash at the newcomer, more blood splashing across my face, then laugh as I disappear into the mist, picking up my humming once more.

Minutes tick by as I dash and twirl my way through the forest, cutting down the hunters one by one like the song I hum is one for death itself. I lose myself in the chaotic and violent rhythm, enjoying the way their dying screams echo throughout my trees and the way their blood feels against my skin as more of it pours into the earth to nurture the roots beneath.

This is all I have now.

Another hunter falls before me, but not before he manages to slice his fiery blade across my thigh. I barely acknowledge the burn.

My people left me. Parents. Mate. *Sister.*

Everyone fucking leaves me.

They left me all alone with this fucking rage. With this godsdamn mantle.

The Witch of the Woods.

What a fucking joke. Hot pain races up my back, and I whirl before sliding one of my scythes deep into the gut of the hunter who snuck up behind me. He coughs, blood spraying my face, and I shove him off my blade and keep going.

They don't even believe in me anymore. All I have is this stupid legend that I've built up over decades of bloodshed, and these fucks laughed when they saw me.

"You can't possibly be her. I mean . . . look at you."

The only people who look at me these days are dead men walking. Nobody sees me anymore.

The wolf saw you, a treacherous voice whispers in my mind. *They saw you—and ran.*

The memory of dark, hate-filled eyes surfaces. A yellow sheen rolling over them.

I snarl and snap both my scythes into another hunter's neck, and he drops his sword before falling to his knees. I jerk my blades free and surge forward, almost desperate for my next kill.

Fuck Talon. They made me . . . feel things. Then they saw what I am and hated me for it, and they stole my fucking sister.

Another hunter collapses before me, his entrails decorating the ground around him. I don't care if it was Talon's sister who stole my Astria's heart. In my mind, Talon is responsible. They took everything from me.

And I hate them for it.

My fingers tighten around the familiar wood handles of my scythes as I turn in a circle.

Listening.

Waiting.

Nothing.

It's as if even the forest has gone silent at my rage. There is no one left for me to cut down as blood coats every inch of my skin. Some mine. Most of it theirs. I need more. Why couldn't he have brought more hunters?

I drop to my knees and scream. The mist rolls back, dissipating between the trees, but I keep screaming until the last of it is gone and my throat is raw.

Carnage litters the forest floor. I stare at the broken bodies of the forty mage hunters who came to kill me, and once again, I hate them a little for not succeeding.

A dark form drops down from the trees and trots over to me. Necos bumps her large head against mine, a purr rumbling from her chest. I leave my scythes on the ground as I wind my fingers through the panther's fur before pressing my forehead against hers and asking in a trembling voice that I barely recognize as my own, "Am I okay?"

Her only response is to purr louder. After a minute, I take a deep breath that only rattles a little and tuck all my loneliness away. Getting to my feet, I survey the fallen hunters.

More will come. They always do. The last few months though, they've come even more frequently. Five years ago, every mage hunter who walked into these woods knew of my existence. My reputation didn't halt the attacks, but it did give them pause. Made them think about just how much they really wanted to risk it.

That is no longer the case. I don't know what strange propaganda the Eleoyn King has been spreading, but now these cocky assholes traipse into my forest constantly, raiders and mage hunters alike, and they all act surprised that it really is just me defending these woods.

I wonder if my companion to the west is seeing the same influx. It's been almost a year since I heard from them, but that's not all that unusual. They're probably just hidden away in that musty library of theirs.

Maybe the world needs a reminder that I'm still here and that this forest is under the protection of the Last Witch of the Woods.

I prod the body closest to me with my toe and smile. I have the perfect idea of how to remind them.

CHAPTER FOUR

~

Talon

THE WIND WHIPS the tall grass around my legs as I stare at the forest. It's late summer, and the leaves are still a deep and vibrant green thanks to the frequent thunderstorms this time of year. The trees along the boundary between the forest and the meadowlands don't look any different from the trees throughout the rest of Eleoyn, but I can feel the difference. I also know that these trees are nothing like the ones farther in the woods where the witch lives. Those ones have towered up impossibly tall and hide homes in their canopies.

I still remember looking up into the trees and searching for her while Ravyn helped Astria pack a year ago. I made it seem like my offer to escort them was merely to provide a lending hand—which it was—but I also wasn't able to resist the idea of seeing *her*. The woman who haunts my dreams.

Not a woman. A witch, I remind myself.

My fingers curl at my sides like they remember what it was like to have claws, but that's just a memory passed down through my bloodline because this is the only form I've ever known. From what Astria has told me about her sister, I know the witch wasn't the one to curse my ancestors. Even at two hundred, she's still far too young for that, but still, witches like her are the reason I feel like part of my soul is missing.

A werewolf who can't shift into a wolf but still craves it. What a fucked-up curse.

For all my senses and keen observation skills, I didn't know what she was when I danced with her around the fire on the blood moon almost two years ago. Her strawberry-blonde hair swirled around her while her blue eyes gave me heated looks. She told me her name was Cerelia, and that was the name I panted like a prayer while I buried myself inside her, my fingers gripping her ass as her legs wrapped around my waist.

Then the moon laughed at us both as the clouds glided away, revealing my cursed nature. She saw the sheen roll over them, and her tattoos flared through the charm she'd had in place to disguise herself.

Two beings who are meant to be enemies, drawn to each other for reasons they don't understand.

My mother would have sighed at the romantic nature of it all, while my father would have asked where I buried the witch's body.

I miss them. Not only because they were my parents, but also because they were the only other cursed wolves I ever knew. Ravyn is my sister, and I love her more than anything—she's the reason I'm about to walk to my possible death—but we don't share the same blood. Something I'm thankful for, because it means my adopted sister will never be tormented by the feeling of something crawling beneath her skin, fighting to get free. Of hearing the other half of her soul calling to her . . . but being unable to answer.

It is a unique type of torment my parents understood well. In my thirty-four years of existence, I've never met another cursed wolf. Maybe they're in the other kingdoms—I've rarely left Eleoyn —or maybe I'm the last one.

The werewolves of the Wilds never travel below the Obsidian Mountains, so I have no idea what they are like. When I was a kid, I often wondered about them. Sometimes made up stories about how strong or noble they were. That stopped the first time my body tried to shift only to be locked in pain for hours. The witches had cursed my bloodline and a few others'—but only at the request of the other werewolves.

I've been damned to a lifetime of pain, all because of some fucking rebellion I wasn't even alive for.

If ever meet a wolf from the Wilds, I'll bury my dagger in their fucking heart.

"What a pair we make," I mutter as I scan the darkening forest. "The last cursed wolf and the last witch."

The wind picks up, and I glance at the dark grey storm clouds. It would probably be smarter for me to wait until morning. The sun is almost set, and I can smell the rain in the air, which means the clouds will be opening up any second now.

But my sister's life—along with Astria's—is on the line. I need the witch's help if I'm to find them. Astria once confessed the last words that her sister had spoken to her were that she wouldn't come save her, but I don't believe it. The young witchkin has rarely spoken of her sister after that, but nobody is more skilled at reading people than I am. The love between the sisters is unbreakable—no matter what harsh words have been spoken.

The witch would help. I just need to make it to her alive to ask.

I reach over my shoulder to draw my sword because I'd rather have its reach than my daggers for this trip, but I pause when my fingers wrap around the pommel. *The witches are the forest, and the forest is the witches.* My mother told me that. She loved telling me all kinds of stories. Now, there is only one witch, but it's likely still true. I don't know if killing something in self-defense is a pardonable offense, but I can't risk finding out. My hand drops away from my sword.

Fast and quiet is my best bet.

Shifting might forever be out of my reach, but I'm still a wolf at heart, and the woods are home to me. I take off at a steady jog, my feet always falling to make the smallest amount of sound. The farther I travel, the darker it becomes until I'm getting by mostly on instinct. My night vision is far better than any human's, but even I need some light, and the clouds are covering any hint of the moon and stars tonight.

Thunder cracks, and the sound of rain smacking against leaves comes a second later. I pick up the pace, but there's no outrunning this storm. Soon, rivers of water race down the trees, and my tattered cloak gets drenched.

I've only been to the witch's home once, but my sense of direction has never failed me. Her home is unexpectedly close to the edge of the forest—only about five miles in—and I've already gone about two miles. Given how much territory these woods cover, I'm surprised she doesn't live somewhere closer to the Wilds on the other side, but I'm not going to complain.

Another mile goes by when I sense something keeping pace with me. I maintain the same speed, even as I glance out of the corner of my eye to the left and then to the right. Several somethings. Maybe these are the infamous devil cats so many people talk about in hushed tones while drinking in taverns. Astria talks about them like they're just overgrown house cats.

I suspect they won't let me use their bodies as pillows the way they did for her though.

My ghostly escorts keep out of sight, but they never stray, following me until I halt at the clearing Astria gave us directions to a year ago. Here's hoping the witch hasn't moved . . .

"*Witch!*" I bellow over the increasingly loud rainfall. "Your sister—"

A silver blade kisses the skin of my throat before I feel warm blood trickle down my cold, wet flesh. I turn my head carefully to the right, where the bearer of the scythe stands. Lightning cracks across the sky and flashes against silver eyes.

"Why are you here, wolf?" she asks in a voice devoid of any emotion.

"Our sisters are gone," I reply, getting to the heart of the matter.

A tremble runs down the scythe, and I go completely still as it digs into my skin a little more. For a few bated breaths, neither of us moves, then she pulls the weapon away, and it vanishes—to where, I have no idea. Tricky little witch. I wonder if she can do that with her own magic or if, like me, she has a fae friend. Could be a mage, but that'd be odd, considering how much most mages want to kill her.

"Come," she commands. "You will tell me everything."

Without waiting for an answer, she strides off towards a massive tree. I don't really like being bossed around, but I need her help, so I bite my tongue and follow her. The witch starts up some stairs, and my stomach does a small flip when I realize her intention. When Ravyn and I came here before, I stayed on the ground while my sister helped her lover pack. Heights are not a thing I enjoy. To my increasing horror, the stairs keep winding farther and farther up the tree . . . and there are no handrails.

Wind cuts through the trees as the storm rages above us, so I keep as close to the trunk as I can, one hand against its rough bark, even though there's nothing for me to grab if I do slip. Clearly, the witch doesn't suffer from a fear of heights, nor does the wind seem to bother her at all. She just keeps climbing, as if we're out for a peaceful stroll around a pond.

After what feels like an eternity, the stairs open up to a large covered balcony. On the way up, I was barely able to see three feet in front of me, but up here, lanterns light up the home. I blink. Like the stairs, the structure is an extension of the tree. There are small divots and rises in the floor, where the tree has done its best to flatten out, and the walls appear to be made of tightly wound branches.

The witches are the forest, and the forest is the witches.

Despite everything, I can't stop myself from smiling faintly.

"You find something amusing?" The witch cocks her head at me in a purely predatory way.

It makes my cock harden, and I've never wanted to strangle the thing more, and not in a fun way. It hasn't so much as twitched in my pants at anyone since my night with the witch almost two years ago. Now, five minutes around her, and it's practically begging for attention. The witch is still looking at me with a gleam in her eye.

I answer her question before she notices the hardening bulge in my pants. "My mother would have loved this."

She furrows her brows; she clearly wasn't expecting that. I open my mouth to explain more about our sisters when a dark form leaps down from the branches onto the balcony, landing next to Cerelia. At the same moment, wet fur brushes against my fingertips.

Instantly, one of my curved daggers is in my hand, and I'm two feet away with my back to the outer wall of her home.

"Feeling skittish?" Cerelia smiles widely as the two panthers crouch at her feet, watching me curiously with bright red eyes.

"Been a while since anything has snuck up on me," I admit. The fact that I didn't sense either of the panthers approaching makes me inclined to believe they purposely let me sense them earlier in the forest. Maybe they are the reason nothing accosted me the whole way here, as if the devil cats were my personal escorts to the witch.

I tap the dagger against my tattooed palm three times so it disappears again. I can tell the witch is curious about the magic; it's almost funny the way her mouth pinches as she chokes the question back. She crosses her arms where she's standing near the edge of the balcony—which also has no railing, but clearly that doesn't bother her—and looks at me with those strange, silver eyes.

"What happened to my sister?" Her voice is calm and even, but I see the flash of outright panic and desperation in her eyes. I was right; despite whatever declarations had been made in her fight with Astria, she loves her sister beyond reason—which is good because I stand a much better chance of tracking them down with her help.

"Astria fit in well with the troupe," I tell her. "At first, she just helped out with other performances, but soon, she started her own. Kind of a mix between fortune telling and love advice. She has an uncanny ability to make people like her and always makes them laugh. Within a month, she became one of the most profitable performers."

The witch's jaw tightens, but she doesn't say anything, and I can't read anything further in her expression, so I keep going.

"After leaving Shalewood, we traveled to the coast, stopped for a while at the capital, but things are extra tense right now in Tenresan. The mage hunters are out in full force, and while there are no Obscuras in our troupe, we still prefer not to be under the scrutiny of the crown," I say wryly. Our troupe, like most other traveling performers, identifies as Tovenian rather than true Eleoyn citizens.

Tovenian culture is . . . flexible . . . when it comes to obeying rules. We never do anything big enough to draw undue attention —in fact, one of the few rules we do have is that you are never to put the rest of the troupe in danger simply to further your own gains—but it's common for us to cut through forests to avoid toll roads. Plus, there are others like me who like to pull in some extra money by coordinating heists.

The heists are always sanctioned by the troupe elders, and we only take carefully selected items that are valuable, easy to sell, and won't necessarily be missed. Things such as a crystal vase gathering dust in an unused room or the lady of the house's winter wardrobe from two seasons ago. They're drowning in riches, and we're more than happy to help them with that.

But my thrill and addiction to heists is why I wasn't there the night Astria and Ravyn disappeared.

Guilt hits me hard and fast, and I look away from Cerelia's unrelenting gaze.

"We moved on, further down the coast, to Albadrid. Everything seemed fine, the locals were glad to have us. I went out on a job one night and didn't return until late," I say tightly. "In the hours I was away . . . Astria and Ravyn left."

"Left?" the witch asks in a harsh tone. "Like they went out for the night? Or they left the troupe?"

I slide the leather satchel off my back and reach inside, pausing when the devil cats let out low, warning growls. Slowly, I pull out the folded piece of parchment and hand it to Cerelia.

She skims the note in my sister's handwriting before raising her eyes to meet mine. "Why didn't you drag their asses back? You were responsible for them!"

"I know," I grind out. It doesn't matter that both Astria and Ravyn are in their early twenties. They're our little sisters, which makes us responsible, and since I'm the one in the troupe . . . it makes *me* responsible. And I failed.

Cerelia paces—right next to the damn edge of the balcony. Part of me wants to shove her off, but another part wants to tug her away from it. I tell myself that part is only concerned about losing the person who can help me find Ravyn. The panthers settle down to stretch out on the floor, and she just steps over them as she continues pacing. "Are you sure that's Ravyn's handwriting? Did you try to track them?"

"It looks like her handwriting but could be a good forgery. There is no trace of them anywhere in Albadrid," I continue. "No horses were taken from our troupe, and I checked with all the stables to see if anyone who matched either Astria's or Ravyn's description had rented or purchased one. Nothing."

"Astria couldn't possibly be this rash," the witch mutters. When she reaches the end of the balcony, she pivots gracefully on her bare feet mere inches from the edge and continues pacing. I bite back my demand that she get the fuck away from there. Mostly because I don't like the fact that I feel protective over her.

I need her to save the girls. Nothing more.

If there is one person I could never love—it's a witch.

The rain continues to pour through the trees, and more panthers slink onto the covered patio. When one of them shakes its coat right next to me, I glare at it, and that's when the exact phrasing of what the witch said hits me.

"Are you implying *my* sister could have been this rash?" I ask incredulously. "Unlike yours, she actually grew up in Eleoyn, so she knows exactly how dangerous it is. There is no way she would leave the safety of our group. Not to mention, Astria is the one who left her home and sister behind for a girl she knew for less than a year. I do believe that better fits the definition of *rash*."

It's a low blow, I know that, but she's the one who started it, and nobody talks shit about my sister.

"Fuck you!" The tattoos down her arms glow brightly like silver fire. "Why did they leave?"

"That's why I'm here!" I shove off the wall and over one of the panthers to get in the witch's face. She's almost as tall as me, so she only has to tilt her head back slightly to hold my gaze. "It doesn't make any sense. I *know* my sister—she wouldn't do this—and Astria seemed very happy as well."

The fury in her eyes doesn't go out, but I get the sense it's no longer directed at me. "You think someone took them?"

I let out a harsh exhale and step back. "A few people did see them walk off together," I admit. "All the evidence points to them really going off on their own . . . It just doesn't make sense."

She stares at me for a long moment. "There's something else you're not telling me."

I look away from her and rub my hand across the lower part of my face. What I'm not telling her is important to me, but she might not get it. Despite how glaring of an issue I find it to be, I know it's flimsy as far as proof goes.

"Did you notice how the letter was signed?" I drop my hand from my face and glance towards the witch, only to find her gaze on me.

"Rav," she says immediately.

"My sister has never gone by anything other than Ravyn her entire life. She doesn't *do* nicknames. Her name is important to her because her mother gave it to her, and—" I stop myself. "Just trust me. If Ravyn truly did write that letter, her signing it as '*Rav*' was done purposely to grab my attention."

"Or it's a forgery and the person who signed it didn't know better." She jerks her head in a nod and resumes pacing. "Does anyone in your troupe know Astria is witchkin?"

"I don't think so." I shake my head and make my way back to the safety of the outer wall of the witch's house, stepping over the lazy-ass panthers as I go. "But that doesn't mean someone couldn't have figured it out."

"Maybe they threatened her . . . said they would reveal her secret or sell her out to the mage hunters." Her fingers twist a silver ring around on her pinky as she continues courting death by stalking back and forth so close to the balcony edge. "If someone from your troupe betrayed her, I'll kill them."

The silver scythe tattoos across her neck flare brightly along with the ones down her arms as her wet, lilac hair clings to her body past her waist. Before tonight, the only time I saw her, she hid away most of her witch traits, which only broke free when her magic reacted to finding out I was a cursed wolf. That night, she had strawberry-blonde hair and blue eyes. She was pretty and mesmerizing.

But that was a lie. This is the real her. An otherworldly beauty with more than a touch of feral wickedness. I ignore the way my cock hardens again and try to redirect my thoughts when she speaks once more.

"So you've come to ask for my help in determining what really happened to the girls?" She tilts her head in a very feline gesture, and I'm starting to suspect that maybe she spends too much time around the devil cats. "You know what I am, and you made your opinions of me very clear the night we met. Are you sure you want to work with me, wolf?"

"For my sister? Absolutely. I didn't come here for the woman who bewitched me with lies." I look down to the silver ring on her little finger before meeting the witch's eyes once more with a wolfish grin. "I came here for Scythe."

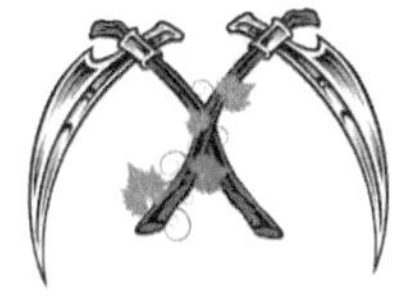

CHAPTER FIVE

~

Scythe

I LOOK around the tree house I've called home my entire adult life and to the bridge made of intertwining branches, which leads to my parents' old home. Witches live a long time—typically a thousand years or more—but we do return to the earth eventually. Sometimes young witches move into vacant houses that have been passed down through the generations. I chose to sing my home into being because I wanted something that was truly mine—and Astria's.

After the other witches left, Astria selected one of the newly vacated homes to be her own so we could have more space. Although most nights, she ended up sitting on the floor of my balcony, lounging against one of the panthers, who adored her beyond reason.

The cold grasp of fear grips my heart again. I knew the second I sensed Talon enter my forest that something had happened to Astria. The cursed wolf never would have come back here otherwise. They made their opinion of me perfectly clear that fateful night.

"*Witch,*" they spat. The strong, clever hands that had held me so tightly abruptly leaving my flesh. "*Is there anything in your nature other than deceit and cruelty?*"

We managed not to kill each other that night. Mostly because immediately after realizing what the other was, our damn sisters had skipped through the woods, holding hands and gazing at each other, completely lovestruck.

My mind might remember the hatred in Talon's eyes when they saw my silver tattoos flash, but unfortunately, my body remembers *other* things. It's confusing and I don't like it, and now I'll be traveling with them for the foreseeable future because there is nothing I wouldn't do for Astria.

I'd forsake it all. I'm still not entirely convinced that the two young women didn't go running off, but I know Talon must truly believe something is wrong because there is no way they would have asked for my help otherwise. Plus . . . I told Astria that if something happened, I wouldn't come. If they really are in trouble and I don't go looking for her, I'll never be able to forgive myself.

What if she is hurt somewhere and thinks that I won't come for her? What if she believes that I'd really abandon her?

A pained sound slips from my lips.

Vexus—one of Necos' littermates—butts his large head against me. I'm not sure where Necos went—probably to keep an eye on Talon, who was very keen to get back to the ground after I agreed to come. Their discomfort hadn't escaped my attention every time I'd gotten close to the edge of the balcony. I might have deliberately paced along it just to see the panic flare in their eyes a bit.

I'd also been curious if they were going to try to push me off or pull me away. Although, I refuse to analyze why I'd wondered that.

"Don't think there is anything else for me to pack." I look down at the panther. "Unless you have any suggestions?" He lets out a chuffing sound and jogs out to the balcony, leaping into the trees. Guess not then.

I sling the small leather pack over my shoulder, which only has a few changes of clothes and some other odds and ends that I picked up from my mage friend. I love my witch magic, it connects me to the earth and all the creatures who call it home, but I have to admit that mage magic is damn useful.

The charm that disguises my hair, eyes, and usually my tattoos is already hanging around my neck on a silver chain. If my magic flares, the tattoos will break through it, which is why I'm wearing a cloak despite the heat. If I have a particularly strong flare, my hair and eyes will be on display too, but there's not much I can do about that other than yank the hood up and hope no one is around to notice.

I've never traveled more than a few miles outside my forest. While I interact with humans in Shalewood and Neidell—the town a little further to the east—I'm hardly well-versed in the ways of Eleoyn. It irks me that I'll have to be so reliant on Talon to travel through the kingdom without attracting attention, but then again, they need me to search for any clues in their camp.

Our sisters disappeared exactly ten days ago. Albadrid is practically on the southern border of Eleoyn, right above Riritha, so it will take us a week to get there, which means another week of the girls being gone.

Gods, I hope they are just on a beach somewhere sunning themselves. Granted, I'll probably murder them after spending a week with Talon, but at least then I'll know where their corpses are.

I jog down the stairs to the forest floor and head towards the clearing before halting abruptly. Talon is sitting with their back against one of the trees . . . and Necos is stretched out in front of them with her head in Talon's lap. I can hear her purring as she enjoys the attention being lavished on her.

Traitorous feline.

Talon watches me approach and gives the panther's head one more pat before carefully extracting themself from underneath the overgrown house cat. Necos twitches her tail in annoyance before laying her head back down. I suspect she knows I'm leaving and that she isn't coming with me and is therefore giving me the cold shoulder.

It's not like I can bring her or any of her pack along. Besides, I need them here to help keep the raiders out of the forest. Although I do worry about the mage hunters who are equipped to fight off the devil cats.

Death is the natural order of things, and my forest is no exception to that. The panthers are predators, but there is always a chance one of them won't walk away from a hunt. Still . . . they are like family to me, and it would pain me to lose one.

"Making friends, I see," I say mildly as I walk over to the stubborn panther.

"I understand why Astria misses them so much." Talon shrugs. "Once they decide to not eat you, they're kind of sweet."

Just hearing my sister's name sends another pang through me. "I'm assuming it makes sense for us to head east to the coast and then travel south to Albadrid?"

"We need to go to Shalewood first; that's where I left my horse." My stride slows for a moment as I take in this bit of information, and Talon chuckles. "Did you think we were going to walk all the way south?"

My mouth hardens as I close the distance between us. Truthfully, I didn't think about that part. I was focused on what to pack while trying to shove all the fears about the many ways this could go wrong to the back of my mind. "I've never ridden before, but I'm sure I can figure it out."

"I have no doubt," Talon drawls before their eyes roam over me, scrutinizing my appearance. "Will the mages be able to detect whatever magic you're using to change your appearance?"

"No." I shake my head. "An acquaintance of mine made it, and they promised its magic is undetectable to other mages. It's not foolproof though. If my magic rises, my tattoos will break through it, and sometimes my eyes and hair as well."

"I remember." Their gaze lingers on the exact spot where my scythe tattoos are on my neck. My magic flared that night we were together after I realized what Talon was. Talon had seen me—the real me. "If you feel that happening, let me know immediately."

I kneel beside Necos, who's still pretending like I don't exist. "If I could take you with me, I would." I scratch the back of her head. "But there is no way for me to disguise you, and a panther traveling out in the open of Eleoyn will draw too much attention." Her tail twitches, but otherwise, she acts like she hasn't heard a word I said, doesn't even start purring when my fingers find the spot behind her ears that usually gets her going. "Please keep my forest safe, Necos, so my sister and I might return to you."

Still nothing. Stubborn feline.

"Let's go." I rise, wiping my hands on my pants and turning south in the direction of Shalewood. I make it three steps before something slams into my back, knocking me to the ground. Sharp claws dig into my shoulders, piercing my skin, and Necos' head nuzzles against my cheek. A low whine tears from the panther's throat as she butts her head against mine before leaping off and racing up a nearby tree.

Humming a melody to heal the wounds on my shoulders, I once again get to my feet and look up into the trees where Necos disappeared. "I'll miss you too, friend."

AT A STEADY JOG, we've made it almost to the edge of the forest in just under an hour. I'm used to running through the rough terrain, so the pace doesn't bother me in the slightest, and Talon hasn't complained once. Very soon, I will be farther away from my home than I've ever been in my entire life.

Anxiety punches me in the chest. Instantly, I feel Talon's gaze on me.

"What?" I ask sharply.

"Your breathing changed," they note. "Is there something around us I should be aware of?"

Ah. They think I'm reacting to one of the many beasts that prowls these lands. "The most dangerous of the predators are farther north. Only the panthers stay this far south, and that's only because I'm here. Don't worry, wolf." A mocking grin stretches across my mouth. "I'll keep you safe."

Talon snorts. "So kind of you, witch."

My grin fades as the anxiety tugs at me a little more. I hate to admit this, but I need to be prepared. "Astria may have mentioned this, but I don't really leave my woods, aside from short visits to Shalewood and occasionally Neidell."

They're looking away from me, scanning the other side of the forest when they answer. "She actually doesn't talk about you much."

"Oh." I fight to keep the pain off my face in case Talon turns their attention back to me, grabbing every fragment of it that would have tightened the corners of my mouth or caused my eyes to water before shoving it deep down. The same way I did when my mate told me he was leaving me. I can't help but glance at my left hand—to where the mate bond tattoos once decorated the backs of each finger.

Talon stops suddenly, and I awkwardly halt as well so we're facing each other. "It isn't that she doesn't care. Astria misses you, and I think talking about you hurts. She's never stopped being loyal to her big sister. I don't think she wants to risk any information, no matter how trivial, being overheard by the wrong person."

"Oh," I say again. Witch of the Woods. The Last Guardian. Skilled Slinger of Words.

Maybe only having the panthers to share conversations with over the last year has left me a little rustier than I thought.

"Just . . . uh . . ." Talon purses their lips together before looking away again. "Assume I don't know much about you, but anything you're willing to share is useful. It'll help me plan accordingly. The towns that border your forest are very different from the rest of Eleoyn. The people who live there don't ask many questions, and the mage hunter presence is pretty light."

I nod. "Okay, so tell me what to expect on our travels."

We start walking again. "The Obscuras have been more active than usual this past year," Talon finally says. "The mage hunters have increased their campaign against them, and paranoia has spread. Entire families suspected of harboring rebel mages have vanished overnight."

My brows furrow together. Strange that my fellow guardian to the west hasn't mentioned anything. If the Obscuras are acting up in Eleoyn, it almost certainly has to do with something going on in Sekaria—the Mage Kingdom. I guard the forest above Eleoyn, and my mage counterpart does the same for the forest above Sekaria. I know little personal information about them—not even their name—only what they are, that they don't mind being referred to as he, and that they despise the Mage Council that rules Sekaria, but they don't seem fond of the rebel mages who have formed the Obscuras either.

Perhaps after I make it back home, I'll pay him a visit. It isn't that I care that much about what happens to the Mage Kingdom, but if some big plan is in play, it may very well spill over into my forest. I prefer to be prepared for such an event.

"Any thoughts on how we will avoid scrutiny?" I ask as I continue to ponder what could be going on with the mage rebellion.

Talon sighs before slipping their hand underneath their brown cloak and pulling something out of their shirt pocket. "Congratulations." A plain, dark silver ring glints between their fingers as they hold it up. "You have the spectacular fortune of being my wife."

They toss me the ring, and I snap it out of the air. "You can't be serious."

Talon keeps moving but spins around so they're walking backwards, somehow sensing the roots and uneven spots on the ground without even seeing them. "We're already going to be traveling together, so this is the best option. Pretty young women don't often gallivant around by themselves."

"I'm two hundred years old." I glare at them, hoping they'll trip and fall, but no such luck.

Talon's lips quirk up. "Not going to argue the pretty part, eh?"

"I'm well aware of my looks." I shrug. "There was a lot of competition amongst my generation for who I would choose as a mate."

Something flashes across their face faster than I can catch it. "Did you?"

"Did I what?"

"Have a mate?"

"Yes." The word slips out seemingly of its own volition, and I wish I could claw it back. It's none of Talon's damn business.

Talon's dark brown eyebrows bunch together. "Don't witches mate for life?"

"No, that's a wolf thing," I respond, and then, before I can think better of it, I blurt out a question I really shouldn't. "Do you have one? A mate, I mean?"

That same twisted hate I saw in their eyes two years ago flashes again. "There are no cursed wolves left, and I can't mate with a human."

Then they turn so they're facing forward again before stalking farther ahead. I know by "*mate*," they hadn't meant "have sex." The witches have bonding ceremonies that link our magic together. When werewolves mate, their souls become connected. It is an intimate and powerful natural magic. Every wolf longs to find their mate, and in the Wilds, they usually do.

Talon will never find theirs though, and a witch like me was the reason for it.

I never really thought about the full implications of that curse before meeting Talon because I rarely interact with cursed wolves. They are the first one I've seen in decades, and the previous encounters were all brief. The original ones were cast out of the Wilds and into the four kingdoms . . . and generations later, their descendants have been forgotten, even while they still pay the price.

We walk in silence until we reach the boundary of my territory. Tall, golden strands of wildgrass greet us, interspersed with blue and pink flowers. I inhale the rich scents of my forest one last time before stepping past the tree line to where Talon is already waiting.

The hatred is gone from their eyes, replaced by a cool mask of indifference as they watch me approach. "Interesting decorations." Dark brown eyes drift over to where roots have erupted out of the earth, twisting towards the sky. Bodies torn into pieces and in various states of decay hang off the roots like adornments.

My nose twitches at the smell, but the wind is thankfully blowing away from us.

"Just thought I'd make it really clear what the fate of any uninvited guests would be. Perhaps seeing this "—I wave a hand at my macabre display—"has changed a few minds."

"I don't think that was your goal." Talon's dark eyes fall on me.

"You don't know anything about me," I respond sharply, not liking the way they're looking at me, because it's not with disgust or scorn . . . but something akin to pity.

Fuck that. I'm fine. Using your enemies' rotting corpses as a warning is a time-honored tradition. Or at least it is now.

I'm a trendsetter. Talon can take their pity and shove it up their ass.

"You're right. I don't know you. The real you anyway." They give me a grim smile and lean over to pluck the ring I'd been rolling between my fingers out of my grasp. "But I know what picking a fight looks like." They jam the ring onto the fourth finger of my left hand. "And that"—they point over my shoulder to the bodies —"is absolutely a challenge."

"It's not like they weren't going to come anyway." I step away, creating much-needed distance between us as my fingers immediately twist the foreign silver band now on my ring finger.

"And what would your sister say about such a display? It's one thing to guard your woods, it's another thing to do something that fucked up."

"Astria left." I shove past them and start walking. "She doesn't get to have an opinion. Once we rescue her, she can go back to her life, and I can go back to mine."

CHAPTER SIX

~

Talon

BY THE TIME we reach Shalewood, I'm not sure who is in a pissier mood—me or the witch. During those six months we were camped outside the town—after Cerelia and I had our tryst—I got anxious every time Astria came to visit Ravyn. Despite the witch and me parting on threats, I wanted to see her again. Whether that was to slice my dagger across her delicate throat or to pin her against a tree again . . . dealer's choice, I suppose.

But she never came, and then we left Shalewood, and Astria came with us. In the year after that, I did everything I could to get her out of my mind. Took more heist jobs and volunteered to help even more around the troupe, but nothing worked.

Now she is here and soon she'll have her body pressed up against mine while we ride a horse together. I still don't know if I want to strangle her or part those perfectly toned thighs and find out what they feel like wrapped around my head.

Fuck. I did not expect it to be this confusing around her. If I go through all of this and it turns out my sister really did leave that note and she's just having some fun with Astria somewhere . . . I'm going to refuse to speak to both of them for at least a year.

On the plus side, I can tell Cerelia is equally unnerved by my presence. She does a piss-poor job of hiding her emotions because everything she feels flashes across that pretty face for all the world to see.

Scythe, I correct myself. The woman I danced around the bonfire with is a lie, even if Cerelia is her real name. Scythe is so much more fitting for the bloodthirsty witch.

We're going to have to work on hiding her expressions a little better though. It's going to undermine everything if I introduce us as a newly married couple only for her to stare at me like she's envisioning peeling the flesh from my bones.

Despite Shalewood being a small town with a population of only a few thousand, it's midday, which is always a busy time. The locals are racing around, trying to complete errands or bartering in the markets. People traveling through are stopping in the local taverns to grab a quick bite to eat. The witch pulls her hood up, clearly uncomfortable with the surrounding chaos and probably paranoid about being recognized as a witch even with that charmed necklace on. She doesn't realize that her attempts to hide are only drawing more attention to us. It's not a big deal in Shalewood because everyone here minds their own damn business, but it'll be like a beacon for the city guards or mage hunters in the larger cities.

"Wait here," I order sharply when we reach the stable attached to one of the main taverns. All the small towns like this keep the stables more towards the populated center, making it harder for raiders to steal their horses.

I don't look back to see if the witch obeys my order as I stalk in, but I can feel her staring at the back of my head, likely thinking about sinking one of those blades strapped to her thigh into it. Unfortunately for her, the witch needs me to find her sister, but as soon as that's done, we'll part ways.

Hopefully for good. We parted abruptly the night we first met, and she didn't come down from her death trap of a house when I helped Astria collect her things. I'm sure by the time we find our sisters, I'll be sick of her presence and will no longer be plagued with the memory of her like I have been for the past year and a half.

Five minutes later, I've paid the boarding fee and am leading Draco back out to the spot where I told Scythe to wait. To my surprise, she's actually still there. Part of me had expected her to move just out of spite. She did back up a couple of feet so that her back is to the wall of the tavern though. Her hood shrouds her face, but I can tell by the stiffness of her posture that she's on full alert, like a wolf that's been cornered and is waiting for the next threat.

Yeah . . . we'll definitely have to work on that a bit. Although I'm surprised she's struggling so much with this because I know she's been to towns before. Maybe because it's daytime? I met her on the road just outside town and then persuaded her to come to the blood moon festival that night. I think about the corpses she put on display outside her forest. Maybe something has the witch more on edge than normal?

Well, she'll just have to get her shit together before we reach the coast. I lead Draco over to her. "Give me your bag."

She steps away from the wall and slaps her bag against my chest. I growl at her, but she doesn't even notice because all her attention is on Draco, who is standing tall and watching the witch with dark, intelligent eyes.

"He's Arandian," she says in surprise.

"Maybe don't say that out loud?" I admonish her as I drop her pack onto the ground next to mine. "My pack has plenty of space —are you okay with me moving your stuff into it? Since we're riding together, you'll have to carry everything."

She hums her agreement, clearly more interested in the horse than what I'm telling her. I'm curious about how she instantly recognized him as being of Arandian blood. The horses from the continent across the ocean are rare. The fae originally brought them over almost a thousand years ago when they first visited these lands. They left long before the witches did, but they abandoned most of their horses here.

Like most Arandian horses, Draco looks like a normal horse—a gorgeous one, but no different from any other. His dark bay coat has a reddish sheen to it, and he has a thick black mane and tail. Astria and Ravyn love doting on him, so it's always free of tangles. At sixteen hands with a strong build, he would make an excellent mount, even if he wasn't descended from the fae horses.

Thanks to his heritage, Draco never tires, and carrying two people a long distance is nothing to him. He's also considerably smarter than most horses, who have a tendency to panic since they're prey animals, whereas Draco just watches and evaluates the world around him with his patient, dark eyes.

Just like he's doing now with the witch as she slowly reaches up to stroke his cheek. It's strange because it's like they recognize each other for what they are. Not only do they both have Arandian blood running through their veins, but they were also both left behind.

The witch finally looks away from the horse, although she keeps petting him. "How do I get on?" she asks tentatively as she eyes his height and bites her bottom lip almost nervously.

"Really?" I arch a brow at her. "You'll walk up those death trap stairs and then skip around next to a two-hundred-foot fall, but this is too high for you?"

"It's not the same." She narrows her eyes at me. The blue is pretty . . . but I find myself already missing the silver.

"Come on. I'll help you up." I motion her over to Draco's side and move so I face the back of the horse and she faces the front. Intertwining my fingers, I lean forward a little. "Put your left foot in my hands and hold my shoulders. When I lift you, just swing your right leg behind the saddle and hop on. He won't go anywhere."

Draco snorts his agreement, and the witch smiles before giving me a look. "Don't drop me."

"If you keep stalling, I will absolutely drop you."

"Prick," she mutters before doing as I instructed. Despite the awkward pose, I can't help but be very aware of how close her body is to mine, particularly her chest to my face. She seems to realize the same because she quickly pushes upward, and I straighten as well. Even with her nervousness, she easily gets onto Draco, and some of the tension eases out of her shoulders.

"Here." I pass her the leather satchel with all of our belongings, and she swings it onto her back. Then I hop on in front of her and settle into the saddle before nudging Draco into a walk.

"Wait, where do I hold on?" she asks frantically, and I feel her trying to clutch the edge of the saddle between us, but there isn't much to grip.

I let out an amused laugh. "Scoot forward a little and wrap your arms around my waist."

After a few seconds of hesitation, her chest presses against my back and she loops her arms around me, linking her hands together. "Why didn't you say that *before* we started moving?"

I grin at the indignation in her voice. "Because you would have argued and refused to do it even though there really isn't any other option. My way was faster and easier. Now hold on."

"Why?" Her grip around me tightens as we turn onto one of the more lightly traveled pathways that gives us a straight shot out of town.

"Because I want to make it to Neidell by nightfall, which means we need to go fast."

Before she can protest, I urge Draco into a canter and laugh as the witch clings to me while releasing an impressive amount of swear words.

"So?" I grin at Scythe as I hold out my hand to help her dismount. "Enjoy your first ride?"

"You're an asshole." She slaps my hand away and slides off Draco, wincing a little when she lands on her feet. "I wasn't expecting to be so sore from that, considering how much running I'm used to doing."

"Different muscles." My grin widens. "It'll be even worse tomorrow."

"Wonderful." She watches me untie my sword and lean the sheathe against the wall before taking off Draco's saddle and then his bridle. "Can I help?"

"Should be a bucket out in the breezeway with some brushes. You can grab one and start brushing him down while I see about getting him some food."

Scythe disappears for a few seconds before reappearing with a soft-bristled brush. Despite her aversion to riding, she's perfectly comfortable around Draco on the ground, even though he towers over her, which I guess makes sense, considering the devil cats seem to be her primary company these days.

"Be right back." I slip out of the stall and return with several flakes of a rich-smelling grass hay. Scythe is humming quietly, and Draco has his eyes closed as the witch brushes his back, but she goes still when I move behind her and lean forward to whisper in her ear, "Are you using your magic right now?"

She turns her head slightly. "No. It's just an old Arandian song I used to hum to Astria when she was younger."

I'm not entirely sure I believe her, but the scythe tattoo isn't showing on her neck and I don't feel anything, so I let it go.

"Remember what I told you earlier?"

"Before or after you deliberately went through the river to scare the shit out of me?" She narrows her eyes across Draco's back, which she can barely see over.

I laugh under my breath. On our way here, part of the trail ran by a river, and I turned Draco into it to "cool him off a bit." Her squeals were adorable and completely at odds with the witch who had held a scythe to my throat just last night. Of course she jabbed me so hard in the side afterwards that I almost blacked out from the pain. She must have hit a nerve or something. *That* was definitely closer to the scythe-wielding witch I knew.

"Before." I lean down to check each of Draco's hooves.

"Nope, I forgot everything," she replies in a breezy tone.

I finish checking the last hoof and straighten to shoot her an annoyed look. The witch just rolls her eyes before closing the distance between us, and I go completely still as she wraps her arms around my neck and plasters her body against mine.

"We're happily married. *Newly* happily married," she whispers in my left ear, and I can't help but inhale her rich and wild scent. "I'm supposed to give you doe-eyed looks and defer any questions to you because I'm just"—she nips my earlobe, and I bite back a groan—"a small-town girl"—another nip—"and you're my well-traveled *kalri.*"

Fates damn this witch. I can feel her breath against my skin as she lets out a low laugh, clearly proud of herself for catching me off guard.

Two can play this game, and I'm betting I'm better at it than she is.

She exhales sharply when I grip her ass and lift her up, slamming her back against the rear of the stall. I can feel her body instantly going from languidly amused to tense and on full alert, but her arms are still around my neck, and she automatically wraps her legs around my waist. "*Kalri* is a Tovenian term." I tilt my head so some of my dark hair falls against the side of my face. "The Eleoyn just say spouse."

"You're obviously Tovenian. I was trying to blend." Her words come out a little breathy, and I swear flecks of silver bleed through the brown in her eyes.

I duck my head and nuzzle her neck, and she shivers as I lightly brush kisses against her skin, my fingers digging into the soft flesh of her ass as my lips blaze a path upward so I can whisper in her ear, "You did a shit job of blending in at Shalewood." Her body stiffens before she starts to drop her legs from around me, but I'm not ready to let her go yet, so I thrust my hips, grinding her against the wall as I wrap a hand around her long hair and pull on it. Hard.

A stifled moan slips from the witch as her legs tighten around my waist again and her fingernails dig into the back of my neck. For a second, I almost forget myself and surrender to my desire to feel every inch of her. Would she let me? Or would she remember who she is and who I am before pushing me away?

I refuse to be the one to fully give in to this only to be denied. If the witch wants me, I'll make her beg for it. My grip on her hair gets harsher and she lets out a hiss of pain. This time, it's definitely silver I see flashing in her eyes along with the scythe tattoo on her neck. Good. Hatred is so much easier to understand than this all-consuming desire between us.

"Tomorrow night, we'll be in a city, and you need to fucking blend in instead of practically screaming, 'Look at me,' to any nearby mage hunter or city guard," I say in an even, bored tone, like feeling her body pressed against mine is doing absolutely nothing for me.

She bares her teeth. "I've survived two hundred years—"

"In your forest," I cut her off. "And if we were hunting in your forest, I'd defer to you, but we're not. I know the cities far better than you, which is why I'm telling you that you're going to get yourself—and probably me—killed long before we find out what happened to our sisters if you don't. Do. Better."

The wrath on her face is delicious, and I can't resist leaning forward to kiss her jawline. I debate moving to her lips so I can taste her anger, but given the outrage rolling off her, I'm pretty sure she'd bite me. The thought almost has me groaning, but I don't want the witch to know just how much my body craves her, so I drop to the crook of her neck and nip her again.

When I pull back, her face is flushed but her eyes are pure ice.

"Message received," she says flatly. "I'll do better."

"See that you do, Cerelia." The name slips out before I can stop it. I drop my hands from her ass, and she drops her legs from around my waist. Immediately, I step away, taking a small amount of pleasure at the way she stumbles to catch her footing, even as part of me misses the feel of her body against mine.

Before I can dwell on that unwanted thought, I catch a flicker of red across her lips. Her tongue darts out and licks it away. I frown because I didn't bite her lip at any point. Only nipped her neck.

She strides towards the stall door, back rigidly straight, and picks up our bag before holding it out to me. When I take it from her, she starts to raise her cloak's hood but halts at my pointed look. With a grimace, she lets it fall and runs her fingers through her hair a few times to straighten out some of the tangles after my rough treatment. Once she's satisfied, she beams at me with a false smile. "Shall we?"

I sling the bag over my shoulder and open the stall door for her. "Let's see what you got, witch."

CHAPTER SEVEN

~

Scythe

My lip fucking hurts, and it's my own damn fault. I'm so used to knowing my environment better than the back of my hand and always having the answers to everything, but Talon—that arrogant asshole—is right. This isn't my forest, and they are far better equipped to navigate these treacherous waters.

It isn't like I haven't left my forest before, but as much as possible, I try to avoid going to town during the day. Everything is so much brighter and busier. People are nosier, and I'm not used to being stared at. At least not by people who are actively trying to kill me. While I was waiting for Talon to collect their horse in Shalewood, I kept getting paranoid that my charm was failing and people could see my true appearance, so I pulled my hood up.

In hindsight, I can see how that would have only attracted more attention, especially considering the heat of the midday sun. Seeing someone standing there in not only a cloak but with the hood up probably looked sketchy as all the hells. I really should have known better, but I wasn't thinking straight.

Just like I absolutely didn't think it through when I kissed Talon in the stables. I was annoyed at them barking orders at me all day and wanted to get a reaction.

I definitely got that.

Yet once again, I found myself out of my depth as Talon easily played my body. We didn't even really do anything. Neither of our hands slipped beneath clothing during our groping, and we didn't even touch anything that intimate. Although Talon did have a pretty good grip on my ass. But when they nipped my neck at the end, I had to bite my lip to claw back the moan that tried to slip free.

It's ridiculous how I reacted, considering I'm far from some inexperienced maiden. I had a bit of a wild youth before I settled down with my mate, and after he left me, I regularly found human males to have some fun with.

Yet my entire body was on fire the second Talon touched me in the stables.

It's confusing. They're confusing. The loud and chaotic conversations of this damn tavern are confusing. I mean, how does anyone have a conversation in all this noise?

I flinch when a group behind me slams their tankards down onto the table. This tavern is similar to the few I've been to in Shalewood, just larger. I deliberately choose the smaller taverns on the outskirts of town because they're less . . . everything. People. Noise. Scents. Just less of all of it.

Before Astria left, we'd gone into town more frequently, sometimes as often as once a month, but I've only ventured into town one time in the last two years, and I left quickly.

Given what they said about how poorly I was handling being away from the forest, I suspect Talon deliberately chose the busiest tavern for us to stay at tonight to test my resolve. This one is definitely the main one used by travelers passing through because it has the stables out back and several floors of rooms above it. Other than the size, it looks the same as any other tavern I've been in—

worn wood walls interspersed with brick and a bar in the back of the room. Stairs are tucked away just to the left of the bar, and a raised platform sits on the wall to the right of the stairs for musicians or bards to perform.

Thankfully, tonight, there is nobody performing. While I enjoy music, there is no way I could handle that right now on top of all the other sounds. Dozens of tables are scattered around, and a huge unlit fireplace takes up most of the wall to the left. I have no doubt they make good use of it during winter, when the temperatures often hover just above freezing.

I would have preferred one of the tables towards the back, but of course Talon directed me to one practically in the middle of the room before sauntering off towards the bar.

Despite the leers I'm getting, I keep my hood down and a bemused expression on my face. In my mind, I've already killed the man who leaned over me to drunkenly ask if I would sit with him . . . and I've broken every finger of the one who pulled my hair to get my attention. Apparently, personal space is just not a thing here. In reality, I sent both of them away with a laugh and polite refusal, even as my fingers itched to slide under the cloak I laid over my lap to pull out one of my daggers.

The real question was whether I'd be throwing my dagger at the next drunk asshole who tried to talk to me . . . or at Talon's face.

I glance at them for the third time in the last five minutes, and my smile slips. Talon is still standing by the bar, chatting with a barmaid. A *pretty* barmaid. I watch, unable to look away as they lean across the counter to brush a loose strand of her curly blonde hair behind her ear. Jealousy shoots through me as the barmaid giggles at something Talon says before reaching out to playfully pat their cheek. Is this what Talon is like with everyone else? With people they truly like?

With me, Talon runs hot and cold, and I'm worried they're aware of my attraction to them and are toying with me. I really shouldn't have kissed them and started that game in the stable. I'm going to stew over that miscalculation all night. Both Talon and the barmaid glance my way, and she says something to make them laugh. I can't hear anything they're saying, but I get the distinct impression that they know each other—intimately.

I jerk my gaze away from them. This isn't fair. It's hard enough for me to blend in as a normal human female, but how in all the hells am I supposed to know how a newly married Eleoyn woman would act upon seeing her charming spouse flirt with an old lover? Break their legs? Cut off a few fingers? Maybe I can ask Talon exactly what the proper etiquette is later after I shove a few daggers into their gut.

"All alone, pretty lass?" A burly man with dark brown hair and a reddish beard thuds onto the bench next to me, spilling his ale across the table.

I pull my hand back before any of the amber liquid touches me. "No, actually. My *kalri* is getting us dinner and a room for the night." Despite Talon's correction earlier, I feel it makes more sense to use the Tovenian word for spouse. Anyone who looks at Talon for more than a second will know they're Tovenian, and perhaps if I have a few social missteps, they'll blame it on the culture difference.

"Don't see nobody." The man looks around, shrugs, and extends an arm over my shoulders. "Have a drink with me."

"I'm sure they'll be back any moment," I say a little less politely. My gaze flicks to Talon, who's *still* chatting with that damn barmaid, now with their back to me. Perfect. Fucking. Perfect. If I make a scene or do anything rash, they'll lecture me about it later.

The man leans even closer, his body and thigh flush against mine. Magic ripples beneath my skin, and I twitch my pinky finger, the silver ring containing my scythe flashing in the dim light. Once again, I look towards Talon, only to find both them and the barmaid gone.

My temper snaps.

"How 'bout we go upstai—" My new inebriated friend's words die on his lips as the tip of my blade nudges his groin.

"How about you go find another place to sit?" I smile widely, and he pales but nods enthusiastically. "Perfect. Off you go."

I pull the blade away enough for him to move, spilling even more of his ale as he quickly flees, but my annoyance remains even after he's gone.

"Making new friends, I see." Talon slides into the seat across from me and places two ales onto the table.

"Greeting old friends, I see." I give them my best innocent doe-eyed look before snatching one of the ales and downing half of it in one go. Talon arches an eyebrow at me, and I arch one back, just daring them to say anything.

They laugh and reach across the table with their palm upright. I hesitate for a moment, then with an internal sigh, I slip my hand into theirs. None of this is real, and I can't let my temper get the better of me. Talon is just a means to an end. I'm already feeling overwhelmed just by being in a tavern, so trying to find Astria in the chaos of Eleoyn without Talon's help would likely prove disastrous.

Talon toys with the fake marriage band adorning my ring finger. "Our meals should be coming out shortly. I figured we would eat down here and enjoy the ambiance before retiring to our room."

Next to us, two men start yelling at each other before one lunges forward to slam the other's head down onto the table. Ale tankards crash to the floor, and the man who just had his nose smashed wipes at the blood, then throws his head back and releases a bellowing laugh.

"More ale!" screams the one who gave him the bloody nose.

"Ah, yes," I say wryly. "The ambiance."

Talon snickers, and then we both lean back as the barmaid they were flirting with places two plates in front of us. "Thank you, Eliza."

I debate flinging my dagger under the table at Talon's crotch for the heated smile they give the barmaid—*Eliza*, apparently. The angle is tough and I'm not the best at throwing knives to begin with, but I'm feeling pretty motivated, so I think I might be able to—

"Are you enjoying Neidell?" Eliza asks, cutting off my train of thought. "Tal said you grew up in one of the border towns to the west and haven't seen much of Eleoyn?"

I search her light green eyes, trying to figure out if she's asking this question in earnest or just messing with me. It doesn't seem like Talon told her our cover story, probably because they know each other and she wouldn't have believed it, but they also didn't tell her who I really am . . . I glance at Talon, trying to figure out how to respond, but they just give me a lazy grin in response.

I'll have to practice my knife-throwing. Something tells me it'll be useful while traveling with Talon.

"It's nice," I finally settle on. "Talon is being so *helpful* about everything."

"I'm considerate like that," they agree easily.

Yep. Definitely going to stab them later.

Eliza laughs. "Tal's a great catch." She wiggles her eyebrows suggestively, and now I'm just extra confused. "Room's all set for you two when you're done." She hands Talon a key and winks at me. "Enjoy your night."

I stare after her. Did I misread things earlier? Weren't they flirting with each other? Does everyone in Eleoyn just shamelessly flirt? Am I the asshole here? Before I can dwell on how confusing everything has been, I get a solid whiff of the deliciously spicy meal in front of me, and my stomach rumbles. Temporarily pushing all other thoughts aside, I grab a fork and take a heaping bite of the curry and rice dish.

"Fuck," I groan as the aromatic spices dance across my tongue.

The distinct piney flavor of cardamom hits, and I make another embarrassing sound. How the fuck did they get cardamom all the way up here?

"Do I need to leave the two of you alone?" Talon asks, their dark eyes lit up with amusement. "You can take it upstairs if you need to. I'll let you have the room for a bit."

I shovel another bite into my mouth, this time managing not to moan, and wipe my face with a napkin while I swallow it down. "Haven't had curry in a while, and it's one of my favorite things," I admit.

"Why not?" They dig into their own plate.

My appetite dims a little. "The . . . cook . . . from my . . . small town," I say for the sake of anyone listening in on our conversation. "She left a year ago, and there isn't anyone else around who can make it." Or anything else really. I can boil potatoes and cook meat over an open fire, but that's the extent of my skills. Astria made all our meals because she enjoys cooking.

"Ah," Talon replies.

Nothing else. Just that one word. I briefly skim their face, but they have their charming mask firmly in place, so I can't get any hint of their emotions. I wish I could do that. Maybe I'll work on it while I'm practicing my knife throwing.

We finish eating quickly. Aside from a few people complaining loudly about delayed fresh fruit deliveries, I don't hear any gossip of note, but it is hard to pick out the individual voices in a loud room.

Relief floods me when Talon rises and extends a hand. "Come on. I'll take you to our room." I slide my hand into theirs, letting them pull me to my feet and guide me up the stairs at the back of the tavern.

A small flicker of nervousness hits me at the idea of sharing a room with Talon. But surely there will be space for one of us to sleep on the floor and not have to share the bed. We go all the way up to the top floor and then down the hallway to the room at the end.

With every step away from the boisterous crowd, I feel myself relax a little bit more. This might be a large and busy tavern, but we're still only in a small northern town. What will the taverns and streets of the cities be like? I chew on my bottom lip while Talon pulls the key from their pocket and unlocks the door.

"This is considered a room?" I blink as I step inside after Talon. It's clean, I have to give it that, but I'm also pretty sure that if I stretch my arms out, I can touch both sides. The bed, which is just a mattress on the floor, takes up the majority of the space. There isn't even room on the floor for one of us to sleep for fuck's sake.

Aside from the bed, the only other piece of furniture is a chair that looks like it was taken from a table downstairs. "You *paid* for this?"

"Nah," Talon drawls. "Eliza likes me, so we get to stay for free tonight."

"I bet she does," I mutter.

"Jealous?" They laugh at my flat stare. "You've done an excellent job of staying in character as my pretty little wife." Little? Talon is only a few inches taller than me, and while their shoulders are broader than mine, they aren't that much larger. "Thought for sure you were going to lose it when that drunk asshole sat down next to you, but you handled it beautifully."

"You saw that?" My brows furrow together. I could have sworn they missed that whole interaction, first with their back turned and then running off with the barmaid.

"Oh yes." Talon chuckles. "Eliza and I were watching from behind the curtain that leads to the kitchen."

"And you didn't think to help?" I ask incredulously.

"Wanted to see how you would manage on your own." They wink. "Like I said, you handled it quite well. Don't think anyone noticed you pull that dagger and threaten to cut off the poor sod's bits."

I stare at them for a long moment, then smack the exact spot I punched their side earlier in the day. Talon grunts and shoots me a dirty look as I slide past them and sit on the edge of the mattress, dropping my folded-up cloak next to me. Fatigue tugs at the edges of my mind. It's relatively early, only a couple of hours past sunset, but I barely slept last night, too busy thinking about where Astria and Ravyn could have possibly gone. When I wasn't thinking about them, I was remembering the night I'd spent with Talon.

It's strange how quickly I felt the pull towards them. I'd never felt that way about anyone, not even my mate, Vaeril. I first met Talon when I interrupted a heist they were pulling off. The feeling between us had started at that moment. When we danced that night at the blood moon festival, that spark had erupted until it burned hotter than the bonfires around us.

I remember every single thing about that evening. The way they laughed as they spun me around the flames, the feel of their body pressed against mine . . . and the look of pure hatred in their eyes when they realized I was a witch.

None of it matters. Whatever foolish pining I've done over the last two years, Talon clearly hasn't felt the same based on their interaction with the barmaid.

"Eliza likes me."

I unlatch the sheaths from my thighs and stack my daggers neatly on the floor and then start to unlace my boots. I desperately need to get these damn shoes off. Talon walks the two feet over to the chair, grabs it, and proceeds to jam it up against the closed door. I give them a questioning look.

"Another lesson for you." They pull off their own cloak before tossing it onto the bed, and I shove it over onto their side. "Never trust the locks on these doors to keep you safe." They wave a hand at the door and then point to the one and only window. "And always have another way out."

"We're three stories up," I point out. "The window isn't going to do us much good."

"Drainage pipe runs down this side of the building to the left of the window." They sit at the bottom of the mattress and tug off their boots. "It's secure enough that we can use it to climb down if we have to. I don't think we'll have any problems here, but one can never be too careful in Eleoyn."

I set my boots next to my cloak and stretch out on the bed. My muscles are still sore from riding, and they only got stiffer while sitting through dinner. "I still can't believe Astria gave up the safety of the forest for shady inns where she has to barricade herself."

"To be fair . . ." Talon thumps down on the mattress beside me, and I ignore the way my heart speeds up a bit. "Raiders and witch hunters regularly enter your forest with the intention of killing you. Not exactly sure I'd call that *safe*."

My lips twitch. "Fair point."

"I'm also a little more paranoid than most." Talon flops their head to the side so they're fully facing me. "Ravyn is always making fun of me for it, trying to get me to relax a little. The cities are absolutely dangerous, but I think the most serious crime that has happened around these parts is when someone declared Eliza's curry to be bland and disappointing."

"It was really good curry," I say reluctantly.

Talon reaches out to toy with the end of my braid—probably just to mess with me. I try to ignore it and not give them the satisfaction of reacting.

"I suppose I can quit tormenting you now. Eliza's a bit of a free spirit. She's had an on-again, off-again relationship with Mattias—one of my friends—for years. He wants her to travel with us. She wants him to give up the troupe and move here. They don't fight about it or anything, it's more like a game between them, but everyone in the troupe likes her, and she does us favors whenever we're in town."

"So let me get this straight." My patience runs out, and I yank my braid away from them. "*You* came up with the cover story of me being your wife, tell *me* I'm supposed to play along with it, then *you* decide to make it even more difficult by flirting with someone right in front of me? I had no idea how I was supposed to react and was stressing about it while you were having a laugh at my expense. You're a fucking prick, Talon."

"I was just having a little fun." They shrug before reaching for my braid once more. I slap it out of their hand but give up when they grab it again. "Eliza is fun to flirt with, and I'm going to have to behave for the rest of the trip and pretend I like you."

"Well, I have to stare at your face and pretend I find you remotely attractive, so I suppose we each have our hardships."

"Please." They snort. "We both know you think I'm stunning, and that if I slipped my hand into your pants in the stable earlier, I would have found you wet and ready for me."

"Just working on my acting skills," I snap, hating the fact that they're absolutely right and that my panties were uncomfortably damp for most of dinner. Needing a change in topic, I ask, "What can I expect in the next city?"

"Sovarre won't be too bad. But even if we ride fast, we still won't arrive until well after sunset, so we won't be spending much time there." Talon looks away from my hair to give me a wry grin. "I won't subject you to one of the larger inns. We'll grab a room at one of the smaller ones on the edge of town and be out before first light. The problem will be Tenresan."

I've never been to the capital of Eleoyn, but I've heard about it. Not just from the conversations I picked up on in Shalewood, but also from my parents. There was a time when witches could travel freely throughout the four kingdoms. My parents did so when they were younger and they told me all about the sprawling city that had been built by witch, human, and fae hands.

Now, the city is home to almost two hundred thousand people, which is just mind-boggling to me. It's also where the mage hunters are based out of, which means the city will be crawling with them. In my forest, I have no problem going up against twenty mage hunters or more, but in a city, they will have the advantage. My magic is nature-based, and while I can use it everywhere, there will be a lot less for me to call on in Tenresan.

I'm lethal with my scythe, but numbers are numbers. If even ten mage hunters get the jump on me in the city, I'm done, which means I need to make sure my disguise holds up and I do nothing to draw attention to myself.

"Why can't we just go around?" I ask. "Head south from here and then cut over east to Albadrid?"

Talon grimaces and finally drops my braid. "The prince is throwing a summer festival in Mabria, which is located directly south of us in the middle of the kingdom. Half the roads are shut down, and the other half are heavily patrolled. It would slow us down. Any roads that aren't crawling with mage hunters will have raiders hunting along them."

"So Tenresan it is," I reply with a sigh.

"We won't stay," Talon says. "But we'll have to ride through, and the security checkpoints can be tedious. You'll need to be on your best behavior."

"Try not to do anything super annoying and I'm sure we'll be fine."

They smile faintly but don't make any promises. "How does it feel to be so far from your forest?"

"Strange." I look around the bare walls and patched-up ceiling. "Haven't slept in inns all that much."

"Really?" A hint of surprise enters their dark eyes. "Astria hinted that you have a few lovers in Shalewood."

"Lovers?" I snort. "If I need a good fuck, I go into town, see to my needs, and then return to the forest. So apologies in advance if I kick you during the night. Been a while since I shared a bed with someone."

"Ah, the mate." Their tone has an odd flatness to it that I don't quite understand. "How long has it been?"

I ignore their question because I have absolutely zero interest in discussing Vaeril with anyone, least of all Talon. Instead, I stretch my legs out and wince at the soreness. Fuck this. Leaning my head back into the pillow, I hum a gentle melody. I didn't see any signs of mage hunters in town, but I only let the smallest amount of magic out just in case. No one outside this room will be able to feel it.

The ache in my muscles gradually fades, and when I stretch again, my body feels loose and relaxed. It's then I realize Talon has gone completely still. I tilt my head to look at them.

"Sorry," I say slowly, taking in the tension radiating off their stiff posture. "Should have given you a warning."

"It's fine," they say tightly. "Just wasn't expecting to feel it—your magic."

"What's it feel like?" I ask curiously. "I grew up around witches, and I never asked Astria because . . ." I drop my gaze to stare at a spot on the bed.

"Because you didn't want to rub her lack of magic in her face," Talon guesses.

I nod. "Our parents . . . they didn't acknowledge her as their daughter. I was the one who raised her." I don't regret it either. Astria is worth more than all those witches combined, even if she did ultimately leave me just like they had.

"What do the Wilds feel like? What are the wolves like there?" Talon asks instead of answering my question.

I think about it, letting my eyes close so I can picture my last trip there. It's been a while. Forty years, maybe? Traversing the mountains between my forest and the Wilds is no easy feat, even for a witch. The trip takes two weeks just to get there and then another two back. Leaving my forest unattended for that long hasn't been an option since all the witches left me on my own to defend it.

A pang hits me. I hope Necos and the rest of the panthers are alright.

"Untameable," I settle on. "The Wilds are called that because no other name can do it justice. It's enchanting and terrifying. Cruel and peaceful. Enduring and fleeting. There is no name or description that can capture all that it is. And the wolves there reflect that. They love the land, and it loves them back."

When Talon doesn't say anything, I open my eyes to find their expression carefully blank. "I suppose I'll have to take your word for it." Then they flip onto their back, those cunning dark eyes drifting shut. "Get some sleep. We leave at sunrise."

I rise to shut off the lantern hanging by the door, casting the room into darkness, and slide back onto my side of the bed. Several hours later, I'm fairly certain we're both still awake, but neither of us speaks a word.

CHAPTER EIGHT

~

Talon

"Why are we slowing down?" the witch asks. It's the first time she's spoken to me in an hour. Like me, she didn't get much sleep last night. Although I doubt her reasons for being restless are the same as mine. I wasn't able to get her description of the Wilds out of my mind.

It sounded like home.

A home I would never see because witches cursed my damned bloodline. Rationally, I know it doesn't make sense to blame her. I don't blame Astria, and lack of magic aside, she still has witch blood running through her veins. And it was the werewolves who asked the witches for the curse in the first place—something I do hate them for.

But when Cerelia—Scythe, damn it—used that small amount of magic to heal her soreness, I felt it glide over my skin and sink into my flesh.

It touched that hollow place in my soul where my wolf is caged . . . and soothed it.

I hate her, but I also desire her more than anything. She confuses me in a way no one has before, but then she so beautifully describes the home I would never see. Lying beside her all night, inhaling her scent, was a new kind of torture.

Which is why, this morning when we were getting breakfast, I shamelessly flirted with Eliza again just to annoy the witch. It worked—her delight over the freshly baked berry biscuits faded and her expression turned guarded. Eliza caught the shift in Scythe's mood and was not impressed with my antics, based on the cool looks she gave me when we said our goodbyes.

If Ravyn had been there, she would have clapped and said it was impressive that I pissed off two beautiful women in less than two minutes, then asked if I planned on repeating the performance.

I miss my baby sister.

"There's a stream nearby." I point ahead, slightly to the right of the road. "Draco could use a drink since we still have a ways to go."

The fae horse prances a little and picks up the pace from a slow jog to a brisk trot, clearly eager to stomp around in some cool water. Scythe's hands tighten around my waist, and my heartbeat speeds up, then she peers around me to look where I pointed. "Not gonna lie. I'm probably going to throw myself into the water."

I snort. "Same."

As much as I love the heat, even I have to admit that today is damn near unbearable. We're lucky that trees have lined most of the road so far and have provided us with much needed shade; otherwise, we would've had to stop and take a break much earlier. Even with the shade and slight breeze, my clothes cling to my sweat-soaked skin.

"Hopefully it'll be a little cooler on the coast. It'll make the ride down to Alb—" The words die on my tongue as the breeze shifts, carrying their scents to me. I pull Draco to an abrupt stop. "Get off."

To her credit, the witch doesn't question the command. She just unlatches her hands from my waist and slides off Draco's back, scanning the road as soon as her feet hit the ground.

She steps a little farther away to give me room to dismount. "Go hide, Draco." I pat him on the shoulder, and he obediently turns around and trots back the way we came before darting through some trees and vanishing from sight. Honestly, I can never have a normal horse again.

The twanging sound of a crossbow pierces the air, and I jerk to the side, the bolt hurtling past my face. A second *twang*, this time coming from behind me. Before I can do anything, I hear it get knocked away, and I twist around to see Scythe spinning her namesake weapon impossibly fast to guard us from that side.

"You can thank me later," she says over her shoulder.

"All the orgasms, coming up." I turn my attention back to some thick brush ahead of us where I smelled the first group of humans.

"Not what I meant, asshole," Scythe grumbles but steps closer until her back bumps into mine.

"It's our lucky day, boys." A dark-haired man steps out from the brush, followed by another half dozen men. "Looks like we got us some potential bounties in addition to whatever money and weapons they have on them."

I eye the man and then the crew behind him. One of them has a crossbow, and there's at least one more with a crossbow behind me, but with the direction the wind is blowing, I can't tell how many there are. I'll have to trust Scythe to guard my back, which oddly enough, I do despite the animosity between us.

The men aren't wearing the typical leathers of Ririthan raiders. Most of them wear simple tunics and loose-fitting pants. They also don't have the edge that raiders have, that hard look in their eyes that says they've not only seen the worst that humanity has to offer, but participated in it.

"Not raiders," the witch muses, and I can hear her scythe still spinning, at an almost lazy pace now. I step to the side and back so we're even with each other, facing opposite directions, and glance at her. I can't help but be a little surprised she came to the same conclusion as I so quickly. Her eyes drift to mine, and she gives me a knowing smile. "I've killed my fair share of raiders in addition to mage hunters. I know what they look like. Who are these assholes?"

"Eleoyn assholes of some sort." I shrug and then look back at the man who spoke. "My *wife* would like to know what type of assholes you are?"

I can practically feel Scythe's glare boring into the back of my head at the *wife* comment. Gods, this ruse is never going to work with her acting skills.

He narrows his eyes at us, and some of the men behind him shift uneasily, clearly thrown off by how unconcerned Scythe and I are about being outnumbered. If they were smarter, they'd see that as the big fucking clue it is and tuck tail and run, but instead, they all look to the dark-haired man as if he has the answers.

"The human kind," the man sneers, his ruddy skin darkening with anger. "Which you two clearly aren't. No human can dodge a crossbow bolt like that."

"Technically, I knocked mine aside," Scythe points out, her gaze briefly darting away from the men she's been watching to meet mine. "Do I have this right? He's mad at us for not dying so they could rob our corpses?"

"Yeah, that sounds right." I rub the back of my neck. "Also, the whole 'not human' thing."

"Right." She nods and then looks over her shoulder at the dark-haired man. "Just out of curiosity, what do you think we are?"

"I think you're gonna be fucking dead in a minute!" the man growls.

"Sure." Scythe shrugs. "But before we get to that, what do you think I am?"

He frowns in annoyance. Clearly this encounter isn't going the way he thought it would. "Some half-fae whore."

"Ha!" Scythe gives me a triumphant look. "I'm already getting better at blending in!"

I roll my eyes. "Then consider this another test." I waggle my finger in front of her face. "No magic."

"Fine." She turns back to face the group behind us. "But let's kill them quick because it's too hot for this bullshit and I was promised a cold river to swim in."

"Gerald?" A red-haired man glances at the one they clearly all view as the leader. I almost feel bad for this one because he's definitely not qualified to deal with people like me and Scythe based on the clumsy way he's holding his dagger.

"Just fucking kill them already!" the leader, Gerald apparently, snarls before unsheathing the broadsword strapped to his back.

"Can we take the woman alive?" another man with the same dark hair and rough features as Gerald asks. "She could be fun to play with."

"Fine," Gerald growls. "Just don't tell your mother."

"Lovely," I say evenly as the wolf snarls inside my soul. The red-haired man who looked unsure a second ago perks up as he eyes Scythe with renewed interest, and the slight bit of reservation I had about killing him evaporates.

Both crossbows go off, but instead of targeting me, they target Scythe. I hear her knock aside one bolt and I summon my curved daggers in an instant before slashing the one aimed at her right calf. Clearly, they're trying to immobilize her while they cut me down.

"Take out the fucking crossbows!" I snarl.

"No shit!" she snaps back.

I have no time to see what she does after that because the men are on me. The red-haired man tries to dart around me, but he screams when I slam one of my daggers into the back of his neck. He falls like a puppet whose strings have been cut, but not before I grab the small dagger from his hand and fling it at the crossbow man, who is frantically trying to reload.

I dive out of the way of the broadsword aimed at my stomach, and a gurgling sound tells me my blade found its new home in the crossbow man's neck.

Guess he'll never get the chance to learn that crossbows are a range weapon and he really should have stayed farther back. One less fool in the world.

The next couple of minutes are just a red haze of slashing blades and dying screams.

A few of the men have some skills, likely former city guards or some other type of soldier, but it doesn't take long to cut through them all. Gerald grunts as I sink my dagger into the side of his neck before jerking it forward, a spray of blood following its path, then his broadsword falls from his fingers as he crashes to the ground.

My wolf growls in frustration at how easy they were to kill. The beast is still riled up over the casual threat to Scythe, and none of these deaths have quenched the need to cut and rend flesh. They want more blood, but there is no one left to kill. I trigger the magic in my tattoos to hide the Kruxtia's claws once more and stand there panting, trying to get my wolf nature to calm the fuck down. Yet no matter how much I concentrate on my breathing or on the satisfaction of seeing all my enemies lying broken around me, all I can hear is their threat.

"She could be fun to play with."

Scythe. My awareness expands beyond the ten-foot radius around me, and I realize the witch is nowhere to be seen. Where the fuck did she go?

As if my panic summoned her, the witch strides out of the woods, covered in blood with a wild grin on her face. Between one step and the next, her weapon vanishes into that silver ring of hers.

"Couple of them tried to make a run for it," she explains. "I took care of them."

The wolf rattles their cage.

"Talon?" She slows, sharp eyes scanning my body. "Are you hurt?"

"No." The word is more of a growl, but it's all I'm capable of. "You?"

"No," she echoes with a scoff. "They were really determined at first to take me alive and delighted in telling me all the things they were going to do to me." She smiles wider, which helps soothe the wolf, who is still fantasizing about ripping apart the bodies surrounding us. "They were quite surprised when I sliced through half of them. The others didn't even fight, just took off running. Honestly, that wasn't nearly as much fun as I was hoping."

I can see the pent-up energy still rolling through her as she struggles to stand still. We both have too much adrenaline left over from the fight, and I know just how we can work it out.

The witch watches me stalk towards her, those calculating blue eyes wary, but she stands her ground even as one of her hands drops to the dagger she keeps on her thigh. It's not a fight I'm looking for right now though.

She gasps when my hand snaps out and grabs the front of her bloody shirt, yanking her to me. Her lips crash against mine, still parted in surprise, but I don't waste a second as my tongue dives in to taste her.

Gods, she is exquisite. For a second, she doesn't kiss me back. I can practically feel her uncertainty. If I let her think about this, she'll pull away, I know she will. I need her to give in to the wildness that lurked in her expression when she walked out of those woods covered in the blood of her enemies.

I pull away from her mouth and kiss her neck, letting my teeth graze the skin right in the crook where it meets her shoulder. I'm rewarded with a breathless moan, and I laugh huskily against her. Any hint of hesitation is gone as she wraps her fingers in my hair and jerks my head back so she can kiss and lick my neck in return.

When my hands drop to cup her ass and lift her, she doesn't

miss a beat as she hops up and wraps her legs around my waist, her lips never leaving my skin.

"As much as I love how fucking unhinged and gorgeous you look right now"—I turn and walk into the woods—"I don't want to taste the blood of others while I devour every inch of you."

Her hand tightens around my hair as her mouth crashes against mine hungrily. Thankfully, the trees on this side of the road aren't that dense because I'm barely paying attention as I make the short walk to the river. If it were any longer, I would have said *fuck it* and just had her against a tree again.

"Boots off," I order as I reluctantly drop her to the ground. We quickly toe off our boots and weapons before I pull her into the cool water until it's up to our shoulders.

Red swirls in the water around us as the blood rinses from our clothes.

"You owe me orgasms, wolf." Scythe hastily pulls my shirt off and tosses it onto a nearby boulder.

"Don't worry." I quickly get her shirt and chest band off, throwing them beside my discarded shirt. "You'll be screaming my name in a minute, witch."

Both of us yank our pants off and throw them onto the boulder with the rest.

"Promises, promises," she rasps before letting out a throaty moan as I cup her between the thighs. My cock hardens even more at the sound, and I drag her to me, kissing her hard as I rub my fingers back and forth through her slickness.

Her fingers dig into my back, pulling me harder against her as she writhes against my hand. A desperate need to taste more of her rises, and I bite her lower lip hard enough to draw blood. The tangy sweetness floods my mouth, and between that and the growl she lets out, both my wolf and I lose it.

I release my hold on her lip, her blood dribbling down my chin. More. I need to taste so much more of her. She doesn't resist as I tug her over to the shallower area where the boulders rise out of the water. A sharp exhale is her only reaction when I grip her waist and hoist her up onto the rocky surface.

Part of me wants to just bury my cock inside her over and over again until she screams my name, but a larger part is desperate to taste her sweet pussy and feel her come apart on my tongue.

"Talon," she says in a breathless tone that she still somehow manages to make sound like an order.

"Yes?" I grip her thighs hard enough to bruise and wonder if she'll leave them for me if I ask her not to heal them. "Something you need?" Her body shudders as I lean down to kiss the inside of her thigh, going up towards the center, hovering over it before skipping back down to her other leg.

"Stop teasing me and fuck me already!" she snarls.

I tilt my head enough so I can meet her pissed-off eyes and find myself wishing they were silver and not blue. The wolf rises inside me, only instead of fighting hopelessly to shift and break free of this body, they're keyed onto her. An entirely different need surfaces that I don't understand. All I know is that the wolf wants it and that it feels right. Holding her angry gaze, I sink my teeth into her flesh until I taste blood.

"Fuck!" She jerks beneath my grip, but her swearing turns into a moan as I raise my mouth from her thigh to lick her straight up the center before sucking hard on her clit. The intoxicating tastes of her blood and her desire mix in my mouth, and a heady rush swirls through my mind.

More. I still need more.

My hands slide under her ass, pulling her closer, and I lavish her clit with my tongue until she's screaming as her fingers tighten in my hair, holding me in place as she grinds herself against my face. A growl tears from my throat as I jerk my hands to her thighs and force her legs wider.

I lick and suck her hard before thrusting my tongue deep into her pussy. The muscles of her thighs flex as she writhes beneath me, but I don't let go, just continue to feast on her, to feed the wolf inside my soul.

When she comes apart a second time, I raise my head, fingers swirling around that sensitive bundle of nerves as she arches her back. How pretty would she look with that lavender hair spread out around her? How hot would it be to come all over her chest while I admire it?

My dick hardens almost painfully, and again, I feel that desperation from the wolf. One that I'm in complete agreement on. We need her around my cock, so I pull her off the boulder, and Scythe crashes into me, her breasts flattening against my chest. In an instant, I have her pinned against the rock before thrusting inside her.

We both moan as my thick, hard length stretches her walls. "How is it possible that you feel this fucking good?" I pull myself almost all the way out before slowly sinking back in. "It's like your pussy was meant to take my cock."

"I don't know," she says through panted breaths. "Maybe if you fuck me harder, we'll find out."

She kisses me deeply, slipping her tongue into my mouth and teasing me before pulling back and biting my bottom lip as hard as I did hers earlier. A deep groan spills out of me as she releases my lip, a wicked grin on her face and my blood bright against her pink lips. "Harder, wolf."

"Don't give me orders, witch," I growl even as my hips pivot forward and I sink deeper into her.

She laughs, and the sound snaps the little control I have left. I can still feel the wolf riding the back of my mind as I thrust into her over and over. Scythe's legs tighten where they're wrapped around my waist, her heels pressing into my ass and spurring me on as the water splashes around us.

I'm dimly aware of her nails digging into my back as I keep up the relentless pace. When she throws her head back and screams my name, the wolf seizes control, and the next thing I know, I'm biting down on her shoulder, hot blood coursing down my throat, and instead of pushing me away, Scythe just clutches me harder to herself.

Something unfurls within me—a wild claiming—but I don't stop to think about it because Scythe comes again and her pussy clenches around my cock until I'm falling over the edge with her. I thrust deeper, my teeth still buried in her flesh, pinning her to the rock as my hot seed spreads inside her before leaking out where we're joined.

My mind feels . . . hazy and blissed out. Slowly, I release my hold on Scythe's shoulder, savoring the taste of blood in my mouth even as I wonder what the fuck I was thinking biting her like that.

Aside from some playful nipping, I'm not really a biter, but the wolf was so desperate, and it just felt right. Here's hoping she doesn't fucking stab me when she realizes how badly I mauled her.

Silver eyes blink at me as if Scythe is still coming down from the high of all the orgasms I just tore through her body. A warm satisfaction spreads through me that I've managed to fuck the witch senseless until it hits me.

My eyes drop to the silver pendant dangling from the delicate chain around her neck. Her necklace is still on . . . but her eyes are silver and . . . glowing. So are her tattoos. The only bit of herself that hasn't bled through is her hair color.

"Fuck," she groans, a smile playing across her lips. "Good job, wolf." Then she wipes her mouth with her left hand, and I go completely still.

"What the fuck?" I grab her hand and stare at the backs of her fingers. Previously bare fingers now have black tattoos above each knuckle, each one representing a lunar cycle of the moon.

Scythe jerks her hand away from me and holds it up so she can see it, and I watch as the post-sex contentment fades from her face to be replaced by horror. "What the fuck? Get out! Get out! Get out!" she chants frantically as she unwraps her legs from my waist and shoves me back.

"I don't think taking my dick out now is going to fix things!" I snap even as I bite back a groan when I slip out of her delicious heat. Suddenly, my chest starts to burn, and I slap a hand against it. "Fucking hells!"

"Talon," she rasps as her silver eyes widen and she gapes at me. The tattoos running down her arms glow even brighter for a few seconds before returning to an inky black and then fading from sight. She points a trembling finger at my chest. "Look."

Slowly, I drop my hand away and peer down. Directly over my heart is a tree, exactly like the one on the witch's back that I've seen only once that first night we met.

"What. In the actual fuck. Is going on?" I grind out, even though I already have an idea . . . but I'm really hoping she says something else to prove my suspicions wrong.

Because this *cannot* be a mating bond. She's not a fucking wolf, and I sure as shit ain't a witch.

The witch stares at the tattoo on my chest, her face becoming more pale by the second before looking at the ones on the backs of her fingers. "It's a mating bond."

"Not. Possible." I raise my hand to my chest as if I can claw this fucking mark off of me.

The wolf snarls at the thought, and I want to strangle the damn beast. *She's not a wolf, you fucking idiot! She's the reason you'll never be free!* My wolf doesn't care. I rarely get actual thoughts from them. The wolf thinks in feelings more than anything, but one word slams into my mind in a deep growl that is not my voice.

MATE.

Fates fucking damn me. I lunge forward and wrap my fingers around the witch's throat. "Undo it!" I demand, my face inches from hers. "Fix it, Cerelia!"

A fist slams into my face, and I see stars for a minute as I stumble back, my hand torn from her throat.

"Give me a minute!" she snarls, and the scythe tattoo on her neck flashes silver. "This shouldn't be possible," she mutters as her gaze drops to the tattoos across her knuckles. "When witches seal a mating bond, we sing. I didn't sing while we were . . ." She clears her throat and rubs her face with her newly tattooed hand. "The tattoos are witch markings. No singing happened. How . . . how did it trigger . . ." She speaks quickly, clearly talking to herself and not expecting an answer from me.

I have one.

Though I hate to admit it since it places the blame on me.

"Blood," I say flatly. "Wolf mates mark each other as part of the bonding ceremony. You bit me . . . and I bit you."

"You fucking mated us!" she screams, and that damn scythe appears in her hand a second later.

"It wasn't fucking intentional!" My daggers are in my hand in a flash, and I draw comfort from their familiar feel against my palms. "How was I supposed to know your freaky magic would do something like this?" We glare at each other, blood still dripping from the wound on her shoulder, and I can't help but watch as it snakes a trail between her breasts. "Undo it," I repeat, but this time, it's more of a desperate plea than a demand. "You are not my mate."

Pain flashes in her eyes, so raw that I immediately regret my words, even if I did mean them.

Silver fades to blue as she gives me a cool look. "I have no interest in a mate either, wolf, least of all one like you. So don't worry—I'll break this bond between us or die trying."

CHAPTER NINE

~

Scythe

IT DOESN'T TAKE us long to find Draco. Talon whistles, and a few minutes later, he comes trotting through the trees to meet us by the lake. Water drips from his legs and underbelly, so he must have visited the river as well. Clearly, the fae horse senses the tension because he's oddly subdued as we mount up and make our way to Sovarre.

The ride to the coastal city is a new kind of torment for me. Mate bonds have a tendency to up your libido. Usually that means the weeks after mating are a fun time for couples, and it's normal for them to stay locked in their homes the entire time.

Neither Talon nor I want this fucking mate bond, but that doesn't stop the flashes of desire that race down the bond. And it's not like I can stop touching them—unless I want to take a header off Draco and straight into the dirt.

It's actually a bit tempting. Being knocked unconscious for a while doesn't sound too bad.

The streets of Sovarre are loud and crowded, and I grit my

teeth as Talon guides Draco through the chaos. When we arrive at the inn, we both practically leap off the horse.

"I'll see to Draco. Find us food," Talon says flippantly before stalking off towards the stables, tugging Draco after them.

"I'll find you some poisoned food and solve all our problems," I grumble.

"Heard that!"

"I meant you to!" I snap.

They don't even turn to look at me, just raise their hand and make a rude gesture. I do the same to their back before stomping into the inn.

A burly man with salt-and-pepper hair gives me a long look when I crash onto a stool at the bar.

"What can I get you, lass?"

Lass? Ugh.

"Whatever food you have that's hot and three shots of your strongest liquor. And a room for the evening."

He raises a brow at me. "Are you traveling with someone or . . ."

I glare at him. "I'm happily married. Can't you tell? My *kalri* will be here any moment. They'll need food as well. Feel free to spit in it."

The man looks at me for a long moment. "I'm so happy I never married."

"Wise decision." I nod.

Talon arrives just as our food does and sits stiffly in the stool next to me. They reach for one of my shot glasses, but I slap their hand away. "Get your own."

A growl rumbles from their throat, but they call out to the bartender.

Even the brief contact with their hand has the bond buzzing. While it can't create feelings from nothing, the bond can absolutely amplify what's there.

And while I hate Talon, that doesn't stop me from wanting them.

After we scarf down our bland but warm stew, the barkeep places a key down between us and backs away. "Third floor. Second door on the left. Good luck."

Talon grunts and tosses down some money before swiping the key. We walk up the stairs in tense silence that's almost unbearable by the time we stop at our door and Talon unlocks it.

"This room is suffocating. We'd be better off sleeping outside." I frown, looking around as we both step into the small space.

"Too dangerous for us to sleep outside, even with just the two of us," Talon responds, sliding past me to look the room over. This one is a little larger than the one before—still only one bed, much to my dismay. It is an actual bed though with a simple wood headboard as opposed to a mattress on the floor. "One of us would have to stay awake to keep watch, and the mage hunters are suspicious of anyone who chooses to sleep outside of the city."

I sigh and pluck at my shirt, which is already plastered to my skin. Talon skirts around the bed and opens the window on the far wall, and a slight breeze filters in. Better than nothing. There is zero chance of me sleeping in these clothes though, unless I pass out from heat exhaustion.

Talon watches as I grab the chair from the corner of the room and wedge it against the door. Then their eyes widen as I pull my clothes off until I'm just in my chest band and underwear. I hesitate at taking off my chest band—it is wildly uncomfortable because sweat is pooling between my breasts, yet I also don't want to be completely naked.

Given what we were doing mere hours ago, that thought seems a little ridiculous, but if I glance down, I'll still be able to see their bite on my shoulder. Much to my annoyance, no amount of healing has been able to get rid of it. I'm guessing it's because it's a mate bond, but I don't truly understand the magic that ties us together. I had to settle for healing the wound and leaving the slightly raised white scar behind.

Turning my back to Talon with a frustrated huff, I unlace the band and then pull my shirt back on, grimacing at how it sticks to my skin. Hopefully it will dry soon.

When I turn around, my lupine mate is still staring at me, a smolder burning in their dark eyes before they snuff it out.

"We should talk," I say quietly as I sit on the edge of the bed.

"Oh, now you want *me* to talk? After biting my head off for the past few hours?" Talon asks tightly as they pull off their own clothes with jerky movements. It's strange to watch because usually everything Talon does is graceful. I can feel their agitation reaching down the bond to brush against my own emotions.

"Can we not talk about biting?" I say through gritted teeth as I try and fail to shove their emotions away from mine. It must be a wolf mating bond thing because emotions were never shared in my witch mating bond, just magic.

I grimace and glance down at my left hand, to the lunar tattoos decorating the backs of my fingers. They're different than the ones that adorned my fingers before—those were roses—but this mating bond isn't going to work out any better than my previous one did.

If I were to bet . . . I'd say it is going to be even more disastrous.

"This bond . . ." I watch as Talon settles down on the bed, keeping to their half, and I do the same. It's like there is some unspoken agreement between us to maintain a distance—because if we don't, if one of us touches the other, Talon will be buried inside me within a minute, and I'll be screaming their name loud enough for the entire inn to hear.

Because that's what the bond wants. Newly mated pairs can't get enough of one another for the first few weeks. It's usually an intoxicating and fun ride while it lasts, and this one is even more intense than my previous mating bond. I wonder if it's because

Talon is a werewolf and our bond is a weird combination of witch and wolf.

If that's the case, then the next few weeks are going to be slow and torturous if I don't figure a way out of this, which is a problem.

"I have no idea how to break it," I blurt out, frustration coating my words. "I don't think it's just a witch bond or just a werewolf bond. I'm pretty sure it's both."

Talon frowns. "You know how bonds work between werewolves?"

"Only a little bit." I chew on my bottom lip until Talon reaches out and brushes their fingers across it. We both still as I release my lip and Talon's fingers linger. Then they swallow and pull their hand away. "The werewolves in the Wilds were friendly towards the witches, but they din't share everything. Definitely not the more intimate aspects of their culture," I say, trying to keep my voice steady even as my heart races at the brief contact. "I know they have the same . . . impulses . . . as witches do for the first few weeks."

"You mean the all-consuming need I have right now to tear off that thin scrap of fabric between your legs and bury my cock inside you until my seed is dripping out?" Talon says lightly, keeping their gaze locked on the space between us.

"Yeah," I rasp. "That would be what I'm referring to." I clamp my thighs together and shift uncomfortably at the dull ache that's already forming from their words. "Thanks for that, by the way."

Their eyes snap to mine, and I swear I see a hint of the wolf in them. "My dick has been rock-hard since your little strip show. If I have to suffer, so should you."

"Such a generous mate."

"It's not like I chose this." They shrug.

"I didn't either!" I hiss. "I've done the whole mate thing once and was quite happy to never do it again."

Something dark flashes in their eyes before I feel their possessive hunger race across my senses. "Tell me about witch bonds," Talon half growls. "And I'll tell you about wolf bonds."

"How do you even know about them?" I cock my head. "Thought you didn't know any other wolves?"

"My parents." Their expression remains perfectly neutral, but it doesn't stop their grief from stabbing me in the chest. It's strange to have this insight into their emotions, but not entirely unwelcome. It feels kind of like cheating since I'm so terrible at reading people, especially someone as skilled at hiding themself as Talon, but since I'm stuck with them for the foreseeable future, I'll take what I can get.

"Before they died, they told me about bonds," Talon continues. "I was a teenager and starting to be more . . . involved . . . with people. They felt I should know about mate bonds on the off chance I met another wolf, although we all knew it was unlikely."

They look away from me, but not before I catch the anguish in their eyes. A heavy silence falls between us, and I find myself wanting to give them something. Anything to pull them out of whatever dark thoughts they've fallen into.

"After our twenty-first birthdays, witches are considered old enough to seek a mating bond."

Talon's sharp gaze snaps back to me as I settle further into the lumpy mattress. I turn my head to stare up at the ceiling. It's hard to discuss this while looking at Talon. It's hard to talk about it at all because I've spent the last decade doing my best to forget about my old life. "When I was growing up, I would read all these stories about how mates fell in love. How they would look into someone's eyes and just *know* they were the one. It all sounded so romantic." I laugh bitterly. "Maybe once upon a time it was like that, but not anymore. Nobody is looking for love when it comes to mate bonds."

For just a moment, I think about that night Talon and I spent together. Those hours when I actually believed in the fairy tales.

And then they ripped my heart from my chest and cured me of that foolish notion.

"What are they looking for?" Talon asks as they adjust their position beside me, and out of the corner of my eye, I see them mirroring me and staring up at the ceiling.

"Power," I spit out the word. "Whether it be a magical boost or a political advantage. When witches bond, we can share our magic. So if you mate with someone more powerful than you, you get a power boost."

"And the political advantage?"

I stare at a knot of wood on the ceiling until my vision blurs. "Witches have a very strict hierarchy. We're broken up into multiple covens, and each of those have a leader and their own rankings, but all the covens report to the High Coven, which consists of the most powerful witches. The same bloodline has ruled the High Coven since the witches first came to this continent." I raise my right hand and call my magic forth, directing it where I want it. The tattoos stretched across my knuckles display a mountain range glowing silver. "I am the last of that bloodline."

"So . . . you're like a witch princess?" Talon asks, and I can hear the wry amusement in their tone.

"Witches don't have princesses," I say firmly.

"Whatever you say . . . Princess."

"You know, I could smother you in your sleep." I turn my head enough to glower at them. "That would solve this whole bond situation."

The corners of Talon's full mouth start to curl up. "I'll keep that in mind if you snore again tonight."

"I do not snore!" I adamantly deny.

"Okay." That same lopsided grin blooms across their lips, and I feel the sudden urge to trace my tongue across it.

"What are you thinking?" Talon asks, their voice deepening.

"Nothing!" I say a little too forcibly before redirecting my attention to the safety of the ceiling with its whirling pattern, where I can distract myself from what it felt like to have that full mouth worshipping my body. Fuck. I rub my thighs together before killing the motion. "Because of my high-ranking status, I was a desirable mate. It was why Vaeril—" I cut myself off. I don't want to talk about him.

Not now. Not ever.

"Once a mate is chosen and both parties agree, a ceremony is held," I continue. "Most of what takes place doesn't actually matter. What is important is that the witches both accept each other and that they're joined. The magic does the rest."

"Joined how?"

That ache between my thighs grows at the roughness of their voice, and I feel a blush creep across my cheeks. I squeeze my eyes shut. Gods, this is ridiculous. I'm two hundred years old and shouldn't be acting like this. Stupid fucking bond.

It's not the bond, my subconscious whispers, and I know it's true—at least partly. Bonds can't be forced. Ours may have come about in a weird way that I don't understand yet, but it was only able to form because I desired Talon . . . and they desired me.

But that didn't mean the bond made sense. The magic had clearly chosen poorly, and now we were paying the price.

"Scythe?" Talon prompts, and I can feel the damn blush darkening across my cheeks.

"Oh, umm . . ." I stumble over the words. "Sex. Our mating ritual is sex."

Silence. I crack open one eye and tilt my head to look at Talon. Their hands are curled into fists at their sides, and a muscle is flexing along their jawline.

"Talon?" I ask hesitantly.

In a flash, they have me pinned against the bed, their leg shoved between my thighs, pressing hard against my center as their hand wraps around my throat. What I should do is twist my leg around theirs to regain some control or grab their wrist and use pressure points to get them to release my neck. Those would be smart things to do when someone aggressively pins you down.

I don't do any of those things though.

Instead, I arch my back, pressing more of my body into their hold instead of away from it. Part of it is the bond . . . but even I have to admit that it's mostly me at this point. Despite every fucked-up thing between us, I still crave their touch as much as my lungs crave air.

This isn't going to work out well for me, I know it, but I can't bring myself to stop.

A gasp slips from my lips as Talon buries their face in the crook of my neck, kissing and licking my skin. They've pinned one of my hands above my head, but I have the other one entangled in their hair. A growl tears from their throat, and then they bite me again. Hard.

"Fuck!" I let out a strangled moan and grind shamelessly against their thigh, desperate for the friction. The fingers around my throat tighten, and a flicker of fear surfaces before being swallowed by desire.

As fast as it happened, Talon is back on their side of the bed, taking deep, ragged breaths, and their normally dark brown eyes are glowing a luminescent golden yellow.

"Sorry," Talon pants, still obviously trying to wrestle control back from their wolf. "They've never been like this before."

"Your wolf, you mean?" The question comes out a little raspy, and I rub my throat. Something tells me I'll have bruises tomorrow to match the ones on my thighs. I should have healed them earlier when I was trying to fix the bite on my shoulder—which is now bleeding again—but the bond was happy about bearing Talon's marks.

At the time, it felt like appeasing the bond by leaving the bruises was the smarter thing to do; otherwise, it might grow more desperate for us to come together again by amping up the lustful feelings. At least that's what I told myself, because it's not that I *like* displaying the fact that I'm theirs.

I'm not theirs. Talon doesn't want me. Not like this. They just wanted a quick fuck at the river and instead got a damn mate.

Knowing that doesn't stop me from watching with rapt attention as Talon's tongue darts out to lick the remaining blood off their lips—my blood—and we both groan a little. Their glowing yellow eyes meet mine and narrow. "Take off your necklace."

I bristle at the command as my fingers brush across the silver chain, and then I glance at the door. Even in the privacy of our room, it feels dangerous. "No."

"Remove it before I rip it off," Talon growls.

"I don't take orders from you." I hold their demanding gaze while pointedly moving my fingers away from the necklace.

In return, they give me a wolfish smile. "You sure about that, Princess?"

We both move at the same time, but I'm just a hair faster. When Talon tries to pin me down again, I twist my hips and use their momentum to flip them onto the other side of the bed. It's narrow, so we both almost fall off. My left leg drops to the ground. My right knee digs into the mattress on the other side of Talon's hips . . . which puts my hot and dripping center right over their hard length, only two pieces of thin fabric separating us.

"Take off the necklace," Talon orders again, not the least bit worried about the scythe I've called forth and placed against their throat. The yellowish glow in their eyes has changed from a solid sheen to bright golden specks shining against the brown, which is so dark, it's more of an inky black.

Like fireflies in the night.

"Why should I?" I push the blade of my scythe a little harder against their skin. It's the dull side, so it doesn't cut them, but it has to hurt a little.

"Because I'm tired of looking at a lie." Nimble fingers trace a path along the back of my right thigh before cupping my ass. "And I want to see what those silver eyes look like when you come."

I tremble as their fingers slide down to tease the edge of my underwear. "This isn't a good idea. We need to figure out how to break the bond, not encourage it."

"We'll figure out how to get rid of it." Talon's fingers dip beneath the fabric, and I barely bite back a moan as they swirl around in the wetness they find waiting for them. "But I'm not going to be able to think straight until I've felt you come around my cock again. So be a good little witch and let me fuck you until you scream. We both know you want it."

Something vicious and angry cuts through the lust haze fogging my mind. It's easy for Talon to say that because their feelings for me are uncomplicated. We fucked once, then they left and forgot about me until they needed me again. They desired me enough for the bond to snap into place, but it's not anything more than that. Talon's happy to use me to fill this need, but once the bond is broken, they'll walk away again. Forget all about me.

I'm so fucking tired of being used and left once I'm no longer needed.

Talon is right about one thing though. It's hard to think with how hard the mating bond is riding us right now. I bite back another moan as Talon's fingers slip from my pussy, dragging my arousal with them to circle my clit.

Control, that's what I need, and to mess with Talon's head a little. Two birds, one arrow.

A single, harsh melody spills from my lips, and the staff portion of my scythe splits into roots that dig into the mattress, holding the blade at Talon's throat. Their fingers freeze just as they start to slip back inside me, and a yellow sheen rolls over their eyes.

"*Witch*," they snarl and try to move, but the blade is pressed too hard against their throat. Even with it being the dull end, there is no room for them to move unless they want to do some serious damage to themself.

"I have a name," I say mildly as I slide further down their body, away from those infuriatingly talented fingers, and grab one of my daggers that I placed near the bed.

"Prin—"

"Call me that again." A few quick slices, and suddenly their cock springs free from the fabric holding it back. I've never really taken the time to admire it, too eager to have it thrusting inside me, but just like the rest of Talon, their cock is obnoxiously pretty. Thick with a slight curve. Gods, looking at it now, I'm surprised it fits. No wonder I'm always sore afterwards. And that piercing is perfection.

I've felt the pressure from the two silver balls—one resting on the top of their cock's blunt head and the other on the bottom, a silver barbell running vertically straight through their cock, connecting them both. It's a very fae thing to have—they're all about piercings—but I'm surprised Talon has one, considering how elusive the fae are these days. Then again, the tattoos on their palms are fae magic, so maybe the same fae did the piercing.

Maybe I'll get to meet this fae one day and thank them personally for all the orgasms they've inadvertently given me.

"You're drooling, Princess."

My gaze snaps up to catch Talon looking at me with a satisfied look. They're pinned to the bed with blades at their throat and dick yet somehow still acting like they're the one in control of this situation.

Time to fix that.

I spin the dagger in my hand before slamming it down, burying it to the hilt in the mattress an inch away from their balls. Talon's lips curve into a smile that is pure sin as heat flares in their eyes.

My mate is insane.

And it really turns me on.

Suddenly, the need to taste them becomes all-consuming, so I lean down, gripping the base of their cock, and take them into my mouth. Talon groans as my lips wrap tightly around them, and their hips jerk upward. I can taste their salty precum spreading across my tongue along with the metallic flavor of their piercings. It's been a really long time since I've done this, and I struggle to take them deeper, spit leaking out from my lips as I slide farther down their shaft.

"Fucking hells," they rasp, and suddenly their fingers are gripping my hair and forcing my head down. I gag a little as I take them even farther, my hand releasing the base of their cock when my lips bump into my fingers. I feel them hit the back of my throat, and my eyes water. "Swallow," they demand, and I almost come from the deep possessiveness of it.

No. This is my fucking show.

I start humming, and Talon grips my hair tighter as a string of curses erupts from them. Then those hands are ripped away—thankfully loosening their grip instead of tearing out chunks of my hair—and I release their cock with a loud pop.

"No touching unless I say so," I purr as I look at their pissed-off expression.

Oh noes. Somebody doesn't like not being in control. Holding their gaze, I lean back down and slowly trail my tongue from the base of their cock to the tip before licking each end of the piercing.

"Scythe," they warn and jerk against the roots that bind their wrists to the bed.

"Yes?" My tongue darts out again, this time licking their head and making their hard length twitch upward. I do it again, and Talon hisses, driving their hips upward as if they can force me to suck them off. I laugh and raise my head.

"Be a good wolf," I croon. "Lie there and look pretty. If you do"—I take them all the way until their cock hits the back of my throat, and I swallow before sliding them back out of my mouth—"you'll get rewarded."

Talon spews something unintelligible, and I tilt my head, giving them an innocent, questioning look. "Sorry, what was that?"

"Do that again," they demand, those golden flecks in their eyes burning brighter. When I just smile, they quickly add, "I'll be good."

I debate tormenting them a little longer, but despite my cockiness, I'm feeling pretty desperate to have them in my mouth again. It's exhilarating having Talon under my control. I didn't anticipate the rush it would give me, and now, I'm desperate to hear them screaming my name while they're completely at my mercy.

The dagger needs to go though. I've been holding my chest up to keep it from jabbing me, and I don't want anything between me and them. I rip it from the mattress and toss it aside before sprawling across Talon's legs and gripping their cock again.

They let out a harsh exhale that has me chuckling darkly as my lips wrap around their head and my tongue darts out to play with each end of their piercing. Then I slide down their shaft once more, getting it nice and wet. I hollow my cheeks and suck hard as I slowly bob my head, the hand gripping them at the base following the motion.

"Harder," they growl.

No *please* this time, but I can't even bring myself to care because I'm getting wetter by the second. Maybe I'll get myself off in front of them after this. That thought gets me even more excited, and my movements quicken. Talon starts thrusting roughly into my mouth, and I pull my hand away from their cock so I can brace myself on their hips, lifting my head a little higher for a better angle.

"Oh fuck me," Talon groans as I take them all the way to the base before sliding back to their head. I swirl my tongue around it several times, loving the way they thicken further, and then swallow them whole. This time, when Talon hits the back of my throat, I start humming. There's no magic in it, but considering how they reacted previously, I suspect they like it.

Something unintelligible spews from their lips once more, and then they're slamming into my mouth. My nails dig into their flesh as I hold on and keep humming while I take every single one of their thrusts, even as my eyes water.

Their salty, hot release spills down my throat, and I swallow every last drop until I've wrung them dry. Talon's breathing is rough as my mouth glides over their cock and releases it. Then I smirk at them as I lick my lips clean. "Good wolf," I mockingly praise them.

A yellow sheen continues to roll over their dark eyes, and part of me wants to grab their still-hard cock and see just how fast the recovery of a werewolf—even a cursed one—is as I sink onto it and ride them until they're spilling inside me again. I can't help tightening my thighs at the thought as I feel the wave of wet heat drip down them.

I'm definitely going to have to find an empty room to see to my own needs because I'm not going to be able to think about anything else until I do.

Talon's eyes roam down my body, and they inhale deeply, their lips rolling up into a smirk. "Something you need help with, witch?"

"Not from you," I say coolly and start to roll off them.

"You can barely look at me while you say that." They laugh. "Such a terrible liar."

Rage courses through me, and I move before I can think better of it. I straddle Talon again, my hands falling close to theirs on the mattress while I lean down until my face is less than an inch from theirs. "Not. From. You."

"So you're not soaking wet right now?" Talon taunts, that arrogant grin still stamped on their face.

There's no point in lying. Their damn werewolf senses can smell just how turned on I am right now.

"It's a natural response to the situation. I can stroll my ass downstairs and pick any random man from the bar and have a similar reaction." I hope my fury is covering up how bad of a liar I am, because the idea of anyone besides Talon touching me right now is an instant mood killer, but I'll let all the gods damn me before I let this arrogant asshole know that.

I find myself distracted by their eyes for a second, which is why I don't notice the sudden tug on my little finger.

"Hey!" I shout, but it's too late.

Talon holds my silver ring between their thumb and index finger and taps it three times in rapid succession. My scythe is gone in an instant. I gawk at them. That shouldn't be possible. Sure, it's mage magic that allows the scythe to be summoned to and from the ring, but it's specifically keyed to me.

Fucking mate bond. Our souls are now connected, which apparently allows Talon to use my godsdamned scythe ring. No matter. I'm still getting the fuck out of—

A sharp exhale bursts from my lungs as Talon grips me and throws me off themself. I land roughly on the mattress, and it's my turn to have a blade at my throat as Talon pushes one of those wicked, curved daggers against my skin.

"Be a good witch," they croon down at me. "And come all over my fingers."

"As if your mediocre attempts at getting me off would actually work!" I snarl.

Talon chuckles. "Your insults need as much work as your lies." With the hand that isn't holding a knife to my throat, they trail their fingers up my inner thigh before stopping midway. "I don't go where I'm not wanted. Tell me to stop and I will." Their fingers go up another inch. "I'll even be polite and leave this room so you can see to your needs." Another tantalizing inch, and I can't stop my breath from hitching.

My entire body is keyed up, and the mating bond is practically pulsing between us. I want to blame the desperate need to feel

Talon's fingers in my throbbing cunt on that, but I can't lie to myself. I've been through a mating bond before, and I damn well know how to control it, or at least ride it out.

But that all-consuming need to feel Talon's touch is only partly from the bond. I remember what the bond between me and Vaeril felt like, and it was never this intense. Most of these feelings are from me and me alone.

I want this. It's not just the bond.

That doesn't mean I'm going to fucking admit it though.

A sly grin plays across Talon's lips as if they can read all of that on my face. It also doesn't help that I'm practically screaming it down the bond, although something tells me Talon will ignore that because they don't entirely trust what they feel through the bond either and need to hear my consent before proceeding.

Plus the asshole wants to hear me beg.

Fingers dig into my thigh and squeeze, and a whimper slips from my lips before I can stop it. They're so fucking close to my practically throbbing clit. I grit my teeth and choke back the next needy sound that tries to escape, my fingers twisting in the blanket covering the bed.

"What's it going to be, witch?" Talon pushes the blade hard enough to draw blood at the same moment they give my thigh another squeeze. The combination of the two has me almost coming.

It's not like I'm a stranger to sex—aside from the last two years, that is—but I've never slept with anyone who was this . . . intense. Talon has a knife to my throat, for fuck's sake. I should be gripping their wrist while breaking out of their hold, not trying to rub my thighs together in a desperate attempt at some friction.

Gods, I'm so fucked.

"Am I staying?" Talon's fingers slide up until I swear they're about to finally touch that sensitive bundle of nerves before they slide back down my thigh. "Or going?"

My stubborn side breaks. "*Staying*," I growl.

Talon's mouth curves into a satisfied smile. "That's what I thought."

The blade vanishes from my throat, and before I realize what's happening, my panties are being sliced. I start to push up on the bed, but the blade snaps out of existence, and Talon wraps their hand around my throat, forcing me back down. This time, my hands grip their wrist, but any thought of getting them off me fades when they slide two fingers over my clit.

"Fuck!" I scream as my back arches off the bed.

The fingers around my throat tighten, momentarily cutting off airflow before they loosen again, and I suck in a breath as they continue to play with my swollen clit, using the perfect amount of pressure. When Talon dips those clever fingers into my pussy just enough to draw out more wetness, I groan.

There is no timidness to their movements, and I'm writhing on the bed, still clinging to the arm pinning me down by the throat.

"We're stuck with each other for the time being, witch," Talon says in a low, deep voice. Their dark eyes bore into mine for a long moment before they drop to the spot between my thighs as they shove what feels like three fingers inside me. I moan, and their fingers gently squeeze my throat again. "Might as well make the best of it. We both know you've never had a fuck as good as me."

"Likewise, wolf," I gasp in between panting breaths. "How many times"—I groan sharply when they push a thumb down over my clit—"have you gotten yourself off—fuck!"—my hips buck up when Talon's already fast pace turns ruthless—"while thinking about me?"

I let out a raspy laugh as my shot in the dark strikes true based on Talon's growl. My laugh is quickly cut off though when Talon jerks me up by the throat, squeezing hard enough that my vision dims for a second, but just as suddenly, they release me, causing me to suck in several sharp breaths.

It takes me a moment to realize that I'm now kneeling on the mattress facing the headboard. Talon's fingers dig into my thighs and jerk me down onto their face, and I barely have time to grip the shoddy worn wood of the headboard before I'm screaming as they devour my cunt.

Seconds ago, my vision was dimming because of lack of air, but now I'm seeing stars because of the climax Talon just ripped from me. They don't slow their pace and let me ride it out. Instead, they lick, suck, and feast like I'm the most delicious thing they've ever tasted and they're determined to get every last drop.

I know I've lost control of the situation, and I don't even remember the point I was trying to prove when I pinned them down and got them off. Something tells me Talon doesn't have any better control than I do. That we're in this for better or worse, and we'll just have to figure it the fuck out.

Later. I'll figure it out later, because right now, the only thing that exists is Talon's mouth on me, and nothing feels more right than that.

Talon's fingers dig into my thighs hard enough that I wouldn't be surprised if they're drawing blood. The thought has me almost coming again. I give up all pretense as I ride their face, and Talon growls their approval before sucking my throbbing clit into their mouth and curling their tongue around it.

"Oh fuck!" The headboard cracks under my fingers as the second climax explodes through me, my back bending as more curses and screams tumble from my lips. Talon hungrily takes everything I have to offer as I shamelessly grind my pussy. Then they spear me with their tongue, taking several long licks that I'm pretty sure they swallow before sucking on my clit again.

Minutes later, I'm still trembling from the pleasure Talon has pulled from me, and after one more brazen lick straight up my pussy, they lift me up and slide out from underneath me. I brace myself for them to say something cutting, but they stay quiet, as if they don't know what to make of what just happened either.

It's less complicated when we're fucking, but as soon as we're not . . . I close my eyes. Tomorrow. We'll figure this out tomorrow.

Neither of us speak as we lie here, each on our side of the bed. Our hands are only a couple of inches apart, but neither of us makes a move to touch the other. Instead, we just catch our breath, wrestling with every fucked-up thing there is between us until sleep claims us both.

CHAPTER TEN

~

Scythe

"I'd rather not stay in the capital," Talon says ten minutes after we leave Sovarre. We've been civil to each other since waking up this morning, our limbs entangled.

I can feel their emotions leaking through the bond. They're freaked out about something, and I don't think it's from me sucking them off or them finger fucking me into oblivion. I'm willing to bet it's from how quickly we fell asleep together and how peaceful that sleep was.

I know it disturbs them, because it sure as fuck freaks me out. The constant desire humming between us is annoying, but it's something that, in many ways, can be dismissed as meaningless. We're both attractive, we have a history, and the magic of the bond is inflaming the desire that already existed.

But when I woke up this morning with Talon's arms wrapped around me, their face snuggled into the back of my neck, it felt so right.

Until the panic set in and I practically flung myself out of bed. Talon looked equally uneasy about the whole thing.

"Can we make it all the way to Albadrid by nightfall?" I've seen maps of Eleoyn, but it's been a while, and I never really cared because I had no interest in leaving my forest.

"No." Talon's stomach muscles tense when I grip them tighter after Draco shies at something he sees in the woods. It's the third time the fae horse has done that, and I'm fairly certain he's doing it on purpose because he hasn't startled at anything on our trip before now. Arandian horses are unshakeable . . . but they're also annoyingly perceptive. He probably senses the newly formed mate bond along with the tension, and this is his way of helping.

No more treats for you, I think.

"I have a friend just south of Tenresan who will put us up for the night," Talon continues.

"What type of friend?" I ask warily. If Talon thinks I'll stay under the same roof as their lover, I'll gut them right here and take Draco for myself. The horse can probably find his way back to the camp near Albadrid.

"Not that type of friend." Talon reaches back over their shoulder to flick at my ear, and they just laugh when I snap at their fingers. "They're . . . well . . . you'll see."

"How much further do we have to go after we leave your *friend's* place?" I huff, still not convinced that this isn't a fuck buddy.

"Half a day's ride. I'm almost tempted to keep going, but if we get stopped by mage hunters—who have become overly suspicious of anyone traveling at night—we'll be delayed even more."

"I wonder what's got them so riled up." I chew on my bottom lip. "They've been even more aggressive about trying to get through my forest to the Wilds lately too. It hasn't been like this since the first wave of them attempted it after the rest of the witches left."

"I've been curious about that myself but haven't been able to find any definitive answers." Talon steers Draco around a low-hanging branch when the horse seems inclined to go under it. "Just rumors about the Eleoyn King being paranoid about an invasion, but which kingdom he's worried about changes every week."

There hasn't been an all-out conflict in Malovias since the war that resulted in the four kingdoms being formed. The fae withdrew shortly after that with the witches and wolves retreating to the northern lands above the kingdoms. I continue rolling my lip between my teeth. What would happen if a war broke out again? It was one thing for me to hold off small groups of mage hunters, but even I can't defeat an army.

They'd still have to make it over the Obsidian Mountains, which is no easy task, but with enough supplies, it is possib—

"Stop biting your lip."

I jolt a little in the saddle, immediately releasing my lip. *How the fuck did they know I was doing that?*

Draco seizes the opportunity to break out into a prance, and panic grips me as I start to fall to the left. Strong hands clamp down on mine, dragging them back to link around their toned abdomen. In several, very ungraceful movements, I right myself until I'm snuggled against Talon's back once again.

"Keep it up, Draco, and I'll introduce you to Necos," I grumble.

"Still amused over how much you panic at the idea of falling off a horse when you live in a fucking death trap." Talon chuckles as they shake their head. Despite me being secure once more, they don't move their hands away from mine.

"My home is perfectly safe," I defend. "Plus, if I did fall in my forest, I could use my magic to get one of the branches to catch me."

"Or you could just build your house on the ground like a normal person," Talon argues.

"But if I did that, obnoxious werewolves might be more likely to wander in," I snipe back.

"True." They let out a raspy chuckle, and my hands tighten around their waist of their own volition.

We travel for a few more minutes in almost companionable silence before Talon speaks again. "I think I might have an idea about why the bond formed."

"Really?" I perk up immediately. "What?"

"The night we met . . ." they say slowly, "it was a blood moon."

"Those are fairy tales." I scoff, disappointment making me sag a little. "There's nothing special about blood moons."

"They're not fairy tales," Talon argues back. "The blood moon is important to Lunos. That can't be a coincidence. I know enough about wolf mating bonds to know that they don't spring up out of nowhere—I think one was planted that night."

"You seriously think the god of fates played a role in our mating bond?"

The old gods are worshipped by the fae, and when they abandoned these lands, most people forgot about the gods as well. I'm a little surprised Talon even brought this up as a possibility.

As a witch, I don't care about the gods one way or another. Maybe if I grew up in Arandia, where temples still remain in their honor, I'd feel differently.

"My mother told me stories about odd things happening under blood moons," Talon continues, a strange cadence to their voice. Grief, I realize. Now that I'm paying attention, I can feel it brushing against my senses. It's not the sharp pain of new grief, but an old, persistent ache that burrows into your flesh and never leaves. Talon loved their family so much . . .

Suddenly, they inhale sharply, their muscles flexing beneath my hands. "That feeling . . ." they breathe out. "You're . . . jealous?"

I grip that unwanted emotion and strangle it into submission until I'm confident nothing else is leaking through the connection. Talon's scent fills my nostrils as I take several deep breaths. They smell like the forest just before a thunderstorm. Then I close my eyes, and it feels like the charged air is dancing across my skin as the rich scent of the pine trees surround me.

The calmness that has eluded me all morning settles into my soul, and I can't even bring myself to be mad about the fact that Talon's scent did that to me.

I am so fucked.

"You've spoken about your mother a few times now." I'm proud of myself for how casual my voice sounds. "Things were always . . . tense . . . between me and my parents. Then Astria was born, and that tension turned to hostility before settling into indifference. I'm sorry that you lost your parents, but I can't help but feel a little jealous that you experienced that kind of love."

"Astria loves you."

"Not enough to stay," I say bitterly.

Their thumb strokes the back of my hand, and I wait for them to tell me I'm being irrational. That asking Astria to give up her love for Ravyn because of her love for me isn't fair. That we're capable of loving more than one person at once, and that doesn't diminish any of it.

I wait for them to tell me all the things I've screamed in my own mind for the past year, but they don't. To my surprise, Talon doesn't pounce on the weakness with that cunning tongue of theirs. Instead, they just continue to brush their thumb steadily against my skin.

"My father would have called my theory about the blood moon a fairy tale too. He'd always roll his eyes when my mother told me stories about the fae and their old gods, the witches who guarded the woods, and the wolves who roamed the Wilds. He called her a romantic fool." An amused laugh rumbles out of Talon. "But he also picked flowers for her every day and rubbed her feet at night when she was aching from performing. He doted on my mother like she was the sun his world revolved around."

"What did they do?" I ask. "In the troupe?"

"My father, Caill, was the stagemaster. He could charm any crowd and get them so riled up, they would gladly part with their money. Our current stagemaster still talks about him in reverence."

"So that's where you get your swaggering confidence from then?" I snort.

Talon turns their head enough so I can make out their mischievous grin. "Taught me how to pickpocket too." Then they sober. "My father taught me how the world is. My mother told me how it should be."

Before I can second-guess myself, I rest my cheek against Talon's shoulder. "Tell me more."

"My mother, Serenea, had a gentle nature. Despite that, she was *excellent* with knives. Better hand-eye coordination than anyone I've ever met. She performed multiple times a day—juggling daggers, throwing them, fancy spin tricks. Her performances were always some of the highest attended; the fact that she was beautiful probably didn't hurt. I get my good looks from her, by the way."

"Good looks? Please. You're average at best," I smoothly lie.

"How you wound me, Princess," Talon says in mock outrage.

"Just trying to counteract all the women who drool over you as soon as we step into a tavern."

They shrug beneath me. "Sometimes the men drool too."

"Don't make me shove you off this horse," I warn, but there's no heat in it.

Talon laughs again, and I get the impression they find something amusing that I don't understand. It's nice, I realize, this moment between us, when we aren't at each other's throats or tearing off each other's clothing. We're just . . . being.

"My parents were well matched," Talon says, their tone one of reverence. "Their mate bond was strong, and they anticipated each other's needs and emotions effortlessly. I think that's why they both fell for her so hard."

Their words soften at the last bit, and I hazard a guess. "Ravyn's mother?" She looks nothing like Talon, so I always assumed they had at least one different parent.

"Yeah," they say softly. "Alea was a servant in some noble's household. She was coerced into a relationship with him and then found herself with child. She fled immediately."

I don't blame her for that decision. There are safe ways to end an unplanned pregnancy, but they aren't practiced in the four kingdoms anymore. It's infuriating because they don't even involve magic, just a specific preparation of herbs and some aftercare, but because the practice came from the fae, it's forbidden. Other alternatives are allowed, but they're all dangerous. Before the witches left, they'd offered to treat anyone who came to the forest seeking care—either to end a pregnancy or to protect it. Both are equally dangerous in the four kingdoms if you can't afford to pay for medical care.

I know the treatments, but no one ever comes into my forest seeking help anymore. They only come seeking my death.

"I still remember the night she stumbled into our camp." Tender amusement coats Talon's words. "It was a few months before my thirteenth birthday, and I was trying to persuade my mother to let me go into the city on my own."

"For what?" I ask curiously, suddenly desperate to get any insight into Talon's life.

"To test out some of the tricks my father had taught me." I can practically hear the sly grin in their voice. "My father would occasionally go for a walk in the city . . . and those walks might've taken him through some noble households, where he relieved them of the burden of too many riches."

I laugh softly. "How kind of him."

"Indeed," Talon agrees. "I was on the cusp of getting my mom to agree to let me go out on my own when they spotted Alea. Her black hair was a tangled mess, and dirt covered her pale yellow dress. She looked like she'd been walking for days, but she still held her chin high as she cradled the slight bump of her belly. My parents would joke later that she looked like a stubborn queen, refusing to let life beat her down."

"Reminds me of Ravyn." I didn't know the girl who had stolen Astria's heart all that well, but Astria had insisted on me hanging out with her several times in the beginning of their relationship before getting frustrated with my indifference. Ravyn had never let it get to her though. It had made me respect her a little, even if I didn't like her.

"They're a lot alike," Talon says, that quiet grief back in their voice. "Even though my parents were a mated pair and their bond was strong, they both fell in love with Alea and made room for her in their hearts."

"Poly relationships are common amongst the werewolves," I note. "The mate bond will adapt and spread if that's what everyone wants."

"I think if Alea had been a wolf, the bond would have accepted her too."

The thumb that was stroking the back of my hand went still at some point, and I feel the pain echoing down the bond. It's faint, so I assume Talon is trying to hold it back. I slip my hand out from underneath theirs and rest it on top, gently brushing my thumb across the back of their hand the same way they did for me. "What happened?" I ask gently.

"We were all happy for a while. Alea fell into our lives so perfectly, like this piece that had been missing. I think my parents were a little worried that I would be jealous, but I loved Alea. She had this dry sense of humor that always had me laughing, and even though she'd been a servant, she'd seen a different side of the cities than I ever had and was happy to regale me with all sorts of stories."

"The noble never came looking for her?"

"No." Talon shakes their head. "She left before she was showing, and even if he suspected, there are plenty of bastard children around the kingdom. Nobody cares."

"The more I learn about Eleoyn, the more I detest it."

"Can't argue with you there." We ride for a few minutes in silence, me stroking Talon's hand, before they go on with the story that obviously ends in heartache. Even with them holding back their emotions, I still feel them trickling into my soul. The rage is almost suffocating, but I never let my movements falter. "Ravyn was born, and she was absolutely perfect. We had one year of bliss as a happy family. Then the city guards of Mabria stopped our caravan as we were passing through."

Dread coils in my gut. The mage hunters are dangerous and ruthless, but the city guards are known to be cruel and corrupt. Before my parents and the other witches stopped traveling Eleoyn altogether, it was the city guards they were often more concerned about than the mage hunters.

"Alea was effortlessly beautiful," Talon says tonelessly. "Something about her just drew your immediate attention and didn't let you go. Our wagons were at the back of the caravan that day, and the guards waved everyone else on but made us stop. It's not unusual for that to happen, and we have a system in place for it. The rest of the caravan is to keep moving until they're a safe distance away and then a small group will double back to help those who were stopped."

"Why not have everyone wait?" I ask, my brows bunching together in confusion. "Isn't there safety in numbers?"

"That used to be the case, but decades ago, a different traveling group did just that. Things escalated, the details are murky, but the end result is that all one hundred three members were hanged. Children included. Since then, we get the bulk of the troupe to safety and then return. We don't like leaving anyone behind—even temporarily—but everyone agrees that we can't risk our children."

I stare off into the woods, the rage coming from Talon now wrapping around my own. "Does no one ever fight back?"

"Public executions are well-attended," Talon scoffs bitterly. "Bets are often placed on how long someone will struggle against the noose choking the life out of them, and wine pours as freely as the laughter pouring from the lips of those gathered. Mostly nobles, but plenty of the lower class come out too for the spectacle."

"This whole kingdom should be drowned in blood." I feel my magic unfurl inside me, excited at the prospect.

"If you ever want to make that a reality, let me know," Talon drawls. "I'll happily stand beside you, witch, while we burn it all down."

A shudder runs up my spine at the promise in their words and how right it feels, but then it fades and I'm left with the cold reminder that there is no Talon in my future. No blood and retribution. Our paths will diverge once we figure our way out of this mess and our sisters are safe.

As if they sense where my thoughts have headed, Talon tugs their hand free from mine and strokes Draco's neck. "The city guards pulled Alea away from my parents and started dragging her towards their security post. Alea fought hard, but they just laughed. My mother snapped. One second, the guards were cruelly taunting the dark-haired beauty screaming for help, and the next, they were choking on their own blood as my mother's daggers sank into their throats. She never was one to miss."

I close my eyes as if that would stop what is to come. It doesn't.

"My father thrust Ravyn into my arms. She was crying, not understanding what was going on, just that it was bad. He told me to run. I looked into his eyes and saw what he wasn't saying. They were going to die. Even as skilled as he was with a sword and my mother with her daggers . . . there was no surviving that fight, but neither of them was willing to leave Alea to be used, tortured, and killed by these men."

A ragged breath spreads throughout my lungs, tension flooding my body with a need to maim and kill, but there is no one for me to take it out on. This tale has already come to pass. So all I can do is stew in my impotent rage.

"I couldn't run," Talon admits with a hint of shame. "I just stood there and watched my world get destroyed in front of me. My father was first—the cowards took him down with multiple bolts from a crossbow—and when a guard thrust his sword at Alea, my mother flung herself in front of it." They stop and draw in a sharp inhale. "Alea's dark eyes were on me when they slit her throat."

"How'd you get away?" I ask numbly.

"People from our troupe arrived. Too late to help my parents, but they grabbed me, and we ran. The guards gave chase, but we had a well-planned escape route and were able to get away. Had to avoid Mabria for a long time after that."

"What happened to the guards?" The silver ring on my finger suddenly feels heavy.

"My wolf might be chained inside me, but they still appreciate a hunt." The words are barely more than a growl. "The face of every single guard was burned into my mind that day. I've found twelve of the fifteen."

"Tell me you didn't give them quick deaths." My voice carries an edge of violence that matches their growl. "Tell me you made them suffer, wolf."

"Such a bloodthirsty witch. Perhaps this is why Lunos felt we were well-matched." They let loose a dark chuckle. "I trust it will please you to know that their screams rang throughout the night for hours, and blood coated the walls."

"Good. Kruxtia no doubt appreciated the offering." The fae often depicted the goddess of retribution in paintings as covered in blood with a feral smile. Her idea of *retribution* was quite clear. "Perhaps after we find our sisters, I can help you locate the other three before I return to my forest and you to your life."

When Talon doesn't respond, I wince inwardly. It was foolish of me to offer such a thing. Opening my eyes, I blink against the bright sun and start to pull away to create some much-needed space, but Talon's hand shoots back and grips the side of my leather vest, yanking me forward before gripping both of my hands.

"Our mating bond might end, but I'll hold you to your offer, witch. You owe me a hunt."

CHAPTER ELEVEN

~

Talon

We reach Ryllae's cottage shortly after nightfall. It still worries me that they choose to live so close to one of the main roads. It's as if they're daring the mage hunters or some Ririthan raiders to find them, and maybe they are. I know very little of Ryllae's history, but I do know that they carry a massive chip on their shoulder.

I just have no idea who or what the fae warrior is so pissed off at.

Scythe is doing her best to keep her expression neutral but failing hilariously at it. I don't think she realizes how much she gives away all the time. Even if I couldn't feel the traces of her emotions down the bond, the slight crease between her brows and the way her full mouth is pressed into a hard, flat line, it's obvious she isn't happy about staying here despite my reassurances that this is merely the house of a friend and not a lover.

Not that I haven't tried with Ryllae, but they laughed in my face when I made a pass at them like I'd said the funniest joke they'd ever heard. I stood there in shock for a solid ten seconds after it happened because I'd never once failed to seduce anyone.

Ever since then, they've been one of my best friends, even if I know very little about why in all the hells they're living in Eleoyn.

True, it's safer for a fae to live here than in Riritha, where they're aggressively hunted down, but the Eleoyn mage hunters would be only too happy to find a fae living amongst them. The last time it happened, they threw a week-long festival around the execution. It was very well attended, and people still reminisce about it three years later.

The Mage Council of Sekaria offers safe haven for any fae . . . in exchange for servitude. Only a few fae have taken them up on that offer. The only other option is the southwest kingdom of Aestelas. All magic is banned there, but their king is so corrupt and inept at running his kingdom that it's easy to hide. You just have to accept that you live in a shithole.

Yet here Ryllae is, living a thirty-minute ride from the Eleoyn capital and the stronghold of the mage hunters.

Scythe studies the simple wood cottage, which is nearly covered in green ivy, before swinging her gaze back to the winding path that leads towards the main thoroughfare. It's a short enough ride to the road that, if I listen closely, I can hear horses passing by. Despite this, the cottage feels isolated because of the trees that grow densely around it.

I set Draco's saddle and bridle beneath a tree, and the fae horse trots off to the small grassy patch behind the cottage. We've been here enough that he knows his way around. Scythe drops into a crouch and shoves her fingers into the dirt, and the scythe tattoo across her neck glows slightly. What is my pretty little witch doing?

Before I can ask, the front door to the cottage opens, and a tall, lithe figure strolls out. Ryllae tends to bounce between androgynous and femme appearances. Just like the last few times I've seen them, they're leaning heavily towards the former.

Their black hair is currently shaved on the sides and long

enough on top to swoop back, and gold earrings dangle from their right ear, gleaming against their light brown skin. Despite the heat, they wear black pants that have a flowy cut to them and a baggy, deep purple, long-sleeve shirt that has the laces undone at the top.

Technically, Ryllae is the only fae I've ever met. So I don't know if not showing much skin is a fae thing or a unique quirk of my friend, but I've never seen them in anything besides pants and a long-sleeve shirt, even on blistering hot summer days.

"Ryllae." I take a step towards my friend. "Sorry for the unexpected visit, but we need a place to stay. This is—"

"Cerelia," they cut me off, their deep emerald green eyes staring at the witch. "Or I suppose *Scythe* is more accurate these days."

"Ryllae." The witch rises warily, letting the dirt slip through her fingers as she straightens. "Wasn't expecting to find you here."

"Obviously." Ryllae snorts. "Come on then."

I stare at my friend, perplexed as they spin on their heel and head back inside, leaving the front door open. Scythe starts to walk after them, but I catch her arm. "You two know each other?"

She looks pointedly at where my fingers are wrapped around her wrist, and I roll my eyes before letting go. Then Scythe glances towards the cottage, and I try to gauge her expression while also processing the emotions I feel through the bond. The wariness is definitely still there, but there's also an underlying sadness.

"Their secrets are not mine to tell," she finally says. "But we both know what it's like to have your own people turn their backs on you." She purses her lips. "Ryllae even more so than me."

"That's not an answer."

"Isn't it?" Her eyes flick to mine, a sly smile on her lips.

I laugh under my breath as she strides into the house because the exchange reminds me of when we first met. The clever but viscous words she used in riposte. The verbal sparring we engaged in had captivated me even more than her beauty. Somehow, I'd forgotten that about her.

"Coming?" Scythe asks from the doorway.

"I don't actually do that on command," I say smoothly, and I'm rewarded with a light blushing across her cheeks. She chews on her bottom lip as I approach but freezes when I touch her chin and gently brush my fingers against her lip until her teeth release it. Her heart beats faster as I do it again. Once. Twice. Then I lean forward to whisper in her ear, "Good witch."

She exhales shakily as I stride into the cottage, but my own steps slow when I realize that interaction was all me. It was me who wanted to touch her, get that heart of hers racing. Not my wolf and not the mating bond. Just me.

Fuck.

"What have you gotten yourself into this time, Tal?"

I look up from where I stopped in the hallway. Ryllae watches me with those impossibly bright green eyes. In the safety of the cottage, they've completely dropped their glamour, and their diamond-shaped pupils watch me closely. More piercings adorn their face as well—three gold hoops through their right eyebrow and another one through the septum.

"Nothing major," I say casually, joining them in their small kitchen and slumping into one of the chairs at the table. "Ravyn's missing. Unclear if she and Astria decided to be incredibly stupid and go off on their own or if something else is going on. Oh"—I reach for the glass of amber liquor they were clearly drinking before we arrived and slam it back—"and I'm mated to the witch."

Ryllae stares at me, those strange eyes of theirs unblinking. I'm pouring myself another shot of the liquor that blazed a trail of fire down my throat—there's really nothing like fae liquor—when Scythe walks in. She takes a seat in the chair farthest from me, the blush still fading from her cheeks and a scowl on her face. I'm thinking there's a good chance she'll try to stab me later for the "good witch" comment, and I'm kind of into it.

A raspy laugh spills out across the room, growing louder by the second until Ryllae is doubled over with a hand on their stomach.

"Your sister"—they straighten enough to point at Scythe—"left you to run off with their sister"—they point at me—"and now your sister has left you behind to explore the world with the witchkin girl." Ryllae wipes some tears from their eyes. "The two of you fucked, hated each other afterwards, and now you're both looking for your sisters and you have a fucking mate bond?" They slap their hands against their thighs. "The gods have truly blessed me with some good entertainment this evening."

"I hate you right now," I mutter.

"As you should." Ryllae laughs.

I raise the shot glass to my mouth, only for Scythe to lean across the table and snatch it away from me. She downs it in one gulp and then grabs the bottle on the table to refill it. The first time I tried fae liquor, I coughed for a solid five minutes. Either the witches also have a liquor that feels like it's setting your lungs on fire, or Scythe's had fae liquor before.

"While I'm glad we can provide some fun in your otherwise dull existence," Scythe drawls, "our sisters could be in actual danger. Perhaps you can remember who you were for a few minutes and help us."

The amusement is gone from my friend's face in an instant, replaced with something cold and alien. The only time I've seen them like this is when I delivered the news about the fae who was captured and brutally executed.

Something dark and vicious crawls under Ryllae's skin, and I say that as someone who is a cursed werewolf and has seen what Scythe is capable of, but while she and I revel in blood and enjoy killing . . . there is something about Ryllae that gives me pause. If they were to ever cut loose, it wouldn't be a pack of mage hunters or raiders that died, it would be an entire city. Maybe a whole kingdom.

The question is . . . why haven't they? The fae—Ryllae's people—are being exterminated or enslaved, but they just sit here in their cottage. Brooding.

"Careful, *Scythe*. I never much cared for witches." Ryllae's diamond-shaped pupils narrow until they're nothing more than thin slits.

Scythe snorts. "You never much cared for anybody . . . except *him*."

I jolt in my seat when the room plunges into darkness, not just a *the lanterns have gone out* type of darkness, but an impenetrable black that has to be fueled by magic. All of my senses feel off, like they're all being overloaded. When I jump to my feet, I stumble, and it's hard to tell which way is up.

What in the ever-loving fuck is this?

"Ryllae!" I yell, reaching out for the table that is no longer there. "Stop!"

A wicked melody echoes throughout the void, and then Scythe is there—her tattoos glowing a bright silver that cuts through the dark. She reaches out, and I instantly grab her hand. I feel her magic flowing into me and mine into her. Her song pours out, and the oppressive blackness fades until it pops out of existence and we're back in Ryllae's kitchen. My fae friend leans casually against the wall, as if nothing happened.

"Temper tantrums?" Scythe breathes hard, her tattoos still an iridescent silver. "At your age?"

"You always were a foolish girl." Ryllae scoffs.

"And you always were a bitch Sovereign!"

"Sovereign?" I frown at Scythe before looking at Ryllae, who is glaring at my witch like they want to strangle her. I step forward, tucking Scythe behind me.

Some of the intensity fades from Ryllae's eyes, and they angrily push off the wall to stride across the kitchen. "My past doesn't matter, and it's best to leave it alone." They reach up into a cupboard and pull out two more shot glasses. "The witch hardly needs your protection, Tal."

"It's just the mating bond," Scythe says evenly, and I only catch the barest hint of pain down our connection.

I want to tell her it's not. That the bond has nothing to do with me stepping between her and a threat, but I'm not ready to admit to myself why I did it, so I keep my mouth shut.

Ryllae gives me a knowing look that I just return with a lazy grin. Then they shake their head before walking to the table and taking a seat. Scythe and I sit back down and watch as the fae pours each of us a shot.

"To old friends." Ryllae raises their glass to Scythe before doing the same to me and saying, "And new ones."

"We've been friends for almost ten years, Ryllae," I say dryly, holding my glass up.

"Trust me." A sly, closed-lipped smile slides across Scythe's face as she raises her glass. "A decade is nothing to Ryllae."

If I wasn't curious about my fae friend before, I sure as shit am now. Ryllae looks like they're a few years older than me—late thirties—but their eyes have always looked older. I'd guess they were closer to Scythe's age, a couple of centuries old at most, but now I'm rethinking that. Scythe referred to them as "Sovereign," but the Fae Sovereign died in The Great War . . . My eyes lock onto Ryllae's, and they hold my questioning gaze.

For just a second, a black crown with bloodred rubies shimmers on their head, and stunning green eyes become a chilling red. Then the image fades, and it's just my blunt but usually mild-mannered friend smiling at me.

We all clink our glasses and throw them back. Fire burns down my throat before settling in my gut, and I look at the half-empty bottle sitting on the table. "I hope you have more booze, Ryllae, because I sure as fuck need it."

<hr>

"THEY'RE alive and not in immediate peril." Ryllae looks at the bones they cast across the table. Scythe eyes them with interest, but they mean nothing to me.

"Is that supposed to be comforting?" I scowl at the bones and then the cryptic fae. "Because the 'immediate peril' part wasn't exactly reassuring. I thought you could give us specific answers. Did they leave voluntarily? Were they taken?"

Ryllae doesn't respond; instead, they just stare at the bones like they've seen a ghost. Dread sinks into my gut. What are they seeing that they're not telling us?

"Where the fuck is my sister, Ryllae?" I rasp. "What do you see? Tell me what you fuckin—"

"Talon," Scythe says softly, placing her hand gently on my arm. Her silver eyes are on the fae, lavender hair draping over her shoulders. Ryllae asked her to take off the charmed necklace earlier, said they didn't like looking at pathetic mage magic. Scythe rolled her eyes but slipped the necklace off and tossed it onto the table.

I gave her a pointed look that very clearly said, *Oh, so you'll take it off for them but not for me?*

The grin that flashed across her lips said she very much understood my annoyance and was delighted by it. Then she made it worse by mouthing, *bad wolf.*

Which is why I've been sporting an erection under the table for a solid ten minutes like I'm an overeager teenager who just had their hand held for the first time.

Surprisingly, Ryllae didn't make any snarky comments during the exchange, which wasn't like them. My mysterious fae friend is quite good at picking up on what people aren't saying, reading body language and minute expressions with ease.

As soon as they picked up that bag of bones though . . . they went somewhere else. I recognize the symbol on the bag. It's the same one carved into each of the broken-up finger bones. Atotl. The god of wisdom.

I glance away from Scythe back to Ryllae, who is still staring at the bones in a way that makes me think they're not seeing them at all. "Are . . . are you okay?" I ask my friend.

"It may not mean what you think," Scythe says, but we both

jump back when Ryllae swipes their arm across the table, knocking all the bones off. The hair on the back of my neck rises when they all vanish into puffs of smoke before hitting the ground . . .

And appear right back where they were on the table.

Then a chill spreads throughout the room, like there is something else here. I stare at Atotl's symbol on the bag. My mother claimed that the gods turned their back on the fae, and that's why The Great War happened in the first place. Why the fae returned to Arandia.

But not all the fae left. Maybe the gods remained too. Although, based on how Ryllae reacted to whatever the bones told them . . . that may not be a good thing.

"I'll have something for you in the morning," they say, and it takes me a minute to realize they're talking to me because their eyes are still locked on the table. "Won't be ready to use until tomorrow night, but the witch will know what to do with it. Might help you figure out where your sisters are."

Without another word, they grab the near-empty bottle and stalk off down a hallway. It's one I've never been down before, and I assume it leads to their bedroom. Then a door slams shut, hard enough to make the windows rattle.

I stare down the dark hall. The sound of the door slamming came from somewhere farther away than seems possible, given the size of the cottage. Granted, I've only ever been in the kitchen, front hall, and the spare bedroom, but I know what it looks like from the outside, and logic says Ryllae couldn't have gone that far.

"What the fuck is going on?" I turn to Scythe, who is doing her best to maintain an inscrutable expression. Big surprise: she's failing. I can see all the thoughts flash across her face and also feel them screaming down the bond. She's concerned about Ryllae but also wary. It's as if she just watched a wounded predator prowl by and wanted to help it but also didn't want to get her hand bitten off.

"It's complicated," she settles on. "And again, it's not my place to spill Ryllae's secrets. Let's just, uh, give them some space."

I want to keep pushing Scythe for answers, not just to sate my curiosity, but because Ryllae is my friend. They've helped me out of a few tight spots over the years, and they've always been someone I can talk to. I love my sister, and Vesi and Mattias are two of the best friends a person could ask for, but we all have history from growing up together, and sometimes it's just easier to talk about things without all the baggage.

Despite that, I respect Ryllae too much to pry. For now. Once my sister is safe, I'll come back and annoy my secretive fae friend until they tell me what the fuck is going on and who we have to kill. I look over the bones on the table one last time. They don't mean anything to me, but I take note of the patterns to ask Scythe about them later. She clearly understands what at least some of it means and can tell me if Ryllae is in any immediate danger.

"Come on." I release a deep exhale through my nose. "There's a spare bedroom this way."

Scythe follows me down the hall we entered earlier and then ducks in behind me when I open a door on the left. A small bedroom greets us, and after a quick inhale I can tell nobody has used it since I stayed here last. Once in a while, I'll pick up other scents when I visit Ryllae, but to my knowledge, no one has used this bedroom besides me in the last decade. If they've ever had overnight guests, those people have stayed in Ryllae's bed.

Though I suspect Ryllae doesn't have any regular lovers because I've never detected the same scent twice, and they don't seem like the type to bring a one-night stand home. Maybe that's why they're so cranky all the time. They haven't gotten laid in at least a decade.

Scythe takes off her boots and then goes over to the dark wood dresser in the corner. With her back to me, she strips down to her underwear, folding her clothes and chest band and placing them onto the dresser before pulling out a light cream top and tugging it on. It's one of mine, so it falls to mid-thigh on her, and even with it being washed, I can still detect my scent on it.

Despite the strip show, the bond between us remains quiet. Maybe we have too much on our minds to get swept up in desire right now, but I do get some satisfaction from seeing her in my clothes . . . covered in my scent.

You shouldn't be thinking like this. The witch is not yours. My brows furrow together because she is. At least temporarily.

"What do you think Ryllae is going to give us in the morning?" I ask to distract myself from my confusing thoughts. "They said you'll know what to do with it?"

Scythe slides into bed, crawling underneath the blankets. Unlike the sweltering heat outside, Ryllae's house is cool and comfortable. I'm assuming we have their fae magic to thank for that.

I pull my clothes and boots off, dumping them into a pile on the ground that Scythe frowns at. She's being very careful not to look at me standing here in only my underwear, and I'm too tired to tease her about it.

I slide into bed next to her, a careful amount of distance between us. This bed is far larger and more comfortable than any of the ones we slept in at the inns.

"Ryllae used to be a very gifted dreamwalker—I suppose they still are, but they don't do it anymore." The witch folds her hands behind her head, that glorious lavender hair spilling out around her, and my fingers itch to touch it. "I know more about Ryllae than you do . . . but even I don't know why they refuse to use that part of their magic now."

"I didn't know the fae could dreamwalk."

Scythe's eyes close, and I carefully snake my hand across the bed to brush my fingers against the ends of her hair, unable to hold back.

"Ryllae is—was—special. Their situation now is . . . complicated, but even though Ryllae themself doesn't dreamwalk anymore, they can enchant stones with the ability. One-time use only though."

My fingers go still. "We can use the stones to speak to our sisters in their dreams?" Excitement and impatience war within me. In less than a day, I may finally know where Ravyn is and if she really left me voluntarily. If she did . . . I'm not sure what I'll do with that information. Probably still demand that she tell me where she and Astria are so I can drag them back.

I'm starting to respect the witch more and more for staying up in her tree house when I came to collect Astria with Ravyn instead of fighting us to keep her sister there. At the time, I thought she was overreacting, but now . . . now I get it. The world is a cruel place, and it's difficult to not be overbearingly protective of those you love.

"*I* can use it," she corrects me. "I'll try to bring you along, but I don't know if it will work."

It's not ideal, but I'll take it if it means she'll be able to speak to Astria or Ravyn. Just then, a hint of melancholy brushes against my senses. "Has Ryllae helped you dreamwalk before? Is that how you know them?"

She cracks an eye to look at me, and I quickly move my hand away from her hair. Normally, I play with Scythe's hair to mess with her. Her catching me doing it because I enjoy it makes me feel oddly exposed. "Cats are supposed to be the curious ones. Wolves are stoic."

I grin at her. "Can't blame me for trying."

Her lips curl into a small smile as amusement races down the bond. "I've known of Ryllae for a long time—all witches do—but I met them a century ago. We crossed paths a few times after that, but the last time . . ." She swallows. "The last time was a little over ten years ago. It was a year or so after my parents and the rest of the witches left. In a moment of weakness, I wanted to see Vaeril . . . see if he regretted leaving me."

Vaeril. Her mate. The one who rejected her. Scythe is going to be two for two in failed mated bonds. The denial from the wolf at that thought is so strong, I inhale sharply, and Scythe jerks her eyes open to look at me.

"Did he?" I ask, letting my expression relax into one of casual indifference, like I don't really care if she answers or not.

"He was already mated again," she says, her eyes closing as she settles back onto the pillow, and I'm glad she doesn't push about whatever she just felt from the wolf. "Seemed very happy."

"He *seems* like an asshole," I mutter.

She huffs a laugh. "He isn't. Vaeril is actually very kind and charming. There were others vying for my hand when I was searching for a mate, but there was never really any competition. Vaeril is gorgeous. He doted on me and treated me with respect during our entire time together."

"Sounds boring," I tell her truthfully. "Bet he never fucked you against a tree." Her lips twitch, and the sadness in the bond fades a little. "And we both know there is no chance of him being prettier than me."

Scythe opens those silver eyes and scrutinizes my face for a few seconds before closing them again. "You're alright."

"Alright?" I sputter. "I am absolutely *stunning*. In a wicked, evil prince kind of way."

"Please." Scythe snorts, a playful grin on her face. "You're not the prince. You're the charlatan who strolls in and robs the prince blind while fucking his wife. Hells, you probably fuck them both."

"You already know me so well, witch." I lay a hand against my heart.

Her grin falters. "I don't know you at all, really."

She looks . . . defeated. My wild and dangerous witch looks small in this moment, and I can't stand it.

"I accidentally dyed my eyebrows bright pink when I was thirteen and then shaved them off to try to fix it."

"What?" Scythe chokes on a laugh, her silver eyes widening so much that she looks like an owl.

"Up until then, I thought of myself as a boy. My father was, like, the perfect image of a man, and I idolized him growing up, but as I started to go through puberty, it became weird when people would refer to me as male or use masculine pronouns. Like I was performing a role in a play that was never meant for me."

Scythe nods, and I snatch a lock of her hair to play with again. I can't help it. If Scythe asks about it, I'll just blame the bond.

"Exploring your relationship with gender is not only supported in Tovenian culture but encouraged. I was still a teenager though and not super comfortable talking about everything with my parents. This was also only a few months after Alea had entered our lives, and they were busy caring for her. I decided that I wanted to give myself a dramatic makeover and maybe start testing out both nonbinary and feminine fashions to figure out what I liked. We were camped outside Sovarre at the time, so one night, I snuck into the city and went to an underground market."

She winces. "My parents told me about those markets. They said half the stuff there isn't even crafted by mages and the other half is made by mediocre ones who have no business being mages in the first place."

"Harsh." I grin. "But accurate. My hair was lighter back then, more of a dark brown, and I wanted it to be black. I didn't want to deal with dying it constantly though, and the mage stuff lasts for months . . . if you get the good stuff."

"I'm guessing you didn't get the good stuff?" The corners of her mouth twitch like she's fighting off a smile.

"With the arrogance that only a teenager can truly achieve, I browsed through the market and selected some dye that I was positive was legitimate. I was so sure of myself that I didn't even test it out." I arch a dark eyebrow at her, and Scythe giggles. "As soon as I got home, I put it on my hair and then decided to do my eyebrows as well—because it would have been silly to make my hair black and not have my brows match."

"Obviously," she agrees with a serious expression that is ruined when she giggles again, and dear gods, do I love that sound.

"Everything seemed to be going fine," I continue. "My hair darkened to black and I rinsed it out, feeling very proud of myself for pulling this off in one evening. But when I looked in the mirror again, I discovered, much to my horror, that the dye had reacted poorly to getting wet, and the black had turned pink." I lean forward so I can hold the ends of two pieces of her lavender hair over my eyebrows. "Pastel pink."

Scythe loses it and starts cackling, one of her hands falling onto my chest, so I seize the opportunity to grab her and pull her closer. Something inside me settles then, at her cuddled up in the crook of my arm and her hand on my chest, and for once, I don't question it.

"At this point, I'm outright panicking. It was my plan to have a brand-new look to show off the next morning . . . but that plan did not involve pink. My hair, I could cover up with a hat, but I decided the eyebrows needed to go."

"I can't believe you'd rather have no eyebrows than pink eyebrows." She laughs and waggles her lavender eyebrows, which are a slightly darker shade than her hair, at me.

"The lavender suits you amazingly well." I twist it around my fingers again. "I am almost perfect, but even I have my limits. Pastel colors are not one of the many looks I can pull off. But more importantly, that's when I learned that femininity did not appeal to me."

"Not all women like pink," she counters.

"True," I concede. "But pink and pastel are still more associated with femininity, and I found that just as uncomfortable as some aspects of masculinity."

"So your disastrous hair dye experiment helped you figure out you were nonbinary." She smiles, her silver eyes shining.

"That amongst other things I tried over the years," I acknowledge. "But I still had the problem in that immediate moment of fixing how ridiculous I looked and felt."

"So off the eyebrows go!" She pumps a fist into the air, and I laugh, catching it in my hand and pulling it back down to my chest to rest over the tree tattoo.

"Off the eyebrows went!" I scrunch my nose. "Turns out . . . that did not fix things. I looked even more ridiculous. In desperation, I raided Alea's makeup box and tried to draw them on. She found me an hour later, after returning from helping with my mother's performance, and somehow managed not to laugh at the sight of me sitting there with pink hair, no eyebrows, and some very crooked attempts at fixing the situation."

"Alea wasn't a woman—she was a god," Scythe says, her lips twitching. "Because it had to have taken godly strength not to laugh."

I flick her nose. "Rude but accurate. She did have a silly smile on her face, and her eyes were definitely laughing, but she proceeded to help me draw on eyebrows, and then we decided to shave the sides of my hair and braid the rest back in a mohawk. It was still pink, but the overall look had enough of an edge to it that it wasn't the worst. I started a fashion trend that summer, and quite a few of the other kids went to the market to buy the dye so they could have pastel pink hair." I frown. "Looking back on it, I should have demanded that merchant cut me in on the tidy profit they made that summer from selling their shoddy goods."

"Definitely a missed opportunity."

"That summer had a lot of hilarious missteps on my part." I tug the blanket up so it's covering us more. "Let me tell you about the time I accidentally locked myself in a room in the middle of a heist and my friends had to run to get my dad before I was discovered . . ."

An hour and several stories about my misguided youth later, Scythe is asleep in my arms, and I soon fall asleep inhaling her scent.

CHAPTER TWELVE

~

Scythe

"Do you intend to break the mating bond?" Ryllae asks when I step outside their cottage in the morning.

"Good morning to you too," I grumble and squint up at the sky. It's barely past sunrise and it's already hot. Today's ride is going to be brutal.

Other people might think Ryllae is evil because of their magic, but I personally think it's because they're a morning person.

"We both know you don't care about such pleasantries. It's why your best friends are felines."

They're not wrong. I move away from the door and close it behind me. Ryllae told Talon to raid their kitchen for food, and they'd practically shoved me out of the way to get to a wooden box beside a cutting board, mumbling something about honey biscuits.

Everything is . . . confusing. It's already been difficult navigating everything since we'd fucked, but last night felt even more intimate, which is weird considering I'd been choking on Talon's cock less than two days ago.

It doesn't change anything though.

"Yes, I still intend to break it." My fingers toy with the mage necklace I'd put back on this morning. "Talon doesn't want the bond."

"But do you?" They look at me, something unreadable in their expression. I recognize that look. It means they know something I don't. I also know that there is zero chance of getting them to tell me if they don't want to.

I start to say no but then remember the uncanny knack all fae have for detecting lies. "I don't want to be trapped in a bond with someone who did not choose it." *Who didn't choose me.* "If I can find a way to break it . . . and the curse on them . . . I will."

They don't even blink at me saying I intend to break the curse on Talon's werewolf, which tells me I'm right about them knowing something about all of this.

Ryllae crouches to pluck a bright orange blossom from the garden and whispers something across it too faint for me to hear before crushing it in their hand. "You're always so quick to give others what they need." Then they pull a leather satchel from their belt and sprinkle the crushed petals inside it. "It's okay to go after what you desire every once in a while, Cerelia Airgid."

Annoyance flares at the use of my family name.

"Oh? You going to pursue who *you* desire any time soon, Ryllae of the Crimson Wood?" For a second, their eyes turn a solid black except for their irises that glow a deep red. Then the former ruler of the fae tucks it all away and tosses the leather satchel to me.

I snap it out of the air and loosen the strings to peer inside, finding a perfect glass sphere nestled amongst the orange petals.

"It should be ready to go by this evening, but I had to make it in a bit of a haste, so it won't last long. Five minutes at most," they say tightly.

"I'm sorry." I sigh and tie the strings back together before using them to attach the leather satchel to my belt. "Things have been . . . difficult for me lately. No reason to take it out on you."

Ryllae snorts, their emerald eyes gleaming. "Lately? Things have been difficult for you for decades."

"Well, they've been difficult for you for centuries," I say wryly. "Just trying to be polite, Ry."

A genuine smile spreads across their lips. "You always were my favorite witch."

I smile, but it doesn't quite reach my eyes. "The bones told you something else, didn't they?" I was able to interpret some of it last night, but not all.

Their smile fades. "Sacrifice. That's the key to dissolving both the mate bond and Talon's curse. You will need to sacrifice something dear to you." The fae hesitates. "I can feel you slipping, Cerelia. Your soul is on the precipice right now, and I'm not sure if you'll survive if you proceed on this path."

I look away. "I've had a good run."

"Cerelia," they growl, but I still don't meet their eyes. "*Scythe.*"

"Don't," I say quietly before meeting their gaze again. "Don't push me on this, and I won't push you on what else the bones told you. '*Fate is a gift one cannot outrun.*'"

Ryllae glares at me and those damning words I'd seen written in the bones but before they can say anything else the door to their cottage swings open and Talon steps out.

"Ready to go?" Talon looks at me, our pack slung over their shoulder and some type of biscuit in their hand.

"Yes," I say quickly. "Let's get going."

Ryllae's gaze feels like a hot brand on the back of my neck, but I release a sharp whistle and Draco comes charging around the cottage.

"You can summon animals?" Talon shoots me a curious glance before they move to grab the saddle from under the tree.

"She can force them to flee too," Ryllae says through gritted teeth.

My reluctant mate settles the saddle on Draco's back before looking at me and then Ryllae. "Something going on I should know about?"

"No," I lie. "Nothing important."

The pointed look Talon gives me says they don't buy that for a second, but they don't push. I turn to Ryllae and finally meet their heavy gaze. "Thank you for your help, my friend. You've always been kind to me . . . and I hope that you will bestow that kindness on my sister."

The look Ryllae gives me is murderous, but they wipe it away when Talon strides over with a fully saddled Draco following in their wake.

"We should get going. If we keep a steady pace, we'll be able to reach my camp by late afternoon." They step to Draco's side and fold their hands together to help me on. I quickly oblige, and a minute later, we're waving goodbye to Ryllae, who gives us a terse wave in response. Just before we reach the main road, Talon pulls the fae horse to a stop, causing my chest to bump into their back. "Why did Ryllae look like they were one second away from going into scary fae mode again?"

"I don't know what you mean." I quickly pull my hands away from Talon's waist and try to smother every ounce of negative emotion I'm feeling so it doesn't trickle down the bond. Based on how they stiffen though, I know I'm unsuccessful.

"Does whatever you two were discussing have anything to do with our sisters?"

I feel their fear through our connection, and I'm happy that I can at least alleviate that. "No," I say softly. "Ryllae and I just had a difference of opinion on something. It had nothing to do with the girls. They did give me a dream ball though, so I'll be able to reach Astria or Ravyn tonight and we can hopefully get some answers."

Maybe I'll be going home tomorrow morning. It is strange to think that, but if the girls are truly safe and just exploring a different area of the kingdom . . . do I really need to stay? I miss

Astria. I miss her so fucking much, but I also don't think I have it in me to see her happy and in love right now. Not with how I am feeling about . . . everything. I close my eyes. She deserves to be happy, and I won't taint her with my darkness.

If I walk into Astria's dreams tonight and everything with her is going well, if we are just overreacting to all of this, then I will run back to the forest as fast as I can. I probably don't need to be close to Talon to break the mate bond and their curse. Given how intertwined our souls are, I am confident I can do it from my forest. If it turns out I'm wrong, then I will track them down later.

Talon turns their head so I can make out their profile and the way their jaw is stubbornly set. "There's something you're not telling me."

"It doesn't matter."

"So you say," they argue. "But you're clearly upset, and unless you tell me, I have no idea of knowing if it's relevant to our situation or not."

"You still want to find out what's going on with our sisters, yes?" I lean back enough so that I can cross my arms over my chest.

"Yes," they grind out. "But—"

"And you still want to dissolve the mating bond between us, yes?"

Say no. Hesitate. Give me something.

"Yes, of course," Talon says sharply.

Something inside me shatters, but I catch all the pieces and carefully tuck them away before wrapping my arms back around Talon, their hard body rigid against mine.

"It doesn't matter," I repeat. Then I whistle again and Talon barely has time to react before Draco takes off in a ground-eating gallop and the time for talking is over.

TALON TRIES to question me again on our ride to Albadrid about the weird vibe they walked into this morning between me and Ryllae, but I refuse to answer and, eventually, Talon gives up. I do my best to distract myself by observing the landscape on the ride down in the meantime.

The further south we go, the more everything changes. The trees become more sparse than the ones in the north. Eventually, they stop growing altogether and plants with long, wicked spines take their place. I ask Talon, and they say the prickly plants are cacti.

I want to let my magic out to play with them, but refrain because I know it would make Talon uncomfortable. Plus the road we are on is pretty busy, people regularly riding by us on the way to the capital.

The brown dirt also lightens until it looks more like sand, but it is hard and compact with cracks running through it in some areas. Talon notices me looking at it and informs me that the southern area of the kingdom is often referred to as the badlands, and it extends into Riritha for a ways. I don't know exactly what they mean by *badlands* but am pretty sure if I push for more of an explanation, Talon will insist on an answer for an answer, so I let it drop.

Still, the unique and changing landscape provides a pleasant escape from me pulling apart Ryllae's cryptic words. I need to sacrifice something, and that will undo not only the mate bond but also the curse on Talon's wolf. But what? Ryllae said it is something dear to me, but the only thing I can think of is Astria, and I will absolutely *not* be sacrificing her for anything or anyone.

Ryllae knows that though and wouldn't have brought it up if my sister were the intended sacrifice. It has to be something else.

"Fucking cryptic fae bullshit," I mutter hours later when I'm no closer to understanding what in all the fates Ryllae meant.

"Perhaps if you tell me what Ryllae told you, I can help figure it out," Talon says mildly. "But it'll have to wait until later because we're almost to the camp."

"Really?" I peer around their shoulder. There is a crossroad up ahead, and when we reach it, Talon steers Draco to the right, taking us further inland. Once again, the landscape changes. The harsh, dry ground gives way to a grassland. It's not green like the meadows up north though, instead, tall grass with feathered edges fills the land on either side of the road. I can also make out the outline of a few trees up ahead. "This area is pretty, but everything is so out in the open."

"Most of the south is like this," Talon says. "You get used to it after a while, but I prefer the forests of the north." Then they hesitate for a moment. "My wolf likes your forest. I think it calls to them."

"I understand why. It's like a miniature version of the Wilds," I say quietly, and then it's my turn to hesitate. "Do *you* like it?"

For a second, I think they won't answer, but when they do, I'm not sure if they're still talking about the forest.

"More than I should."

I'm still contemplating their response when several people exit from the large and colorful performance tents to wave at us. Based on the cheers inside, I know there are some performances going on, but it's still late afternoon so the crowds aren't too bad yet. At this time of day, it's mostly families or folks who want to come for the cheaper daytime prices. Astria forced me to go to a few performances early on in her relationship with Ravyn, so I know that things get louder and raunchier at night. That's when the bulk of the crowd comes out and the more daring performances begin.

Talon doesn't stop to speak with anyone, just directs Draco towards a cluster of trees behind the large tents. A few people shoot me curious looks, but if anyone recognizes me from the few times I interacted with the couple, they don't show it.

Four wagons are tucked away in the trees, bright canvas tents stretching out in front of them, and a large man throws back the flap of one of them before stomping towards us. Talon tugs Draco to a halt and throws their leg over the fae horse's neck to smoothly dismount, then they clasp the other man's forearms in greeting.

"You made good time," the man notes. I've seen him before—the day I met Talon. That scar across his face isn't something I'd forget. I'm impressed he didn't lose an eye when he got it.

"Luckily my friend didn't need much convincing." Talon looks around. "Vesi around?"

"Finishing up a performance. Should be done soon." The man looks at where I'm still sitting awkwardly on Draco's back, and recognition sparks in his gaze. "It's a pleasure to see you again, *Cerelia*." He strides over, and I'm too shocked to react when his hands wrap around my waist to pluck me off Draco like I weigh nothing. I'm even more surprised when he loops a heavy arm around my shoulders and walks me back over to Talon like we're the best of friends.

"Hi?" I tilt my head back so I can meet his kind, warm brown eyes before glancing at Talon, unsure about what they've told their friend about me aside from my real name. Then again . . . that is how I introduced myself to Talon in our initial meeting, and I spoke to Mattias back then too, at least briefly. I'm surprised he remembers me.

"I should have realized you were Astria's sister." He shook his head ruefully. "She said you were merely a friend, but now it seems so obvious. I can't believe this whole time, Vesi and I have been trying to figure out who Talon was—"

"Not important, Mattias," Talon cuts in, sending their friend a warning look.

A gleam of amusement dances in the big man's eyes, so at odds with the brutal scar running across his face, but he drops whatever he was going to say before he looks down at me again. "I'm sure many recognized you when you rode through the camp. You caused quite a stir when you danced with Talon the way you did."

"It was just a dance." I frowned.

"There were sparks flying, and it wasn't from the fire." Mattias grins. "The fact that you're actually Scythe makes this all so much juicier. The elders are going to love this. Nobody gossips like them."

"You . . ." My gaze bounces between Mattias and Talon. "You know who I am? What I am?"

"Everyone in the troupe knows I went to fetch the Witch of the Woods," Talon says carefully, like they're gauging my reaction. "They just didn't know that the woman I danced with around the bonfire and 'the witch' were the same person."

"And they didn't question why you would ask the Witch of the Woods for help?" I narrow my eyes at them.

Talon tilts their head in a purely lupine gesture. "They know you're Astria's sister, so it made sense I would request your assistance."

"You told them she's witchkin?" I stare at them incredulously.

"I told you before that honesty is important to us. I couldn't ask the troupe to offer Astria a place to stay without telling them she was."

"You trusted my sister's life on your misplaced belief that everyone in your troupe is trustworthy?" Anger spirals within me, and I resist the urge to punch Talon in the face. Repeatedly. "And you didn't think to mention that before now?"

They. Shrug.

Fuck punching them. I'm gonna shove my knife through that perfect godsdamn face. My hand slips to the dagger on my thigh, but I'm stopped from doing anything when Mattias adjusts his position to clamp my arm against my side.

"Be nice," he admonishes when I growl at him. "Talon's right. We don't keep secrets around here. Better to have the entire troupe looking out for her so that they can cover if necessary."

"That's nice," I grind out. "Except for the fact that someone in your precious troupe likely sold out my sister!"

"We do not tolerate traitors," Mattias says, the cheerfulness gone from his voice, now replaced by a vicious edge. "If someone is responsible for the girls' disappearance, then we'll drag every truth out of the traitor before snapping their fucking neck."

My fury settles a little. "I see why Eliza likes you."

His smile is brighter than the sun at the mention of her. "Eliza *loves* me. She's just too stubborn to admit it. I'll wear her down eventually though."

I open my mouth to argue but decide against it. I'm probably the last person to be giving relationship advice. Instead, I glare at Talon. "Still plan on stabbing you later."

They smirk at me. "Honestly, I assume you're thinking about stabbing me at any given moment." Their smirk widens suddenly. "Even when I'm stabbing *you* with something."

A blush spreads across my cheeks, and Mattias chuckles.

He's back on my list of people to punch.

"Our arrival was actually timed perfectly," Talon says, directing our conversation back to the reason I'm here in the first place. "The afternoon performances will be finishing in a few minutes and the crowds will disperse, leaving only the troupe members until the night performances begin."

"Of course." Mattias squeezes me one more time—I'm pretty sure my bones creak—before releasing me. "What can I do to help?"

Talon glances my way, giving me the opportunity to decide how much I want to reveal. Mattias and everyone else knows that Astria is witchkin . . . and that her sister is the infamous Witch of the Woods, but that doesn't mean they really understand what I'm capable of, only the stories and rumors that surround my title. It's been a long time since a witch has walked amongst the kingdoms.

I think about how negatively Talon reacted to me using my magic for something as simple as healing. These two might have faith in their people, but I'm not sure how wise it is for me to flaunt my magic. Then again . . . if anyone is going to be comfortable with a witch . . . it'll be the Tovenians. I mean, they accepted Astria even knowing she was witchkin.

I look away from the two Tovenians to the trees surrounding us and spot just what I need, a flock of starlings tucked away, waiting out the heat of the day.

"There are two ways I can go about this," I tell Talon as I turn back to face them. "I can individually test each person. It'll be less . . . showy, but if you think they'll freak out over a large display of magic, then that would be best. Or I can suss out any traitors within a few minutes, but it . . . won't be subtle." I chew on my bottom lip before releasing it when Talon's gaze narrows on the movement. "You already suspect one of your people; how much do you trust the rest?"

Are they going to run to the nearest mage hunter and tell them about me? I don't say the question out loud, but I know Talon understands my reservation.

They glance at Mattias, and the two of them seem to have some silent conversation before Talon jerks their head in a nod. "Second option. I don't want to waste any more time. Perhaps I'm wrong about there being a traitor amongst us, but if I'm not, they didn't just betray Astria and Ravyn, they betrayed all of us. The troupe deserves to know and act accordingly."

I narrow my eyes at them. "If your suspicions prove correct and there is a traitor, their life is mine." If Talon thinks the troupe would get to claim vengeance before me, they are sorely fucking mistaken.

"I'd never dream of denying you," Talon gives me a smooth smile. Mattias coughs, and I'm pretty sure he's covering up a laugh.

Suddenly, the faint sound of cheering and clapping comes from the large tents we passed by upon arriving at the camp.

"Performances are finished." Talon looks over my shoulder towards the tents. Then their dark eyes flick to my blue ones. "Mattias and I can gather everyone in the large main tent once the crowds clear out if that will be useful."

"Alright." I nod. "Let me know when you're ready for me."

Mattias strolls off with a determined look, but Talon lingers. "Thank you," they say quietly.

"For not stabbing you?" I arch a brow at them. "Still a strong chance of that happening."

They roll their eyes, not the least bit worried about my threat. "I know this is a risk for you, being so far from your forest and for what you're about to reveal to a bunch of people you don't know, trusting my word that they'll keep your presence here a secret."

"Astria is my sister." I shrug and look away from their piercing stare, not comfortable with the sincerity I see in it. "There is nothing I will not do for her."

Before Talon can say anything else, I walk over to the tree with the starlings and gaze up into the branches, and I feel Talon's heavy stare on me for a moment before they follow Mattias' steps.

"Alright, my friends." A deep, echoing note spills from my lips before tapering off, then as one, all the starlings look at me. "Let's freak out some humans."

CHAPTER THIRTEEN

~

Talon

I WAIT by the entrance of the main tent as the crowd filters out. It's almost all families with kids, taking advantage of the discounted ticket prices for these shows. Their excited chatter about all the things they just witnessed flows past me, in one ear and out the other.

Close. We're so fucking close to figuring out what is going on with Ravyn and Astria. A large part of me hopes I'm wrong, that there isn't a traitor amongst the people I consider my family. Scythe will be able to dreamwalk tonight, so one way or another, we'll get our answer.

But I can't let this go now. I need to know if someone here sold out Astria and therefore Ravyn.

Mattias is gathering everyone who didn't perform in the show. I'm curious how Scythe is going to pull this off. In my mother's story, a witch sang to spiders that bit those who had betrayed their own kin.

My lip curls. Hopefully Scythe isn't going to use spiders, because my skin is already crawling at the thought.

As soon as the last customer exits, I duck inside. Vesi immediately spots me and comes striding over. "You're back." No clasped hands or hugs from her, but I can see the relief in her eyes. Then she looks over my shoulder. "Is she here?"

"Yes," I tell her. "Help me keep everyone inside? Mattias is rounding up the others, and then the witch will come work her magic."

"On it." Vesi sprints around one side of the tent and I go to the other. Everyone is tired from several hours of performing, but no one hesitates when I tell them this is about Ravyn and Astria. Everyone loves my sister, and Astria really did fit in immediately. I wasn't the only one surprised and suspicious of the way they departed.

More people flow into the tent and take a seat in the stands, courtesy of Mattias' efforts. Kasia rushes over to me, the young girl's face still painted in bright glittery makeup and a sheen of sweat across her warm brown skin. Like her parents, she's an acrobat, but unlike their elegant and haunting acts, her performances tend to be funny, so she's a big hit with the kids.

"Do you have a lead on where Ravyn and Astria went?" she asks hopefully. At seventeen, Kasia is good friends with both girls, thinking of them like older sisters in a lot of ways.

"Not yet, but hopefully soon," I tell her honestly.

Kasia glances back to her parents before leaning forward and whispering, "Everyone is saying you brought the witch back with you, but no one knows why."

"I'll explain as soon as everyone's here." I try to give her a reassuring smile, but it comes out more like a grimace. There is no part of me that is looking forward to finding out someone here betrayed the troupe. Unfortunately, my faith in humanity is pretty low. The Eleoyn people either actively engage in cruelty or turn a blind eye to it.

These people though . . . they're my family. My entire life is here, and there is nothing I would not give to protect them. Before my sister vanished, I never had any reason to doubt they felt the same.

As soon as the trickle of people slows and everyone is settled in the rows of seats, I give Mattias, who's standing at the entrance, a nod. He disappears to fetch Scythe while Vesi comes to stand by my side, a grim look of determination on her face.

"You're all correct," I say loudly, and the chatter dies down. "I have returned with Astria's sister, the Witch of the Woods. Just like me, she wants to know where our sisters have gone and to ensure that nothing nefarious took place."

Several people shift uncomfortably in their seats, and everyone has a solemn look on their face. Nobody likes the idea of a traitor amongst us.

"Whatever you need, Talon," Elaine says calmly. The tremor in her voice isn't from fear but simply age. She's one of our elders and was a dear friend of my parents. "I haven't been able to sleep since the girls left. These old bones need to know that they're alright."

Others nod in agreement.

"Scythe will be here in a moment and will use her magic to reveal any traitors amongst us." I keep my gaze steady as I look over those gathered. "If someone here knows something, this is your last chance to step forward. I'm not feeling particularly merciful at the moment, but I promise you, I will feel even less so after the witch is done."

No one moves.

So be it.

Not long after my declaration, Scythe stalks into the tent, and several people inhale sharply at the sight of her. She took off her charmed necklace, and her hair flows like lavender waves down to her waist as her silver eyes take in those gathered. She bears no weapon; instead, on her extended right hand, a bird is perched on her finger.

It pecks its yellow beak against her hand before cocking its head up at her. Black feathers with speckles of white cover its body, and every time it moves, a rainbow of teal, purple, and magenta gleams against the darkness. A southern starling.

Thank fuck it's not a spider.

Scythe stops beside me and looks over the crowd like a predator sizing up a herd. I don't love that she's looking at people I care about like that, even if one of them could be a traitor. Tension fills the tent, and everyone has gone completely still, like they don't want to be the one to draw the witch's attention.

Vesi is the one to break the tense silence by barking out a laugh. "Oh my gods." She stares at Scythe's hair like she's trying to envision it strawberry-blonde instead of the lilac purple it is now. Then her mouth splits into a wide grin. "This is her, isn't it? The one you've been pining over this whole time? You danced with the fucking Witch of the Woods!" She slaps her thigh and points at Elaine. "Bet you didn't see that one coming!"

The old woman rolls her eyes.

Some of Scythe's lethal edge bleeds off as she gives me a puzzled look.

"Vesi and some of the others have nothing better to do than sit around and gossip all day," I say nonchalantly while also willing my friend to shut the fuck up. "They've been a little obsessed with my love life lately."

"You mean lack of a love life." Vesi laughs.

Fuck it, I'm going to murder her. I have Mattias. Does a person really need *two* best friends?

The soon-to-be-dead woman strolls over to me and pats my cheek. "Poor Talon has been a sad, grouchy wolf pup the last year."

Scythe's eyebrows shoot up comically high, and I sigh. "No secrets, remember? They all know what I am."

There are quite a few nonhumans in our little group, no pure faes but more than a handful with fae blood in them, a couple of mages who just want to be left alone, and a few other . . . oddities.

It's one of the reasons nobody batted an eye at Astria being witchkin.

"Riiight." Scythe draws the word out as she peers at Vesi. "And you think Talon has been—what did you say?—*pining* over me for the last year?"

"Well, you have to understand"—Vesi waves her hands while she speaks, and I have to step back so I don't get smacked in the face—"our Talon had a bit of a reputation before they met you."

"Reputation?" Scythe's silver gaze falls on me, and it takes an extreme effort on my part to keep a bored, bemused expression on my face while I reach around Vesi and clamp a hand over her big, fat mouth.

Unfortunately, Vesi isn't the only problem.

"We were all convinced Talon was going to actually drown in pussy one day," Elaine chimes in.

Several parents clap their hands over their children's ears even as they nod in agreement.

"Not a bad way to go though," Nicola says dreamily and then yelps when the blonde woman next to her smacks her on the back of the head. Then the pretty brunette looks at her wife with innocent doe eyes. "I meant *your* pussy, love."

"Good cover, Nicola," Mattias rumbles as he steps into the tent, earning himself a very obscene gesture from Nicola. He chuckles as he strides over to join us.

"I can't believe I have to say this, but can everyone please stop talking about pussy?" I glare at Elaine, and the old woman huffs at me before pointing at Scythe and then drawing a heart in the air.

"Are they always like this?" Scythe asks, her eyes darting around the tent. Instead of a predator hunting down prey, she's now a wolf who realizes all the deer she cornered are eccentric and possibly suffering from rabies. "I'm about to use my magic to find a traitor . . . I thought they'd be . . . you know . . . scared?"

A little tension creeps back into the air at the reminder. "We're not scared, child," Elaine explains. "We're pissed off at the notion that someone here would have betrayed our girls, but this is Eleoyn. Shit is all kinds of fucked-up, so we seize any opportunity for joy that we can."

"Not a child," Scythe mutters even as she stares at the old woman in wonder. Something tells me the witch elders didn't have Elaine's mouth. The woman swears more than anyone I know.

"And any chance to give Talon shit cannot be missed," Vesi adds.

I give Vesi one last dirty look that promises she'll pay for this later before directing my attention to Scythe. "Ready when you are."

"Once it begins, do not move," Scythe instructs. "As long as you sit still, you will not be harmed." All the parents clamp their arms around their children. I don't think any of the kids are traitors, at least not intentionally, but we've never shielded our children from the reality of what happens if you betray the troupe. It is ingrained into us at a young age. They need to be a part of this, but I don't believe for a second that Scythe would harm children despite her often vicious nature.

Scythe starts to sing a high-pitched melody that builds on itself until I'm gritting my teeth against it. The wolf inside me hunkers down, and I can practically feel them whining. *Yeah, I don't like it either, buddy.*

The starling on Scythe's hand hops around a couple of times as Scythe's singing becomes louder, and then I hear it. The sound of hundreds of flapping wings.

A flock of starlings surges into the tent, narrowing into a needle as they fly through the entrance flaps before encircling the ceiling. Their chirps blend into Scythe's song as the witch's tattoos glow and magic seeps into the air.

Mattias' eyes are locked on the birds flying rapidly in the small tent, his expression a mix of alarm and wonder. I glance at Scythe, who is staring straight ahead, eyes glowing like silver fire. Suddenly, she lets out a final, sharp note, her song ending before the birds dive down towards everyone.

It's a testament to their faith, not only in me but in the witch as well, because nobody moves an inch, although more than a few close their eyes.

Silence falls across the tent as everyone tentatively opens their eyes and looks around. Then Scythe lets out a harsh exhale before staggering back a step. In an instant, my arm is around her waist, holding her up. She smiles at me, and that's when I know she must be really out of it.

"Whoever doesn't have a bird on their shoulder"—she inhales a few breaths as if she's fighting to stay conscious—"is a traitor to the troupe."

Some small tension in me unfurls at seeing both Vesi and Mattias with a bird. I never had any doubt, but still. Vesi is standing perfectly still, like she's worried the bird is going to peck out her eyes at any second. Meanwhile, Mattias is grinning stupidly at his starling and trying to coax it onto his finger.

I shake my head and scan everyone else. There are more starlings than people, so some of them have a few birds using them as a perch. My eyes search the crowd before landing on two people who don't have a bird, both trying to hide their nervousness with stone-faced expressions.

"A traitor in general?" I ask Scythe quietly. "Or specifically ones who betrayed our sisters?"

"General," she breathes out. "Easier that way."

"Good witch." I kiss her on the brow, and she manages to glare at me, the silver fire dimming from her eyes. "Mattias?" I look at my friend and then down at the witch, who is now fully leaning on me for support.

"Hang on, Mr. Bird," he tells the starling that is still perched on his shoulder. The bird starts to flutter its wings but settles when Scythe lets out a low whistle. Mattias scoops her up into his arms, her head flopping against his broad chest. A growl rumbles through my mind, and I don't know if it's coming from me or the wolf at seeing her in someone else's arms. It's a little startling to have such a visceral reaction, and I have to give myself a moment to get my emotions under control.

Mattias is only doing what I asked him to do, and he's being very polite about his hand placement. I blame my reaction on the situation in general. Emotions are running high.

"You don't need to carry me," she protests, but the fact that she doesn't put up a fight is quite telling. I'll need to make sure she rests after this.

"Maybe I'm scared of birds and need you to protect me," Mattias tells her, his expression completely serious.

She looks pointedly at the starling on his shoulder that he'd been doing his best to make friends with before sighing. "Fine. I'll protect you. Only for a couple of minutes though."

"Only for a couple of minutes," Mattias agrees solemnly, his eyes crinkling at the corners with amusement as he looks down at the witch. Though that lightness vanishes when he turns his attention to the two traitors.

Everyone is still sitting on the wooden stands, but space has been created around the two men who have no starlings on their shoulders.

The dark-haired man with hazel eyes is Dain. He's a few years older than me, and his family has been a part of this troupe for generations. His parents passed two winters ago when a sickness swept its way across Eleoyn. We lost quite a few people to it and almost lost Elaine as well.

The second man is also dark-haired but has light green eyes and a more stout build. Eldrin. Unlike Dain, he wasn't born into this life—he married in. His wife of five years, Katrin, is staring at him in disbelief.

"Eldrin?" Her voice shakes. "What—what did you do?"

Instead of answering, he leaps off the stands and bolts for the hidden slit in the tent walls that performers use to sneak in and out.

He lets out a shriek when some of the starlings bolt towards him and start pecking at his face, but he keeps running—until my dagger slices into his calf.

The birds circle around in the air above him a few times before returning to perch on people's shoulders.

Dain wisely stays perfectly still while this is going down, although his jawline hardens.

"Can I move now?" Vesi asks Scythe.

The witch lets out one low whistle and then nods, as if she's too tired to speak.

"Wonderful." Vesi strolls over to Eldrin and jerks him to his feet. He struggles in her grasp, but whatever he sees in her eyes makes him stop. Once he goes still, Vesi gives me a pointed look.

"Right." I clap my hands. "It's time for the adults to have a chat. Kids, off you lot go."

Everyone glances at the starlings still sitting on their shoulders, and Scythe lets out a longer, more melodic whistle. As one, the birds lift off and race towards the door. The parents quickly usher their children out, murmuring that they need help getting things ready for the night performances in a couple of hours.

Soon, the tent is clear except for the elders and another dozen or so people who chose to stay. We'll inform those who left about the fate of Dain and Eldrin, although everyone likely knows death will be the outcome.

I look to where Katrin's mother and Vesi are talking to the young woman, probably trying to convince her to leave so she doesn't have to stay and watch this. It won't work though. Katrin is only a year older than me, and she's always been wildly stubborn. She deserves to hear straight from her husband's mouth how he betrayed us.

Elaine's oldest grandchild, Arel, drags Dain over. He didn't bother trying to run like Eldrin, and I can see in his eyes that he's already accepted his fate.

"Speak," Elaine orders, no tremble or humor in her voice now.

Dain looks around at those gathered before his eyes fall on me and he holds my stare. "I didn't sell out your sister." His eyes flick briefly to Scythe. "Either of your sisters."

"But you betrayed the troupe." I phrase it as a statement, not a question.

He lowers his eyes. "Got in a bad way with a gambling den in Tenresan. I owe them a lot more than I'll ever collect in performance tips."

"Funny," I drawl. "I know for a fact that several people have offered you a spot on their teams for more well-paying gigs. You've turned them all down."

I wasn't the only one who ran heists. There were half a dozen other groups that did the same, usually smaller ones than Vesi, Mattias, and I pulled off, but they brought in good money all the same.

"Those are dangerous!" His head snaps up, and I see a flash of defiance in his eyes. "Nobody got hurt from what I did! It was low-risk and just"—he winces—"cost the troupe a little money."

Elaine and several of the other elders frown. "What do you mean?"

Dain's gaze drops to the ground again, and I lose the remaining hold on my temper.

"No." In the space of a breath, I summon one of my claw daggers and place it under his chin, forcing his head up. "You look us in the eyes while you tell us what you did."

He swallows and looks at Elaine. "Sometimes, when we're trying to bypass a toll road, I tip off the city guards so they know where to find us. Nobody gets hurt! We just have to pay a penalty, and the guards give me a cut of it! That's all I've done, I swear!"

I almost cut his throat then and there.

"That's. All. You've. Done?" I repeat. The words are barely

more than a growl as the wolf inside me rises. My fingers tremble around the dagger's handle. I know what's coming and barely manage to loosen my fingers, letting the blade fall to the floor before a pain like no other racks my body.

Then I stumble back from a wide-eyed Dain as the urge to shift and tear him apart becomes all-consuming. The curse running through my blood holds the wolf back even as it claws at my soul, and an agonized groan rips from my throat as I struggle to stay on my feet.

I know from experience that I have less than ten minutes before every muscle in my body seizes up and I black out.

Dain's breathing quickens when he looks at me and sees a wolf looking back. A very pissed-off wolf. "It's just money, Tal! That's all they've ever wanted! And it's not like we don't have plent—"

My fist slams into his face, and blood splurts as cartilage snaps, then he staggers back when Arel releases him. Most of the troupe has seen me lose it before, so they know I need to at least take the edge off my rage. I punch Dain again, and this time, he falls to the ground. He doesn't even get a chance to scramble away because I'm immediately there, punching him over and over again until somebody finally pulls me off.

Dain struggles to breathe and cries out when Arel drags him to his feet again. Blood drips from my knuckles, not just Dain's but my own too, where I sliced my skin open on his teeth. It's barely noticeable though compared to the sharp tremors attacking my muscles. Over three decades of existence, and my body still refuses to accept that it's been denied half of its nature. The wolf paces within me, desperate to taste the blood of our enemy. The best I can offer them is beating the shit out of him.

Still, it won't be enough. It's never enough.

Elaine steps towards Dain, her usually kind eyes cold. "We don't avoid the toll roads to keep more coin in our pocket. We skip *specific* stops because they're the ones that have the least amount of traffic and the guards tend to be bored." Her expression hardens further. "When city guards get bored, they look for ways to entertain themselves. Your father was one of the people who rescued Talon the day the city guards attacked their parents. You damn well know what the guards are capable of. Talon's parents were not the first to fall prey to them."

"Nothing happen—" His words are cut off when Elaine backhands him hard enough for his head to snap to the side.

"And what if it had, Dain?" she asks with a lethal softness. "What if they decided to slit someone's throat for fun? Or maybe take some of our young people and break them until they wished *their* throats were slit instead?" The old woman leans forward until her face is only an inch away from Dain's. "Would you have grown a spine then and fought for them? Would you have sacrificed your life for theirs?"

He blanches, and we all know the answer.

Elaine steps back and looks at me. "Do what you need to do, wolf."

I'm in front of Dain in the next second, my dagger slicing his neck before he can even try to get away. It's a far quicker death than he deserves, but the clock is ticking until the pain overwhelms me. Arel doesn't bother holding him up, and the traitor drops to his knees, falling forward, dead before his face hits the dirt.

Suddenly, silver and lavender fill my vision, and I blink. *Scythe.*

The witch, standing on her own now, stares into my eyes, and for once, I can't decipher her expression. Everything through our bond is too chaotic, probably thanks to my wolf losing their mind and trying to break free of their cursed prison.

"Eldrin," I rasp, breaking my stare-off with the witch to look at the remaining traitor, who is shoved forward by Vesi. His eyes dart to Dain's cooling corpse, and I see the fear in his eyes. He knows he's going to die here.

I step away from the witch to face him, and Katrin joins me, staring cooly at her soon-to-be ex-husband. I knew they wouldn't be able to convince her to leave. She probably blames herself for not seeing her husband's betrayal before now. I'll have to reassure her later that I don't hold her responsible. Katrin is good people. If she knew of Eldrin's betrayal, she would have slit his throat, dumped his body in a shallow grave, and then apologized to the troupe for her poor taste in men.

"Did you betray my sister?" I ask.

"You always swagger around here like you're the gods' gift to humanity." Eldrin's jaw hardens as his green eyes flash with anger. "I know you're going to kill me so you can fuck off, Talon. Your sister is probably already dead."

I surge forward, but Katrin grabs my arm. "We need answers, Tal," she says urgently. "You can't kill him yet."

Fuck. She's right. My body jerks as another muscle spasm races down my spine. I close my eyes and let Katrin tug me back while I concentrate on breathing and keeping my need for violence under control. The wolf wants Eldrin's blood decorating the dirt, but even they understand we need to be patient.

The problem is, the second I start cutting into him to loosen his tongue, I'm going to lose my shit and tear his body apart with my bare hands until nothing is left but mounds of blood and gore.

Eldrin looks at me, and the bastard smiles, like he knows how close I am to losing control.

His satisfied smile fades though when Scythe starts humming.

Everyone's gaze swings to Scythe then, who is staring at Eldrin, those silver eyes of hers alight again. She dips her hand into a leather satchel at her side, letting her fingers dangle in it, and saunters over to Eldrin.

"Everyone fears the devil cats of my forest or the bears that occasionally wander down from the mountains, but those are far from the most dangerous creatures."

She pulls her hand from the pouch, and a centipede is looped around her fingers several times. Now that it's out of its container, it stretches out across the back of her hand and up her forearm. It's at least eight inches long. A gleaming black makes up most of its color, but fine, bloodred lines create a mesmerizing pattern down its back. It scurries around the witch's skin on its multitude of legs before raising its body up above her fingers and moving the two giant pinchers back and forth.

"This is a morfrin centipede." Scythe flexes her fingers, causing the centipede to aggressively bite its pinchers in the air. "They're the favorite snack of several small predators, and so they've evolved to have a highly venomous bite." She walks towards Eldrin, who tries to move away, only for Mattias to grip the man's arms and wrench them behind his back, holding him in place. Then Scythe stops beside me and glances at my palm. "May I?"

It takes me a moment to figure out what she's asking. Brushing my thumb against the death tattoo on my palm, I call forth one of my daggers and hand it to her. She smiles at me like I've just handed her a rose and takes it in her free hand before continuing over to Eldrin.

With one smooth strike, she cuts through his shirt and vest and, based on how he screams, some of his skin too. The scent of his blood hits me a second later, and I grit my teeth as the need to shift becomes more demanding.

Scythe then places her hand with the centipede on Eldrin's bare chest, her palm against his bloody skin. "Their venom isn't deadly, but it's quite painful." She hums, and the insect scuttles off her hand and onto Eldrin, who lets out rapid, loud breaths but seems to be frozen in place out of fear. "It only takes one bite from them for every predator in the forest to learn the pain isn't worth the meal."

Her hand shoots out to grip Eldrin around the neck. "Let's see how long you last." Another hum pours from the witch's lips, and the centipede dives forward, its pinchers digging into Eldrin's skin. He screams and thrashes against her and Mattias' hold, but neither lets go as the centipede buries its pinchers farther into Eldrin's flesh. After a minute, Scythe stops humming and Eldrin sags in her grasp.

Darkness encroaches on my vision, tinged with red, and every breath feels like I'm inhaling jagged glass. I scrape together the last of my energy to saunter over to the witch and put my arm around her, then, on a whim—and probably because I'm at least a little insane—I hold my hand out for the centipede. It didn't harm Scythe, and she's my mate . . .

The insect releases Eldrin and scurries up my hand, blood dripping off its pinchers. New accessory unlocked. It'll go nicely with my crown.

Eyes full of derision stare at me and then slide to Scythe. "Of course you would find the only other living creature as fucked up as you."

I give him a wolfish smile. "Have you rethought your answer to my previous question? Or do you need more time with your new friend?" I move the centipede back towards him, and Eldrin flinches.

"Sold them to the mage hunters," he snarls, his eyes on the morfrin. "They only wanted the witchkin bitch, but it was easier to grab them both together."

Scythe goes absolutely still. "The mage hunters have my sister?" Her voice is death incarnate.

"Yes. They paid me her literal weight in gold." He laughs and then looks at Katrin, who is staring at her husband like he's shit she just stepped in. "Was going to leave your ass in a few months. Never should have let your nice rack blind me to what a shitty life this is."

"Why bother to wait?" Katrin bares her teeth at him.

"Would have been a bit suspicious for me to slip off into the night after the girls went missing." He returns his spiteful gaze to me. "When you said you were going to get Astria's sister, I assumed she'd kill you. Nobody has entered that forest and lived. What the fuck makes you so special?"

"He cares about my sister," Scythe says. "That's all I needed to know."

"What do you think your sister is thinking about right now?" Eldrin sneers. "I overheard her telling Ravyn one day what you said to her. That you wouldn't come to save her. I'll bet that's what she's thinking about when the hunters are—" He suddenly gurgles, blood dripping from the corners of his mouth as he stares down at his chest, where Scythe has buried my blade.

"Shit!" Vesi curses and rips Scythe away from Eldrin, who collapses to the ground. Then she puts pressure on the wound, trying to keep him alive so we can question him further, but I can already hear his heartbeat slowing.

Scythe turns to me, her expression practically feral, my knife still in her hand, coated in the traitor's blood. It's the last thing I see before my body goes rigid as it tries to tear itself apart to free the wolf, and then everything goes black.

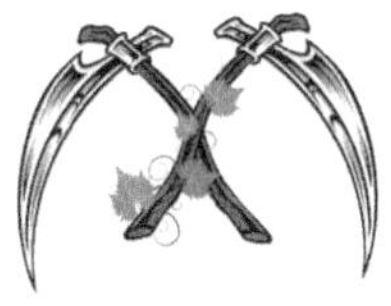

CHAPTER FOURTEEN

~

Scythe

"Here." I look up from the crackling flames and find Vesi and Mattias standing before me; the former offering me charred meat on a stick and the latter a dark green glass bottle.

"Mmm." I take them both. "Mystery meat and Tovenian wine. Just what I was craving."

"Pretty sure the meat you're craving is still passed out." Vesi grins as she points towards Talon's tent behind me. I sat by their side for hours after Mattias carried them back, but they didn't stir once. Finally, I couldn't sit there any longer . . . but I also couldn't bring myself to go far.

So I started a fire in the center of the clearing, took a seat, and thought about how much I'd fucked up. I shouldn't have killed Eldrin. We might have been able to get more information out of him. I know the girls are safe because Ryllae saw it when they threw their bones, but Eldrin knew he wasn't walking out of that tent alive and baited me into giving him a quick death.

When I wasn't thinking about that, I was obsessing over what is going on with Talon. I felt their pain through the bond, and at first, I thought they were just pissed off about the betrayal from two people they'd trusted, but then it kept getting stronger, more vicious. When I looked into Talon's eyes after they killed Dain . . . I knew what it was . . . what was ripping them apart.

That godsdamn curse.

I didn't truly understand the cruelty of the curse until that moment. Why some of the original cursed werewolves had gone insane afterwards. It hadn't just been that they'd missed their wolf side—their bodies had refused to accept they couldn't shift anymore and had tried it anyway. Over and over again.

Unlike Talon, those first werewolves had remembered what it was like to shift, for their soul to be whole, but then the witches had locked half of it away but had not suppressed the need . . . only the ability. There were stories that some of those first cursed were-wolves had ripped out their own hearts while lost in bloodlust.

"Told you the witch would need wine," Mattias says.

My attention snaps back to them when I realize I've just been staring at Talon's tent. They've both joined me on the overturned logs encircling the fire. I take a large swig of the wine before passing it to Vesi.

"You two don't seem worried about Talon. Does this happen a lot?" I tear a chunk of meat off the stick Vesi handed me and pop it into my mouth. Overdone, but the seasoning is decent.

"Sorry about the lackluster food. Elaine is normally a good cook, but when she's angry . . . she has a tendency to set things on fire," Vesi explains. "Luckily, she rarely gets this upset over anything, so we're not subjected to burned-to-a-crisp venison all that often."

I nod and take another bite. Food is food, and my body needs the energy. I didn't actually use that much magic in the tent, but when they left me with Talon earlier, I tried to heal them. It didn't help. The minor cuts they'd given themself healed right away, but those dark brown eyes never opened.

"This doesn't happen as much as it used to," Mattias answers me before taking a swallow of wine and handing it to Vesi. "After Tal's parents died, they were like this every few days." Suddenly, Mattias looks so much older than the three decades he's seen.

"We had to tie 'em to the bed so they wouldn't hurt themsel —" Vesi swallows sharply, as if the memory just surged to the forefront of her mind, then takes several drinks from the bottle. "Tal was so angry after that . . . and they never really stopped."

Mattias nods. "Their baseline became angry. Tal hides it well behind that charming mask of theirs, but that smoldering fury has never gone out . . . and sometimes the flames flare up again."

"It's been at least a year since the last time this happened," Vesi says and passes the bottle back to me. "But today was . . . it was a lot. I was having a hard enough time wrapping my head around the fact that we had one traitor—but we had fucking two of them."

"I didn't know witches could do magic like that . . ." Mattias trails off, leaving it up to me to respond or not.

"In Arandia, the witches and fae are far more intermingled than they are here."

When they originally came to these shores as guests of the humans and mages, the witches were immediately called to the beauty of the wild, whereas the fae were intrigued by the mages. It led to the belief that the witches and fae weren't friendly towards each other, a belief that still persists based on the surprised looks on Vesi's and Mattias' faces.

"How 'intermingled' exactly?" Vesi asks. She—unlike Mattias—has no problem being nosey.

I smile tiredly at her. "My grandmother was a fae, and there are other fae further back in my bloodline."

"Shit." Vesi squints at me. "So you can do witch *and* fae magic?"

"Not exactly," I hedge and take another drink of wine before passing it to Mattias. "I can only do witch magic. I need to be able to hum or sing to access it, but the fae blood in my veins allows me to tap into more empathic magic than I would otherwise be able to. A fae could search the mind of everyone here. I can't do that, but I can use the birds to channel my magic and nudge it towards anyone with a traitorous heart."

"Huh." Vesi's eyes drop to my hands and then the leather satchel hanging from my belt. "Is . . . uhh . . . your *friend* safely tucked away again?"

I smile. "He scurried off when Talon fell, but I called him to me before following all of you to Talon's tent. I didn't want any kids to find him. He's back in the safety of his box with a nice juicy grub to munch on."

Neither Vesi nor Mattias looks pleased by this information. What did they think I'd done with him? Thrown him into the fire? Maybe I should have brought one of the huntsman spiders instead . . . Were spiders more or less disturbing than centipedes?

"Astria doesn't talk much about you or the forest," Mattias ventures, his words careful, even as curiosity gleams in his eyes. "But when she does, she often mentions the devil cats. Do you really have an entire pack of them living with you?"

"Yes." I chuckle. "For ferocious predators, they seem to prefer sleeping in the soft beds the witches left behind."

"Okay, you have to tell us about them," Vesi pushes, holding out her hand to Mattias, who gives her the wine.

"Alright." I chew my bottom lip as I glance at the tent where Talon sleeps. "I'll trade you stories of them for ones of my sister and what her life has been like here."

Vesi's eyes soften. "Deal."

"How does this work exactly?" Vesi asks.

I brush Talon's dark hair out of their eyes. They stirred briefly when the three of us entered the tent after talking for a couple of hours but didn't wake. Vesi and Mattias seem pretty convinced they won't wake until morning, and I guess they would know.

"It's simple, really." I tug the blanket up higher on Talon's chest and then climb down the wagon steps to join the others in the tent. They piled some of the pillows into a makeshift bed, and I can't help but smile at it. I don't need anything special, and it's not like I haven't slept on the ground before . . . but it's a nice gesture from people who barely know me. Based on the stories they shared, I know they quickly took to Astria and that she enjoys her life here.

It makes me both sad and happy at the same time.

"I hold on to this"—Vesi and Mattias look wide-eyed at the glass sphere I'm holding up—"think about Astria, and then let the magic do its thing."

"Really?" Vesi arches a skeptical brow at me. "That easy?"

"Fae magic." I shrug and settle onto the cushions. They really are comfy. I might have to steal some to bring back home with me. I frown at that thought because I'll have to figure out how to keep the damn panthers off them.

"So they would work for anyone?" Mattias asks.

"Anyone with fae blood running in their veins," I correct him. "Witch magic is mostly nature-based. Fae magic is empathic. The spell within the sphere will seek out the consciousness of the person I'm thinking about once I activate it. As soon as that person falls asleep, it will pull me into their dreams. So let's hope my sister is sleeping; otherwise, we might be here for a while." The clear glass starts to glow faintly with a pale blue light. Soon, other colors begin to rise until it's a maelstrom of blues, purples, and reds. "Don't freak out if I pass out mid-sentence. That's why I'm lying down for this."

I clasp my hands over my chest with the glass sphere nestled between them and concentrate on Astria. Vesi and Mattias continue chatting, something about Vesi being stubborn for not reconciling with two people she has an ongoing relationship with. I'm only half listening when the spell yanks me under.

"Astria?" I call her name immediately when I wake in a cell and see my sister curled up in the corner, her matted blonde hair around her. She doesn't stir as I rush over to kneel beside her. "Astria."

Nothing. She's out cold. I run my fingers down her cheek, feeling the warmth of her skin. Maybe she has a fever? I quickly check her over but don't see any injuries. Not that I'd be able to do anything about it. I might be here, but my magic isn't. Luckily, aside from being dirty, she looks completely unharmed. The relief that rushes through me is so intense, I let out a low whimper.

"She won't wake up," a familiar deep voice with the hint of a lilt says from behind me.

I whirl to face the beautiful, dark-haired woman. Like Astria, she's seen better days. Her long black hair is tangled, and her captivating eyes look tired and worried.

"Hello, Ravyn," I glance back at Astria and then at the glass sphere in my left hand. The rainbow colors are glowing brightly now, but they'll fade the longer we hold this connection until the spell burns out or something wakes Astria. "It must have pulled you into the dream as well."

"Is that what this is?" She peers around at the rough grey stone and worn bars. "I thought I was losing my mind for a second because it looks like the cell we're currently in . . . but something is off about it."

"There are no doors," I say softly.

Ravyn's eyes widen as she looks around. "Oh."

I sit and gently lift my sister's head so I can slide under her. Ravyn watches as I cradle my sister in my arms. It's a little awkward because I can't let go of the glass sphere, which is already starting to lose some of its vibrancy, but I can't resist holding Astria like I used to when she was young and believed I could shield her from the world.

"All this time, I thought I could protect her by being the monster the world feared." The fingers of my right hand twirl in her matted hair.

"There are always bigger monsters." Ravyn strides over to kneel on Astria's other side.

"Do you know where you are? Anything useful?" I look over her carefully, but like Astria, she only looks dirty and tired. It's possible she's injured in real life, but typically, when dream spells are used, the person pulled into the dream is in a similar state to their actual body. Only those who are gifted with manipulating dreams, like Ryllae, can change how they appear.

"No, they knocked us out when they captured us near Albadrid and kept us that way until we woke up here. Astria only came to briefly before they forced her to drink something that knocked her out again." Ravyn's head suddenly jerks up, her eyes frantic. "You need to find Talon and tell them that Eldri—"

"We know," I cut her off. "Talon came to find me. We know Eldrin sold Astria out to the mage hunters and you got caught up in it."

Ravyn's shoulders slump. "He said he needed our help picking out a gift for Katrin. We knew they'd been having problems in their marriage lately. I always thought he was a bit of a scumbag, but Astria wants to see the good in everyone."

"She's always been that way." I stroke more of my sister's hair before glancing at the glass sphere. "Talon and I will find you, but if there is anything you can tell me to at least give us a direction, that would be helpful."

The young woman purses her lips, dark brows bunching together. "I've been trying to figure out where we are, but nothing has hinted at it. We don't even have a window in our cell." Her eyes grow distant as she thinks, and then they snap to me. "There's a man—Stelian. He's a mage hunter and I think the one who orchestrated this whole thing. The guards outside our cell the other day were complaining about him being demanding while constantly partying. They mentioned that he was going to a masquerade the prince is throwing and were pissed that they weren't selected to be part of the group that accompanied him."

"Okay." I nod excitedly. "We've heard people talking about the festival the prince is throwing. Nothing specifically about a masquerade, but we'll figure it out."

Maybe we could separate this *Stelian* or one of his mage hunters from the crowd and interrogate them? Or maybe follow them after the party? Eventually, they'll have to return to where the girls are being held. I chew my bottom lip. Talon will know what to do. I just need them to point me at a target.

"We *will* find you." I raise my gaze from Astria to look at Ravyn, letting her see my determination.

She swallows, and I notice it then—that protrusion of cartilage at the front of her throat. Her slender fingers go to her neck when she sees where I'm looking. "Normally I wear a necklace, but it got torn off when they apprehended us."

"Did they hurt you?" I ask sharply. Just because I couldn't see any injuries didn't mean they weren't there.

"They weren't exactly gentle while shoving us into the back of the prison carriage," she says dryly. "But after that, they didn't lay a finger on us. Stelian expressly forbids it, and they all seem scared of him." Her full mouth flattens into a hard line. "I'm relieved they haven't tried anything . . . but also surprised."

My breathing quickens, and I have to force myself to remain calm. Nothing has happened to them yet, and we'll get to them before it does. I'll tear this entire fucking kingdom apart if I have to.

"Not much is known about witch magic because we mostly stayed out of the four kingdoms, and the majority of witches left these shores long ago," I say evenly, focusing on each word to maintain my calm. "Stelian likely doesn't know enough about witchkin to risk his mages being injured or her getting the ability to contact me."

Because he's obviously plotting something, likely hoping to lure me out of the woods by dangling Astria in front of me. He'd want to do it on his terms though. Set the stage and time. The fact that he doesn't know I am already on to him is to our advantage, and I need to keep it that way for as long as possible.

"That makes sense." Ravyn's gaze falls back to Astria, and she runs her fingers through my sister's tangled hair. "They've been keeping her out like this since we arrived. I don't think they know what she is or isn't capable of, so they're playing it safe."

There is no mistaking the love and concern in her eyes as she stares down at my sister. I was doubtful in the beginning and even when Astria left, thinking that this couldn't possibly last. Astria had never been in a relationship before Ravyn. The witches had left when she'd been young, and while she'd had trysts with people in Shalewood, it had never been anything serious.

But I see it now. That devotion. It's like the fairy tales I read as a child. The ones I hoped I'd get to live someday—of meeting your true love. My eyes trace the lunar tattoos on my fingers.

"You are not my mate."

There is no epic love in store for me. I have one failed mate bond behind me, and soon, I'll figure out how to break this one between me and Talon. Two failed mate bonds in two centuries of living. I have no interest in attempting it a third time, I don't think I would survive it, but at least my sister has found the love they write poems about. That will have to be enough.

"I know you blame me for all this. That you've hated me all along," Ravyn says, and I look up to meet her defiant gaze. She brushes her finger across the front of her throat again. "I thought it was because of this. Gender may be fluid within Tovenian culture, but I'm well aware that's not the case outside of it, but I love your sister, and I would nev—"

"You're right," I cut her off. The colors are fading from the glass sphere, now a pastel rainbow. My time is almost out. "I do hate you. Astria was the only person I had in this world. The only one who saw me. Who ever truly gave a damn about me. And then you came."

I reach out and cup Ravyn's face with my hand as she stares at me with uncertainty and wariness.

"The beautiful young woman who stole my sister from me, not with deceit or treachery, but with love. You make her happy, Ravyn. Better than I ever could." I drop my hand from her tear-streaked face. "And *that* is why I hate you."

She lets out a choked laugh as the colors in the glass turn almost translucent.

"We're out of time," I tell her quickly. "But do not lose faith. We're coming."

Ravyn's lips curl up into a wolfish grin. "I never doubted Talon would find me. There is no one more devious and cunning than my sibling, but with you at their side?" She chuckles darkly. "I almost feel sorry for everyone who stands in your way . . . almost."

I give her my own feral smile. "See you soon."

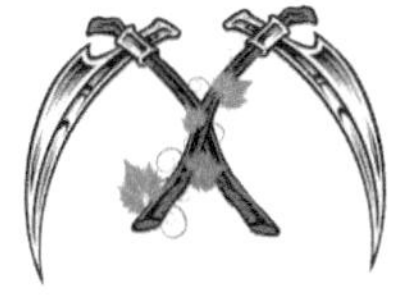

CHAPTER FIFTEEN

~

Scythe

I WAKE the next morning to find Talon's dark eyes watching me. In the dimness of the wagon, their deep brown eyes appear black. I tried to sleep on the pile of cushions in the tent area, but after getting up to check on them for the third time, I gave up and just settled down in the wagon. The entire space had been converted to a bed, so I was able to put a healthy bit of distance between us.

I meant to leave before Talon woke. Something told me they wouldn't be pleased to see me—a witch—first thing in the morning after what the curse had put them through.

"You're awake," I say awkwardly when Talon continues to stare at me with an unreadable expression. My gaze slips down to their chest and the tattoo over their heart—the perfect miniature copy of the one on my back.

"You're staring." One side of their lips curls up into a lopsided grin, and I feel the amusement stretching between our bond. I'm surprised when I also feel a hint of desire, because I had expected anger and disgust.

"You were staring first," I say defensively, pulling the thin blanket further up on my chest to hide the fact that I stole one of their shirts to sleep in. The nights are cooler here with the sea breeze rolling in.

Given the way Talon's smile widens, I know I'm unsuccessful, so I let the blanket drop. The nights might be cool, but by the way the morning sun is already beating down on the dark blue canvas of the wagon, I can tell it's going to be a hot day.

"How long was I out?" Their voice is a little rough, whether that's because they just woke up or it's leftover from the pain they went through, I'm not sure.

"It's morning." I move so I'm sitting upright with my legs crossed and the blanket across my lap.

Talon grunts and sits up to stretch. I try to keep my gaze on their face, but after two seconds, it drops down to admire the way their abs flex. Talon isn't a large person; they don't have a ton of bulk. Instead, they have a lithe frame and are corded with muscle—built for speed and endurance.

Still strong enough to hold me up and pin me agains—

"Staring again."

My gaze snaps up to find them smirking at me. "I need tea," I grumble.

"Mattias might be able to help with that." Talon dangles one arm across their propped-up knee, dropping the other to their lap. "Vesi and I prefer coffee."

"Coffee?" My brows furrow together. It sounds vaguely familiar, but I can't quite place it.

"It's popular in Riritha," they explain. "Hot like tea but with a stronger flavor, more bitter. More like a morning slap to help you wake up."

"Maybe I'll stick with tea." I make a face, and Talon laughs.

"It's morning . . ." Their lighthearted mood slips from their face, and tension races down the bond. "Did you dreamwalk? Did you talk to Astria?" They lean forward, their dark eyes searching my face for an answer.

"Yes," I say quickly. "Well—no, not Astria. Ravyn." I draw in a breath. "The girls are being held in a cell—unharmed but they're keeping Astria completely unconscious with some type of tonic. Witchkin were never all that common, and they certainly aren't now that most of the witches have left. I don't think they know what she's capable of, so they're being extra cautious."

"But they're alright?" Talon pushes. "My sister . . . they haven't hurt her or done anything?"

"No," I assure them. "The guards watching over them have been instructed not to harm them in any way, and they all seem to fear the mage hunter who orchestrated all of this."

Talon sags back against the wall, their shoulders slumping. "Well, that's something at least. Was Ravyn able to tell you anything useful about where they're being held?"

"No." I sigh. "They kept both girls knocked out after capturing them, and the cell they're in doesn't have any windows, but the guards did let it slip that the hunter in charge—the one they all fear—is going to be at the prince's masquerade. He's bringing some of his chosen mages with him as well."

Talon nods, their eyes growing distant like they're already thinking through a plan. "Okay, that's something we can work with. Based on the chatter we heard on the way here, the festival is in two days, which means we need to leave today to make it to Mabria in time."

"Ravyn said it's actually a masquerade. You should probably go to the party on your own," I say hesitantly and pluck at the shirt I'm wearing. "I barely managed to keep it together at the taverns before. A party thrown by the prince . . . it'll be crowded, Tal, and we know there will be mage hunters there. I'll be a liability, so it'll be best if—"

The rambling words die on my tongue as Talon pivots forward until they kneel in front of me. We're not touching, but I'm acutely aware of every inch that separates us. "You called me, Tal. Usually, you just call me *wolf*."

My breath catches in my throat, and I don't think there is any force in the world that could make me look away from them right now. I swallow. "Your friends always call you Tal . . . It just kind of slipped out."

I expect them to give me an arrogant smirk. Maybe say some lewd remark or aggravating comment that will make me want to strangle them. Instead, they tilt their head as a wolfish yellow sheen rolls over their dark eyes. "You saw the truth of the curse last night," they say. "What the witches did to my ancestors. To me."

"I did," I rasp, guilt reaching around my throat to strangle me from feeling anything else.

I might have had nothing to do with the curse, but I never thought about it either, even knowing the cursed werewolves lived on. Even after having met Talon . . . I never considered what type of unique torture it would be to have part of your soul locked away like that. If someone bound my magic and prevented me from interacting with the world around me as I do . . . I don't think I could have survived it.

"You understand," Talon says.

I don't know if they feel it through the bond or if they can read it on my face. Probably both.

I just nod. "I understand." Their gaze drops to my lip when I start to chew it, and I stop immediately before looking away. "I'll break it. Once we get the girls safe and before I leave, I'll free you, Tal. From both the curse and the bond."

Warm fingers lift my chin, forcing me to meet dark eyes filled with flecks of gold. "Scythe . . . Cerelia . . ." My heart beats faster at hearing my true name on their lips. "I—"

"Tal! Get your lazy bones out of bed! We need to—"

The curtains at the end of the wagon separating it from the rest of the tent rip open. Talon throws themself back to the other side of the wagon, and I flinch at their desire to get away from me before someone saw us doing . . . whatever it was we were doing.

"Oh." Vesi's eyes dart between me and Talon. "I didn't realize I was interrupting . . ."

"You're not," I say quickly and roll to my feet. A blush spreads across my cheeks when I realize I'm wearing Talon's shirt—and *only* their shirt. It falls to the middle of my thighs, but still, I'm well aware of what this looks like. "I was checking on them during the night and fell asleep. Nothing happened. I'll get dressed."

I race past Vesi, who shifts to the side before I can barrel her over.

"Tal?" I hear her ask, a slight hesitancy in her tone. "What—"

"Nothing, Vesi," Talon replies, their tone clipped. "Do me a favor and make us some coffee—and tea. We've got a lot of planning to do and not a lot of time."

"Planning for what?" Vesi asks, a little bewildered.

"We're going to crash the prince's masquerade party," I answer her over my shoulder as I quickly pull on my clothing.

"Well . . ." Vesi leaps down the wagon stairs and heads towards the front of the tent. "I'll get you lot some coffee. Mattias will handle the tea. And I'll find some whiskey for myself."

I FROWN AT THE MIRROR. The color of the dress is beautiful, a light silver with hints of ice blue. The ethereal color isn't the problem though—it's the style. I twist to the side, and the fabric flows around my body like liquid silver, showing off my leg up to the rise of my hip.

The only thing keeping me from giving the dressmaker a really good show are the thin chains on the sides of the dress holding the two panels of fabric together. The woman, someone named Kayla, insisted I take off my underwear so she could get a feel for the look.

The top half of the dress is . . . aggressive.

A deep V-cut runs straight down the middle to my navel. Something tacky is on the inside of the fabric that Kayla swears will keep the dress in place even while dancing. I have my doubts about that and think it's likely I'll be flashing someone, or everyone, an eyeful of my breasts.

The back of the dress is every bit as dramatic, in that there is no back of the dress. It's completely open, and that feels even more exposing than my cleavage being on display. My tattoos are hidden from sight, thanks to the charms I wear, but I usually also wear long sleeves and a cloak—something to cover them in case the spells fail while I'm around humans.

The large tree tattoo that spans my back would be on display to everyone if something happened to my charms. Not to mention my unusual hair and eye color along with the rest of my tattoos.

Light silver chains identical to the ones on the skirt crisscross over my back.

I look dangerous. Powerful. Wicked.

"Is this really what people wear to these parties?" Aside from witch celebrations—which happened decades ago—the only parties I've been to have been the small ones in the towns that border my forests.

This is not the type of dress that would be worn there.

"Usually, no," Nicolai says from where he sits in a chair, sipping some sort of bubbly, alcoholic drink. I don't understand what his deal is or why he's here, but Vesi and Talon left me here to get the dress sorted and said I am in good hands. They clearly trust these two . . . although Vesi had a tight expression on her face when she introduced everyone.

"But Prince Caspian has a certain reputation," Kayla says. She tilts her head, causing her curly brunette locks to cascade over her shoulder. Her delicate features pinch in concentration as she messes with the fabric at my waist. "He tends to . . . push boundaries at his events. The more outlandish your outfit, the more you'll fit into the vibe of the party, and the more people will accept that you belong there."

"I don't know much about the prince . . . or Eleoyn society as a whole, I guess," I admit as I try to figure out how much is safe to say around them.

These two clearly have some connection to Talon, and I suspect their connection to Vesi is a lot more intimate, although clearly on the outs. I might not be the best at reading others or understanding social cues, but even I know the signs of a bad breakup when I see it.

"Something isn't working." Kayla releases the fabric in frustration and frowns at me. I shift on my feet as she scrutinizes my features, her frown only deepening. I know she's just trying to figure out what to do, but it feels weird having someone just openly stare at me for an uncomfortable length of time. "Talon specifically said that the plan hinges on them being able to draw attention. Flashing a lot of skin isn't going to cut it, and she doesn't look bold enough for this dress."

Nicolai rises from his chair and strides over, giving the dress—and me—a critical eye. Great. Now two people are staring at me. "Maybe the light pink dress instead? It shows off even more skin."

"Scythe has some curves, but she also has a lot of muscle," Kayla muses. "I was trying to lean into that instead of trying to soften her appearance, but it's not working with the face and hair." She grabs a handful of my fair curls and glares at it like it just insulted her.

"Standing right here," I mutter, but they both ignore me.

"We could straighten it," Nicolai says, his honey brown eyes looking at my hair. "That would give it an edgier appearance."

"Maybe," Kayla says, doubt still clear on her face. "But the color . . . it's nice, but the strawberry-blonde isn't particularly eye-catching."

"Wig?"

Kayla releases my hair and glances towards a wall, where wigs are displayed on several shelves. "I'm worried about it staying attached if they need to get physical with someone but then return to the party afterwards." Kayla tilts her head back and forth. "Mage hunters don't go down easy."

I raise my eyebrows. Exactly how much do these two know?

"We were already going to give her a crown. If we select one with a lot of points, that will add to the overall effect," Nicolai suggests.

"Do you two know why Talon and I are doing this?" I study both of them, trying to decipher if what I'm contemplating revealing is a good idea.

"The mage hunters have Ravyn and Astria," Nicolai says.

"Astria is witchkin." Kayla drops that truth as if it's nothing, all her attention on my appearance. Her lips are still pursed as her gaze bounces between my hair, face, and the dress. "You're her sister, which means you're a witch. Pretty sure there is only one of those around these days."

My jaw almost drops at the nonchalant way she admits to knowing who I really am.

Nicolai chuckles, but he looks away to avoid meeting my eyes. "We're not Tovenian, but we're not exactly loyal Eleoyn citizens either."

"Hard to be when you could get killed at any moment if they learn the type of blood that runs through your veins," Kayla says tightly.

"What do you mean?"

Magic is only detectable when it's being used. I haven't sensed anything from either of them, but that doesn't mean much.

"I have fae blood." Nicolai shrugs. "Kayla is a mage."

"Barely." She rolls her eyes. "Aside from basic illusion spells, I hardly use my magic."

"Because you don't want to die or be recruited." Nicolai looks at her sharply. There is so much love and concern in his expression, it breaks my heart a little.

I want someone to look at me like that someday.

Kayla's lips press into a hard line. "I will not use my magic to kill my own kind. I just want to live my damn life."

"I know, love." Nicolai reaches over to kiss the side of Kayla's hair, and she relaxes a little.

I've been so busy defending my forest and the Wilds beyond them from the mage hunters that I never thought about what it would be like to live in Eleoyn as the *other*. Mage. Fae. Hells . . . maybe even some witches still live here. Cursed werewolves.

Every day, knowing that if the truth of who you are is discovered, your life is over. If you're lucky, you get a quick end. If you're not, torture followed by a public execution. Or I suppose if you're a mage, recruited to serve one of the major factions.

"Does this help?" I grip the silver charm dangling from the delicate chain around my neck and tug it over my head. Nicolai lets out a sharp exhale as the strawberry-blonde locks turn lilac. Then both he and Kayla raise their gazes to look into my silver eyes.

"Yeah . . ." Kayla breathes out. "This will work."

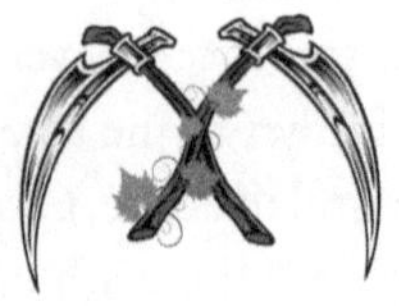

CHAPTER SIXTEEN

~

Scythe

"Almost done," Kayla says two hours later.

"Thank fuck." I let out a relieved sigh.

Kayla and Nicolai think my hair is perfect. My silver eyes are pushing it, but given that I'll disappear after the party, it's fine. For the tattoos they decided instead of hiding them, to just cover them up with silver paint which they've packed up along with the makeup and accessories.

After giving me very explicit instructions on what to do with all of it, they traded a look that said they'd be repeating those instructions to Talon whenever they come back. I've never worn makeup before, so it's probably for the best, because I just nodded along with everything they said without understanding a single word.

"What about shoes?" Nicolai frowns, their eyes falling to my bare feet.

"Scythe, how do you feel about—" Kayla's words cut off as we all turn at the sound of the back door—the locked back door—

opening.

Talon slides in, several slender pieces of metal disappearing from their hands as they enter the large fitting room in the back of Kayla's dress shop. Vesi stumbles in behind them and quickly closes the door, and a roguish grin spills across Talon's face as they whisper something to Vesi about doubting their skills. Vesi rolls her eyes, and Talon directs their attention to the rest of us.

"You lot about done . . .?"

I see the moment Talon's gaze lands on me. In a rare second of complete honesty, their face reveals everything. A mixture of surprise, desire, and satisfaction settles onto their features as they drink in my appearance. A thrill races through me at knowing I am what put that expression on their face. The mating bond hums happily, but I ignore it.

This isn't about the bond. It's about me and them. For once, I knocked Talon off their game.

"Surprised, wolf?" I grin wickedly.

They blink, and their genuine reaction vanishes as a lazy grin rolls across their lips. "Never had a doubt. Kayla is the best dress designer in all of Eleoyn, and nobody has a better eye for style than Nicolai. If anyone could make you presentable, it'd be those two."

Talon winces when Vesi smacks the back of their head. "Don't be a prat, Tal."

"Rude." They glare at her before glancing around at everyone. "I've got a few things to discuss with Scythe before we leave. Can you three give us a minute?"

I frown. Did something go wrong with securing us an invitation? Talon said they'd handle that part while I was getting outfitted. Apparently, they already own several fancy outfits and masks, so they didn't need to get anything else. I'm a little concerned about where they would procure an invitation on such short notice because I imagine most of the nobles attending the masquerade have already left for Mabria.

Even if they managed to steal one, I don't understand why the nobles wouldn't immediately report it. Surely they'd notice if an invitation from the prince went missing?

"Of course," Kayla draws out as she arches an eyebrow at Talon. "We'll be upstairs."

Nicolai and Kayla head up a set of stairs in the corner while Vesi looks like she's debating between following them or bolting back out the door.

"Get your ass up here, Vesi!" Nicolai yells from somewhere upstairs.

The petite redhead scowls at Talon, who just grins at her. Then she marches up the stairs like she's going to her execution but is determined to be defiant about it.

Okay, so the bad breakup was her fault then.

"What exactly is their dea—"

Talon's mouth crashes against mine and swallows my gasp. I was distracted by Vesi's impending drama and didn't even see them move. Their kiss is demanding, and I give myself into it, parting my lips and teasing their tongue with mine. Talon's hands slide down the sides of my dress, running over the smooth fabric until they get to where it parts, revealing bare flesh.

Their fingers then trail down my hips, toying with the silver chains that connect the two panels. When they pull away from my lips to trail kisses down my jawline, I arch my neck to give them better access.

"I should have known those two would dress you in something to taunt me," they whisper against my skin, their teeth grazing the pulse on my neck before licking and sucking the spot.

A low moan slips from me, and I freeze. The others are right upstairs. I can hear them walking around above us. There is no way they won't hear us if we continue.

"Tal . . ." I breathe out. "We shouldn't. Your friends are upst—"

My protest is cut off when Talon tugs me against themself. I feel their erection pushing against their pants at the same moment they bite down on the mate mark on my neck. The spell in the choker hides the mark from view, but apparently, Talon can still sense it.

I struggle to contain my groan, and Talon laughs huskily against my skin when they release my neck. "You're not wearing any underwear," they state matter-of-factly.

"Kayla," I pant, "said it wasn't possible with this dress."

"I'm sure that's why she chose it." They roll their eyes. "Vesi likely filled them in on who you are, and now they're all excited that we're together."

"We're not together," I squeeze out. "It's just the bond." It's hard staying focused with the way Talon draws their fingers against my skin and kisses around the mate mark. Rationally, I know this isn't a good idea; I'm already in way over my head with Talon, and the closer we get, the more confusing everything becomes. I should stop this.

I should. I really fucking should.

My hand slips between us to cup their hard length, and this time, I don't hold back my groan. Gods, why does Talon have to have such a perfect dick?

"Your words and your actions seem to be saying two different things, Princess." Talon's hips jerk forward, pushing their erection harder against my palm. "So let's make sure we're in agreement."

I exhale sharply when they grab me, spin me around, and force me to bend over Kayla's worktable. My forearms are braced against the table, and I start to push myself back, but they place one hand between my shoulder blades, pinning me down. I can tell, based on how Talon gives a little against my movement, that if I really tried to get free, they would instantly release me.

My heart beats faster, but not from fear. That rational voice that was whispering how bad of an idea this is has fled, and instead, all I feel is anticipation that keeps me rooted to the spot as Talon's hard body leans over mine.

"I'm going to tie your wrists to the top of this table." I hear the clink of a belt being unbuckled as they shift away from me for a moment before slapping the brown leather belt onto the table next to my face, causing me to jump a little. "Then I'm going to slam my cock into your pussy—that I can already smell is wet for me— over and over again."

My thighs clench together, and I feel the traces of my desire running down my legs. "You're going to be a good witch and not make too much noise." Then their hand glides over my ass, but when I lean into it, they quickly draw their hand and slap my right cheek. Even with the fabric between their hand and my skin, it still stings.

"I'm not done explaining things yet, Princess," they say evenly as I let out a hiss. "You have to wait."

"Tal," I start, but I have to bite back a moan when they smack my ass again.

Then warm breath tickles my neck as they bend over me again. "One of these days, I'll fuck you nice and slow. Make you feel every single inch of my cock as I slide into your tight little cunt inch by inch."

"Fuck." I shift my thighs against each other, trying to relieve the growing ache between them. When Talon's hand tightens warningly on my ass, I go still.

"But the only way you're getting my cock today is hard and fast. For taunting me."

"Kayla is the one who chose the dress," I point out.

"Are you saying you want me to go upstairs and *punish* Kayla?" When I growl at how much innuendo they snuck into that word, Talon just laughs. "That's what I thought."

I hate that they can read me so well. Almost as much as I hate how wet it makes me.

"So tell me . . ." Talon starts to bunch the fabric of the dress up in their hand. "Do you want me to punish you?"

I grind my teeth together as the ache between my thighs becomes unbearable. Talon's fingers trail down the curve of my ass before stopping an inch from where I need them. Fuck. I jerk my head in a tight nod.

"Use your words, Princess."

Asshole.

"Yes!"

At this point, I'm so desperate to have them inside me, it almost hurts. I tell myself it's the bond that's making me feel this way, even though I know it's a lie. It's definitely happy right now and is amping up my need, but mate bonds don't create desire. Or love. That has to exist on its own.

"Not so loud." Talon chuckles as they draw back, and I instantly miss their hard body pressed against mine. "We wouldn't want my friends to hear."

Heat flares in my cheeks. How did I forget that little detail?

I open my mouth to tell Talon I changed my mind because there is no way I'll be able to keep quiet, but their fingers slip between my thighs and glide through the hot slickness waiting for them. My teeth jab into my bottom lip as I smother the moan that tries to escape.

Talon swirls their fingers around several more times before dragging them out and smearing them across my ass, which they promptly slap again. A litany of swear words tumble from me, and Talon makes a tsking sound before pushing me down when I start to rise off the table. Their hand lingers a moment between my shoulder blades, then they remove it, but before I can move up, they're on the other side of the table and wrapping that leather belt around my wrists. I feel the magic in it as soon as it touches my skin. Talon makes a loop to bind my hands while tying the rest of the belt to something I can't see. I test the hold and find there is no give.

"I'm not going to be so mean to say that you won't enjoy this." Talon unbuttons their pants and pulls their cock free, the silver piercing shining in the bright lighting. I can't help but lick my lips as I stare at it. "But you're still being punished. So you'll have to take all the pleasure I'm about to give you—and be quiet about it."

I let out a strangled whimper. Being quiet isn't something I'm good at—definitely not with Talon—but I'm also not an exhibitionist and don't want to face their friends again after they've heard me screaming Talon's name.

A low, devious laugh rumbles from Talon as they read the dilemma on my face and probably sense it through the bond.

"Here." They brush the broad head of their hard length against my bottom lip. "You can practice being quiet with something in your mouth." Talon lets out a low groan as I take them in, swirling my tongue around the piercing.

Fuck, I love the way they taste. The subtle metallic flavor mixing with the saltiness of their precum. Talon can play this up all they want, but they're every bit as desperate to fuck me as I am to be fucked by them. We're both on this messed-up ride together.

I hollow out my cheeks and suck harder as Talon's shallow thrusts turn harsh and demanding. A growl slips from their lips as they fuck my face in earnest. Despite being the one tied up, I feel very much in control. Something I relish as I swallow more of their cock until it hits the back of my throat.

As if realizing they're losing sight of their punishment plan, Talon withdraws their cock after thrusting it in one more time— hard enough to make my eyes water.

"Naughty." A golden sheen rolls over their eyes as they take me in—breathless and panting—before they survey the cabinets along the wall. I frown and turn my head to watch as they stride over to one and go through its contents for a minute before pulling out a small blue bottle.

They walk around the table, and no matter how much I twist my head, I can't see what they're doing. I tug on the restraints again, but there's definitely no give. If I use magic, I can probably break free, but where's the fun in that?

I hear what I think is Talon placing the bottle on the table, then I yelp as they kick my legs further apart. Talon notches their cock at my entrance and leans over me. I bite back a groan as they slide in a few inches, that damn piercing heightening the feeling of my body stretching around them.

Then warm lips kiss my spine. "Good luck staying quiet, witch." Their tone is deep and wicked, causing my heart to pound even faster.

That's all the warning I get before Talon straightens, their fingers digging into my hips as they slam all the way to the hilt. I bite down hard on my lip until the taste of blood fills my mouth. No screaming. No moaning. No crying out their name.

I'll get my pleasure from this and defy them in the process.

A frustrated growl rumbles from Talon when I don't break the way they were expecting. "You want to play, Scythe?" they rasp. "Let's fucking play."

SLAP.

I strangle back the groan that almost bursts from my lips when Talon's palm connects with my ass again. Fuck. I had no idea I would like that so much, and I absolutely cannot let them know that.

Unfortunately, my pussy has other ideas as it clenches around Talon's cock like a vise.

"Fuck," they groan. "Do you like that?"

"No," I pant. "Do something interesting before I fall asleep."

That earns me two more slaps—one to each cheek. The climax that was building tears through my body, and before I can wrestle it back, a moan escapes.

Talon doesn't give me a moment to enjoy it, just continues fucking me like I'm not falling apart with every thrust.

"Your mouth is a gift from the gods, you love rough sex, and your pussy"—another slap followed by a groan—"fucking strangles my cock the harder I hit your ass." Talon lets out a wolfish laugh that has my aforementioned pussy clenching again, already greedy for the next orgasm. "It's a shame you're a witch, because otherwise you might be my perfect mate."

"It's a shame—fuck!" They kick my legs farther apart and slam into me deeper than before. I bite down hard to keep from moaning. More blood fills my mouth. "You talk so much. Overcompensating maybe?" A hand releases my hip as Talon leans forward enough to grip my throat.

"Is that so?" Talon rasps, their other hand dropping from my hip to sneak around and rub my poor clit, which is still overly sensitive from the last orgasm.

"Yes," I grind out. "Trying to cover up your lack"—a half-strangled scream tears from my throat when they push down hard on my clit just as they bury their cock to the hilt—"of skills!"

"Hmm . . ." Talon muses, their fingers gently squeezing my throat as their thrusts slow, which only increases the torture because that piercing leaves behind a delicious burn. "I suppose I'll have to try harder."

They suddenly straighten, their hands disappearing from both my throat and clit—something that has me whimpering before I can stop. Satisfaction pulses through the bond. They know exactly what they do to me and love that I'm a writhing mess beneath them.

I love it too.

"It's a shame you're a witch, because otherwise you might be my perfect mate."

Shit. This isn't real. None of this is real.

I. Am. So. Fucked.

The sound of a bottle opening draws my attention. What are they doing? Talon's cock is still seated firmly in my pussy, but they've stopped thrusting.

"You've done an admirable job up to this point," Talon says in an idle tone that puts all my instincts on alert.

I hold back another moan as they move inside me again at a languid pace that matches their voice. One hand lands on my ass, parting my cheeks slightly, while the other's slick fingers toy with my tight hole. Instantly, I tense up. I've done a lot of things in my centuries of living, but not this.

"Relax, Scythe," Talon purrs. "Have I ever done anything you didn't love?"

"All the time," I hiss.

They laugh. "Have I ever done anything *to your body* that you haven't loved?"

I want to lie, but they'll just call me on it, so I keep my mouth shut. Talon changes it up and pulls their cock almost all the way out before slowly sliding back in. It's fucking torture. I try to push back with my hips, but I'm tied tight enough to the table that I can barely move.

Sensing my frustration, they laugh and start to fuck me faster. A finger presses into my ass, and I exhale at the sudden pressure, then Talon reaches around to play with my clit with their other hand.

They add a second finger, stretching me out further as they push down on my trembling clit. This time, I can't hold back the moan as pleasure breaks over the orgasm they wring out of me.

"Such a good witch," Talon praises as I tremble beneath them, panting for breath while trying to stay quiet. "Your mouth and pussy take my cock so well. I bet your ass will be perfect too."

My mind is still swimming from the two orgasms when Talon pulls their fingers from inside me and replaces them with their cock. Whatever was in that bottle made everything deliciously warm . . . and slippery.

"Oh, fuck!" I start to squirm when their thick, pierced head pushes in. It's not going to fit—too tight. It's not going to—

"Breathe," Talon commands, and my traitorous lungs instantly pull in a breath. The pressure lessens, and then Talon pivots their hips forward, filling me all the way. A small flash of pain followed by immense pleasure floods my system.

"Tal," I moan, and they go still for a second.

Something I don't understand flickers down the bond, but before I can try to decipher it, Talon is moving again. Their hips slap against me as they take me over and over. I don't even understand how I can climax this way, but the pleasure building feels intense.

Too fucking intense.

"Tal!" I cry out as my fingers dig into the hard wood of the table.

"Come for me, witch," they demand as they hammer into me at a punishing pace. "Come for your fucking mate."

A scream tears from my throat as I do exactly what they order. Talon empties themself inside me, fucking me through our orgasms until they finally slow and then lean forward to rest their forehead against my spine.

It takes me a moment to realize the feeling of contentment—of rightness—isn't coming from the bond. Talon stole my heart years ago under the starlight, and they've never given it back. Love. Hate. It's all blended together into one truth. Talon is my true mate, in every sense.

But they are still going to leave.

"I think you might be the end of me, Cerelia." Talon chuckles.

My throat seizes up at hearing my true name on their lips. Their tone is light and teasing. This is all just temporary fun for them. They have no experience with mate bonds, so it's probably just driving them towards me. Once the bond is removed, the only thing Tal will feel is hate.

"Then we'll be the end of each other," I answer in an equally casual tone even as my thoughts grow darker.

You'll be the end of me.

CHAPTER SEVENTEEN

~

Talon

"THIS IS . . . A LOT." Scythe eyes the people walking down the rose petal pathway from where we stand off to the side, draped in shadows. The prince's palace is in the center of the city of Mabria, its towers rising far above everything else. We haven't seen any mage hunters yet, just guards and the partygoers making their way down the brick pathway to the stairs that lead inside.

A small orchestra plays welcoming songs, and performers in masks ranging from funny to demonic wind their way through the guests. The prince of Eleoyn adores drama. I've never actually been to one of his parties, but I've heard about them—everyone has, because every time he has one, it starts a new trend across Eleoyn.

He always hosts them here, at his palace.

And *palace* is the only way to describe it. The prince's preferred home is even grander than the king's residence in the capital. Smooth, white stone walls rise up to the night sky. Occasionally, spiraling towers break up the walls. I suspect there are

215

pathways connecting them where guards patrol, but I can't see any of them from down here.

The architecture alone sets the building apart. Most structures in Eleoyn—other than the king's sprawling monstrosity of a palace in Tenresan—are simple and efficient. The palace before us, though, was built by the fae through magic. It is elegant and refined, not a stone out of place, but what truly makes it unique is the mural made of various minerals, precious metals, and gems. On the smooth white walls is the story of the fae and witches crossing the ocean to reach Malovias. Over a hundred boats are shown with serpentine monsters rising up from a sea made of sapphire gems.

The design glitters underneath the starlit sky. Based on what I've heard, this is the grandest of the murals but far from the only one. The fae wrote their stories on the walls of the palace. It makes me wonder why the prince has taken it as his own, given the unpopularity of anything related to the fae. Then again, the prince's reputation as a partier is only rivaled by his reputation as a boundary pusher.

No one else would get away with what Prince Caspian does. Last year, he hosted a party where everyone was given fake tips to put on the ends of their ears. They'd been spelled by mages to make it appear as if everyone had pointed ears like the fae.

Even his father hadn't been happy about that one and had publicly rebuked the prince, likely to appease the Ririthan king. The border was closed between the two kingdoms, but there had been talks of opening them over the last couple of years to increase trade.

The prince's shenanigans did not endear him to the Ririthan king, who was fanatic about eliminating all traces of the fae from Malovias.

"We can wait here for a few more moments." I glance at Scythe, who warily watches the parade of masked partygoers. "The masquerade only started an hour ago, and the prince's events always go until the early morning. We have time."

I smirk as Scythe starts to chew on her bottom lip, stops, and glares at me in annoyance for a second before turning her attention back to the partygoers. "Have you been here before?"

"No, but I've always wanted to see it," I admit.

"It does kind of seem like your scene." She watches a group of people walk past us. It's hard to tell with the masks, but I would guess they are all young, early twenties. They're practically dripping in jewels. One of the women wears a mask covered in glittering diamonds, emeralds, and rubies.

"Lots of easy marks," I agree.

"And people to fawn over you," she says lightly, but I don't miss the way the corners of her mouth tighten as she speaks the words. My little witch doesn't like it when others flirt with me, and oddly, I like that possessive streak in her.

Unfortunately, she'll have to keep it under control tonight because we each have our roles to play. Of course, that means I'll have to keep myself—and my wolf—in check tonight as well.

Which is going to be difficult, considering that godsdamn dress.

I'd foolishly convinced myself earlier that it wouldn't matter. That the impact of it would be lessened, considering how thoroughly I'd taken her when I'd walked in on her being fitted for it at Kayla's. As soon as she slipped it on tonight though, that intense need to claim her rose up, and I had to excuse myself for a few minutes before I gave in to my baser desires and bent her over the nearest piece of furniture until she screamed my name again.

The dress is sin incarnate, and I want to thank Kayla for it while also berating her for this unique form of torture, because our plan tonight hinges on Scythe attracting attention, which she absolutely will. The slick silver fabric clings to her every curve, leaving nothing to the imagination, and that's before the slits on either side that end just below her waist. I'm beyond skeptical of those delicate silver chains keeping the two panels of fabric in place. It's blindingly obvious she's not wearing anything beneath the godsforsaken dress.

The top half isn't any less tempting. The bodice hugs her breasts and is low enough to show off an indecent amount of cleavage.

I want to grab a cloak from a passing nobleman and drape it over her shoulders so no one else can see what is mine.

It's getting harder and harder to deny that fact. The first time the witch and I met years ago on that fateful day, we allowed ourselves to get swept up in each other. My wolf had been on edge, and learning the truth of who Cerelia was had been the tipping point.

I'd lost myself to the agony of my curse and woken up feeling like my soul had been shattered.

This time though, it wasn't hatred I felt when I opened my eyes after my body had tried to tear itself apart. It was relief to see her sleeping beside me, like that was how it was supposed to be and I'd been missing it all my life.

This is so far beyond a physical attraction.

I like her.

I like the wry smile she gives me when we trade barbs. She has a cunning tongue, and it's fun when she lets it out to play. I like the way she pretends to be annoyed when I call her Princess. I don't think many people have ever given her a nickname, an endearing one anyway. Perhaps the thing that terrifies me is that I like the way she feels when she falls asleep in my arms at night and wakes up before the sun rises to listen to the birds sing.

Maybe she will be able to break the curse on my wolf, but every time she reiterates her determination to break the mating bond, there is a cold dread that sinks into my gut that has nothing to do with how my wolf feels or the effects of the bond itself.

"Like" isn't the right word. I'm in love with the witch.

I need to tell her, I know I do, but my sister has to come first, and I know Scythe feels the same about hers. We'll have to figure out our confusing and messy situation afterwards.

Which means, tonight, I'm going to have to deal with watching people flirt with her. Touch her. My wolf rumbles inside my chest. They really don't like this plan, but we need to separate the mage hunters, and in my experience, the easiest way to do that is using sex as a lure. Scythe looks absolutely delicious and should be able to snag at least one of them. Ideally not Stelian. Whoever we interrogate isn't going to survive the night. The leader going missing would attract far too much attention. The disappearance of a lower-ranking hunter will be looked into but not to the same degree, especially at a party with the reputation of the prince's.

"Are you ready?" I brush my finger across the tattoo behind my ear along with a push of intention. In the span of a breath, my silver jackal mask appears over my face and the crown of silver and gold adorns my head.

Scythe looks me over, taking in the effect the mask and crown have on my outfit. If Scythe is the beauty of early morning, I'm the glory of moonlight. My high-collared shirt is black and so are my pants and boots. The shirt is sleeveless, showing off the lunar phase tattoos that run down both my arms, and a black, corset-style vest with intricate silver stitching is molded to my upper body.

"Azdall. The god of thieves. How fitting."

"Because I stole your heart?" I smirk at her, knowing how corny the line is and that she'll be amused by it.

Sure enough. My witch rolls her eyes, but I don't miss the blush across her cheeks, which causes my heart to beat a little faster. Maybe she'll be more open to my proposal about holding off on breaking the mating bond than I thought.

"I've actually yet to see your thieving ways in action," she drawls as she places the silver mask across her face. Kayla had some masks for her to choose from, and Scythe chose one that features an elaborate design of vines and flowers. At first glance, the mask is beautiful, but it's only when you look closer that you see the sharp thorns and realize the thorns are violencias—a carnivorous flower that lures in small prey to devour it whole. "You have a tendency to boast about your skills without ever actually proving anything."

Her chin dips as she struggles to secure the mask. Unlike mine, hers is held on by silver chains similar to the ones on her dress.

I slip around her and gently take the chains from her fingers so I can clasp them into place. There are six of them on each side, and once together, they create a network of silver across her lilac hair.

"Have you found my skills so lacking, Princess?" I murmur as I lean down to kiss the sensitive spot at the crook of her neck. Her breath quickens, and I smile against her skin. "I'll have to work harder next time."

She whirls around to face me, silver eyes lit up with desire and amusement. "See that you do, wolf."

I laugh and hold out my bent arm, and she slips hers into mine before we step out of the shadows and head towards the palace.

It's time for us to hunt.

WE PAUSE when we get to the top of the stairs that lead into the palace. A woman wearing a gold dress and a swan mask awaits us along with six armed guards standing behind her, all decked out in black with plain gold masks. I pass her the invitation I swiped from the noble back in Albadrid, and she arches a dark eyebrow at me.

"My uncle couldn't make it," I explain, adding a touch of concern to my voice. "The heat the last few weeks has aggravated an old ailment of his. Our family physician ordered him to stay on bed rest. I offered to come in his stead, and my lovely companion was kind enough to allow me the pleasure of her company."

The woman's gaze flicks to Scythe, who just smiles at her before the woman looks down at the gold ring on my left index finger and the crest of the Gannon family. She stares at it long enough that I wonder if maybe I missed a spot of blood when I was cleaning it off, but then her crimson-stained lips curl into a polite smile.

"Please give our best to your uncle. We hope he recovers quickly."

Given that I slit his throat and shoved his body into an empty wine barrel for Vesi and Mattias to dispose of, that seems unlikely.

"I'm sure he'll be fine and is no doubt looking forward to the next one," I assure her. "He does love a good glass of wine."

"Please." She gestures to some stairs winding up to the right side of the palace. "We have a special entrance for guests who have truly embraced the villainous theme of the evening."

"Who doesn't love the chance to be a bit wicked from time to time?" I grin, and she giggles before composing herself.

"Really?" Scythe asks dryly as we make our way up the stairs. "*'Who doesn't love the chance to be a bit wicked from time to time?'*" She does her best to deepen her voice, and I let out an amused huff.

"Couldn't resist." I shrug. "We're already off to a solid start, you have to admit."

"This is the easy part." A thread of tension shoots through the bond before sharply tapering off. She must be getting better at controlling what she sends through it. That's fine. Her face is still an open book to me.

We reach the top of the landing, and a grand set of silver doors awaits us with guards posted on either side. There are always two entrances to the prince's outlandish parties. The main one, which is where the majority of the guests enter, and a secondary one that allows certain guests to have a much grander introduction. Unlike the parties other nobles throw, having a fancy title does not automatically mean you get to use the second entrance at the prince's parties.

It's always awarded based on appearance and dedication to the theme. The more outlandish, the better the chances. I like to think I would have gotten in on my own, but Scythe . . . I laugh under my breath.

This is a daring plan, even for me.

When Scythe takes a step towards the door, I tug her to a stop. My fingers glide down her mask, nimbly avoiding the jagged points, and brush her hair back over her shoulder. I thought about suggesting she pin it up in some elaborate braid, but leaving it loose is more fitting. Although, oddly, I find myself not liking the idea of anyone getting to admire her hair but me.

I brush a kiss against her pink-stained lips, not caring that some of the color likely rubbed off on mine, and pull back enough to whisper quietly, "You will be glorious, I have no doubt. Just think of Astria and that you'll be seeing her again soon." Her silver eyes bore into mine, and she gives me a shallow, determined nod. "And if you have any doubts about how to react in a situation, just ask yourself what I would do."

Her lips twitch. "So my choices are fighting or fucking those gathered inside?"

A low growl spills from my throat, only for Scythe to swallow it a second later when I crash my lips against hers. I'm vaguely aware of her grabbing my hand and pulling it away from her hair before I can rip off the chains holding the mask in place. My other hand slides into the slit of her dress and around to cup her ass, my fingers squeezing the soft flesh.

She pushes her body flush against mine as my tongue plunders her mouth, hungrily taking everything I give her.

Mate. Mine.

Reluctantly, I end the kiss and pull back, my hand smoothly sliding out from under her dress, careful not to break the chains. If Scythe accidentally flashes someone tonight, I'm pretty sure I'll be more pissed about it than she will.

She doesn't say anything as I use the tip of my finger to clean up the pink stain smeared around her swollen lips. Silver eyes search mine, clearly trying to figure out what in all the hells that was about. I can feel the barest hint of her emotions down the bond. Desire. Need. Wariness.

Once again, I remind myself that this conversation has to wait. I can feel the gaze of the guards like an itch between my shoulders, but I ignore them as I meticulously wipe away the last of the smears.

Scythe exhales sharply when I lean forward, like a predator expecting an attack, to whisper in her ear, "You can fight whoever you want, witch, but you only fuck me."

I start to move back, but her hand shoots out to grip my forearm, nails digging in hard enough to draw blood. Then Scythe's breath tickles my ear, and I freeze. "Careful, wolf," she warns in a raspy voice that has me thinking all kinds of wicked things. "Nobody has given me orders in a long time."

I turn my head just enough so I can see more of her face as my lips twist into a smug grin. "Ah, but you enjoy the orders I give you, don't you, Princess?"

The nails bite harder into my skin, and I laugh before stepping back and laying a hand on hers, capturing it against my arm. Her eyes are a burning silver fury behind her mask because she knows I'm right and it pisses her off beyond reason. Before she loses it and calls forth her scythe to stab me, I tug her towards the guards at the door.

They open them at our approach, and music pours out, revealing a small landing for another staircase, this one winding down. Beyond it, I can see grand, white stone walls and chandeliers hanging from the high ceiling. It's not obvious where the stairs lead, but the space looks massive, so I'm assuming this is where the main floor of the party is.

A slender man wearing a dark blue tunic and a gold lion mask steps forward. "How shall I introduce you?" he asks in a smooth, melodious voice, his gaze flittering over both me and Scythe with interest. It doesn't feel salacious, more like he's admiring the craft that went into our clothing. Kayla really is quite talented.

I lean forward and whisper our titles for the evening into his ear, then he chuckles before striding over to the railing. The music lowers as he raises his right hand to his lips, a blue sapphire gem glittering in the light. It's a sound amplifier, most likely courtesy of mage magic.

"My friends!" His voice echoes across the large open space. "We may all be villains this evening, but some of us are trickier than others, and some are far more dangerous—more wicked. Do take care as you find yourself in the company of Azdall, the mischievous god of thieves, and their date for the evening, the Witch of the Woods!"

Scythe and I move before the announcer finishes, and gasps explode from the crowd gathered below when they get their first glimpse of us. My lips are curled in an arrogant smirk, and when I see a matching expression on Scythe's face, a thrill shoots up my spine.

We make our way down the winding staircase at a leisurely pace. I use the height advantage to scan the crowd, and I have no doubt Scythe is doing the same. There must be at least five hundred people in attendance. When I see that it extends farther back beneath a large balcony that wraps around half of the room, I double my estimate.

Scythe's smile doesn't slip, but I can feel her astonishment as she takes in the vast, grand ballroom. Even I have to admit that I'm impressed at the beauty of it all. The floors are a shiny obsidian black with threads of gold woven through them. That same gold runs up the white stone walls, thickening until they become the trunks of trees in the murals painted along the walls. Each tree has different-colored leaves—blue, green, red. Most of them have been painted onto the walls, but interspersed in the leaves are sparkling sapphires, emeralds, and rubies.

There are traces of the fae in other buildings and artifacts, but this palace was built entirely by them, and it shows. Despite the thousands of people who have walked down these steps, there are no scratches or scuff marks, and the murals look like they were painted yesterday, not centuries ago. Unlike the gaudy homes of the nobles, the richness on display here doesn't look ostentatious —only breathtaking. I realize now that this is what the wealthy of Eleoyn have been trying to replicate.

Even the light blazing from the silver and gold chandeliers hanging from the ceiling are from fae magic; mage lanterns have more of an orange hue.

Excited whispers rise to greet us as we continue down the stairs. I'm already looking forward to telling Vesi she was wrong— again. Apparently, when Scythe and I were . . . occupied . . . Vesi was arguing with Kayla and Nicolai that Scythe couldn't possibly walk through the front doors of the prince's palace dressed as herself, given that the Witch of the Woods was the most wanted person in the Eleoyn Kingdom. Even I have to admit that it is a bit bold.

Though nobody would believe that the actual witch would come here, so what better way to hide than in plain sight?

The hair and eye color can be explained away with minor mage spells. And I can smudge the silver paint over her tattoos to imply they aren't real. As long as she doesn't use magic in front of anyone or where the mage hunters can sense it, we'll be fine. People will be talking about this party for years. Honestly, I'm a little put out that Scythe is upstaging me, but if I'm going to be shown up by anyone, it's fitting that it would be my mate.

As Scythe and I take in the sights, I realize that people really weren't exaggerating about how extravagant the prince's parties are or how much he pushes the boundaries of his father's rule. Last year, he even dedicated some of them to the old fae gods. This time, I see plenty of people dressed as fae and some of the other gods, although no other Azdalls yet.

To my knowledge, nobody has ever been punished for what they do at these events. It irks me, considering the mage hunters and city guards happily punish the working classes for simply wearing a sigil of an old god, but nothing will happen to me for dressing like one.

A woman wearing a siren mask waves at me, a coy, flirty smile on her red-stained lips. I look away, but not before I note the diamond-encrusted bracelet on her wrist. If the witch is going to parade around as herself tonight, perhaps I'll embrace my god's knack for lifting jewels.

When we reach the bottom of the steps, Scythe lets me guide her forward, and the crowd parts for us. I'm getting my fair share of admirers, but I'm far more aware of how many people are looking at Scythe like she's a delicious treat. It's not just that she flashes skin with every step, it's the tantalizing way it's being shown. Based on the way several men stare at the slits of the dress, I know they're debating sliding by us and "accidentally" tearing one or two of those chains away.

"Dance with me, witch." I drop my hand from her back and offer it to her, although my tone makes it clear that it's a command, not an invitation.

Scythe gives me a warning look, but those gathered just chuckle. If we stand still, we'll get bogged down by people wanting to speak to us. Better to stay on the move and keep up the mystery while we search for the mage hunters.

"Careful, little god." Her lips curl into a cruel smile as she accepts my hand. "My teeth are sharper than yours."

I give her a wolfish grin as we stride towards the dance floor. The couples already dancing glide out of the way, and I twirl the witch before pulling her tightly against me. Then the slow beat of the music starts to pick up as the musicians switch to a new song.

The people around us cheer as they swirl a little faster to match the song. I hold the witch's stare, and it feels like the crowd slips away as I remember the night we met—our wild dance around the bonfire to a different song, but one with an equally fast beat.

Based on the bit of fire that flickers in her eyes, I know Scythe is remembering it too.

It feels like the moment stretches into an eternity, then the band hits a high note, and Scythe and I move in the same breath.

She spins away from me, the dress flaring out around her, the silver catching the light of the fae lanterns and making it shine like starlight.

The crescendo starts to peak again, and just before it hits, I intercept Scythe's spin. One arm slips around her back, and she trusts me completely as I dip her body until she relies solely on me supporting her. My other hand skims down the front of her dress, brushing her cleavage and blazing a heated trail towards those tantalizing slits around her hips.

Scythe's eyes darken, and I hear her heartbeat race, but just as my fingers touch the bare skin of her thighs, I pull her up, and we whirl around the dance floor once more. The band has clearly latched on to us because they start to throw challenges out: increasing the beat, randomly changing it, and holding long, drawn-out notes.

Pure delight shines in the witch's gaze, and I'm so fucking glad I'm looking at silver eyes instead of glamoured ones. How did I forget how much Scythe loves to dance?

She dances the same way she fights. Wild and untamed.

I could dance with her forever.

A tall, broad-shouldered man moves along the outside of the dance floor, watching us. Scythe hasn't noticed him yet, too caught up in the joy of the music. He wears a simple silver mask with a black tunic and pants. Each of his rings has a silver band, and I spot the pendant of the Eleoyn mage guild. As bold as the guests often are at these things, it seems unlikely they would risk the wrath of the mage hunters by dressing like one.

As far as they're concerned, there are no gods or witches to punish them, but the mage hunters are an ever-present threat.

The question is, which mage hunter is this? The leader? Or one of his lackeys?

He watches Scythe intently, and I can see the desire in his brown eyes. This isn't the stare of a mage hunter who has spotted their prey—this is the look of a man who wants to get laid. My hands tighten around Scythe's waist. I can tell, based on the way she angled her body, that she's now spotted the mage and is getting ready to enact the next part of our plan.

This is exactly what we want. I just need to spin her in his direction. They'll dance, she'll lead him off, and then we'll get our answers. I just have to let her go.

My grip tightens.

"Tal," she whispers harshly under her breath.

"Fuck," I mutter sharply before spinning her away from me. The mage steps forward, moving to intercept Scythe as she twirls, her hair a lilac wave around her. Most people are staring at the dress like they can will those chains to give a little more and grant them the glimpse they've been hoping for since seeing us walk down those stairs.

I can't do this.

I move towards her, even though Scythe is going to bump into the mage in seconds. That's fine. I'll just rip her out of his arms. Maybe pick a fight and get him to follow me out that way.

Suddenly, fear sinks its claws into my heart and the wolf rattles their cage because it's not the mage who steps forward to claim Scythe.

It's the Eleoyn prince.

CHAPTER EIGHTEEN

~

Scythe

ONE MOMENT, I'm spinning, putting all my faith in these damn silver chains to hold my dress together so I don't flash everyone, and the next, I'm exhaling sharply as I run into a hard chest. Hands fall onto my upper arms, gripping them tightly, and I look up, expecting to see the mage hunter who was making eyes at me, but I exhale sharply when I find myself staring into a beautiful pair of mismatched eyes. One an impossibly vivid green and the other a blue so deep that it reminds me of the ocean.

The Eleoyn prince.

Even with the mask, I know it has to be him. No one would pretend to have eyes like his, and there is an air of power radiating off him that can't be faked.

Shit.

I turn my head to look for Talon—although what I expect them to do about this, I have no idea—but a hand leaves my arm to grip my chin, forcing me to look forward once more.

"I will have this dance." The prince's voice is smooth like

honey, so much so that I barely notice it was an order and not a request. When I do, I bristle and dig my heels in; he's already pulled me farther onto the dance floor. Whispers swirl around us as the other guests give us space while still trying to linger.

I can feel Talon thanks to the mate bond, but I don't see them anywhere, and I suddenly feel very alone.

"You could look a little happier," the prince teases in that soothing voice of his. "Everyone here is vying for a dance with me. In fact, I believe a few have paid some of the staff and other guests to increase their odds." He leans forward, and I feel his breath tickle my neck. "Whisper a favorable word in my ear. Point out a particularly attractive young woman." Then he moves back and smiles at me, displaying a row of perfectly white teeth; I can't help but think there is something wrong about them though. "Nobody had to point you out though, *witch*."

Fear crawls up my spine as the prince tugs me closer and leads us around the dance floor. I don't know if the "witch" comment was because of how I'm dressed or if he knows. Surely if he knew, he'd have summoned the mage hunters already? I should say something. Even I know it's strange that I haven't spoken once, but I don't know what to say.

Something isn't right about the prince, and it's all I can think about. His face is covered by a mask made of silver and gold. It's a very stylized design, but I recognize the flower.

Nightshade.

Out of the corner of my eye, I see a flash of silver. Talon. I feel their panic race down our bond before they manage to abruptly cut it off. They aren't any happier about this than I am, and they're clearly struggling to keep their emotions in check. Cold settles into my bones. What if Talon does something to reveal who and what they are? The mage hunters will kill them.

That thought grounds me. I just need to survive this dance, excuse myself, then Talon and I can get the fuck out of here. We'll have to find someplace to hole up and trail the mage hunters as they leave.

"Forgive me, my . . . lord?" I stumble over the word because it never occurred to me to ask what in the hells the people call royalty in a situation like this. Should I have used Prince? Your Highness? "I grew up in a small village, and I'm not accustomed to such refined company."

He gives me an amused grin. "Is that so?"

We glide across the floor as guests quickly move out of our path. The dance is simple, and the prince is good at leading. I just have to concentrate on not stepping on his feet. One of his hands rests on my back, and the other is on my hip, right above where the slit of my dress starts. I'm a little surprised his hand hasn't dipped lower to cop a feel. Firm . . . but almost polite.

"Yes," I say quickly. "My friend is probably worried about me. It's my first time in a major city, and they're feeling a bit overprotective."

"Are they?" Again, that amused look, like he's playing a game all his own and waiting for me to catch up. I don't want to play though. I'd rather stab him.

"I don't believe I've seen either of you at one of my parties before." He says it like a statement, but I know it's a question.

"Like I said"—I shorten my steps to avoid stomping on his foot when he turns us suddenly—"I haven't been outside of my small village before."

"That, I believe," he murmurs. "But your . . . friend. This *is* their scene."

My heart beats faster. Talon said they've never been to one of these parties before. Surely they would have mentioned it if they know the prince?

"Even wearing a mask, all your emotions are on display." The prince laughs. "You'd best guard your thoughts—and your heart— better, my witch."

"I'm not yours," I snap.

"No." He spins us around. "I suppose you're not." His eyes rise to look over my shoulder. "But are you theirs?"

Suddenly, the world tilts as the hand on my hip disappears and my feet are knocked out from under me. My hands, which were resting lightly on the prince's shoulders, dart around his neck as he dips me, and his hand on my back supports me as I'm lowered parallel to the floor, the fabric of my dress sliding between my thighs. I suspect my ass is at least somewhat visible as my legs are stretched out and the prince trails a hand down my bare thigh.

For the first time in our dance, his touch feels . . . possessive.

It's not me he's looking at though. It's the jackal wearing a silver crown . . . with glowing golden eyes.

FUCK.

The prince knows. What exactly, I'm not sure, but it feels like he's baiting Talon, which means he suspects that they're a werewolf or at least something *other*. I feel everyone's gaze on me, likely glued to my ass that I'm now quite sure is on display, but any second now, someone is going to glance at Talon, and there is no explaining those glowing eyes.

I rip my hands away from the prince's neck, and his eyes widen before I feel his grip tighten, but it's not enough for my sudden deadweight. I crash to the floor, and the music stops.

Caspian freezes for a moment, and it's almost comical how unsure he looks about what to do in this situation. Apparently, he's never dropped anyone on the dance floor before.

"So sorry," I gush loudly. "Dancing has never been one of my talents."

The prince's lips twitches as he holds out a hand to help me up. "I'm sure you have many other talents."

I swear I hear a low growl over the laughing and chattering of the guests watching us, but I don't take my eyes off Caspian.

"Apologies, my . . . prince?" I guess again at how I'm supposed to address him as I wince while getting to my feet. I did actually land hard on my hip, and those damn chains bit into my skin. "I fear I've sprained my ankle," I lie. "Perhaps my friend can—oof!"

Strong arms scoop me up before I can finish.

"It's my fault." The prince looks down at me as I'm cradled against his chest. "Let me attend to you." Then he carries me off the dance floor, the guests parting around us.

Fuck. I should have just stabbed him.

As we go, I lock eyes with Talon, who is standing in the crowd with thankfully nonglowing eyes. "*Wait*," I mouth to them before doing my best to send calming thoughts down the bond. Something is up with the prince. Everything about this encounter has been strange, and I want to know why.

Plus, if I have to kill the prince to keep him from spilling our secrets, it'll be easier to do so away from the crowd. A growl rumbles inside my head, and I jolt, causing the prince's arms to tighten around me and his pace to quicken. We're almost to a hallway at the end of the ballroom now.

That was definitely a wolf growl in my head. Either the mating bond is already getting stronger—not good, considering I need to break it—or the wolf is *really* pissed. Probably both.

"Let no one pass," the prince orders the two guards standing in front of the hallway. They nod and step aside. "If this one's friend tries to follow . . . tell them Atotl means the witch no harm."

I frown. Why would the prince reference the fae god of wisdom?

We only make it halfway down the dimly lit hall before the prince steps into a dark room and carefully sets me onto my feet. Then he turns to tap his fingers against a symbol carved into the wall near the door, and fae lanterns spring to life, these ones not as bright as the ones burning in the grand ballroom. Their smokeless fire casts the room in a soft, welcoming light as the prince shuts the door.

"This room is soundproof." The prince tugs his mask off and tosses it onto a nearby table. "I have a bargain for you, Cerelia."

I have my scythe at his throat in an instant. It's not fear but interest sparking in the prince's eyes.

Great. Another insane man who has the hots for knife play.

"There are very few people who walk these lands and know my true name," I say coldly. "How did you learn of it, *Caspian*?"

"What?" He grins over my blade. "No more 'my lord' or 'my prince?' I have to admit, it was highly amusing watching someone centuries old get so tripped up over titles."

A trickle of blood forms as I press the scythe in a little harder, but based on the groan he lets out, it's doing little to deter him. Guess I'll have to try harder.

"It's been a long time since I've had to concern myself with such formalities. These days, I spend most of my time listening to the screams of dying humans." My scythe cuts a little deeper as a feral smile stretches across my lips. "I've grown to like it."

"How fortunate for me then"—he blinks, and his formerly round pupils twist to become diamond-shaped—"that I am not human."

I stare at the beautiful prince, and he grins broadly, displaying two sharp fangs.

"You're a changeling," I breathe out and slowly pull the scythe away from his neck before absently tapping my ring and dismissing it. "How?"

Caspian holds his fingers over the cut on his neck, and light similar to the ones from the fae lanterns flashes. When he pulls them away, both the wound and the blood are gone. A changeling with a good amount of magic then.

Children between fae and witches are fairly common, but those offspring always lean heavily one way or another. They're either fae with a hint of witch magic, or witches with a hint of fae magic like me.

When fae reproduce with humans however, the outcome is a little more random. The offspring always take after the fae in appearance, but sometimes they're born with little to no magic.

More often than not, they have a modest amount, but occasionally, the fae-human hybrids, referred to as changelings, have considerably *more* magic than most fae. It's why, when hostilities started rising between fae and humans before the Malovian War broke out, such pairings were forbidden.

No one can explain why changelings always have fangs, since that isn't a trait either the fae or humans have. It's just a weird quirk of the hybrids.

"Well, you see, when two people love each other very much—"

"My patience is thin, and I promise you that my friend's is thinner," I cut him off.

Talon's wolf growls in my mind, startling me a bit, but once I get over feeling them there, I try to send soothing thoughts down the bond to let them know I'm alright and to not do anything rash.

"Ah yes. Your *friend*." Caspian cocks his head as he studies me, sending his wavy, chestnut hair over his shoulder. Without the mask, I can see that the tales of the prince's handsomeness aren't exaggerated. He has a strong, square jaw, full lips, and chiseled cheekbones. No wonder every young noblewoman in the country has been hoping he would notice them.

Although, they'd probably run screaming if he dropped the glamour to reveal the otherworldly eyes and fangs.

"How exactly did the infamous Witch of the Woods find herself mated to a cursed werewolf of all beings? Thought all those poor bastards were dead." He closes the distance between us and reaches for my left hand. I stiffen but don't stop him from gently clasping it and raising it up. His other hand hovers over my fingers, and I feel fae magic dance across my skin. The silver paint slides off like water, revealing my true tattoos beneath. "I've never heard of such a thing happening before." He studies the designs curiously.

"That makes three of us." I snatch my hand back, and the tattoos vanish from sight again. "How the fuck are you a changeling? Does the king know? Have you enjoyed attending the executions of the fae who have been caught over the years?"

A coolness slips into his expression, and it makes those strange eyes seem all the more predatory. "If the king knew that not only was I not his son but also a changeling . . ." He lets out a humorless laugh. "Well, let's just say that the fae executions held so far would be nothing compared to the one held for me."

I narrow my eyes at him. "You can't possibly have been hiding something like this your entire life."

"Says the witch who just strolled into a party with the elite of Eleoyn society dressed as *herself*."

My fingers pluck at my dress as I cock my head and let out an exasperated sigh. "Do you really think I wear this around my woods?"

His eyes trail down my body, and he grins. "No. I suppose not."

"Keep looking, and I'll gouge out those pretty eyes," I warn.

"You think my eyes are pretty?"

"I've seen better." A pair of wolfish yellow eyes flash across my mind.

"No, you haven't." Caspian's grin takes on a carnal edge that, no doubt, usually has people ripping off their clothing and throwing themselves at him.

Maybe I would have been one of those fools a century ago, but I'm far more jaded now.

"Gods, I've known you for less than half an hour and I already find you exhausting." I rub my forehead. "I miss my cats. They're assholes, but not nearly as annoying as people."

He snorts. "Pretty sure the fact that you prefer the company of things referred to as 'devils' says more about you than us." The prince drops his wicked smile like one would change outfits, and it makes me wonder if it has all been an act.

I follow him as he walks over to a couple of chairs arranged in front of an unlit fireplace. For some reason, Caspian wanted to get me away from Talon—and not to fuck me. I want to know why . . . then I can decide if I'm killing a prince tonight.

"So if the king is not your father, who is?" I take a seat in the chair across from him.

With the flick of his hand, the same smokeless flames that light the room blaze to life in the fireplace, but not a lick of heat comes from it. So the prince doesn't just possess a decent amount of magic . . . he's well-versed in using it. The question is . . . who taught him?

Those mismatched eyes with their diamond-shaped pupils stare into the flames. "My mother didn't have a choice in marrying the king. She was young and pretty, from a high-ranking noble family. Two years into their marriage, she met my father. I don't know much about it because she died when I was five and she was very cautious about what she told me of him. Looking back . . . I think it also hurt her to talk about it."

"You think your mother—the human queen of Eleoyn—fell in love with a fae?"

People fear the witches, even though most have been gone from these shores for some time now, but they don't hate them the way they do the fae. The witches always kept to the woods and the Wilds above them. The fae lived across the four kingdoms before the war. After it ended, the kings who rose to power in the four kingdoms did everything they could to paint the fae as the villains. Given how well-attended the fae executions have been, I'd say it worked.

"I think so." He nods, still looking at the fire. "Never met him. He was captured and publicly executed. I was told it took him two days to die, and they only put him out of his misery because they ran out of wine. My mother was excused from attending because she was pregnant with me at the time."

"Fuck," I mutter.

"So you'll find me absent from the fae executions for several reasons." He gives me a smile that doesn't reach his eyes.

I frown. He might have decent control over his magic now, but it's not like he was born with that control. It would have been obvious he was a changeling as soon as he opened those eyes. "How have you survived all this time?"

"My father—my *real* father—knew my mother was pregnant before he died. He spelled a piece of string for her to tie around my wrist or ankle. It glamoured my eyes and fangs—the rest of me passes for human. Luckily, I look like my mother, so my appearance was never questioned, and my differing eye color was just accepted as an anomaly."

"But you clearly know how to use your magic now," I push. "Someone must have taught you."

There is an innate desire to use the magic one is born with. All witch and fae children begin to test out their abilities without ever being taught, but only for minor things. To do things like create fire with no heat or smoke . . . that requires knowledge and training.

"Someone did," he agrees, "but I'm not willing to reveal who at this time."

I think about everything that's occurred so far in our interaction. The prince knows who I am and that Talon is a cursed werewolf. He also made the comment about the party being Talon's scene, which means he knows at least something about Talon's life, and he knows that we are mates.

Some fae are quite sensitive to magic, so it is possible he sensed my witch magic, although that seems unlikely since I haven't used it here. He might have been able to figure out what Talon is based on the reactions he pulled from them while dancing with me— although cursed werewolves aren't that common. Maybe he felt our bond?

"*Tell them Atotl means the witch no harm.*"

The bones Ryllae used to gain insight had been blessed by Atotl himself. The fallen Fae Sovereign was rattled after the bone reading, and I was only able to interpret some of what they saw.

"*Fate is a gift one cannot outrun.*"

"Fuck me. You're *him*. Ryllae's fated mate." I shoot up from my chair. "Is it just the god of wisdom pulling your strings? Or have the others gotten involved too?"

The prince just smiles. "Tell me where Ryllae is, and I'll help you rescue your sister."

My heart stills. If anyone can help me find my sister, it's the bloody Eleoyn prince. Hells, he could probably just order the mage guards to release her.

But Ryllae is my *friend*. And they have gone to great lengths to avoid ever meeting their fated mate after their disaster of a first love.

"I'll sweeten the deal." He leans forward, and half of his face is lit by the fire while the other half is cast in shadow. "I'll request that the gods dissolve the mating bond between you and the wolf, if you so desire."

For a second, it feels as though my breath has frozen along with my heart. I could save my sister. Talon could go back to their life, unchained to me. Everyone would be happy.

Not you, a voice whispers in my head, but I stomp on it. The prince is offering the solution to everything. It would be so easy . . .

"No." It's like my body unfreezes, and suddenly, my scythe is in my hand and pointed at the changeling prince. "I don't agree with all of Ryllae's choices, but they did *everything* the gods asked of them, and the gods still chose to fuck them over." I call enough of my magic forth that it blazes through the mage spells to make my tattoos glow silver. "I will not add myself to the list of people who have betrayed the fallen Fae Sovereign."

"My time is running out." Caspian leaps to his feet and summons a sword with a black blade. He points it at me, and even from several feet away, I can feel the magic radiating off it. "I'm twenty-nine, but I still look like I'm in my early twenties. People are going to start noticing soon that I'm not aging the way I should."

He's not wrong. Changelings with little to no magic age like humans, but Caspian clearly has magic in spades. It's entirely possible he'll live for a thousand or more years.

Not my fucking problem.

"So leave." I gesture at the room with my scythe. "Or have you grown so accustomed to living as a prince that you refuse to give all this up?"

"I will not run away," he snarls. "There are still fae living in these lands! I can save them! Ryllae can save them! I have no interest in being their mate, but the gods are very clear that we need Ryllae's magic if we're to succeed."

"We?" I laugh ruefully. "Never trust the gods, princeling. Ryllae learned that the hard way. If you want to save the fae, charter a ship and fucking sail them all back to Arandia! They should have left the first time." I shake my head. "There is nothing but death for those who remain in the four kingdoms."

"I don't accept that." Caspian lowers his sword.

"Yeah?" I scoff and plant the end of my scythe onto the floor. "Tell that to your father."

The prince flinches before recovering quickly. "At least I'm trying to do something to help the fae instead of wallowing away in self-pity!"

A cruel laugh spills out of me. "Save the speech. You're trying to save your own skin. The clock is ticking on your birthday and all your secrets being revealed. Imagine the execution party that will be thrown in your honor," I mock before baring my teeth at him. "Ryllae isn't a tool to be used. Not by the gods. And definitely not by a mate who doesn't fucking deserve them."

I sure as fuck won't be the one to sell them out now. Not even for my sister. I'll find a way to save Astria without the prince's help.

Caspian stares at me for a long moment before swearing and tossing the sword towards the couch the way one would a discarded piece of clothing. It vanishes into shadows before it ever hits the cushions.

My eyes widen a bit at that. Shadow magic is a rare talent

amongst the fae. Ryllae is the only other one I've met or even heard of who possesses that ability.

"Just . . . consider what I've requested," Caspian says tightly. "I only want to speak with Ryllae in person. I am not the gods, and if Ryllae is worried about being trapped with a mate, they don't need to be. We might be fated, but nothing says we have to remain that way. All I want from them is to help save the fae—and myself. Then they can continue to live the life of a recluse. I don't fucking care."

Once again, I debate if I should just kill the prince. I mean, he's destined for an excruciating death if he's still here on his next birthday. So, really, it'd be a mercy kill.

Ryllae is a . . . complicated person. On one hand—thanks to having gotten drunk on fae liquor with them one night—I know they like the idea of a mate. Not just a fated mate, but a soulmate. Someone who is their match in every way.

But I also know Ryllae has no intention of ever meeting their mate. The fallen Sovereign lives their life by one rule—if the gods want them to do something, they do the opposite.

I don't want them to ever learn that their mate is a spoiled prince. Sure, maybe he has some aspirations of saving the fae, but I have no doubt he's more concerned about his own hide, and if he really takes the gods at their word, then he is also a fucking idiot.

"You know your expression is practically screaming, 'I'm about to commit murder,' right?" Caspian drawls. Despite his words, he doesn't seem the least bit concerned about me actually killing him.

Ah, the arrogance of youth. I almost want to kill him just to cure him of that.

"Your death would solve a lot of problems." I shrug, not denying it.

He chuckles darkly. "I like you, witch,"

"Can't say the same, prince."

"Lies. Everyone loves me." Between one breath and the next,

his glamour is back in place. "I'm the charming Eleoyn prince, after all."

"You'll make a beautiful corpse," I muse.

He rolls his eyes. "In exchange for sparing my life"—his tone makes it clear he doesn't actually think he's in danger—"I'll grant you a boon this evening."

"Oh?" I eye him warily, not sure if I trust any gifts from him. They likely have strings attached, even if I can't see them.

"I assume you risked coming here tonight because of the mage hunters in attendance, yes?"

I nod. Either he's a good guesser or one of those pesky gods whispered it into his ear.

"Wait here, and I'll have one of them check on you. I don't care what you do to them, as long as you take care of the body afterwards."

I blink.

Caspian smiles slyly. "If you would just work with me, I'd make your life a lot easier. I could have your sister returned to you with a bow wrapped around her head."

"You should be thanking me," I say smoothly. "Ryllae will rip you apart if they ever see you."

"They won't." Caspian moves confidently towards the door.

"How can you be so sure?" I stare after the prince. He might have the gods in his corner, but their loyalty is fickle, and Ryllae is quite possibly the most powerful fae to have ever existed.

The prince looks over his shoulder, and for a few seconds, his glamour drops and he gives me a toothy grin. "Sorry, love, I don't even whisper my secrets during pillow talk, but you're welcome to find me another time and try." He winks at me, and his glamour settles back into place before he strides out the door.

Yep. Definitely should have killed him.

CHAPTER NINETEEN

~

Talon

THICK, humid night air threatens to choke me when I burst out onto a stone balcony just off the main ballroom. It's narrow but wraps around the palace as I stalk down it to get farther away from the music and loud conversations of the party still raging inside.

I tried to follow after Scythe when the prince led her down that hallway, but the guards told me, *"Atotl means the witch no harm."*

I didn't even know what the fuck to do with that, but it was very clear that I couldn't follow after them. Scythe keeps sending me soothing thoughts down the bond, so I have to trust that she is okay. I am definitely not okay though.

When I saw the prince run his hand down Scythe's exposed thigh, I almost lost it. The wolf *did* lose it. I'm lucky I had that failed shift a few days ago and my wolf side isn't as strong as usual; otherwise, I have no doubt it would have happened again right there in the middle of the prince's fucking party for everyone—including the mage hunters—to see.

This fear and irrationality isn't something I'm used to. Sure, I always have this thread of anger underneath everything, but I'm also cool and collected. I do *not* lose my mind in high-pressure situations. I fucking thrive on that shit. The rush of walking that fine line between getting caught and being victorious is something I crave.

Yet here I am, outside, trying to calm both myself and the wolf. Scythe is the one who should be freaking out since she's the fish out of water. I'm used to masquerades and idly chatting with people who would kill me if they knew what I was, but she's spent the last year with only those damn panthers for company and doing nothing but hunting down trespassers in her forest. It was supposed to be me supporting her, not the other way around.

I realize I've stopped walking and I'm just rubbing my chest, right over my heart—where the mating mark is—and I drop my hand away. Scythe needs me to get it together. My sister needs me to do the same. Our plan might have spun out of control, but we can still recover from this. I'll go back inside, mingle with the crowd, and see if I can keep an eye on our quarry until Scythe comes back out.

The image of the prince's hand on her thigh flashes to the forefront of my mind. I'm not sure if it's the wolf or me who lets out a growl. I shake my head, clearing the image away.

I don't know what game the prince is playing. Scythe is absolutely gorgeous, but it felt like he was taunting me. It doesn't make any sense. It's not like he knows who or what I am.

I frown. Does he?

No, I'm reading too much into it. Scythe looks absolutely stunning. He probably just wanted her and wanted to rub it in my face that he could take her away from me so easily, but I know my vicious little witch. She wants *me*. The prince doesn't stand a chance, and if he tries to force anything, she'll bury her scythe in his neck without a second thought, which means I need to be inside and ready to run if she walks out with blood splattered on that pretty dress.

A grin spills across my lips, and I feel the wolf rumble in contentment at the thought of her wearing the prince's blood. Just as I start to turn around to head back inside, I sense the presence of another. My thumbs hover over my palms, not calling the daggers forth yet, but ready to do so if I need to. Then I fix a happy grin on my face, one that someone would have after guzzling down several glasses of the prince's expensive wine, and finish turning to face the newcomer.

A mage hunter, but it's not the one who was trying to get a dance with Scythe. This man wears no mask, and the only jewelry he has on are some rings and a silver pin with the emblem of the mage hunters on the collar of his black button-up shirt. He's dressed the same way mage hunters always dress. I'd bet my life that this is the leader, Stelian.

I'd also gamble on it not being an accident that he followed me out here. The question is . . . why? Is he simply curious about the person who came on the arm of the woman the prince swept away? Or does he suspect something? Killing him will lead to questions, but I may not have a choice. If it comes down to that, I'll have to at least try to get some answers out of him before slitting his throat.

"Hello, friend." I slur my words a little while taking a slightly wobbly step towards him. "Come to join me on this lovely evening? Don't suppose you brought any wine with yo—"

"Your sister is going to be dead in three days." He throws the words out casually, like he's just informed me I have a stain on my shirt.

I stop in my tracks and go completely still, my fingers curling but not calling the blades forth—yet. He stands a few feet away from me, an easy arrogance written across his face, and his dark blue eyes watch me as he patiently waits for me to come to terms with what he just said.

The mage hunter knows who I am, and he wants to chat. Fine.

"Interesting way to open negotiations," I drawl and take a step back so I can lean against the wall, letting my mouth curve into an unconcerned smile even as my heart hammers within my chest. Here's hoping this mage hasn't charmed his hearing to be better than that of an average human.

"You'll find that I like to get to the point, Talon." He pauses for a moment, as if to see if using my name unnerves me at all. It doesn't. The bastard already has my sister, and it's no surprise that Eldrin told him my name. Whether or not Eldrin told him I am a cursed werewolf is a better question. When I don't react, he continues, "You know, I almost killed your sister immediately—it was the witchkin girl I was after—but I've learned over the years that having backup plans is important."

"Do you have a backup plan to get out of this alive?" I ask lightly. "Because from my point of view, I'm talking to a dead man right now."

"Please." He laughs. "I've received threats from fae, rogue mages, and all sorts of creatures over the years. They've all failed. I don't think a human thief is going to succeed where they didn't."

So Eldrin didn't tell him what I am. Good to know.

"How about you get to that point now?"

"It's the witch I want." He shrugs. "I was planning on using her sister to lure the bitch out—I've lost too many hunters to her forest—but Eldrin passed along a message that you were going to get the witch. So you actually got her out of those damn woods for me."

That treacherous bastard didn't suffer enough. Panic fills me, but I fight to keep it off my face. Did the prince lure Scythe into a trap? No. That doesn't make any sense. This asshole wouldn't be out here talking to me if they already had Scythe captured, and I can still feel the mating bond, so she's alive.

"I'm well aware that the Witch of the Woods walks amongst us this evening," he goes on as if he read my thoughts. Maybe my mask is slipping. "Did my research on you after Eldrin told me about your connection to her. He really didn't like you by the way. Also told us about your heists and how you dress for them. That mask of yours is a bit of a giveaway, and you do have a certain . . . *presence* about you. Walking Scythe in here as her true self was a stroke of genius, just your bad luck that I recognized you and knew she was in your company as the two of you hunted for your sisters."

I don't say anything because, for once, I don't know how to play this.

"Unfortunately for me, I don't have enough men here tonight to take the witch down, and if I damage this palace, that useless prince will likely call for my head—and his father might let him since he hasn't managed to bring another heir into existence. Despite all his fucking around, he doesn't even have a bastard to trot out, so I'm a bit stuck, you see."

"My heart bleeds for you," I say flatly.

"Oh, don't be like that," Stelian chides. "I have an offer for you. I'll tell you where your sister is being held—you can even have the witchkin she's in love with—and you just have to make sure the witch takes the left tunnel."

"The left tunnel?" My voice comes out a little raspy as the wolf grows more irate with this conversation.

Stelian nods. "They're being held underground. You'll enter through the main tunnel, then there will be a fork. You go to the right, save the girls, go home. It's not like I'm asking you to do anything to the witch. Based on the way you've been looking at her this evening, I'm guessing you've grown . . . attached, but who is more important to you? Her or your sister?"

Suddenly, it feels like my rapidly beating heart seizes and a fiery pain burns inside my chest. Ravyn is my responsibility. I promised our parents I'd always take care of her. I love her. She's my little sister. If you asked me a week ago if I would sacrifice Scythe for her, it would have been an easy choice. Sure, I've been obsessing about her for over a year, but that was over the *idea* of her. I might have felt unsettled by the choice and had some regret . . . but I would have done it.

But now . . . now I *know* Scythe. She's my fucking mate, and with every hour that passes, the bond between us feels more and more right. The thought of betraying her makes something tear inside me, but Ravyn . . . I can't let my sister die.

I stiffen when Stelian steps towards me, ready to summon one of my daggers, but he stops with some distance between us and holds out a piece of paper. "Directions to where they're being held. If you accept my offer, simply spill your blood onto the sigil at the bottom. I've already added mine." He holds up his hand, displaying a cut across his index finger. "There is a simple contract that will bind us, and then the map will be revealed."

Fuck. He really thought this through. Mage contracts are unbreakable once all parties have agreed by spilling their blood on the sigil. The penalty for breaking the agreed upon terms varies but usually involves a gruesome death.

"Think about it," Stelian says smugly. I snatch the paper from his hand, and he moves back with a smile. "Though it will take you about a day and a half to get there. On the third day, I'll kill your sister, so I suggest you don't delay too long."

The paper shakes in my hand as I feel the wolf rise. I turn my head slightly away from the mage, casting my eyes down so he can't see the change in them. If I try to speak now, I know it will come out as a barely controlled growl. I might not be able to shift into a wolf, but lupine blood still runs through my veins. I'm stronger and faster than any human. He doesn't know that though, and I can't risk him finding out. There has to be a way to save my sister and protect Scythe.

Stelian starts to turn to head back inside before pausing, and I can feel his gaze on me even though I don't look up. "Also, just so you know, your sister and the witchkin are in a cell primed for fire magic. If you fail to sign the contract or if the witch takes so much as one step down the right hand pathway, you'll find out what your sister's dying screams sound like as she burns to ashes."

Ten minutes later, the fury subsides enough for me to think again and look at the paper Stelian handed me. We can probably make it to where the girls are being held in a day, thanks to how fast Draco travels. The contract at the bottom is straightforward and to the point. I have to agree to get the witch to go down the left pathway, and I have to swear that I haven't informed her in any way of this plan nor will I in the future.

Which squashes my hopes of being able to just tell Scythe all of this, because I know she would choose to save her sister's life. I would do the same for Ravyn. For a brief moment, I think maybe I can plan to have her walk into the trap but then escape once I have the girls safe, but if I sign this . . . I won't be able to warn her. She'll believe I betrayed her. What if I can't rescue her in time? What if she dies believing I fucked her over?

"*Fuck!*" I slam my palm against the stone wall. There has to be some way out of this. One that doesn't require me to betray my mate and send her to her death. I doubt Stelian will kill her right away. He and the Eleoyn king will want to get information from her about not only her forest but the mountain paths that lead to the Wilds beyond them. They will torture her for the information, and when she fails to tell them—because I have no doubt Scythe will spite them until the end—they'll torture her for fun.

The execution of the Witch of the Woods—of the Last Guardian—would be an event like no one has ever seen before in Eleoyn.

And it would be my fucking fault.

"There has to be a fucking way!" I snarl, and my hand hits the wall again, causing the skin on my palm to sting. "You're smarter than this!"

"I mean if you're hitting a wall . . . are you smarter than whatever *this* is?"

I whirl, shoving the folded-up piece of paper into my pocket. The wolf and I are really slacking to let two people sneak up on us on this fucking balcony. An androgynous person stands six feet away from me. Gold earrings dangle from their right ear, their eyes a bright golden brown, and long black hair that is shaved on one side tumbles over their shoulder in a shiny, dark wave.

They're not wearing the symbol anywhere I can see—and mage hunters are loathe to take off those fucking pins. I've never seen any mage hunters that use the Tovenian custom of jewelry to denote gender either.

Party guest? Their clothes are fancy. I frown. They're actually dressed a bit like me. Only, their corset vest has gold threading instead of silver and they're wearing something like a skirt over their pants. The sheer, dark gold fabric flows out from underneath the vest over their black pants to end at the knees.

No mask though.

"Apologies, friend," I say briskly and step away from the wall to stride past the stranger so I can head back inside. "'fraid I'm not in the mood for whatever brought you out here." I need to find Scythe. Come up with some excuse about how I found the location of our sisters. We can get the fuck out of here, change, then grab Draco and—

The stranger steps into my path, stopping me in my tracks. "The witch requires your help."

For the second time on this damn balcony, I have to avert my eyes quickly as the wolf rises. *Calm the fuck down,* I order. The wolf growls back, but I feel them settle.

"What do you mean?" I raise my gaze to look at the stranger once I'm confident my eyes haven't changed color.

"The beautiful woman who came with you this evening?" they prompt. "Dressed as the Witch of the Woods?"

Right. They must be one of the prince's servants.

"Ah, my companion." I give them a pleasant smile that I suspect is more like a baring of teeth, but I seem to have lost my ability to shuffle through expressions like cards. "We got separated a while back. I was actually just coming in to find her."

"Allow me to escort you. She's still in one of the private rooms."

The wolf growls, but I swallow it down before it can spill from my lips. "Lead the way," I say tightly, trying not to think about what Scythe has been up to all this time. Did the prince make a move on her? Did she have to kill him and is now freaking out about it? I should have figured out a way to follow her into that damn room, then Stelian wouldn't have been able to corner me and make that wretched offer.

Of course, if the mage hunter hadn't done so, he still would have come up with some other way to set a trap. It was my idea for us to attend this party in such a grand fashion. If I hadn't been so fucking arrogant, we might have been able to slip in here without Stelian ever being aware.

This is all my fucking fault. I have to figure out a way to fix it.

I fall into step beside the stranger as we make our way down from the balcony. A gold coin appears in their hand, and they start flipping it in the air. Catch. Flip. Catch. Flip. It distracts me for a moment because they're not watching the coin. Their gaze is on me.

"I like the jackal mask." Golden brown eyes flow over the mask to my earrings with a smirk. "Azdall would approve. Although, I do believe they prefer gold over silver." They continue to flip the coin and catch it with unnerving accuracy.

"I prefer silver to gold." I shrug and quicken our pace. Now isn't the time to get distracted by the prince's strange servants and their parlor tricks.

"How *interesting*." I glance back at them and almost trip when I see that the gold coin they're flipping . . . is now silver.

I must remember the color wrong. No, it was definitely gold. Slight of hand maybe? I frown as I think it over.

We step back into the ballroom, and I forget about the coin as we skirt around the edges to avoid the crowd. I don't see Stelian or any of the other mage hunters. To my surprise, the prince is out here. He's drinking wine straight from the bottle and speaking with a group of pretty young things. Strange. Why would he leave Scythe all alone in the room?

Prince Caspian's mismatched eyes connect with mine from across the ballroom, and he raises his bottle in a salute before returning his attention back to his sycophants.

I decide that if I ever have the opportunity, I'm going to punch him in the face. Twice.

The hallway the prince took Scythe down earlier comes into view. There are now four guards stationed at the start of it, standing against the wall, two on each side. My escort takes us behind a large decorative wall erected behind the tables of food, momentarily hiding us from view.

"Here." Silver flashes in the air, and I catch the coin the stranger tosses to me. "Hold on to that for a moment."

A faint tingle runs across my skin where the coin is pinched between my fingers. It doesn't feel malicious, but I can feel it spreading throughout my body. We reach the hallway, and the guards don't react to us at all. They don't even look at us, which is strange. I expected the coin-flipping stranger to maybe explain that they were escorting me on orders of the prince, but it's as if the guards don't see us at all.

I glance at the coin as we make our way down the hall. One side of it has a stylized eye that is closed. I flip it over. A jackal head stares up at me.

It can't be. There is no way I'm in the company of a fae god right now.

"Here we are." We come to a stop in front of a closed door

around the corner, and I stare at the stranger, whose eyes look a lot more gold than brown right now.

"Are you really—"

"I'll take that." They cut me off, and the coin disappears from my fingers. "By the way, you might find the middle portrait on the left wall of interest."

"What?" I glance at the door and then back at the stranger, but empty space greets me. I dart back around the corner only to jerk back. The stranger is gone, and the four guards are still stationed at the far end of the hallway. None of them call out, and I don't hear any footsteps, which means they didn't see me.

I rub my forehead as I stride back over to the door we stopped at. Did I really just meet Azdall in the flesh? And if I did, what in the fuck is a fae god doing here? A chill runs up my spine. They might have helped me in this moment, but the gods had turned their backs on all the fae who had stayed in Malovias.

Just because I like the idea of Azdall, doesn't mean the god won't fuck me over if it's in their best interest. The gods are not to be trusted. I reach for the door to see what surprise I'll find next. Hopefully, things are going better for Scythe than they are for me this evening.

CHAPTER TWENTY

~

Scythe

I FROWN at the blood soaking into the silver fabric of my dress. A hum flows from my lips to heal the deep gash the mage hunter managed to open across my abdomen. If I had been a second slower, he would have disemboweled me. As it is, Kayla's beautiful dress is ruined, between the blood and the tear across the middle.

Oh well. It's not like I'd have another opportunity to wear it. No use for dresses in my forest.

The hunter in question glares at me from where he sits on the floor with his back against the wall. I used the same scythe trick on him that I did to pin Talon to the bed, so he's not going anywhere. His attempt at glaring daggers through me isn't working, thanks to the swelling in his right eye and his nose being bloody and crooked.

After Caspian left, this asshole came strutting in. I'm guessing the prince told him I was waiting for him in this room and he was eager to make my acquaintance.

I had some anger to work out, so I punched him several times in the face because I was pissed off and hitting something felt good.

It was a foolish move, because he went for the kill, which was how I ended up with a blade across my gut.

"You're going to die a slow and painful death, witch," he snarls when I finish healing myself. "And I'm going to be there to watch every second of it."

"Unlikely." I snort. "You're not going to survive this night."

He gives me a sharp smile. "So you don't deny that your death will be painful then?"

I shrug. "Death comes for us all. I doubt I'll pass painlessly in my sleep." The hunter probably thought his comment would unnerve me, but I grew up in the forest and have a front row seat to how brutal nature can be. A peaceful death would be nice, but given the life I live, that seems unlikely.

The hunter flinches when I walk over to crouch before him, and he strains against the roots. There is no give to them. It's my turn to smile.

"If I were you, I'd be more worried about the painful death in *your* near future and maybe pray for an easy one instead."

"You'll get *nothing* from me," he spits. "My fellow hunters will notice me missing and—"

The door swings open, and I whirl, a song already dancing on my tongue, but relief flows through me when Talon quickly walks into the room and closes the door. I scan them quickly from head to toe. Unlike me, they appear perfectly fine. They must have had a less interesting past hour.

I can feel the moment they see the torn and blood-soaked fabric. The wolf roars in my mind at the same moment Talon's fury burns down the bond.

"Who the fuck did that to you?"

Faster than I can track, they're standing in front of me, moving aside the torn fabric to look at my now-healed skin, and only a little bit of their rage abates at seeing I'm already mended.

"It's fine. *I'm* fine." I gently tip Talon's face so their dark eyes meet mine. A yellow sheen rolls over them. "The mage hunter who ruined Kayla's dress is there if you want to kick him."

"I don't give a fuck about the dress," they growl, but their eyes skim down it once more. "Okay, maybe I care a little about the dress, but only because I had plans to rip it off you later."

"It'll have to wait." I drop my hand away from their face and look at the guard. "We have to figure out how to get him out of here so we can question him properly. I have . . . a lot to tell you."

This room might be soundproof, but I can't be sure how much time the prince will buy us, and I desperately want to get out of these walls. Talon needs to know about the prince's connection to Ryllae as well. I don't want to betray the former Fae Sovereign's trust, but I also believe Talon will do right by them. The prince seems like the type of person to use Talon's ignorance against them, and if they don't know about the prophecy between Ryllae and their fated mate, the prince might be able to get information out of Talon without them realizing it.

We came here tonight to get answers about our sisters, but I can't help but feel like we've stumbled into something so much bigger than us. Unease crawls up my spine.

When Talon doesn't answer, I look up to find them staring at the mage hunter. I expect to see a bloodthirsty gaze, but instead, it's more like they're not even seeing the mage in front of them. Their dark brows are bunched together, and I sense trepidation down the bond . . . and guilt.

"Did something happen?" I ask carefully.

Their expression instantly smooths out, and the bond between us goes quiet. "No. Let's get him out of here."

I chew on my lip. Talon is lying to me. I don't know how I know it, I just do. It'll have to wait though because getting out of this palace with our captive is the priority.

I move towards the outer wall and glance out the window. The stairs we went up when we entered the palace are considerably higher than the ones we went down to get into the main ballroom. We're on the second story. Talon and I could jump, but it would be cumbersome to carry the mage while doing that, not to mention the grounds are well patrolled. It's not like we could walk through one of the gates with the mage draped over our shoulder, and scaling the stone wall around the palace would be a problem.

Something clicks behind me, and I turn to find Talon standing in front of a huge portrait of some stuffy monarch. Then they push on the portrait, and that section of the wall springs forward on hinges. A secret door.

"How'd you know that was there?" I hurry over as Talon swings the door all the way open to reveal a passage.

"Noticed the seam in the wall," they say with a shrug. "A lot of nobles have hidden stairwells and such in their homes. Makes sense the prince would have one too."

I look away from the dark passageway to Talon, but they've already stepped back to collect the hunter. It makes sense that they would know about the peculiarities of nobles' homes, but this is awfully convenient, and this palace was built by the fae. No mere noble can boast about living in a place that is fae built.

Something is wrong.

"Talon," I start, "are you sure nothin—"

"Can you release him?" they cut me off and wave a hand at my scythe wrapped around the mage.

I brush my fingers three times over the silver ring on my pinky, and the scythe with all its roots vanishes from around the hunter. Talon ponders him for a moment before stomping down on his ribs. Several times. Something cracks, and the hunter screams, but it's cut off when Talon hammers a fist to the mage's jaw. His head snaps to the side, and he spits out a glob of blood, then he glares up at Talon.

"You don't *ever* touch her."

The mage just lets out a cruel laugh. Talon punches him again, and this time, the hunter slumps over, knocked out cold. They reach down and pick the man up, slinging him over their shoulders.

"Let's get the fuck out of here." Talon ducks into the dark secret passageway without looking at me and vanishes out of sight.

The unease grows. I jog over to the fireplace and sing out a melody before shoving my hand into the flames. Then I pull my hand back, palm up and fingers pointed towards the ceiling with a bright ball of fire hovering above them. The fae magic within the flames flows over my skin in a welcoming embrace, and I hurry back over to the passageway, stepping into the darkness and closing the door behind me.

Talon's wolf howls in my mind. It's not a sound of victory at finding our quarry though . . . It feels like sorrow.

"THIS WILL WORK," Talon says half an hour later when they unceremoniously drop the mage hunter. Dust rises from the floorboards, and the mage groans as he stirs to consciousness.

We didn't speak as we made our way through the secret passage. It snaked down the palace before leveling out for what I guess was a quarter of a mile. Then we hit a dead-end. It took Talon a few minutes to find the latch that released the hidden door. It seemed odd that they'd found it so fast in the palace but struggled in the tunnel. I added it to the list of things that don't make sense.

The room we entered after the passageway was a basement in an abandoned house, and now we are on the third floor. I don't love that we're in the building where the secret passageway ends, but I also don't think the prince is going to follow us or send anyone after us. He's playing his own game, and our capture serves him no benefit. Taking the mage hunter anywhere else risks exposure.

Those are my reasons for staying here. I have no idea what Talon's are.

Just as I'm about to grab Talon by the throat and demand they tell me what the fuck is going on inside that head of theirs, the mage starts to stir.

Talon jerks off their belt and uses it to bind the mage's hands behind his back to a support beam running up through the middle of the room. I took all the mage's rings off on the journey here. He'll still be able to use magic, but I'll sense it if he tries, and mage spells aren't particularly fast. It's why they prefer to enchant rings and other items so they have spells at the ready.

I call my scythe forward and close my fingers around the worn wood staff, taking comfort in it. Talon has mostly cut off their emotions from going down the bond, and based on the way their jaw flexes, it's tiring them out. I'm a little rusty, but I've had more experience with controlling what flows down the mating bond, so it's not as difficult for me. That doesn't stop it from feeling wrong though. It's like the river that is meant to flow continuously between us has been dammed on both ends and the water is straining to break through.

There's too much pressure building inside me right now. So many things that I need to do.

Find and rescue my sister.

Break the bond and Talon's curse.

Warn Ryllae about the prince.

Should probably give Talon a heads up about that situation too . . .

Speaking of which—

Figure out what the fuck Talon is up to.

The mage's blue eyes flutter open, and he takes in his surroundings before looking at Talon and then me. We're both still wearing our masks. I'm itching to take mine off, but Talon still has theirs on, so I leave mine on as well. The mage isn't leaving this room alive, so I'm not worried about him identifying us, but I'm also well aware of the fact that I can't hide what I'm feeling and the mask will help with that a little.

"Where are our sisters?" I ask, not taking my eyes off the mage as I spin my scythe out of habit.

"You'll have to be more specific." His voice has a bit of a nasal tone to it on account of the broken nose. "We've taken a lot of people's sisters over the years."

"Not a lot of witchkin though." My blade continues to slice through the air at the same steady pace. "And let's not play games —you know who I am."

"Can't believe I almost fucked you." He grimaces, and I roll my eyes. He didn't *almost* anything.

The mage jerks and screams when one of Talon's daggers sinks into his thigh.

"Talon," I say tiredly, "you almost hit an artery. We can't have him bleeding out."

They roll their eyes before leaning over and ripping the blade out. "I'm well aware of the vital spots, witch." Talon wipes the blade on the mage's pants before straightening and pointing the dagger at him. "And keep in mind that we might need your tongue, but I could just as easily have aimed three inches to the left. You don't need your dick for this conversation, and I'm more than happy to send you into the afterlife without it."

"I don't know where your sisters are, and even if I did, I wouldn't tell you shit." The mage leans back against the thick wood beam. "You can carve into me all you want; I won't betray my fellow hunters."

Talon looks like they're eager to take out their aggression on the mage, but I know hunters. They're hard to break. He'll scream and swear while we cut him apart piece by piece, but he won't tell us what we need. Pain alone won't get him to loosen his tongue.

But fear and panic will.

I start to hum. The melody stretches out with long and dark

notes, and the mage pales. I give him a small, close-lipped smile while I keep up the song.

"We're in the middle of a city, witch," he says quickly. "There are no wicked beasts to call on here, and we're three stories up. No roots for you to summon either."

Talon cocks their head and looks at a wall to our left. I keep humming.

Then the sound of scratching fills the empty space, punctuated by my constant hum and the mage's panicked breathing.

"Whatever you're doing, it won't work," he insists even as he struggles to break free. I point my scythe at him and adjust my song. Then the silver blade melts away, and the handle splits apart into multiple branches that stretch out to pin down the mage's legs and push his body against the beam to further secure him.

"You're right." I weave the words in between my melody. "The city is so different from my forest."

The scratching in the walls grows louder as hundreds of small creatures try to break through. Talon steps towards the wall and studies it.

"No sharp-clawed predators." I crouch down so I can look the mage in the eye. "No venomous serpents." The mage is almost hyperventilating now, his previous defiance weakening. He knows what's coming. "You know what there are a lot of in cities?" Talon slips the tip of their dagger into a gap in the wall and starts to pry a board forward. I smile widely at the mage. "*Rats.*"

The board falls away from the wall and bounces off the ground, and Talon steps back as hundreds of rats flood out. A wordless song pours from my lips, and the rodents rush over to the mage, covering him like a flood blankets a grassy plain.

He lets out a bloodcurdling scream as they bite and claw their way into his body. Talon moves to crouch next to me, watching the scene unfold with fascination.

I shift my song back to a soft hum, and the rats immediately stop biting the mage, but they don't disperse. A few start cleaning their now-bloody paws.

"Did you know a group of rats is called a mischief?" I hold my hand out, and a large rat with dark brown fur jumps onto my palm. Then I lift my hand and pet her fuzzy head as she twitches her nose at me. "This is more like a swarm. There are multiple family groups here that were kind enough to answer my call."

"Get them the fuck off me!" The mage strains against his bindings, but nothing budges.

"They're also quite hungry," I continue like the mage hasn't spoken. "There are quite a few young ones here and more back in the nests. It's a lot of mouths to feed."

"I didn't realize they would eat people," Talon muses.

"They're opportunists." I shrug. "Food is food."

A pained sound slips from the mage when two of the rats start play fighting and tumble over an exposed area on his thigh with a significant chunk of skin missing. Most of the bites across his body are shallow and spread out, but there are a few places where some of the rats really dug in. Nothing is even close to life-threatening, but I'm sure it all hurts.

"Sometimes, my panthers will eat hunters alive." I lower my hand so the big female rat can hop back down to join the rest of her mischief. "The hunters never last long—usually only five or ten minutes before they die of shock or blood loss. Rats are quite a bit smaller though, so you might last for hours."

"You're fucking sick!" Leather creaks as the mage tries to pull his hands free. "This is why you all deserve to die! We're just cleaning up the fucking garbag—"

He flinches when my hand snaps out to rip the silver chain from his neck. I spotted it when he was struggling to break free the first time. I ponder the charms hanging from it.

A small amount of Talon's feelings leak through the bond. Disgust. They recognize what these are too.

The mage hunters are always men, but anyone can be a mage.

They're simply humans with a gift for magic. Why some humans are born with the ability to manipulate magic and others aren't, nobody knows, but only the mage hunters of Eleoyn care about gender. Even the fucked-up mages in Sekaria don't give a shit.

It's well-known that many mage hunters take a particularly sick delight in hunting down members of Obscuras who are women. Young women especially. The deaths of the rebel mages at the Eleoyn mage hunters' hands never come quick enough; they suffer for weeks.

Some mage hunters have taken to hanging little charms on necklaces or sewing the symbols into their vests of how many Obscuras they personally have killed. Clover for men, roses for women, and lilies for the nonbinary and genderfluid.

A dozen small silver roses hang off this chain.

"Quick death," the mage says in a rush. "I tell you where the girls are, and you put me out of my misery."

"I'll know if you lie," I say tonelessly.

He holds my gaze for a long moment before his eyes dart to the necklace hanging between us. He winces when Talon's dagger pricks the underside of his chin.

"Where are our sisters?"

"You swear," the mage rasps, his eyes now on Talon, "you'll grant me a quick death. Slit my throat. Stab me in the heart. I don't care."

"It's more than you deserve," Talon growls. "But we have places to be."

I start humming low enough that it's barely audible. The fae can sense lies; despite the fae blood that runs in my veins, I don't have that gift, but the hunter doesn't know that. The tattoos on my arms glow faintly.

"Speak," I command before humming again.

The mage hisses when one of the rats chomps on his leg. "Cave system," he pants and proceeds to describe the area and where the cave is located. I only catch the name of a town, but the rest of it is meaningless to me. Talon's mouth hardens into a flat line, and they catch my eye, jerking their head in a nod. They must recognize the location.

We step away from the mage and move to the other side of the room. "He could be lying," I murmur.

"Maybe," Talon says doubtfully. "But I know that area. It would make sense that the mage hunters use it to hold captives."

I chew on my lip. If it turns out the hunter is lying and we kill him, then we did all this for nothing, but it's not like we can bring him with us. He'd be too difficult to control, plus we'd increase our chances of being seen by other mage hunters.

Talon's thumb brushes against my lip, and I stop chewing on it. "It's where we have to go," they say, drawing my gaze. There is no hint of deception in their dark eyes. Maybe I've been imagining the distance between us. This night has been . . . a lot.

"Okay," I say slowly. "Do we need to wait until morning to leave?"

"No." Talon shakes their head and drops their hand. "It's a day's ride, and I know some back roads we can take, so we can leave tonight after we change and grab our stuff."

"Let's take care of our friend then." I look back to where the mage warily watches the rats milling about around him. "How attached are you to that belt?"

"I can get another one."

"Good." Then I sing a long note, and the rats go still before they all turn their heads towards the mage.

"You promised!" he screams and frantically tries to break free. The wood of my scythe creaks but holds him.

"Technically, I only said that we had places to be." Talon's eyes turn hard as they stare at the mage.

"And I promised you nothing." I toss the necklace onto the floor next to him. "Did any of them beg for a quick death? Did you make them false promises?"

The mage starts to chant, and I feel their magic gather. A song rips from my lips in the next second, and the rats dig into the mage's flesh. Then his screams interrupt the chant, and I feel his magic slip away.

I sing for a few more seconds before fading off. They're stirred up enough that they'll keep going. I can feel more of them rising up in the walls, eager to join in on the meal, so I'll wait a few hours before summoning my scythe back.

Talon and I make our way to the stairs as the mage thrashes, trying to knock the rats loose, but there is nowhere for him to go.

And the rats are *very* hungry.

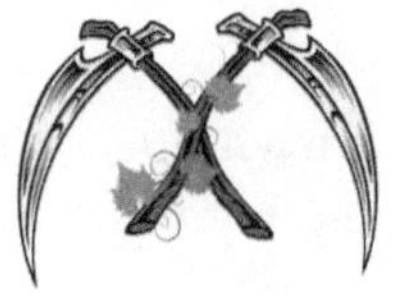

CHAPTER TWENTY-ONE

~

Scythe

"Let's rest here." Talon pulls Draco to a stop, and I slide off the fae horse, only wincing a little when I hit the ground. We've been riding nonstop for some time, but dawn is still a few hours away.

"Shouldn't we keep going?" I glance around the meadow with its sparse trees. It feels like we're exposed, but then we haven't passed another traveler the whole night.

Talon shakes their head before dismounting. "In about two miles, we'll hit a main road. It's usually heavily patrolled because there is another city nearby, and the guard regularly checks the roads around it. At this hour, we'll stand out, but after sunrise, we'll just be another pair of travelers passing through."

I squint towards the west as if I can see our destination. "How much farther do we have to go?"

"Half a day's ride, maybe." Talon settles Draco's saddle and bridle onto the ground, then pulls a brush from our bag and quickly runs it over the horse's silky coat before checking his feet.

I walk over and rub Draco's forehead. He must have sensed the shift in our moods and urgency because the fae horse didn't pull any of his usual shenanigans. "Good boy." I kiss him on the nose, and Draco bumps his head gently against me before trotting off to snack on some grass.

Talon settles down with their back against a large tree, and I take a seat next to them while we watch Draco graze.

"Here." Talon holds out a small, dark red cloth bag . "Best I can do for a meal, I'm afraid."

I take it from them and peek inside. The bag contains a mixture of dried meat and seasoned nuts. I pour out a handful before passing it back. "It's fine."

"Sorry I couldn't find a place by a river." They pluck at their shirt and smell it with a grimace. "Would have been nice to rinse off."

"I think we've gotten into enough trouble rinsing off in rivers," I say dryly, and Talon snorts in response. They acted a little more normal on the ride here, although we didn't speak much. I only felt small flashes of emotion that were difficult to decipher.

Something happened at the masquerade, I'm sure of it, but maybe it had nothing to do with me or our situation?

Talon loosened the stranglehold on their emotions, so some of it is coming down the bond now. It's mostly exhaustion and tension, which makes sense, considering all that's happened to us and what we're going to walk into.

I feel Talon's wolf through the bond too. They've been leaning on it more lately, which I don't mind. I like Talon's wolf, even if I find their existence a bit strange. In all my interactions with the werewolves who live in the Wilds, I never got the impression that their wolves were a separate consciousness within them.

I suspect this is a side effect of the curse. Something about not being able to shift into their wolf form causes the two halves of a cursed werewolf's soul to separate. Will Talon and their wolf merge when it's gone? Unease ripples through me. Talon's wolf feels like their own being, and I don't like the idea of them disappearing.

A low whine echoes through my mind, and I try to send comforting thoughts to the wolf. They don't like the idea of disappearing either. I might not be able to read Talon all that well, bond or no bond, but their wolf is certainly more forthcoming with their feelings. I'll miss them when the mate bond is gone.

"What did you and the prince speak about after he took you into that room?" Talon asks, their tone casual.

My lips quirk up, because even with them clamping down on their emotions, I can still feel the small hint of jealousy. I debate teasing them, but then the reality of who the prince is and what his existence means to our mutual friend comes crashing down.

"The Eleoyn prince is a changeling."

Talon's hand freezes halfway to their mouth. "Come again?"

"And he's also Ryllae's fated mate."

I give Talon a moment to process all that and grab the bag from them. Just as I swallow down another bite of meat, Talon drops their own news on me.

"I met a god at the masquerade."

"What?" I choke and slap my palm against my chest several times. The prince's reference to the god of wisdom pops back into my mind. "Was it Atotl?"

"No." Talon grabs the bag back. "Azdall."

"Fuck." I rub my face. "Ryllae needs to be warned."

"You don't seem all that surprised about the old fae gods being involved," Talon notes.

I worry my bottom lip. It's not my place to tell Ryllae's secrets, but I'm beginning to feel more and more like this entire situation has been manipulated by the gods. Maybe they aren't directly responsible for our sisters being kidnapped, but they saw an opportunity and seized it. I think more about what they did to Ryllae. Maybe they were the ones to whisper a suggestion into Eldrin's ear about selling out his fellow troupe mates.

"It's said that after the Malovian War, the fae retreated back to Arandia after being defeated by the combined forces of the humans and mages." Talon nods at my words. "But that's not exactly true. The humans—and some of the mages—were divided. Many of them didn't want the fae to leave, and many of the fae had mates and families here they didn't want to part with."

"Couldn't they have taken them back to Arandia?"

"No." I shake my head. "There is strong magic all around the continent; you have to have a certain amount of magic to walk through it. Humans do not, nor do most mages."

"So the fae who married humans or mages were forced to choose between leaving them behind . . . or staying."

"Most chose to stay," I say softly.

"When the witches returned to Arandia . . ." Talon glances at me. "They couldn't bring the witchkin, could they? That's why you chose to stay. You wouldn't leave Astria. But your asshole mate —he left you."

An old ache stabs me in the chest, but I try to keep it off my face and make sure it doesn't snake its way down the bond. "I made my choice, and I don't regret it," I say calmly. "Astria is worth more than he ever was."

The silence stretches between us, and I feel frustration from Talon through our bond before they claw it back and clear their throat.

"So most of the fae with human or mage mates chose to stay . . . and Ryllae stayed with them?" Talon guesses.

"More than that. Ryllae's parents died during the war. Ryllae was only the Fae Sovereign for a year when the decision was made for the fae to return to Arandia. The fae who wanted to stay rallied a force to fight against the Ririthan army and carve out a place for themselves in the southeast kingdom. The gods refused to help. Technically, they can't directly intervene, but that's all bullshit," I snarl, suddenly feeling very angry. "They skirt the rules all the time when it benefits them, but in this case, they chose to do nothing—give no warning."

"That battle . . ." Talon's eyes grow distant like they're remembering something. "It took place on the coastline?"

I swallow and nod, and they continue.

"The Ririthans boast that the bones of thousands of fae litter the beach." Talon's head rests back against the tree. "I always thought it was an exaggeration."

"It's not," I say softly. "The gods did interfere though. Atotl himself lured Ryllae away . . . They had a relationship of sorts. I get the impression it was mostly one-sided. Ryllae loved him and thought the god loved them in return. But Atotl trapped them with magic and walked away. Ryllae listened to the dying screams of their people for hours."

"Why would he do that?" Talon jerks their head forward to stare at me, black eyes glowing with flecks of gold. "Why do that to them?"

"The gods do not like to be defied." Understatement of the century. "And when he told Ryllae to walk away from the rebellion—when Atotl told them to leave it alone—the Fae Sovereign refused. And so Ryllae learned the price for telling the gods no."

"How does the prince fit into all of this?" Something in Talon's tone makes me think they're thinking of killing the prince, and I smile faintly.

"After the battle . . . when their people lay dying on the sand . . ." I close my eyes briefly before opening them once more, clearing my throat. "Atotl told Ryllae that the sacrifice had been a necessary distraction to ensure that the bulk of the fae could get away. But if Ryllae was a good little fae, someday, they and their *fated mate* could rescue what was left of the fae who remained."

"What a fucking prick," Talon growls.

"Ryllae thought the same." My smile turns grim. "They tried to kill the god."

Talon's eyes widen. "Is that even possible?"

"Don't know." I shrug. "Despite their rage and power, Ryllae didn't succeed, but they did swear to never trust the gods again—especially not Atotl."

"I'm pretty certain it was Azdall I saw, but the guards did mention Atotl." Talon frowns. "What's your take on the prince?"

"It's hard to say." I think back on the conversation. "We only spoke for half an hour or so, but I think he buys what the gods are selling. He wanted me to take him to meet Ryllae."

"Why don't the gods just tell him where Ryllae is?"

"Not all the gods were happy with what Atotl did. There were rules set up after the fae returned to Arandia about how much the gods could interfere with things here. Many of the gods blamed everything going to the hells in Malovias on the gods being too involved in the business of humans, mages, and fae to begin with."

I snicker as I remember the story my grandmother told me about a very pissed-off blonde goddess storming through our coven and cursing Atotl's name.

"The gods used to visit the witches frequently, the werewolves too. In many ways, we were seen as neutral in all this. Kruxtia and Erdite were particularly pissed off on Ryllae's behalf."

"The goddesses of retribution and love," Talon muses. "Seems like an odd pair."

"You've clearly never been in love." I say it as a joke, but the amusement fades from my lips at the intensity I find in Talon's eyes. Confused, I quickly look away. "An agreement was struck that the gods would never again directly interfere with those living in Malovias, and Kruxtia and Erdite specifically stated that nobody could force Ryllae's fate."

"I take it you refused the prince's offer?" Talon asks.

"Ryllae is rude and difficult, I'm not even sure if I'd call them a friend, but they've been through enough, and they're important to me," I say evenly. "I do not betray those I care about."

Something flashes down the bond, too quickly for me to interpret what it was. When I look at Talon, their expression is relaxed and their eyes are once again a dark brown as they raise them to meet mine. "We need to warn Ryllae in case the prince figures out where they are some other way."

I study them for another moment, trying to determine what it was I felt, but their face is giving me no clues. I sigh. "Do you have any paper in your bag?"

Talon nods and gets up to fetch the travel bag next to the saddle. Then they pull a folded-up piece of paper from it and walk back to the tree, handing it to me before they sit down.

I unfold the paper and smooth it out. "Can I see one of your daggers?"

Talon brushes their thumb against their tattooed palm—the fae symbol for life— and one of the beautiful, curved blades appears. I pluck it from their hand and slice open my palm before handing it back to them. Talon stares at the blade for a moment before holding it up to their face and licking my blood off it.

Then they wink at me before the dagger vanishes once more, and I realize I stopped what I was doing to watch them lick the dagger clean. A familiar, needy ache starts between my thighs, and the lingering concern about whatever it was I sensed through the bond fades away.

"Okay, that was hot," I admit.

A lopsided grin spreads across their face. "You know most women would have freaked out about that, right?"

"The women you've been with have been human. I'm a witch." I turn my attention back to the paper before I let myself get too distracted.

"True." I feel Talon grab the end of my long braid and twirl it between their fingers. "I like that I don't have to downplay my baser instincts around you."

"I like your baser instincts more than your snobby ones," I say honestly.

They snort. "Such a charmer you are, witch."

I huff out a laugh while holding my bloody palm above the

paper. As the blood splashes across the surface, I start singing. Unlike my usual wordless songs, this one is more like a chant. It's inspired by an old story of a sister fighting her way through a forest to save her older sibling. I don't remember where I originally heard it—definitely not from my mother—but I told Astria the story when she was a babe.

Usually, it's easier for me to draw on my magic and weave it into spells or summonings without words, using the vibes and tones to craft what I want. Yet for some reason, when I create this specific spell, it's the old story that comes to me.

"Over the roots.
Through the trees.
I seek. I seek. I seek."

THE BLOOD on the paper flows until it's covered and I continue chanting. As the blood soaks into the paper, it leaves behind words crafted from my thoughts: warning Ryllae about the prince, the gods meddling. All of it.

"Deep in darkness.
Racing through earth.
I run. I run. I run."

I FEEL Talon hovering next to me, but the disgust I felt from them when we first started traveling is nowhere to be seen. Somewhere along the way, they lost it, and now all I sense is wonder as I pick up the paper and slam it onto the trunk of the tree behind us.

. . .

"Up through the bark.
To the fallen one.
I speak. I speak. I speak."

MY VOICE HITS A HIGHER note on the last word as I command the magic to do as I bid. The piece of paper with my bloody words gets sucked into the dark bark of the tree and vanishes from sight. Then I rest my hand against the trunk and pant slightly.

"Fucking fae magic," I mutter.

Talon rubs my back. "Fae magic?"

"Sort of." I close my eyes and rest my forehead against the back of my hand. "It's the witch version of a fae spell. Even small ones like this take a lot out of me for some reason."

"So, will the note, like . . . show up on their table or something?" Talon keeps rubbing my back and applying just the right amount of pressure. It feels nice to be touched like this. Intimate but also relaxing.

I breathe out a laugh. "No. It'll be on the tree outside their cottage, viewable from the kitchen window. It's how Ryllae and I have always communicated. The paper will appear blank on their end until they use their magic to reveal the words."

"Ah." Talon's hand vanishes, and I instantly miss its warmth. "We should rest while we can. If we keep up a fast pace tomorrow, we'll get to that cave system by late afternoon."

"Alright." I move to lie on the ground in front of the tree, and Talon does the same. Even though we have plenty of space, we end up leaving less than a foot between us. It's like neither of us wants to be farther apart than that . . . but neither of us is willing to close the distance either.

"What do you think Ryllae will do?" Talon asks.

"Honestly?" I close my eyes. "I have no fucking idea."

I GAZE UP at the night sky, seeking guidance from the stars, but they don't answer. They never do.

The elders in my coven used to tell me all the time that I lacked patience. That if I would just settle my mind and *be*, the answers would reveal themselves. They all had different ways of doing this. Some would watch the tides roll in and out, and others would look to the stars.

Talon's breathing evened out as they drifted off to sleep, but it evaded me. Eventually, I gave up and quietly moved away from them and the tree to find a spot with a clear view of the night sky. I've been looking up at the stars for a while now, pondering all my problems while waiting for them to chime in with their infinite knowledge.

"Asshole fucking stars," I mutter.

"You alright over there?" Talon asks from where I thought they were sleeping beneath the tree.

"Fantastic." I scowl up at the stars. They fail to tremble in fear.

Clothing rustles, and then Talon plops down beside me, stretching out and folding their hands behind their head. "I'm not sure picking a fight with the stars is the best use of your energy. You should be sleeping."

"Can't." I shrug. "My thoughts keep bouncing between seeing Astria again, how my forest is doing without me, and breaking your curse—and the mating bond."

Talon goes quiet. I expect them to ask if I've made any progress on breaking either. Or maybe discuss the options for how we'll handle things once we get to where our sisters are being held.

But that's not what they do. Instead, they ask me a question nobody ever has before.

"Does any part of you regret not going back with the rest of the witches?"

"What?" I turn my head towards Talon and find their dark eyes already on me.

"You gave up so much to remain here," they go on. "I swear I'll never tell Astria. I'm just . . . curious."

"I thought we went over this already. Cats are curious. Wolves are stoic."

"That sounds boring."

My lips twitch. "I suppose it does."

"There is a forest in the northwest portion of Eleoyn—nothing like yours, but still a decent size—that I enjoy. Sometimes, when we pass it, I think about what it would be like to stay behind. Let the troupe go on and just live in the woods for a while. I may not be able to shift into a wolf, but I still have the heart of one."

Surprise filters through me, drawing my attention back to them.

"I thought you enjoyed life on the road and in the cities?" Based on how Talon spoke and the stories Vesi and Mattias told me of their many heist adventures, I assumed Talon loved their life. "Not a lot of reason to wear fine clothing and jewelry in a forest."

"Like I need an incentive to look good." Their eyes spark as they grin at me, and I can't help but grin back. "I might even steal some fancy dresses from Kayla just for you. We can have our own ball in the forest. The panthers can come too."

"Pretty clothing isn't really my thing," I say with a snort before I think about it more. "I do kind of like that silver crown of yours though."

"Then I promise to wear it and nothing else for you someday."

I bark out a laugh. "You are ridiculous."

Talon chuckles, and I hope they miss the way I briefly rub my thighs together. Something tells me a naked Talon in only that silver crown is going to grace my dreams at some point.

"There are parts of my life that I enjoy—I don't think I'll ever get over the thrill of pulling off a heist, and I do appreciate nice clothing, expensive wine, and dancing all night with my friends."

I wrinkle my nose. "I really don't see what's so appealing about that."

"You can't judge all parties by just that one." They reach over and flick my nose. I mock biting their finger, and they laugh. "I'll take you to more parties—ones that aren't run by someone as snobby as the prince."

I shake my head, not seeing how I'd ever enjoy parties. Then again . . . it was nice to hang out with Vesi and Mattias while we waited for Talon to wake up. Maybe they're right and it is the people that make parties truly enjoyable. A way to celebrate with friends.

Except I don't have those. Vesi and Mattias are Talon's friends, and very soon we'll have our sisters back. Once Astria and Ravyn are safe, I'll just need to break Talon's curse and the mating bond between us, then I can go home. Despite Talon's talk of the forest that calls to them, I'm not going to delude myself into thinking they see themself living happily in *my* forest—as my mate.

That idea is a dream and nothing more, and I am too old to believe in happily ever afters.

I thought about both the curse and the bond a lot on our ride, since Talon wasn't particularly chatty and we were going pretty fast most of the time. Even without Ryllae's input, I'd suspected what would be required of me to break the curse. Curses always require sacrifices, either to create them or break them.

Usually, when curses are placed on a person or object, that sacrifice could come from anywhere, but bloodline curses—ones that follow each generation—become stronger over time. If I want to break it, I'll need to give up something vital to myself. Many people think that means giving their life, but that is too easy, because while the thought of doing so can be agonizing, once it's done, it's done. Curses cause pain to the people they are placed upon. The sacrifice has to cause pain upon the curse breaker.

Something that lingers.

In my heart, I know what that is, but I'm not willing to even think it just yet.

"I've never regretted staying behind," I say softly and turn my head so I can look at Talon. "Even after Astria left."

Talon moves until they're on their side, propping up their head with a bent elbow, dark eyes flecked with starlight, watching me. "I haven't known Astria long, but I see why my sister fell in love with her. She's so full of passion, it's almost contagious, like everything becomes better as soon as she steps into a room."

"She's always been that way." I smile, but I know it doesn't reach my eyes. "My parents never understood; they only saw a child with no magic."

"What about Vaeril?" There is an underlying growl when Talon speaks the name of my first mate. One that is echoed in my mind by their wolf. "What did he think of Astria?"

"He was polite to her." The fake smile falls from my lips. "I don't think he understood my devotion to her, but he was willing to overlook it because it didn't cause him any hardship during the century we were together."

"You were with him for a century?" A golden sheen rolls over Talon's eyes. "And he just left you?"

"Technically, he broke the bond first and then left."

The muscles along Talon's jaw flex, but they don't say anything. What can they say? Talon will be leaving me too. The dull pain that has been thrumming inside my chest since we started this conversation sharpens.

"My parents, Vaeril, everyone in our coven was so obsessed with magic that they never saw what I did in Astria." I turn my attention back to the stars as heat begins to pool in my eyes. "I was 179 years old when Astria was born. When you live as long as witches do, it's so easy to slip into a haze. Seasons come and go. Years slip by in a blink. It happens so gradually, you don't even realize it. When I was a child, life was full of wonder. I loved my forest and the way it whispered to me." A small, genuine smile crosses my lips.

"'The witch is the forest, and the forest is the witch,'" Talon whispers.

"Yes." I swallow. "I think the other witches forgot that though. The talk of returning to Arandia started a century ago, and they began to pull back from the forest then. There were other changes too. They became more solemn and withdrawn. I did as well."

Tears leak out of my eyes as I lose the battle against them.

"I remember holding Astria the night she was born, after my mother screamed to get her out of the room. She didn't even want to look at her." More tears streamed down the sides of my face. "I bundled her up and climbed to the top of the forest canopy." I raise a hand and point to a cluster of stars. "*Astria*."

"Naming her after a flower constellation is quite fitting." Talon smiles softly. "If anyone was made of starlight and flowers, it would be your sister."

I squeeze my eyes shut for a second, trying to get the tears under control. "I had to beg my mother to nurse her, which she was only willing to do for six months. Aside from that, I took care of her completely. Vaeril tried once to convince me to give her to some humans in one of the nearby towns, but whatever he saw in my eyes made him never bring it up again."

"You know if he was still on this continent, I'd kill him, right?" Talon says casually.

"I'd probably let you," I respond honestly. "It felt so right holding Astria that first night. A few weeks later, she smiled. Then, when she was two months old"—a choked sob slips from my lips —"she laughed, and I laughed with her. My life had become so devoid of joy, and all I'd been doing was going through the motions. I probably would have kept on that way for centuries— maybe even forever—but before she could even speak or walk, she made me laugh. The world suddenly had color again, the flowers became so beautifully fragrant with their rich aromas, and the forest sang to me again for the first time in decades." I open my eyes and turn my head to look at Talon once more. "Is that not magic?"

Talon reaches out and brushes away my tears, but more come because I can't seem to stop now that I've opened the floodgates. Talon moves forward and wraps an arm around my waist, tugging me closer, and I shift until my back is against their chest, then I breathe in their wild and pine-infused scent.

"The witches were blind not to see how wonderful Astria is and that she should be cherished." They nuzzle my hair, and something inside me loosens as the pain in my chest starts to fade, contentment replacing it. I know it's foolish to feel this way in Talon's arms, but I can't help it. My time with them might be running out, so I'll allow myself this last night.

I'm starting to drift off when Talon whispers in my ear, "They were fools to let you go." Then sleep pulls me under, but I swear I hear three more words before the darkness claims me. "You're mine, mate."

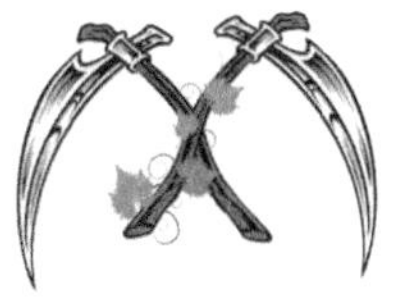

CHAPTER TWENTY-TWO

~

Scythe

"THAT WAS EASY." I toe the body of the mage hunter that's lying on the ground. Well . . . half of it. The other half is resting a few feet away.

"We don't know what's waiting for us inside." Talon wipes their claw-like blades clean on the hunter's tunic. "We have no way of knowing if these ones sent a warning."

"I didn't feel any magic." Which seems a little odd to me, but then we have no idea what we'll find inside. Maybe Stelian wants any interlopers to feel overconfident.

Talon just nods. They've gone back to that silent and tense mood they were in when we initially left the prince's palace. I understand because I'm feeling pretty keyed up myself. While I love the thrill of a good fight, my sister's life is on the line. Though, as soon as we get her and Ravyn free, I'm coming back here and slaughtering my way through every mage hunter who played a role in this. And if Stelian isn't here, I'll hunt him down afterwards. Nobody threatens my sister and lives.

281

"Let's go." Talon sets off towards the tree line. We found the cave entrance earlier, but we doubled back to clear out the mages hiding in the trees so they couldn't close in behind us. It seems a little odd that there aren't more hunters posted out front—or maybe even some human guards—but Talon is right that we don't know what awaits us inside. If we didn't know this cave was here, it would have been be easy to walk past it, and it's far off the road. Having a bunch of people guarding it outside would only draw attention to its existence.

Still, I've hunted in my forest for two centuries, and I've learned to trust my instincts. Something about this doesn't feel right, but I can't exactly stop now. My sister is very likely inside, and I know there is no way I can convince Talon to walk away from saving Ravyn either. I'm sure whatever trap has been laid for us, Talon and I can fight our way out together.

The mouth of the cave is small—barely six feet tall and maybe four feet wide. Between the thick undergrowth around it and the tree that has fallen across the top with its branches hanging down, the opening is well hidden. Talon and I approach it slowly before stepping inside. After half a dozen steps, the ground begins to slope downward. Another half dozen, and it becomes even steeper with darkness spreading.

"I can't see," I murmur and come to a halt. "If I create light, the mages might be able to sense my magic."

Plus, I'm not particularly gifted at creating light. I can do it, thanks to my fae blood, but it's not exactly pretty and sometimes takes an embarrassingly long time.

Talon slips their hand into mine, our fingers intertwining. Then they start to walk, and I follow, trusting them completely to lead me through the dark.

After what feels like an eternity, a dim light comes from ahead. A minute later, we step into a spacious cavern. Moss grows on the cave walls, and the air has a damp, musky odor. Other than the mage lanterns hanging on the walls, there is nothing else in the large, open space.

Opposite the tunnel we entered are two others.

"Left or right?" I stride forward, heading to the right and stopping to peer down it. Unlike the tunnel we came through, these ones have mage lanterns running down the side to light the way.

"I don't want to be here any longer than necessary," Talon says as they come to my side. "You take the left, and I'll take the right."

I frown. "I don't think us splitting up is a good idea." I turn towards Talon, unease rolling through my gut. "Don't you think it's strange that we haven't encountered any more mages? There's no way Stelian left the girls unguarded."

"We have no idea how far those tunnels go," Talon argues. "He probably didn't want to waste hunters being posted here."

I frown, liking this less and less with every second. Maybe we should leave . . .

"We'll each go down the tunnels for a bit just to check them out." Talon grasps my shoulders and moves so they stand in front of me. "If you see or hear anything, just turn around and come back. I'll do the same. We might get lucky; hopefully the hunters guarding the girls aren't paying attention and we can overtake them easily. They must be bored being stuck down here with nothing going on."

"Maybe," I say, even though I don't believe it.

"It'll be okay." Talon cups my face in their hands. Despite their reassurance, I find an intensity and desperation in their eyes that sets me even further on edge. Before I can say anything though, Talon's mouth crashes against mine. They pull me against their body as they kiss me like they want to claim my soul.

And I want to let them.

I'm breathless when Talon pulls back a few seconds later, that desperation in their eyes even stronger. "We need to do this," they rasp and lean forward to press their forehead against mine. "Just wait for me, Cerelia. I will *not* leave you behind."

Then they're gone, disappearing down the right tunnel. I stare after them for a long moment—both my mind and my heart racing—before I call my scythe forth. My fingers run down the handle, brushing against the glyph midway down the staff, and it splits into two smaller weapons that will serve me better in the narrow passageway. With one final glance at where Talon went, I stride forward and step into the left tunnel.

MY FOOTSTEPS SOUND IMPOSSIBLY LOUD as I stalk down the tunnel, and it only increases my anxiety. There are still no signs of any mage hunters. This has to be a trap—the question is, where are they going to spring it?

I step a little closer to the cave wall and run the back of my knuckles along it. I don't feel any traces of mage magic, but that doesn't mean it's not there. Truly skilled mages are quite good at hiding their spells, especially if they're in a dormant state.

Up ahead, the tunnel curves to the left. I pause and kneel, setting my scythes down, and my fingertips push into the hard, compacted earth. The hum that ripples up my throat is faint and barely audible. I close my eyes and let the feedback filter back up into my skin and resonate within my bones. If someone is waiting for me around the bend, they're doing an exceptional job at hiding themselves.

This cave isn't my forest, and my range for detecting life isn't nearly as good, but I'm relatively confident that there is no one within a forty-foot radius. The mages might be able to hide their magic, but I doubt any of them are skilled or powerful enough to hide their life force from me at this short a range. Even my mage friend who made my scythe struggles to do that.

Go around the corner. Evaluate what's ahead. Then decide if I want to carry on or return to that cavern where the tunnels split off and wait for Talon. They still have their emotions clamped down, but I can feel their presence through the bond, so I know they're okay. And I suspect if they run into any serious trouble, some stronger emotions will make it through.

I grab my scythes and rise, spinning them once to loosen my wrists before moving around the corner. The tunnel goes on for another forty feet or so before opening into another cavern. Cautiously, I move forward, stopping when I'm almost there and once again kneeling and sending some of my magic out to seek other life forms.

Nothing.

Gripping my scythes, I move with purposeful strides towards the opening. A song is already on my lips, one that will pull rock from the ceiling to bludgeon whoever I direct it at.

Just as I step into the cavern, I realize my mistake.

I felt *no* life—and that's not possible. Life is everywhere. I should have felt insects at the very least. Maybe some small mammals. But I felt nothing.

"Shit," I growl, most of my ire directed at my own stupidity. I'm better than this, damn it! But I let myself get so distracted by Talon's odd behavior and the strangeness of this entire situation that I didn't see the blaring warning sign in front of me.

Suddenly, mage magic flares, and iron bars slam down, cutting me off from the tunnel. I spin around, looking for the attack, but there is nothing here. The tunnel is the only way in or out. I look up to the ceiling, and my breath freezes in my lungs.

Etched into the center is a five-foot-wide spiral. A dozen lines spin out from it to form their own spirals that create a circle around the one in the middle. The larger spiral in the center starts to glow, and I suddenly feel like someone is stepping on my chest —crushing me.

This is the spell that was made infamous by the Mage Kingdom because it's how they keep traitors contained—the ones they don't execute, anyway.

Arcane mortus. The death of magic.

I didn't realize anyone outside of Sekaria even knew how to do it. *Arcane mortus* is complicated, and the Mage Council guards the workings of the spell viciously. It also requires life to be powered up. Stelian must have used the denizens of the cave to give it the life force it needed.

The spell doesn't work fast. It's used as much for torture as it is to contain the mages that have gone against the council. My friend told me about it during one of the brief times I got him to speak of the Mage Kingdom. He said that the spell typically takes a few days to drain someone of magic. For those particularly strong—like myself—it can take weeks.

On the plus side, it won't kill me. It only requires life to finish the spell. However, it will continue to feed on the trickles of my magic as it returns, which, according to my friend, is quite agonizing.

I may not know the specifics of how this spell works, but something this complex would require a decent amount of time to set up. At least a week. Which meant Stelian must have started as soon as he had Astria in his grasp. But he still needed to guarantee that I would take this path . . .

"You take the left, and I'll take the right."

I squeezed my eyes shut.

"We need to do this."

It hurt. The betrayal. Even if I can't bring myself to blame them for it. There isn't much I won't do for my sister either.

Talon must have made some sort of deal. Had they sought out Stelian? Or had the mage hunter approached them? And was it for just their sister? Or Astria too?

No. Despite all the complications between us, Talon cares for my sister. They have always been supportive of her relationship with Ravyn and there is nothing Talon won't do for their sister's happiness.

Me being in this trap is proof of that.

"Just wait for me, Cerelia. I will not *leave you behind."*

Were those words a lie too?

"Fuck this." I race back to the iron bars. I'm not some damsel in need of rescue. I'll break myself out of here. And if Talon gets the girls out safely, I won't even kill them over this. Maybe just hurt them a little for not telling me. It's not like I wouldn't have walked willingly into this trap if I knew the godsdamned plan.

My gaze narrows at the symbols carved into the iron bars. These ones, I don't recognize. "What type of nastiness do you have in store for me?" Cautiously, I extend one of my scythes towards the bars. The symbols glow a bright purple, and black flames erupt. I leap back, and the mage fire disappears.

Okay. Not going out that way.

I look up to the ceiling again. Maybe I can collapse enough of it to disrupt the spell? Or I can do my best to ignore the agonizing pain in my chest, concentrate on breaking through the rock around the doorway, and just cut a new path to that tunnel, bypassing the iron bars.

My gaze falls back to the space beside the tunnel entry. I'll only need to carve out five or so feet. Stone is difficult to work with, but I can do it.

I have no idea what will happen if I directly attack the stone that has the magic-draining spell carved into it. It likely has some sort of defense built into it because surely I'm not the only one who thought of fighting back that way.

I can work through the pain.

My scythes vanish back into my ring. I won't need them for this. A pained groan slips from my throat, and I rub my chest. "Ignore it," I command myself.

I step closer to the cavern wall, a safe distance away from the iron bars so that I hopefully won't activate the black flames again. A deep, rumbling song starts to pour from my lips as I hold my hand out, palm facing the rocky surface.

The grinding of shifting stone fills the cavern. I can do this. I just need to concentra—

My knees slam into the earth, and my song becomes nothing but a blood-curdling scream as more symbols flare a bright gold on the cavern floor. It feels like I'm being burned alive from the inside. Despite letting go of my magic, the spell keeps attacking me until it's too much.

I collapse entirely, my head slamming into the hard floor. Then, there is nothing but darkness.

CHAPTER TWENTY-THREE

~

Talon

EVERY STEP I take down this tunnel feels wrong, like I'm shredding my own soul and then setting the pieces on fire. The wolf has retreated somewhere deep within me. They understand the impossible choice we had to make, and they don't disagree. Despite us feeling like two separate entities, they love Ravyn as much as I do, and they care for Astria as well.

This is the only way to save the girls. It's the choice Scythe would have wanted us to make. We both know that.

Nothing changes the fact that we just betrayed our mate though.

We'll get the girls, and then we'll find her, I promise the wolf. A growl not of my own making rattles in my throat. No one will keep us from Scythe once our sisters are safe. I'll carve my way through every fucking mage here if I have to.

I have yet to see Stelian or any hunters, but I can smell them. My fingers tighten around my Kruxtia's claws. I might be pissed off at Azdall right now for the role they've played in all this, but at least, according to Scythe, the goddess of retribution isn't pleased with what the other gods did to Ryllae; maybe she'll become my new favorite deity and Azdall can fuck right off.

The tunnel takes another abrupt turn, and I stop in my tracks. Ravyn and Astria. I can smell them. It's faint but definitely there. Relief slams into me hard and fast, and I almost fall to my knees, but instead, I take several deep breaths, parsing the scents just to make sure I'm not imagining them.

A flowering meadow on a warm summer day. A creek after a rainstorm. Astria and Ravyn.

I'm running before I realize it, and only the wolf's warning rumble in my head gets me to slow down so I can be more aware of my surroundings. Stelian might have signed that mage contract, but I'm not arrogant enough to believe there aren't ways around it. He might not be able to act directly against me, but maybe some of his hunters could.

Now isn't the time to get sloppy.

Once again the tunnel twists, this time to the right, and the scents of the girls grows stronger—but now I smell mages too. The ground is also starting to slant uphill again. Hopefully there is another way out because I really don't want to walk all the way back through this winding tunnel. I'd rather get the girls somewhere safe and then double back to where Scythe and I originally entered and go from there. Stelian will likely move her, so I'll need to return fast before that happ—

Pain tears through my chest, and I barely remember to dismiss my daggers so I don't stab myself as I frantically pull at the front of my tunic. I rip it back enough to see the tree tattoo on my chest glowing silver. That's not the source of the pain though. It feels like someone has reached a clawed hand into my chest and is taking great joy in shredding each of my organs.

One hand covers the tattoo, my nails sinking into my skin, while the other braces against the cave wall as I struggle to stay upright. I inhale sharply, panting with every agonizing breath as I try not to black out.

Scythe. What the fuck are they doing to her? Are they killing her? I gambled everything on them keeping her alive for a public execution and therefore buying me time to get her free. What if Stelian has decided she's too big of a threat?

I caused this. This is my fucking fault. The wolf is going livid, and their rage is probably the only thing keeping me conscious. It's like I can feel them sinking their teeth and claws into my mind and rooting me to this spot.

As suddenly as the assault started, it stops.

"Fuck." I suck in a rattling breath and look down at the tattoo, pulling my hand back. Blood trickles from where the nails bit in deep. The tree is no longer glowing, but the tattoo remains. That has to mean she's still alive, right?

I reach through the bond but grasp at nothing. "Damn it!" I slap my palm against the rock surface before forcing myself to straighten. I should have asked Scythe more about how the bond works or practiced using it more instead of putting all my effort into keeping my emotions held back.

She could be dying right now and I wouldn't fucking know. I rub my hand against the lower part of my face. The wolf ripples beneath my skin, and I pick up on their feelings. They're upset over feeling our mate in pain . . . but they don't share my despair that she could be at her end.

My ability to use the bond might be crippled, but I trust my wolf. I'm pretty sure they instinctively know how to use it. If they don't believe Scythe is in immediate danger, then I need to get to the girls and get them the fuck out of here as fast as possible.

Just hold on, love, I silently beg down the bond.

I shake the last of the pain from my limbs and take off at a fast jog down the tunnel. After another turn, it seems I might have reached my destination because at the end is a door with two mage hunters posted outside of it. They watch me warily as I slow down to a walk.

Neither of them speak, but the dark-haired one to the right pushes the door open and steps back. The spot between my shoulder blades itches as I stride between them and into the room. No attack comes, but they do close the door behind me.

"Tal!" Ravyn cries and lunges forward to grip the bars separating her and Astria from the rest of the room.

Every part of me wants to close the distance, but I stay where I am, just inside the door, and scan the room. Stelian stands a few feet in front of the holding cell, while two neat lines of hunters wait on either side of the room, their backs against the wall. Each of them is holding up their right hand, black flames flickering in the dim lighting.

"You know, a few of my men doubted that you'd come through." Stelian chuckles. "But I never did. Good job, my friend."

"Not your fucking friend." A vicious growl rumbles up my throat as I speak. Stelian's eyebrows creep up, and I claw back the wolf. "I'll be taking the girls and going now," I say in a more even tone.

"A deal is a deal." Stelian flicks his fingers towards the cell, and one of the mages peels off from the wall to my left, the flame winking out of existence from his hand as he strides towards the cell door.

"What deal?" Ravyn asks, her tone calm, but I don't miss the hint of accusation in it. A muscle in my jaw ticks, but I can't bring myself to answer her. "What fucking deal, Tal?" she demands a little louder.

"Pushy little thing, isn't she?" Stelian muses. Ravyn's hostile glare snaps to him, but he just gives her a placating smile. "Your older sibling isn't a fool. They saw an opportunity and took it. The witch's life in exchange yours . . . and the witchkin's." His lips slip down as disgust creeps into his expression.

My fingers itch to call my blades forth and bury them in the mage's heart. He's making it sound like I sought out this deal and not that he blackmailed me into it. Ravyn tears her gaze from Stelian to look at me with disbelief . . . and disappointment.

It kills me to think that she believes the worst of me, but I understand why she does. Ravyn has no idea how much things have changed between me and Scythe over the last couple of weeks. Gods, it's crazy even to me how much everything has shifted in such a short time. The last Ravyn knew, I claimed to despise Scythe. She knows it's more complicated than that, so it makes sense why she thinks I sold the witch out.

Once we're free of this place, I'll explain things—quickly—and then rescue my mate.

The mage unlocks the cell door, and Ravyn hurries to Astria. I wait until the mage has stepped back from the door before walking towards it, but I don't go in because I don't trust them not to lock it behind me.

"Just get her to me," I tell Ravyn. "I'll carry her the rest of the way."

"I'm not going to lock you in, Talon," Stelian says dryly. "I promised to hand over your sisters in exchange for the witch. She's currently passed out in a prison cell designed just for her and having her magic stripped away. I got mine—you get yours." He waves a hand towards the girls before moving to the cavern wall, some of the hunters stepping aside to make space. "I'll even give you an easier path to get out." He speaks a word, too faint for me to hear, and a symbol glows on the wall. A second later, a portion of the rock disappears to reveal another tunnel.

"Life has taught me to never be too careful," I say, doing my best to keep one eye on Ravyn—as she struggles to half lift, half drag Astria to me—and one on the mage hunters. The witchkin girl doesn't stir at all as my sister less than gracefully gets her to me. I quickly pick Astria up, nestling her against my chest. She looks so pale, and her cheeks are sunken in. Whether it's from lack of food or whatever they dosed her with to keep her unconscious, I'm not sure.

Ravyn stays close as we walk quickly towards the new tunnel. Just before I step into it, Stelian speaks again. "I'll consider our deal complete once the sun hits your face. I'd advise you to leave the area . . . and keep going. The fate of the witch is not your concern."

I turn my head to meet his steely gaze. "Never was one to care about the whims of fate." Stelian's eyes narrow further on me, but he doesn't say anything else or stop us as Ravyn and I step into the tunnel heading towards freedom. Even though I also rescued Astria—something I know Scythe would have prioritized above her own life—it doesn't feel like a victory.

It feels like betrayal.

As soon as we breach the surface, I take off at a run, only slowing when Ravyn stumbles a few times, but the determined look on my sister's face keeps me from easing up too much. We need to put enough distance between us and the mage hunters for me to feel comfortable leaving the girls alone so I can go back for Scythe. I angle our direction so that we are moving south, back towards the original entrance Scythe and I used.

Once I figure we are about a mile away, I stop and carefully settle Astria on the ground. The forest isn't all that thick here, more a meadow interspersed with trees, but we aren't too exposed either. I let out a long, piercing whistle that I know Draco will hear, and once he arrives, I'll settle the girls on top of him. I know there is zero chance of convincing Ravyn to leave, but at least if they are on Draco, they can run if they need to.

I frown at Astria. She still hasn't shown any signs of waking, but her breathing is even. Ravyn will have to hold on to her while they're on Draco.

"Tell me everything."

I tear my gaze away from Scythe's sister to meet the pissed-off glare of my own as the sound of Draco's hooves pounding into the dirt reaches my ears. He's almost here. I close the distance between me and Ravyn and yank her against me, my arms wrapping around her, squeezing tight. Despite her anger, she hugs me back and sobs.

"It's okay," I soothe. "I'll explain everything, I promise, but Draco is going to be here in a moment, and I need you to get on him. I'll pass Astria to you." I pull back and cup my sister's tear-streaked face in my hands. "Promise me you will run if you hear anyone approaching? Do not hesitate. Just get out of here. Trust Draco if he takes off at a run."

"You're going back for her?" Ravyn's voice wavers as she struggles with her emotions. My sister is one of the strongest people I know, but she was kidnapped and held hostage for weeks, watching as her lover was drugged and grew weaker by the day. She held herself together for the escape, and now it's all threatening to come out, but I need her to keep her head a little longer.

"Yes." I nod and let out a relieved breath when Draco tears through the trees and slams to a stop next to us. "Come on."

Ravyn doesn't argue as I grab her hand and tug her towards the fae horse. She mounts without my help, and as soon as she's in the saddle, I race towards Astria and gently pick her up off the ground. After some trial and error, we end up draping Astria over the front of the saddle, because if they have to run suddenly, Ravyn isn't strong enough to hold her upright.

I hate leaving them here—so close to Stelian and the rest of the mages.

"Go," my sister orders. "We'll be fine, I promise."

Draco snorts and jerks his head as if in agreement.

"Be safe, sister." I place a hand on her leg.

"You too, Tal." She lays her hand over mine for a second before pulling it away. "Now go save the witch."

I don't hesitate as I take off at a dead run back towards the cavern entrance. The wolf stirs within me, lending me their strength and speed as we race to save our mate. Once again, I find myself wishing I could shift, if only because I know I would be faster on four legs.

When we're close, I slow our pace. There had only been a few mages guarding the entryway when Scythe and I arrived, but Stelian could have increased that now that he has his prize. At the very least, the hunters we killed have likely been replaced. I wonder if Stelian is upset about that. He had to know they would be in harm's way. Maybe he chose the mages he liked the least to guard the entrance—a pragmatic way to not give away the trap while also getting rid of those he didn't like. In my brief interactions with him, that seemed like something he would do.

Cautiously, I creep through the trees, which are thankfully thicker here, then I swear internally. Stelian has doubled the guards. He must have suspected I would return for Scythe and planned accordingly.

Shit. There is no way I can sneak past all of them, and I don't think confidently strolling up to the main entrance will work this time. I either need to find another way inside or figure out how to distract them.

"Tricky, tricky, tricky."

My dagger flashes in my hand and is at the throat of the person who spoke before they get the last word out.

Azdall grins at me, their gaze dropping to the curved, claw-like dagger. "First you insult my penchant for gold, and now I find that you bear the blades of another. I'm beginning to doubt that I'm your favorite god after all."

"That's because you're not," I say in a low, dangerous tone. "I'm in no mood for your games. What the fuck are you doing here?"

"Just here to help." They hold their hands out to the sides and raise their gaze to meet mine, an innocent look stamped onto their features.

"Bullshit," I spit out. "Even if I were inclined to believe that, aren't you forbidden from directly interfering?"

"Never met a rule I didn't love to break." Their golden gaze briefly flicks to my fingers, which are tight around the dagger. "Not so much the ones around Ryllae. Kruxtia was quite clear on not forcing the fallen Sovereign to do anything—even if it is for their own damn good, I might add."

I press the dagger harder into their throat, but Azdall just grins and licks their lips. "Mmm . . . *harder.*"

My lips harden into a flat line, and I pull the blade away.

Azdall sighs. "You're no fun like this."

"Either help or fuck off." I look away from the god and start going through my options again. The only other way in is where Stelian opened up an exit for us, and I don't think going in that way is going to be much better.

Silver flashes in my peripheral vision, and out of nothing but instinct, I dismiss one of my blades as my hand snaps out. Then I open my fingers to look down at a gold coin.

"Don't say I never gave you nothing, kid."

I look up from the coin to Azdall, only to find them gone. Magic nips at my fingers, and I study the coin; it similar to the one they gave me at the masquerade. Did Azdall just solve my problem? I think they did, but the question is . . . why? I may have limited experience with the gods, but something tells me this isn't from the kindness of their heart.

That will have to be a problem for the future though, because I'm getting Scythe the fuck out of here.

Clenching the coin in my palm, I stride out of the forest, my heart racing as I come into view of several of the mage hunters, but none of them react to my presence. When I reach the cave entrance, I have to angle my body to slide between the mages guarding it because I'm not sure if the coin also works on physical touch. Despite being inches away from them, it's clear that none of the mages sense me.

I take off at a sprint once I'm in the tunnel, only stopping when I reach the cavern where Scythe and I parted ways. Stelian is still nowhere to be seen, but there are several mage hunters waiting here. They're playing some sort of card game, occasionally glancing down the tunnel to the left.

I'm guessing they're all too scared to venture where Scythe is being held to check on her. They're waiting until the spell has drained enough of her magic that she won't kill them on sight.

Part of me wants to stop and kill them for the role they've played in all this, but it's not worth the risk of revealing myself just yet, so I keep going. Scythe's scent grows stronger the farther down the tunnel I go. Thankfully, this one is shorter than the one I went down the first time, and after only a few turns, I come to a stop as the tunnel ends in iron bars. My heart also stops when I see Scythe lying on the ground a few feet away, curled up in a fetal position.

She's not moving. I sense it then, a cold, oppressive feeling, and look up at the ceiling of the cavern she's imprisoned in. Spiral symbols have been carved into the rock surface, giving off a faint glow. That must be the spell that's draining her magic.

How much of her magic has it taken already? I glance at the coin in my hand. Hopefully it will work for two people because something tells me that Scythe isn't going to be able to fight anytime soon.

"Scythe." She doesn't move or give any indication that she hears me. "*Cerelia.*" The growl in my voice comes from the wolf as we utter her name like a prayer.

Her hair shifts as her head lulls to the side. "Tal?"

"Yes," I breathe out. "I'm here, and I'm going to get you out," I promise quickly as I examine the bars between us. There is some type of symbol carved into them. I grip them and pull as hard as I can, just to test their strength, but nothing gives. Fuck. My eyes quickly dart around . . . but there's no lock.

There's no fucking lock.

I can't pick anything if there's nothing to fucking pick, and my daggers won't cut through iron. *Stop*, I tell myself. *Don't panic.* There has to be a way out of this. Something I'm not seeing. I did not lead my fucking mate down a trap that I can't fucking spring her out of.

Just fucking look, damn it.

"You came back."

I shift my attention from the bars I'm hopelessly staring at to Scythe. She's managed to push herself up and is standing, looking a little unsteady, but at least she's on her feet. It kills me to see how dim her silver eyes are though. Whatever magic is in that necklace must be gone, because she looks like her true self now. Although her tattoos aren't a crisp black like they normally are when she's not calling on magic—more like a faded grey.

"I told you I would." My fingers tighten around the bars. "I'm so fucking sorry. I didn't have a choice. Stelian cornered me at the masquerade, and if I didn't go along with his plan, he would have killed our sisters, but they're safe now," I say quickly.

"Good." She nods, and I see the relief in her face even as her shoulders sag a little—like she's accepted her fate.

"We just need to get you out of here." My mind races as I try to think of how we're going to accomplish that.

"I don't think I'm going anywhere." She looks at me with a ghost of a smile on her lips.

"Bullshit," I growl. "We just need to figure out how to get a few of these bars loose." I look up towards the ceiling. "Can you use your magic to shift the rock around them? I can pull while you do that. They can't go that deep into the—"

"They do," she cuts me off. "Stelian designed this well. Those iron bars are embedded deep, and shifting rock is not easy. It takes a lot of magic . . . and time. Both of which I don't have."

"So you're just giving up?" I snarl and slam a palm against the iron bars, the symbols on them glowing faintly, and I have to pull my hand away when black flames ripple across them. Then I glare at Scythe through the bars. "The witch I know never stops fighting!"

"Oh, I very much intend to go down fighting," Scythe replies, a flicker of defiance in her eyes. "But you won't be here to see it, my wolf. Everyone leaves me eventually. It's time for you to go too."

I lean closer to the bars, just out of reach of the flames dancing across them. "I'm. Not. Going. Anywhere."

Again, she gives me that faint smile that crushes my heart every time I see it. "I know how to break the curse—and the bond."

Icy fear shoots through me. "No." I shake my head. "The bond stays. You're my mate."

"You didn't choose me." She snorts. "This was the meddling of the gods."

"I choose you now!" Desperation coats my words. "I don't care what the gods are doing. I don't care about breaking the curse. My wolf and I have survived this long, and we're both in agreement. We want you. Only you."

Scythe's beautiful face crumples as tears start to flow from her eyes. "I love you, Tal, and I choose you too, which is why I have to do this. There is no breaking me out of this prison, but I have just enough magic to do this. I need to know that you will survive. That you'll watch over Astria for me . . . and Ravyn. She's good for my sister."

"We won't go!" The wolf's raspy growl mingles with my own voice.

"Ryllae was right, you know." Her voice is soft as she speaks. "I can summon animals to me . . . but I can also force them to flee."

Panic grips me. She can't . . . she wouldn't. I step closer to the bars, ready to try ripping them out again, mage fire or not. I don't fucking care. But then Scythe starts to sing and the flames surge, forcing me to step back as dark magic licks my skin.

I fall to my knees as the bond between us goes rigid, as if it was a flowing river before but now it's freezing over. Azdall's coin slips from my fingers and rolls across the ground.

"Stop!" I scream desperately.

Scythe keeps singing, and my fingers claw at the rock as my vision starts to shift. It's hard to see, but when I raise my hands . . . my nails are now claws. I can feel it. The cage around my wolf is growing weaker—I can feel them starting to break free. I scream as my back arches, the pain almost unbearable, but this feels different from all my failed shifts.

Her song rises to a crescendo, and even through my own pain, I can hear the agony in her voice. Through the black fire on the bars separating us, I see Scythe kneeling too, her back arched and head thrown back while dozens of symbols light up on the ground. I have no idea what they're doing, but Scythe sounds like she's dying.

I'm vaguely aware of footsteps and shouts coming from farther down the tunnel. The hunters must have heard my screams and are coming to investigate despite their fear of the witch. Another scream rips from my throat but ends in a howl as I find myself no longer kneeling but standing on four paws.

My curse is broken . . . and so is the mating bond.

Scythe's song fades, and with it, the fire on the bars dim, and I can see her more clearly. Sweat coats her skin, and blood is leaking from her eyes, nose, and ears.

"You're beautiful."

I whine, unable to speak. The wolf and I are still separate beings, but I can tell their presence is stronger in this form—the way that mine is stronger when we're human. *Don't run*, I plead with them. I can feel their determination to stay . . . but I also fear it's pointless.

We're a wolf. We obey the forest. The witch is the forest, and the forest is the witch.

My new lupine body whirls as half a dozen hunters turn the corner. I can feel them rallying their magic, and several of them bear swords coated in varying colors of flames. Scythe screams, a deep, rallying note, and large chunks of stone split from the cave wall, slamming into the hunters, pinning them against the other wall of the tunnel.

Not enough to kill them—which I know she would have if she had the strength—just enough force to keep them in place.

I turn back to her, and silver, glowing eyes meet mine. I don't need the mating bond to know everything she's feeling right now. I can see the love in her eyes. It's not sweet and tender. No. This is the kind of love that is all-consuming. Fierce, wicked, and a little unhinged. It's us.

Don't! I scream, and the wolf howls.

The Witch of the Woods smiles at us and sings one word. "Run."

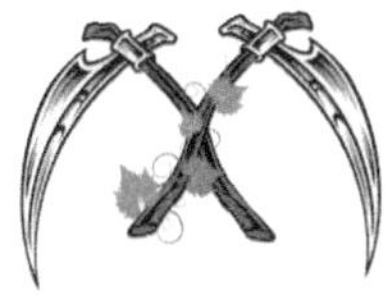

CHAPTER TWENTY-FOUR

~

Scythe

I STARE into the tunnel that Talon in their wolf form raced down seconds ago. The song has died on my lips, but I had to start humming again to keep the stones pressed against the mage hunters. Blood flows freely from my nose now as the spell in the cavern floor punishes me for using magic. I don't really feel the pain anymore. It's like my body has moved beyond it.

That's probably not a good thing. I have enough of my mind left to understand this.

Still, I keep humming.

Talon really was glorious in their wolf form. Midnight black fur tipped with silver, as if they were moon-kissed. I hope they don't hate me for what I did today. When they declared that they wanted the bond—that they chose me—I almost wavered in my conviction.

They would have died trying to break me out of here though, and while I can accept my death, I refuse to accept theirs.

Blackness starts to encroach on my vision. Have I contained

303

the guards long enough? I'm sure there are more mage hunters out there, but they won't be expecting a wolf to bolt out of the cave, and I sank a lot of command into that word. Talon is going to run for miles and miles.

They'll be free.

Some of the stones start to slip, and I hum louder. Through blood and pain, I *will* buy Talon whatever time they need to save our sisters. Because I have no doubt that's what they're doing. I just wish I could have seen Astria once more.

"For fuck's sake," somebody snaps.

My vision has blurred, and it's too dim for me to make out who spoke. I hear what sounds like metal grinding against stone before something dark fills my vision. Boots? When did my gaze drop to the floor?

Pain explodes on the side of my head, and I fall to the floor, my hum abruptly cut off. Suddenly, sound and color flood my senses. The mage hunters swear as they fall from where they were pinned against the wall. My vision sharpens, and I twist my head enough to look up and see Stelian sneering down at me.

"You don't get to die that easily, witch." He snaps his fingers, and the symbols lighting up the floor fade. Now that it's no longer attacking my body, it's like I can feel the lingering wounds it left behind. Everything hurts, and for the first time in my life, I can't feel my magic. Not even a flicker.

A steel-toed boot connects with my ribs. *Crack.* Several bones snap, and a ragged scream rips from my throat, only to choke off as I spit up blood. Stelian shoves me again with his boot until I lie on my back, my breathing rough. I'm pretty sure one of my now-broken ribs has punctured a lung.

"I knew there was something between you and Talon." Stelian tilts his head as he ponders me. "But I'll be honest, I didn't think it was the kind of thing that would have them coming back for you. Cursed werewolf, right?" He jabs me with his foot again, and a hiss of pain slips from my lips. "Must have taken some intense magic to break that. I'd planned to drain you for days, if not a week, so you could be moved."

He steps back, and another mage takes his place before kneeling down next to me. Out of habit, I try to call my scythe forth, and when nothing happens, it takes my mind a second to catch up as to why. The scythe was made of magic, and just like my necklace that charmed my appearance . . . it's been drained by the spell above me. My magic will eventually come back, but the enchantments are gone.

The ring on my pinky is now just that and nothing more.

Grief hits me. It's weird to mourn a weapon, but today has been pretty fucked, and it would have been nice to bury that silver blade in Stelian's smug face. Definitely would have made me feel better, even if his men would have killed me seconds later. Some things are worth it.

Thick irons are clamped onto my wrists and ankles. Aside from hampering my movements, I feel the spell in them that will leach my magic away as it comes back. On their own, they wouldn't be enough to drain me of magic, but I'm tapped out, and the manacles will be more than enough to make sure I stay that way.

Two hunters yank me to my feet, not giving a shit about my broken ribs. I bite my tongue to hold back the scream that tries to claw its way out, and coppery blood fills my mouth. For a second, I think I'm going to pass out, but I manage to stay conscious.

"Nothing to say?" Stelian moves to stand in front of me and grabs some of my hair, twirling it between his fingers. "A pretty woman who knows how to keep her mouth shut. Pity you're a witch."

It's not his words that drive my response, it's the fact that he's touching my hair the same way Talon does. The bloody glob of spit flies through the air before he can move and smacks his cheek, dripping down into his close-clipped beard.

Stelian stumbles back, wiping at his face in disgust, and I give him a feral smile through bloody teeth. His eyes go hard, and words spill from his mouth as the emerald ring on his pointer finger starts to glow. The guards holding me step back a bit before Stelian flings his hand towards me and black flames tinged with green slam into my body, sending me crashing against the rock wall.

Crack. Pain explodes in my spine, followed by my head a second later as both hit the hard surface. This time, I do scream when I collapse to the floor and the flames dance across my skin. They don't burn, but it feels like I'm being stung by a thousand bees. I'm still screaming when a boot comes down and smashes into my face.

SOFT CONVERSATIONS SLIP through my mind as I pretend to still be knocked out. After throwing his little magical tantrum and breaking several more bones in my body, Stelian healed me enough to keep me alive and then had me thrown into the back of a carriage. I drifted in and out of consciousness during the ride, my mind still fuzzy from slamming into the cavern wall, but I'm pretty sure we haven't been traveling too long, only an hour or two. I held my eyes shut when they dragged me in here—wherever here is— and have kept them shut in hopes I could glean some useful information while they think I am still unconscious.

The air smells of wine and too much perfume. Between that and the cold metal of the manacles biting into my wrists and ankles, I have to swallow down the nausea.

"Is this really her?" a light, posh feminine voice asks. "The infamous Witch of the Woods?"

"It is. The last of her kind." The masculine voice that responds is deep with a commanding undertone.

"And it's safe to have her here?" Her tone implies that she's more curious than actually scared.

"Of course, my dear." Something happens because the woman giggles. It's that obnoxious, exaggerated giggle I overheard more than once while at the prince's masquerade. For a second, I hope that Prince Caspian requested to see me. I still won't give up Ryllae, but maybe I can bargain with something else. That thought dies a swift death when I hear the next words spoken.

"King Thain!" a strong voice calls out clearly. "Dinner is ready to be served."

"Go on ahead, my lady," the man—King Thain—says. "I'd like a moment alone with my new prize."

Another airy giggle and then the sound of retreating footsteps.

"I know you're awake. Saw you wince when she laughed. Understandable—it's not the most pleasant of sounds."

Deciding there's no point in feigning sleep anymore, I open my eyes and move until I sit cross-legged.

In a cage.

It must be several feet off the ground because even sitting, I'm eye level with the king. I knew, based on what Caspian said, that the king and the prince looked nothing alike. Still, I'm a little surprised exactly how much they differ in appearance.

Caspian has dark chestnut hair and a strong but lean muscular build. He's handsome in a charming sort of way with just the right amount of wicked glint in his mismatched eyes to be intriguing. King Thain, on the other hand, is massive and looks like he enjoys breaking bodies. He has to be at least six-and-a-half feet tall with a broad build that says he can shatter you with one punch. His golden blond hair falls to his shoulders, and a thick beard covers his face.

Everything about him implies power, but it's his eyes—a dark green—that convey his true personality. Cunning and cruel.

Because I suspect it will annoy him, I look away and survey my surroundings. The bottom of my cage is a cold white marble that matches the floor. It's probably supposed to look rich but instead it just comes across as lifeless. Talon would call it gaudy.

The gap in my soul where the mating bond used to be burns with an icy desolation. Nausea rises again, and I have to swallow it down.

Focus.

The cage bars are iron, but they're coated in silver to make them look pretty. Thanks to my fae blood, I'm sensitive to iron. It doesn't impact my magic, but it does make my skin crawl. Unfortunately, the manacles still attached to me are doing their job, and I can't feel even a flicker of my magic.

The high-pitched-giggle woman makes her way across the room to where at least twenty other guests sit at a long table. Unlike Prince Caspian's palace, this one was not built by fae hands, and it shows. There are seams in the floor showing the individual tile squares, and the lanterns lighting up the space are powered by mage magic—not fae.

It's also just . . . less.

Although that might have more to do with the man in front of me than the lack of fae magic.

The heads of various animals hang on the wall like trophies, and there is an ugly oppressiveness to everything.

"All this money," I drawl as my eyes drift around the room before settling back on the king, "and still such poor taste."

Talon used that line on some woman who wouldn't stop flirting with them one night when we were staying at a tavern, and her face had turned a lovely shade of purple. The king doesn't have quite that reaction, but the corners of his mouth pinch together, and I see anger flash through his eyes.

I let out a low chuckle. Human. Mage. Witch. Fae. It doesn't matter. One universal truth is that people who are obsessed with power don't like others laughing at their display of it.

"It'll be interesting to see if you keep up the flippant attitude once King Oluin gets his hands on you." It's the king's turn to laugh as I fail to hide the fear that shoots through me. "I'm pleased that Stelian didn't ruin the surprise."

"You're taking me to Riritha." A statement, not a question, and any hint of bravado I felt dies. "Why?"

"It's been a long time since one king from the four kingdoms has proposed an alliance with another."

He trails his fingers across the bars of my cage. I know it's a taunt, a test to see if I'll try to grab him, but I also have no doubt that there is magic in those bars that will likely do something nasty to me if I try it. Someday, I hope someone rips out the Eleoyn king's throat and that I'm there to see him choke on his own blood.

"Once upon a time, it was customary for the visiting king to bring a unique gift as a token of goodwill." He smiles at me through the bars. "And what better gift for the man who has prided himself on hunting down every person of Arandian blood than quite possibly the last witch on these shores?"

I knew when I sent Talon running from that cave that I would never see them again. Never get to hug my sister. That a drawn-out, painful death was all that waited for me, but it isn't death that awaits me in Riritha.

Death would be a gift.

There are tales of the prisons King Oluin keeps beneath his fortress. Of the fae he's kept down there for his sick amusement for decades—possibly centuries. It's one of the things that keeps Ryllae rooted to these shores. A desperate need to free what is left of their people.

But the Ririthans don't practice magic. They abhor it. There are no mages there—loyal to the king or not. No one is more skilled at brutally neutralizing magic than the Ririthans. I don't know why their king hates the fae so much, but his father was the same and his father before that.

A poison passed down through the generations.

I'm not fae. A bit of fae blood runs through my veins, but I am still a witch. I don't know if that will make him hate me more or less, and I really don't want to find out.

"There it is." My gaze shoots up to meet the king's as he lets out a contented sigh before grinning at me. "*Fear*. I was wondering when it would truly sink in. It looks good on you."

He's not wrong. I'm terrified of what awaits me in Riritha, but I'm not there yet, and this fucker doesn't get to see me break.

"Someday"—I hold his penetrating stare—"you *will* die. Painfully. Brutally. I bet you'll scream and plead for your pathetic life. I hope I'm there to see it, but if I'm not, I'll watch from whatever afterlife claims me." The smile stretching across my lips is more of a baring of teeth. "And cheer your demise."

"We both know you'll be rotting away in a cell for centuries, *begging* for death." His stare doesn't waver from mine. "Perhaps I'll meet a violent end. Perhaps I'll die peacefully in my sleep. You'll never know, witch."

I will though. There are few things that I'm sure of, but his death is one of them. The gods are plotting with the prince, and while I might hate them, I'm well aware of what they're capable of. And then there is Ryllae. Someday, they're going to explode and burn this entire kingdom down.

Hells, maybe Talon will avenge me and sneak into the king's room one night to slit his throat.

The Eleoyn king grunts, clearly done with this conversation, and turns away to join his dinner guests. He stops mid-step when I start laughing. It's the raspy laugh of a wolf, and it makes my heart ache. The king looks back over his shoulder at me, the light from the mage lanterns giving his dark green eyes an ominous glow.

"The earth will always speak to me. I don't need magic to hear it." I lean forward, palms down on the cool surface of my cage, my face an inch away from the bars. "And even if I'm in the lowest levels of that godsforsaken prison, the roots will sing of your death, and I'll sing along with them." I shift away from the bars, leaning back onto my hands, and give him a lazy smile. "Enjoy your dinner."

CHAPTER TWENTY-FIVE

~

Talon

"Tal?" a voice asks cautiously. "Talon?"

I know that voice. The wolf's mad dash slows, and for the first time since Scythe uttered that command, I feel my human self surface. Whatever she did caused the wolf to fully take over, and it felt like I was adrift. I felt the wolf's panic, not only at being forced to flee like that, but over my absence.

Yeah, I didn't like it either, buddy.

"She broke the curse," another light feminine voice half whispers. Or maybe she only whispered it. I thought my hearing was good before, but it's nothing compared to what it is now. Everything around us is just so . . . loud. This will take some getting used to. I wonder if my human form will have heightened senses.

I look out through the wolf's eyes and see Ravyn still astride Draco, but Astria is awake now and sitting upright in front of her.

Can we shift back? I ask the wolf. *It'll be easier for me to speak with them.*

It's a little surreal that I'm in wolf form right now. That the

311

curse is gone. But just like I couldn't truly celebrate when I walked Ravyn and Astria out of that cave, I can't feel too happy about being whole now.

Because I'm not. The bond between Scythe and me might be broken, but she's still my fucking mate, and I will get her back. Then I'll spend the rest of our lives punishing her for making me run.

"Why is he growling?" I hear Ravyn whisper to Astria.

The fair-haired girl grimaces. "My sister has that effect on people."

I can feel the wolf pull back, letting me take over for the shift. The only problem is—I don't exactly know how. Everything is such a blur from the cave, I don't know if Scythe forced our shift or if it was just a side effect of the curse being broken. The only other werewolves I knew were my parents, and they were never able to shift, so we never talked about it.

Fuck. What if I'm stuck like this? The wolf feels restless in my mind, letting out low growls and whines as they grow more impatient at my inability to shift so we can explain everything to the girls. So we can get Scythe back.

Not helping, I growl at them, and they snap back.

"You okay, Tal?" my sister asks, and I halt when I realize I've been pacing.

It has to be instinctual—the shift. It's not like I can speak in wolf form, so there is no spell that does this, and all the times I tried to shift over my life and failed were reactions to situations. I feel a little stupid, but I close my eyes and think about being human. Not just my human body, but the emotional connection I have to it and the driving reasons for wanting to change back.

At first, nothing happens, but then I feel it, the magic dancing across my skin. For a few seconds, I'm elated and relieved to have figured it out, then the pain hits.

My skin burns as the fur recedes beneath it. Bones break and snap into new ones as my organs violently shift around. It feels like

I'm being broken and remade, which I suppose I am, but fuck, it didn't feel like this in the cavern.

"Oh shit!" one of the girls screams, though I'm not sure which.

Finally, the pain is over, and I lie in the dirt, coated in sweat and trembling slightly. Okay. That wasn't fun. Gods, I hope it's not like that every time. The wolf rumbles their agreement.

I push myself to my knees and look up just in time to see black hair flying before Ravyn crashes into me. "Thank fuck!" She throws her arms around me, and I grunt as her impact causes me to fall on my ass.

"Glad to see you too, s—oof!" Astria slams into us, and this time, I fall over completely as both of them hug me tightly.

"There was all this shouting and we saw several bursts of light in the air," Ravyn explains quickly, her words muffled slightly because her face is pressed into the crook of my neck. "Draco took off and wouldn't listen when I told him to go back. Then he suddenly changed direction, and we found you in your wolf form and—*oh my gods, you're naked*!"

Ravyn and Astria fling themselves off me and cover their eyes.

"Did you not notice that before you hugged me?" I snort and rise to my feet before striding over to Draco to grab a pair of pants from the travel pack.

"I was happy to see you, asshole!"

As soon as I tug on the pants, I walk back over to my sister and pull her into a hug. "Fucking same, sis."

Ravyn hugs me tightly, and I breathe in her scent for a few moments, letting it calm both me and the wolf before pulling back and facing Astria.

Sky blue eyes look at me, and her bottom lip quivers. "You weren't able to save my sister."

"I'm so sorry, Astria." My voice is raspy with guilt. "It's my fault she was captured. I thought I'd be able to get her free after getting you two to safety, but Stelian laid his trap for her well.

They're draining her magic, and I'm fairly certain she used the last of it to break the curse on my wolf."

I can't bring myself to say that she broke the mating bond too. They don't know about that part, and I'm not ready to say it out loud yet. That Scythe was my mate and that she sacrificed our bond to break my curse.

Now that I'm back in my human skin, the despair I felt in that moment comes hurtling back. On its heels is an absolutely blinding rage. How fucking dare she? As soon as she's safe in my arms again, I'm going to tie her ass to the bed and punish her for weeks.

I rub my hand over the spot on my chest where the tree tattoo used to be. Now, there is nothing but unblemished skin, as if it was never there. If there are any traces of the mate bond left, I can't feel them. Can mating bonds be formed again? Or have we lost it forever?

It doesn't fucking matter. Scythe is my mate, bond or no bond, and I'm getting her back.

"What do we do now?" Astria asks. "Will the three of us be able to get her out of that cave?"

There is no way in all the hells I'm putting Astria and Ravyn in danger, but I don't bother saying that right now because it will just cause an argument. I might have been able to get Ravyn to go along with my plan of running earlier, but that was only because Astria was unconscious. Now that they're both awake, I can see the stubbornness etched into their features.

Astria wants her sister back, and Ravyn will follow her to the ends of the earth. I'll figure out some way for them to be useful without putting them directly in danger.

"We'll go back to the cave." I click my tongue, and Draco trots over. "You two can ride—I'll run beside you." I can tell already that I'm faster than I was before, even in this form. And everything is just . . . more.

The color of the forest. The scent of the earth. Birds chirping in the trees. I want to find out just how far I can push myself now.

"Do you think she's still there?" Astria chews her bottom lip in the same way Scythe does, and it feels like someone just sucker punched me.

"No," I say a little roughly as I look away from Astria. "That trap was set to drain her magic—and it did. He'll move her now to prevent any further rescue attempts, but I should be able to track them from the cave."

"Then let's go." Astria strides back to Draco and smoothly mounts. Unlike her older sister, Astria took to riding right away, as if she was always meant to be on horseback. Ravyn wraps me in one more quick hug before she jogs over to where Draco patiently waits. Astria reaches out her hand, and Ravyn grabs it, then swings up to sit behind the fair-haired girl.

As soon as Ravyn loops her arms around Astria's waist, the girls take off, Draco quickly breaking into a ground-eating gallop. The wolf surges forward in my mind, and while my body remains human, I can feel their strength flooding through me. We race after the fae horse—and keep pace with him the entire way.

"SAY IT AGAIN," I demand in a low tone.

"I go to the bar and pretend to be drowning my sorrows because I found out my husband has been cheating on me," Ravyn says steadily. "I do *not* leave with anyone, and if someone offers to buy me a drink, I watch the bartender pour it. Keep myself angled out towards the rest of the tavern and see if anyone acts strangely once you start asking questions."

"I keep my hood up and stay near the door," Astria answers, her tone just as calm as Ravyn's. "Watch who leaves and enters. If I get a signal from you to follow someone, I do but stay back at least twenty paces, and I do *not* take any risks."

Both young women look at me with determined faces, and while I have faith in them, I wish Mattias and Vesi were here instead. My friends are well-versed in running recon. They know the signs of trouble, and they know how to play a situation to their advantage on the fly.

We're nowhere near Albadrid though. It would take too long to get them or send a message via courier, and I don't have Scythe's nifty ability to transport notes through trees.

We made it back to the cave quickly and found it mostly empty aside from Scythe's blood smeared on the walls. The wolf and I lost our mind and shifted again. It hurt, but apparently anger is a better motivator than fear and frustration because I changed forms much faster than before, although not as fast as when Scythe had used her magic.

It was then we learned that not all the mage hunters had left. They heard my howling rage and came to investigate.

Ravyn and Astria plastered themselves against a wall while I ripped through the hunters. A few of them hit me with magic that burned off patches of my fur, but I was so lost to the rage and bloodlust that it barely slowed me down. I was still ripping into them and flinging their body parts across the cavern long after they were dead.

It was Astria who calmed me down by screaming that she'd turn me into a fur coat if I didn't get my ass out to the front and start tracking where they'd taken Scythe. Ravyn stared at her like she had two heads, but I guess a girl who grew up with devil cats as playmates wouldn't be that intimidated by a werewolf venting their rage.

As soon as we neared the city, the girls found me some clothing while I changed back to my human form. Every shift seemed to be a little easier and hurt slightly less.

"It'll be fine, Tal," Ravyn assures me, her voice gentle but her eyes hard and full of resolve. "We'll watch the room. You use your charm on the locals."

"Alright. Astria will go in first, Ravyn a few minutes later, and then me last." I glance towards the exit of the grungy alleyway we ducked down to the shabby wood building across the way. The thing looks like a strong breeze would knock it over. "Remember to not make eye contact with each other while we're in there, but don't avoid looking at each other either. If you're scanning the room, it will stand out if you specifically don't look at someone."

"Got it." Astria pulls the hood of her cloak up and strides towards the tavern, and I have to curl my fingers at my sides to keep from pulling her back. When we get Scythe back, I'll have to convince the girls not to mention this part of the plan.

Ravyn's eyes stay locked on the worn wood door after Astria slips inside. Despite her confidence in this plan, I know she's still worried about Astria. Ravyn is well aware of the reputation of this area. The trail from the cave led us to Kesdril, a city that sits close to the southern border with Riritha. I'd expected Stelian to take Scythe to Tenresan, where the king usually resides and the stronghold of the mage hunters.

I don't understand what drew them here. Kesdril is a rough city. It's heavily patrolled by the mage hunters and city guards, but that doesn't make it safe by any means. It's a well-known haven for Ririthan raiders, whose bribes keep those in power from looking into their business.

Tenresan is at least a four-day ride, but Mabria is only two. They could have stopped there and seen the prince before riding on to the capital.

Something about this isn't right, which is why, after hours of wandering around, trying and failing to figure out what is going on, we're about to walk into one of the seediest taverns in the city in hopes of getting information.

A few minutes tick by, and then Ravyn nods at me before walking out of the alley. She hunches her shoulders as she walks, and I can hear her sniffle a few times, even over the loudness of the city. Ravyn has always been an excellent actor; she's more than capable of playing a dejected woman drinking her sorrows away at a bar.

My heart rate picks up as a group of mage hunters laugh amongst themselves before entering the tavern after her. This is why we targeted this establishment in particular. I don't spend much time in Kesdril because the place is a shithole, but I've always made it a point to have the basic lay of the land for all the major cities, and I know The Drift is a favorite place for hunters to gather after their shifts end.

It's well past sunset, so the mages who had a day shift are all looking for something to do with the rest of their evening. We stopped in a few other taverns while skulking around the city, yet we didn't hear a peep about Scythe, but the mage hunters will know, and hopefully their tongues will loosen after a few rounds and some carefully phrased comments on my part.

As much as I want to race inside after the hunters, I force myself to wait. Usually, I'm quite good at being patient, but not today. All I can think about is Scythe and what they might be doing to her. It's hard, but I have to try to keep those thoughts contained because they won't help. I need to be completely focused. We need to find out where she's being held so we can plan accordingly.

I will not fail again at rescuing her.

When enough time has passed, I leave the alleyway with a cocky swagger to my stride. My dark hair hangs around my shoulders, and I roughed up my clothes a little to make sure I don't look too clean or well-kept. I look shady enough, even by Kesdril standards, that people distance themselves as I make my way across the street to The Drift.

As soon as I open the door, I'm greeted by the scent of stale ale and body odor. Ugh. In this enclosed space, my keener sense of smell makes the stench almost unbearable.

I swallow my grimace and instantly plaster a lazy grin onto my face as I make my way to the bar and order a drink. Out of the corner of my eye, I note Astria posted up by herself at a table off to the side, sipping her ale, while Ravyn sulks at the end of the bar.

Perfect, because I'm about to start voicing some very loud questions. We might get the answers we need here, or I might get my ass kicked, and in the ruckus, someone might slip out to report the loudmouth asking about Scythe. In which case, Astria will follow them and hopefully at least give us some sort of lead while Ravyn watches my back.

Grabbing a pint of what I can tell, based on the color and scent, is a very watered-down ale, I head towards the long table, where the mage hunters have settled. I sit at the end of the table, not wanting to crowd them right away, and guzzle down half my drink, letting some of it slosh onto my shirt.

A couple of mages glance my way but dismiss me as a drunkard and go back to conversing. At first, I'm disappointed because the conversation is all about women they're bedding—or trying to—as well as some Obscuras rotting away in the prison awaiting a public execution, and a new poison enchantment that is being tested out. It seems like standard, day-to-day mage hunter business.

I'm half listening, half planning our next move when one of them says the words I've been waiting for.

"So . . . have any of you seen *her*?" a ginger-haired man with a thick beard asks after downing his ale and slamming the glass onto the table.

"Nah." Another man snorts, his fingers spinning an empty shot glass around. "Tried to right after Stelian brought her in, but she's in the king's *entertaining room*." He rolls his eyes. "She should be in the fucking dungeons with the rest of the vermin."

"Don't mind, Victor," a mage with dark chestnut brown hair chimes in. "He's just upset that he can't get his hands on the witch to show her a proper good time."

The men all have a good laugh at that, which is the only thing that prevents them from noticing my violent reaction. *Crack.* My glass fractures slightly in my hand, and I'm barely able to see through my rage to tip it over so that it crashes to the floor and covers up my momentary lapse of control over my newfound strength.

"Shit." I plaster a forlorn look on my face as I stare down at the broken glass. This isn't the type of joint where the staff comes over to clean it up quickly, and most of the patrons don't even notice. The mages have stopped talking though and are now glaring at me, probably hoping I'll go sit somewhere else.

Not bloody likely.

"Grip has never been right since a run-in with some damn Obscuras last year." I hold my right hand up and force a couple of my fingers to twitch. "Caught up with the fuckers a few weeks ago and made them pay though."

The red-haired mage looks me over with a keen eye. "You ain't a mage. How'd you take out some Obscuras?" The disbelief in his tone is reflected in the expressions of all the other hunters, and I have to hide my wolfish smile. So easy to bait.

I shrug and turn on the bench to face them. "They might have magic, but they ain't that bright. I mean, if they were, they'd be serving the Eleoyn king like you lot, right? Seems that's the way to go if you're truly opposed to the Mage Council and want to actually do something about it." Some of their hostility and disbelief fades. Never underestimate the power of flattery, especially amongst the arrogant and weak-minded. "A few well-placed rumors had the Obscuras scum scuttling to a meeting place where some other gents and I lined up some crossbows. Hard to use magic with a bolt through your head."

Some of the mages laugh, and the one who spoke to me cracks a smile. "That'd never work on us. We'd sense the trap."

"Obviously." I laugh. "Like I said—those who run off with the Obscuras ain't the smartest."

"Here." One of the mages pushes a glass filled with a dark ale over to me. "We got some extras because Claude here"—he points at the chestnut-haired mage—"can't count. Anyone who takes out Obscuras deserves a free round."

"Cheers, mate." I take the ale from him with a grin and hold it up. "Death to the Obscuras!"

The mages hold up their own glasses. "Death to the Obscuras!"

An hour later, I stumble away from the table. The mages cheer me on as I make my way to the door, calling out random insults to Obscuras and the Mage Council as I go. Once I get outside, I aimlessly wander the streets, putting distance between me and the tavern before ducking into the vacant, run-down building that was our agreed-upon rendezvous spot.

Waiting for Ravyn and Astria to arrive is testing the limits of my patience. I kept an eye on them while chatting up the mages, and nothing looked amiss. Nobody approached Astria, who kept her cloak up the whole time. One man started to get pushy with Ravyn, but then she released a loud sob that ended in an explosion of mucus, which quickly convinced the man to spend his attention elsewhere.

Gross, but I had to give her points for creativity.

Footsteps sound from outside the dilapidated cottage. I catch their scents a few seconds before the girls slip through the broken door leaning against the frame. The tension I've been carrying since leaving them alone in that tavern eases. Some of it anyway. The rest won't go away until Scythe is safe.

"What did you find out?" Astria asks quickly, her blue eyes searching my face like she's trying to get a read on just how bad the situation is.

I wish I could tell her it isn't that bad, but I can't because it's worse.

"King Thain is in Kesdril. That's why Stelian brought your sister here. The king means to bring her with him to Riritha as a gift for King Oluin because he's trying to forge a treaty with him."

The color drains from Astria's face, and Ravyn wraps a

supportive arm around her shoulders. "We'll get her back before she crosses that border," my sister assures her.

"Tell me you have a plan, Tal," Astria demands, an echo of Scythe's fierceness in her eyes. "Tell me you know how to save my sister."

"My dear, I always have a plan." I look both of them over. Astria still looks pale and weak, but a bath, makeup, and the right clothes will fix that. The same goes for my sister. "The king plans to leave in two days. Tomorrow night, he's having one last event to show off Scythe before taking her from this kingdom. It's a small affair, with only his advisors, high-ranking mage hunters, and some nobles in attendance."

"You're good, Tal." Ravyn shakes her head. "But you're not that good. It's one thing to crash large parties where there are a lot of people in attendance and everyone is drunk off their asses. But you'd stand out at this, and not in a good way."

"Ah, but there is one other person attending who just arrived in the city tonight." My lips curve into a vicious smile. "Prince Caspian. And he'll be inviting us in. Whether he wants to or not."

CHAPTER TWENTY-SIX

~

Talon

To HIS CREDIT, Prince Caspian doesn't scream or look particularly alarmed when he wakes up with a blade to his throat. Makes me wonder exactly what type of life he leads because I'm pretty sure most princes wouldn't be so calm about this.

Then again, he is a changeling who regularly chats with old fae gods, so he's not exactly a normal prince.

"I had no idea you were so eager to crawl into my bed, Talon." He gives me that same cocky smile he did at the masquerade when he was dancing with Scythe. "I'm flattered."

It's true. I *am* in his bed. The way I'm leaning over him though, my right knee pressed into the mattress between his legs, means I'm in the perfect position to slam my leg right up into his balls.

Which I do. *Hard.*

I dismiss my curved blade so I don't slit the prince's throat when he jerks up with a pained scream that I quickly cut off by placing my hand over his mouth. He glares at me through watery eyes, quickly dropping the flirty, nonchalant act.

"This is your only warning," I say coldly. "Scythe is in the hands of the enemy. The gods played a role in that, and you're quite chummy with them, so I hold you accountable as well." I let the wolf peek out through my eyes as I lean down farther until my face is only an inch away from Caspian's. "Given the option, I would coat the walls of this room red with your blood. Anyone who threatens my mate dies. I don't give a fuck that you're a prince or a changeling. Nor do I give a fuck about the gods whispering in your ear. Do not play games with me. You won't like the outcome. Nod if you understand."

The prince's mismatched eyes widen slightly before turning calculating, but he nods all the same. I pull my hand away and roll off the bed. I know I'm taking a chance—he could still call for help. Even if I told everyone he was a changeling, it would be my word against his. But based on what Scythe told me, Caspian wants to meet Ryllae. He knows I'm a potential path for that—which means the odds of him not screaming for help just yet are high.

"You *want* Scythe to be your mate?" He frowns. "I was under the impression that neither of you wanted that."

"Perhaps you should assume that you know very little. It'll make all of this easier," I say smoothly.

Caspian shoots me an exasperated look before scooting off the bed, wincing a little as he cups his balls through his silk pants. "I'm going to pay you back in kind for that one day." He glares at me as he gingerly sits on the edge of the bed.

"Unlikely." I shrug.

He looks me over again, and I do the same. It's odd to think of him as Ryllae's mate. Caspian is so . . . normal looking. The different-colored eyes are striking for sure, but the rest of him just screams normal, pampered, charming prince. And Ryllae is anything but normal. It's not just their looks; everything about them is just . . . more.

Now that I know Ryllae is the fallen Fae Sovereign, it makes sense, but changeling or not, the prince doesn't seem like a good match for them. How is it possible that they're fated mates?

Scythe and I had the baggage of the wolf curse between us, but we are well-matched in every other way. Both of us are vicious and bloodthirsty. We each have our own strengths, but we *are* equals.

I would have thought that Ryllae's mate would be someone powerful . . .

I push the curious thoughts away because Scythe is all that matters now. Besides, Ryllae doesn't want the mating bond, so it'll never come to fruition.

"Tomorrow night, your father is throwing a feast before leaving for Riritha." I summon one of my blades again and casually toss it up, letting it flip through the air before repeating the move. "You're going to get me and two other people in."

A hint of remorse flashes across Caspian's face before he smothers it.

"Look, it wasn't my intention for Scythe to be caught." He leans back on his hands and stares up at the ceiling. "Given her reputation, I assumed she'd be able to get her sister free. You were more of a wild card, but Azdall seems particularly interested in you, so I figured you'd be alright as well."

"Azdall is interested in me?" I carefully watch the prince's face for any sign of trickery. "Why?"

"Really?" Caspian's gaze slides back to me, a smirk playing across his lips. "You look like *that* and basically dress as the silver version of them at parties, and from my understanding, one of your favorite pastimes is liberating the wealthy of their possessions. Are you really surprised that the god of thieves took an interest in you?"

"So I'm hot and have talented fingers." I shrug.

The prince laughs. "Gods, you even talk like them."

I think back to Azdall showing up outside the caves during my attempt to rescue Scythe. Did they know how things would play out? That Scythe would sacrifice the bond to break the curse on my wolf? Was that Azdall's way of helping me?

"Yes, it was," a familiar voice says from behind me.

I whirl, and the blade flies from my fingers a second later. Azdall catches it a hairsbreadth away from their right eye.

Pity.

I try to scatter my thoughts, because clearly, they can read at least some of them. Which is new information to me. I don't know if all the gods can read minds or if it's just an Azdall thing.

"It's a me thing . . . mostly. And the dagger to the face was rude." They huff and start flipping the knife in the same manner that I was a minute ago. "Thought you'd be in a better mood, wolf. Curse broken and all. In fact"—their golden eyes roam down my body and darken slightly—"I thought maybe you'd get down on your knees and show me just how grateful you a—"

My fist connects with their jaw, and thanks to the wolf flooding my body with their strength, the god's head snaps to the side. Then Azdall whips back towards me, and I punch them again. *Crunch*.

Azdall swears in what I think is old fae. It's hard to tell because their jaw is fractured and the words are mumbled. I dart in to hit them again, but they vanish and appear on the other side of the room, golden eyes glowing, yet they don't appear all that angry. If anything, they look more turned on.

I stalk to where my dagger fell after it went flying out of Azdall's hand and swipe it off the ground.

"I think you miscalculated things." Caspian laughs as he strolls over to a small bar set up against the wall. He pours a light amber liquid into three glasses, carrying one over to me and leaving Azdall to fend for themself.

I summon the clawed dagger back into my tattoo and take the glass from Caspian. It's not like I can't call on the blades again in a heartbeat, and this glass is thick and sturdy—I'm already thinking about smashing it into the god's pretty face.

Azdall snorts as they take in my pissed-off expression. "That explains why Erdite tried to beat the shit out of me earlier today." They walk over to claim their glass and slam it back before pouring another. "Honestly didn't understand why she was so pissed, but it makes a little more sense now."

"Shocking that the god of love would know more about mate bonds than you," Caspian says dryly.

Azdall narrows their eyes at the prince as they walk over to join us. "I liked it better when you were all starry-eyed and didn't talk back."

"I liked it better when it was only Atotl I was dealing with," the prince snaps.

"I don't give a shit about either of you," I cut in, my patience at an end. "All I care about is getting my mate back."

"Not your mate anymore," Azdall points out before sipping their liquor.

"I don't need some bullshit bond. Scythe is *mine*," I snarl.

Azdall cocks their head and looks at me as if seeing me for the first time.

"Did you play a direct involvement in her capture?" I push, knowing that, depending on their answer, I might be finding out sooner rather than later if it's possible to kill a god.

"Fascinating." Azdall tilts their head in the other direction. "You really do love her. I wasn't entirely blind before—I knew there was something between the two of you—but I thought it was just really hot sex and a passing fancy. Not an *I'll burn the world for you and slaughter a god* type of love."

"Answer the fucking question."

"Calm yourself, wolf." They roll their eyes. "I did not orchestrate or play even the slightest role in the witch's capture. Even I don't interfere directly like that. I was pushing it by giving you that coin."

"But they almost certainly knew she was going to be captured." Caspian looks at the god with obvious distaste before downing all of his liquor in one go.

"Not helping, prince." Azdall cuts him a dirty look.

"Wasn't trying to, Az," Caspian says idly before going to refill his glass. As soon as his back is turned, the god smiles, and I get the impression they enjoy the prince standing up to them.

As angry as I am with the gods' involvement in Scythe's capture—even if it was merely knowing what was coming and failing to warn us—it doesn't help to dwell on it now. I can always kill the god later. Ryllae would probably be overjoyed to help me with that.

"You know I can hear your thoughts right?" Azdall snorts. "You have no secrets fro–"

My wolf snarls viciously, the sound echoing through my mind, and the god flinches.

"Fucking werewolves," they mutter, rubbing their forehead.

I can feel my wolf remaining vigilant against further intrusion, something I had no idea they could do but am thankful for all the same, and turn my attention back to Caspian and the reason I'm here in the first place. "I need you to get me and two others into the main castle tomorrow."

"You're going to try to break Scythe free from here?" Caspian shakes his head. "It won't work."

"How about you leave that part to me and just worry about getting us in? We'll handle the rest."

How we'll handle it, I have no idea, but the hardest part will be getting in undetected, which the prince can help us with. If I have to, I can plan the rest on the go, because I absolutely can't let them take Scythe across that border. Things will get exponentially worse if that happens.

"Look." Caspian gives me a tired look, some of his princely facade slipping. "I've been trying to figure out a way to get Scythe out since I learned Stelian has her. She'd be a useful ally in the future, and something tells me I'm going to need those, but your plan of breaking her out from that fortress won't work for a number of reasons."

"I'm listening," I say tightly.

"First, I'm not kidding when I call it a fortress. My father has always been paranoid about having strongholds along the border. When he took over the throne, he had the original palace torn down and that monstrosity built in its stead."

His description of the structure isn't wrong. We scouted it as best we could earlier today, and it's not a pretty building by any means. A thick stone wall surrounds it with turrets spaced along its length. I spotted several mages with crossbows in each turret, and I'm sure there are all kinds of other hidden surprises. I could only see the top of the building rising over the wall, but it was built of the same dark stone and had a very foreboding presence.

"I take it there are no hidden passages we can make use of?" I ask, even though I already suspect the answer.

"There are, but they're well used by the guards and mages," Caspian says, confirming my suspicions. "Trust me. You don't want to go in them."

"You have a reputation across the kingdom." I take a different approach. "It wouldn't be that much of a stretch for you to bring in some guests. Surely you also have a room in that place. We can wait there, and you can claim that you'll be joining us later for an afterparty."

"And then what?" Caspian asks harshly, his demeanor suddenly hostile, causing the wolf in me to perk up. "You think it will go unnoticed that I just happened to bring in three strangers on the night that someone tries to break Scythe out? She's being held in a cage in my father's main entertaining room—the same room where they have dinner—so it's not like you can break her out then. And the room is being guarded by at least forty mage hunters. You will be noticed and likely captured."

"We can handle—"

"You will be caught, and even my reputation will not keep Stelian from looking too close," Caspian snaps and drops his glamour. The wolf in me goes absolutely still as the affable prince disappears and a changeling takes his place.

The prince was pretty before, but without his glamour, he's something else. Something otherworldly and beautiful. Now, his chestnut brown hair has streaks of gold that curl around his pointed ears, the handsome features of his face are a little sharper and more chiseled, and then there are the fangs.

Suddenly, the mate bond between Caspian and Ryllae seems a little more believable, because it's a predator standing before me now. One who feels like I'm cornering him.

"I want Scythe freed too," Caspian says in a low, dangerous tone. "But I'm not willing to give my life for hers. There are too many others counting on me, and I will not fail now. Not after everything I've done to survive up until this point."

"Fine," I bite out. If I thought my plan to break Scythe out of the fortress was still feasible, I wouldn't have backed down, but even I can see at this point that it won't work. Scythe's magic is no doubt drained, which means she won't be able to help us fight, and while Astria and Ravyn both have basic fighting skills, they'd be no match for mage hunters. "What do you know of your father's plan to move her?"

Caspian studies me for a long moment. His eyes are the same color in this form—a deep oceanic blue and a bright spring green—but like Ryllae's, his pupils are diamond shaped.

"I do not know the specifics, only that they're planning on leaving at first light, but I would wager that Stelian will move Scythe before then and my father will likely ride out to meet them somewhere with his personal guard."

"Why?"

"Stelian isn't a fool," the prince says. "He knows that you or someone else will likely try to rescue the witch, and he never misses an opportunity to bait a trap. Stelian's biggest flaw is his arrogance.

It's the reason I've been able to fly under his radar all this time despite his occasional suspicions that something isn't 'right' with me. Because the alternative is for him to accept that he missed what I am all this time, and his own pride won't allow that."

"So he'll be expecting a rescue attempt." My brows furrow together as I try to think it through. "He knows that if someone wants to save Scythe, they'll do it on Eleoyn soil rather than risk crossing into Riritha, but he won't want the king to be at risk, so he'll set a trap with Scythe as bait---and wait—and wait."

"I will do my best to get you some information." Caspian rubs his face, and between one breath and the next, his glamour is back in place. "But I can't help beyond that."

The two of us look at the god, who has been suspiciously quiet all this time. Somehow, he got a hold of the bottle of fancy liquor and is just drinking straight from it. He finishes his long swig and lets out a contented sigh before glancing at both of us.

"Oh . . . do you want my opinion now?" He wipes his mouth with the back of his hand. "Thought I'd been unceremoniously dismissed."

"And yet you remained," the prince says with a flicker of annoyance. "Like a leech that isn't done sucking the blood from its host."

"Careful." Something ancient and powerful ripples beneath Azdall's skin. "I may be more easygoing than the others, but I am a god, and I only have so much patience for outright disrespect."

Caspian's mouth hardens into a flat line. "My words were ill-crafted."

An acknowledgment but not an apology. How very fae of him.

"Do you have anything to add?" I ask the god before he can call the prince on his bullshit response.

Azdall looks at me. Whatever darkness that lurked beneath his flesh is gone, and the mischievous god is back. "There is nothing I can do to help you get Scythe back. I've been warned quite clearly by the others to back off. It's almost as if none of them trust me."

"Shocking," I deadpan.

"But I can share a bit of knowledge that perhaps will fix the wrong I have done in regards to Scythe." The god of thieves smiles at me. "The other gods have always favored the fae and, to some extent, the witches, but when we came to these lands, I felt myself drawn to the werewolves. They were something new, and after living for thousands of years, you have no idea how dear that made them to me."

"You spent time with the wolves?" I arch a dark brow at them.

"I did." They nod. "The forests above the mountains are referred to as the Wilds not only because of the vast wilderness but because of the magic of the lands. You see, unlike the fae and witches, the werewolves do not try to control magic—they accept it as a part of nature. Wild and unyielding."

The wolf settles within me, and I can feel their agreement with the god's words. I'm not sure what Azdall's point is, but I stay silent, letting them continue at their own pace.

"Witch and fae mating bonds are quite similar. It's a bending of magic to their will—to tie two souls together. That tie can be manipulated . . . or broken."

Something sharp twists within my soul at the hollow place where the mating bond should be.

"What do you mean *manipulated*?" I ask roughly.

"Did you know that fate is nothing more than a complex set of paths? Sometimes, individuals are on completely different trajectories. But if one knows just where to push . . . it's not hard to send two paths careening towards each other." The god smiles. "Easier still on the night of a blood moon."

I go completely still.

"Fuck," Caspian mutters, and I hear them throw back another shot.

"What are you saying?" I growl. "That the mating bond between me and Scythe wasn't real?"

Dread and panic swirl in my gut. She was my mate. Is my fucking mate. Azdall is fucking with me.

"Oh it was real. It was just . . . helped along. You see, Atotl needed the witch to leave her forest, so he went to his brother, Lunos, who loves to play with fate . . ." Azdall claps their hands together before spreading them wide, and a glowing spiderweb appears between them. "To follow those strands of possibilities and see where they lead."

Dread turns to rage. How hard had the gods nudged fate? Had they ensured our sisters were captured? That Scythe would be?

"To what end?" I clench my fists. "Why us?"

Those clever eyes slide to Caspian, who is staring at his empty glass.

"Atotl has never liked being denied." Azdall slams their hands together, and the web winks out of existence. "And Ryllae refuses to bend to his will. The prince is on board with the god's plan; he just needed to get the witch in a position where she would give up Ryllae."

"Before you ask—or try to slit my throat—I didn't know," Caspian says quietly. "Not the specifics about why Scythe would be coming to me for help."

"Because you didn't want to know," I snarl. "You seem happy enough to do as the gods bid."

The prince's head snaps up, and he glares at me with glowing eyes, shadows curling around his fingers. Then it's gone, and it's just the charming prince looking back at me.

"None of it matters." Azdall shrugs. "For all their scheming, they still failed." The god snorts. "It seems Scythe is just as unwilling to dance to their tune as Ryllae since—despite her sister's life hanging in the balance—she still refused to give up the fallen Fae Sovereign."

"Why are you telling me this?" The wolf lends their growl to my voice. "I don't give a fuck what they did. Scythe is *mine*."

"Atotl and Lunos might have played with fate, maybe even

manipulated magic the night of the blood moon to ensure a mating bond would fall into place, but it's a big world—there are all kinds of magic." A golden sheen rolls over the god's eyes. "The bonds that tie wolves to their mate is wild magic—and it *cannot* be broken. Not truly. It endures. Always and forever."

Hope stirs inside my chest, and my heart starts to race. I open my mouth to ask how to fix our mating bond when Azdall winks at me—and then vanishes.

Caspian catches the bottle the god was holding just before it hits the ground.

"Godsdamn it." I glare at the empty space.

"Here." Caspian offers me the liquor after they take a solid swig. "I've found it helps when dealing with the gods." I take the bottle from him, and he waves a hand at the chairs arranged in front of an unlit fireplace. "Sit with me, and I'll tell you everything I know about Stelian. Then I'll find out more tomorrow."

"What's your price?" I ask warily, even though I know I'll pay whatever it is.

"Help me with Ryllae." He holds his hands up when I instantly balk at the suggestion. "I've thought things over since my conversation with Scythe, when I asked for the same thing and she more or less told me to go fuck myself."

I smile at the thought. My witch is loyal and protective of those she loves. I'm a little surprised she didn't slit the prince's throat then and there.

"You know you have the same killing smile that she does, right?" The prince sighs as he walks over to sit in a chair. "All I'm asking is that you tell Ryllae about me and tell them that I truly want to help the fae who remain in these lands—and that I need their help to do it. Speak on my behalf and try to persuade them to meet me in person."

"And if they say no?" I take a seat opposite the prince.

"Then I'll come up with another plan without them."

"You mean the gods will and you'll just do as you're told," I sneer.

He gives me a smile that doesn't even come close to reaching his eyes. "I got dealt a shitty hand and I'm doing my best." Those sharp eyes go to where Azdall stood a couple minutes ago. "You can't beat the gods at their own game if you don't play in the first place."

"Seems to me like you're losing."

His gaze snaps back to me and I see a hint of mischief. "Does it?"

I study him for a moment longer. Scythe would probably tell him to go fuck himself. But my time is running out and I won't lose her. Besides, he's not asking me to bring him to Ryllae or tell him where they are.

Nor did he specify a time frame.

"Alright." I take another gulp of liquor. "Deal."

The prince leans forward with their hand outstretched, and I shift forward in my seat to shake it, but Caspian moves at the last second to grip my wrist. "Deal." His voice is infused with magic, and I feel it prick against my skin.

I yank my hand back, Caspian releasing it instantly, and study the tattoo that now marks the flesh of my wrist. A serpent coiling around a dagger. I raise my gaze to meet his, a question in it.

"Just a precaution on my part."

"What does it do?" I ask calmly, even as I now once again debate killing the prince. After he tells me everything I need to know, of course.

"It's a reminder of our bargain."

"That's not an answer," I growl.

Caspian smiles and drops his glamour, revealing inch-long fangs and reptilian-like eyes. "It's part of an answer, and the only one you'll be getting. Now"—he leans back in his chair—"let's discuss how to save your witch."

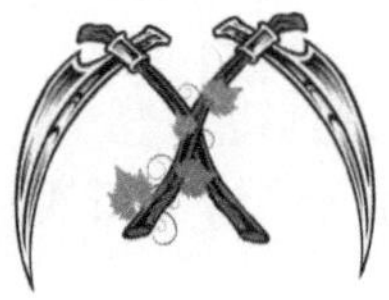

CHAPTER TWENTY-SEVEN

~

Scythe

"Fuck!" the mage screams as he jerks away from me. I spit out the chunk of his hand, and it lands next to the now-shattered bottle he dropped when my teeth sank into his flesh. Thanks to the iron manacles around my wrists, I still don't have any magic to call upon and my movements are restricted, but they didn't think to bind my mouth shut.

The mages might consider themselves hunters, but I am never prey.

I smile at the hunter through bloody teeth. "Tasty."

"You're fucking crazy, bitc—"

"What's going on?" Stelian demands as he rides over on a dark grey horse. "Why is she still awake?"

"We dosed her an hour ago before we left the fortress," another mage explains. This one is tall and broad-shouldered with a face that looks like it's been punched multiple times. Hopefully, I'll be adding myself to the list of people who have given him a permanently crooked nose.

"She burns through the sedative faster every time we give it to her," the mage I bit growls as he starts chanting a healing spell over his hand. Pity I hadn't gotten a good grip on the finger; those take longer to grow back, and the process is a lot more painful.

Stelian glares at the broken bottle and the liquid seeping into the ground. "Just gag her then and use some rope to secure her further. We'll make a stronger sedative when we're on the road." Stelian scans the trees around us before riding off to where at least forty mage hunters are gathered on the other side of the large clearing.

It's true that the sedative they've been giving me on and off the last two days isn't working well. They likely created it for the rebel mages they more commonly capture, which means it was made for a human metabolism. Even without my magic, my body burns through it quickly. It isn't like it has no effect though. I was still a little foggy when they yanked me from the cage before sunrise this morning and hauled me out to the forest.

After days being locked away in a cold cage, my heart aches at seeing the trees around us. It may not be *my* forest, but magic or not, I am a witch, and all forests call to me, whispering their secrets.

Which is why I know that there is a werewolf slipping through the trees right now with two other beings. The wolf has to be Talon. I hope the other two aren't who I think they are. Surely Talon would not endanger our sisters after everything I sacrificed to get them free.

I will fucking murder Talon if my suspicions turn out to be true. Once I'm free of these manacles. And find a blade, since my scythe is no more. And after I kiss them for coming back for me.

After all that, it will be stab fucking city.

And Astria will be getting a long lecture about putting herself in harm's way. Maybe Ravyn as well.

Help, I plead to the forest. *Please help them.*

The forest obliges. Without the influence of my magic, the

forest's wild magic is a little more chaotic and less focused, but it's still there. I can feel it swallowing the girls' footsteps, and Talon is already moving silently, either through skill or the natural magic of their wolf flowing through their blood.

Branches creak as the wind shifts so that it's blowing away from the mages. Then Stelian's horse rears suddenly, and while he struggles to get it under control, the rest of the horses tied to the trees pull back on their leads.

"Secure the horses!" Stelian commands and half of the mages rush over to the panicking creatures. "And somebody knock that fucking witch out!"

The two mages closest to me—the one I bit and the big one— eye me and then drop their gazes to the manacles. Confusion and wariness are clear in their expressions.

They aren't the ones claiming my attention though, because there is a woman standing behind them with pointed ears, radiant light brown skin, and dark hair in tight, spiraling curls. The silver armor that adorns her is more functional than elegant, and I can see where parts of it have been dented. Based on how nobody else is reacting to her, I know I'm the only one who sees the fae goddess standing before me.

Kruxtia.

"Consider this an amends for the wrongs my fellow gods have done to you and a balancing of the scales." She raises her hand and snaps her fingers. Three things happen at once. The manacles fall off my wrists, a new silver ring sizzles to life around my pinky finger, and the goddess of vengeance gives me a feral smile. "Tell the wolf they do me proud with their claws. Good hunting, witch."

Between one blink and the next, the goddess of retribution vanishes.

"What the fuck? The witch is free!" the smaller mage in front of me calls out in warning.

Chaos erupts in the clearing as some mages race towards me

while others continue to try to get the panicking horses under control.

"She still doesn't have any magic!" Stelian shouts as he runs towards me, bits of dirt and leaves stuck to his clothing. His horse must have thrown him when I wasn't looking. The remaining horses finally break loose from their ties and race off, knocking down and trampling several mages as they go. "Forget the horses—just grab that godsdamn witch!"

I spring to my feet and roll my shoulders. The manacles might be off, but my magic is still depleted. It'll take hours before I have enough to do anything useful.

"This will go easier for you if you don't put up a fight," the broader mage says as he draws his sword. It drips with purple flames.

"Nah." The mage I bit grins. "By all means, struggle. It'll make your screams all the sweeter in a minute."

Talon is closing in, I can feel it in my bones, but they're still thirty seconds away, and the direction they're coming from puts them on the other side of the clearing with the bulk of the mage hunters between us. They could skirt around Stelian and his mages, but knowing Talon, they plan to plow right through the hunters.

Crazy asshole.

Fuck, I love them.

"Your magic is still drained." The larger mage takes a step closer as another half dozen mages line up behind him. "This is gonna hurt."

"It wasn't my magic that gave me my name." I bare my teeth at him. "And you're right, this *is* gonna hurt." Three taps to the ring and I call my new scythe forth. The mages freeze as a weapon made of bright silver appears in my hand. Unlike my previous one, the handle is silver, not wood, as if it's all one flowing piece. Magic vibrates within it, and I know, despite its delicate beauty, it's unbreakable. Two wicked, curved blades flow from each end in opposite directions.

"The fuck?" The fair-haired mage whose hand I bit stares at the scythe in shock.

I don't give him or the others a chance to recover though before the scythe cuts through the air then through tissue and bone like a hot knife through butter. The mage's head rolls off his shoulders, and his body collapses a second later.

"*The fuck?*" another mage yells even louder. More start to shout in alarm—not the big one though. He's on me within seconds, and I barely jerk my scythe up in time to block his sword from piercing my heart. Rings with glowing gems adorn each of his fingers. Given how fast his strike was, at least one of them must boost his speed. He pushes his sword down harder on my scythe. I had no doubt he would be strong, considering he was built like a mountain, but not this fucking strong. One of those damn rings must increase his strength too.

"Gods, I hate mages," I grind out as his sword inches closer to my chest. Out of my peripheral vision, I see other mages start to skirt around me, now over the shock of their headless brethren. Then the scent of magic fills the air. Whatever they're up to isn't good for me, but I'm barely managing to keep this fucker from carving me up.

Stelian might want me alive, but something tells me not all of his hunters feel that way. The purple flames of the sword lick at my skin, and a low hiss slips from me. Shit, that hurts, and things are about to hurt even more in a second because I'm going to have to do something drastic if I don't want to let the other hunters finish their damn spell.

The hunter bearing down on me smiles as his eyes light up. He can feel my resistance weakening and pushes a little harder.

A harsh breath explodes from my lungs as the blade cuts into my shoulder. The mage fire burns, and on top of that, I can feel its poison surge through my blood.

"Who's hurting now, bitch?" He laughs, and I get the sense he's toying with me now, not pushing his sword in farther but not pulling it away either.

There's a flash of movement to my right, then the telling twang of a crossbow firing, followed in rapid succession by another. The sword bearing down on me wavers for a second as the mage looks to see what the commotion is about. His head turns to the left . . . so he doesn't see Talon coming from the right.

Even I'm surprised at how fast Talon moves, because they were definitely on the other side of the clearing seconds ago. Now, those wickedly curved daggers of theirs cut into the mage before me, one in the throat and the other in his belly before Talon yanks them up with one vicious tug and eviscerates him.

Blood and gore cover me despite my hasty step back. Then the most beautiful face I've ever seen is instantly there, a golden sheen rolling over dark eyes as Talon takes me in and kisses me deeply.

The kiss is fast and brutal, then Talon pulls back with a wolfish smile. "Want to kill some hunters with me, witch?"

"Always, wolf." More crossbow bolts shoot out of the trees. One mage is taken out, but a flash of green light flares in front of the other, and the bolt turns to dust as soon as it touches it. The shield vanishes instantly. It takes a large amount of magic to destroy something so rapidly. I'm begrudgingly impressed that the mage crafted a spell capable of bringing a shield up and down so efficiently.

Maybe I'll tell him that before I take his life.

"Get those fucking sharpshooters out of the trees!" Stelian orders, eying both Talon and me carefully. He was keen to take me on by himself, but I can see the hesitation in his gaze now. "Take the witch alive! Kill the wolf!"

For half a second, Talon and I spin around so we're back-to-back, then we break apart, cutting through the mages as fast as we can. In the chaos of testing out my new scythe, Talon attacking, and the girls with their crossbows, six mages are down. Another two or three lie broken on the ground where the horses trampled them, either dead or injured enough that they aren't going to be a problem for us.

That leaves roughly thirty mage hunters. Not great odds.

I duck as a mage swings a sword dripping with a sickly green flame. Some of it brushes my skin, and I let out a sharp groan as my flesh instantly boils. Another hunter executes a perfect strike, aiming for the inside of my wrists to disable me, but I knock their sword away with my scythe and put some distance between us, only to have my back slashed by another hunter.

Instinctively, I start to hum, but it's like trying to draw water from an empty well.

The hunter who tried to slash my wrists steps forward, only to stumble over a root that wasn't there before, courtesy of the forest doing its best to help me. With one smooth motion, I stab forward with my scythe and catch the mage in the gut before ripping the blade out with a twist.

My back burns as I dance away from the mage who sliced it. Hard, dark eyes track my movements, and the dark red flames of his sword flicker in them. I've never seen mage fire that color before, but I suspect it has a bleeding effect because blood is dripping from my back at an alarming pace, considering the cut isn't that deep.

Hopefully Talon is faring better than me. I can see them trading blows with three hunters while another two moan on the ground. Stelian is chanting with roughly a dozen mages in the center of the clearing, and something tells me that if they finish whatever spell they're working on, it really won't bode well for us.

That's all I have time to take in before four mages—including the one wielding the sword with the fucked-up red flames—close in on me.

I grip the scythe with both hands, sliding them to the middle —but there is no glyph for me to activate to split it into two. I start to adjust to a better position to fight with a longer weapon, when I feel the magic spark, and suddenly, I'm holding two scythes, each with the perfect proportions to wield two-handed.

Kruxtia really is the best god.

Then everything melts away. Talon snarling as they shred their way through the hunters. The twang of crossbows firing. Stelian and his mages chanting. It's just me and the four hunters, who are foolish enough to dance with the Witch of the Woods.

I dance to the beat of the forest. A song only I can hear.

An obsidian black sword flashes in front of my face as I lean out of the way, then one of my scythes cuts through the arm of the wielder while my other one blocks the sword angling for my gut. I glide away, blades whirling as the mages and I trade blows across the clearing.

Blood steadily leaks from at least a dozen wounds on my body, but I ignore it, even though I know I'm pushing my body to its limits. One of the mages executes a diagonal strike, intending to carve my upper body in half. I don't bother blocking it; instead, I step back, letting the tip of his blade pass a hairsbreadth from my chest. He's a second too slow in bringing up his guard, and my scythe slashes through his throat, then warm blood sprays outward, coating most of me.

I laugh and spin away. The hunter with the fiery red sword follows after me, fury burning in his gaze. Without looking, I take one more step back, knowing with absolute certainty that it's where I'm meant to be.

Talon's back meets mine. "Having fun, witch?"

"Bit bored, to be honest." I pant, wincing with each inhale. Is one of my ribs broken? I suck in a breath and hiss at the sharp pain. Definitely broken. How unfortunate. "Enjoying your stroll in the woods, wolf?"

"It's alright," Talon responds. I don't miss the way their own breath hitches. They're far more injured than they're letting on.

Between the two of us, we're doing pretty good. At least a quarter of the mages lie dead or dying across the clearing.

Neither Astria nor Ravyn have fired their crossbows recently, which means they're probably out of bolts. They're in the tree behind us, its branches stretching over our heads. I don't dare look up to find them though because the three hunters I have yet to put down are spread out in front of me. I have no doubt there are a few squaring off against Talon as well.

The hunters keep their distance as the chanting picks up. I can practically taste the magic in the air. Whatever the spell is, the forest isn't happy about it.

A small amount of my magic has returned. It won't be enough to stop Stelian, but maybe it can buy us some time.

Well . . . it can buy the girls time to get away.

Just as I'm about to reach down deep and cast what will likely be the last magic I ever do before I'm cut down, Stelian lets out a roar. Then there's a loud popping sound, and the chanting stops.

The hunters around Talon and me move to the outskirts of the clearing, while Stelian and the other mages do the same, leaving only one . . . thing . . . in the middle.

"What the fuck is that?" Talon turns, and I do the same so that we stand shoulder to shoulder.

I swallow as the beast that shouldn't exist rises to its full height of at least ten feet at the shoulder. Its body is composed of mismatched parts, with traces of feline, canine, and something vaguely reptilian. Parts of it are covered with fur, but there are gaps here and there, where I can see straight through to the bone and the pulsing innards. Black ichor drips from it onto the forest floor, and the plant life shrivels up at the impact before the forest wails in my mind. The natural magic of the forest can't touch this creature. My magic can, but I don't have enough of it.

Burning red eyes full of hunger look at us from a blunt skeletal face as it opens its maw to reveal rows of jagged teeth.

"Necromancy." Disgust bleeds into my words. "Even the Eleoyn king, for all his corruption, has forbidden this type of magic."

"The king will never know," Stelian replies smoothly. "Once the wolf and those brats in the tree are dead, the beast will bring me your broken but still breathing body, and then I'll carve out your tongue."

Stelian raises his hand, a beating black heart contained within it, and squeezes. Then the necromantic beast made of nightmares charges straight for us.

CHAPTER TWENTY-EIGHT

~

Talon

A RAGE-FILLED melody bursts from Scythe's throat, and thick roots surge up from the ground, forming a tight cocoon that contains us and the girls' tree. On the other side, the beast roars and starts ripping into it. Scythe staggers, and I barely manage to catch her before her legs give out.

She winces as my arm wraps around her waist, making me suspect her ribs are cracked or possibly broken. I try my best to support her without causing her further pain, but given that almost every inch of her is coated in blood—and I can tell a good amount of it is hers—I know my attempts are in vain.

Neither of us are in good shape. The roots tremble around us, and there's already more light peeking through. We have a few minutes at most before that abomination gets through, and then we'll be trapped inside a small space with an undead monster.

"I got to say, witch"—I brush my fingers across her cheek, leaving behind a bright red streak of blood—"my insane plans always worked perfectly before I met you. I think you might be cursed."

She lets out a raspy laugh, and some blood dribbles out from the corner of her mouth before she wipes it away. "Honestly, I think you're right."

Some of the roots creak as the beast climbs up to where they are thinner, and I adjust my already short time frame. We have maybe a minute before it drops right on top of us.

"Can you make an opening?" I ask Scythe, my gaze sliding pointedly to Astria and Ravyn, who have dropped down from the tree to stand in front of us.

She gives me a small nod in understanding. So much has changed over the last few weeks, but one thing remains the same— we both just want to protect our sisters, and their safety comes before ours.

"What do we do now?" Astria asks, tossing her crossbow onto the ground. "We're out of bolts, and even if we had them, I don't think they'd help against that thing."

"No weapon will work against it." Scythe grimaces. "It's not alive, so we can't actually kill it."

"How do we stop it?" Ravyn secures her crossbow across her back and pulls a dagger from her thigh.

"*We* won't do anything," Scythe says. "Talon and I will distract the beast, and the two of you will run. Stelian will likely send hunters after you, so you need to be prepared for that."

"We're not leaving you," Astria snarls, a defiant expression matching Ravyn's.

"Stelian ordered that thing to kill you two." I reach out with my free hand to cup my sister's face and force her to look at me. "Scythe and I can't afford to be distracted by trying to protect you while also trying to defeat it. You've done well, sis, but it's time for you and Astria to go."

Ravyn's eyes soften. "But it has orders to kill you too, Tal."

"I've survived worse odds than this," I lie through my teeth while giving her a confident grin. "I'll be fine." Another lie.

"Don't stop." Scythe steps away from me to yank her sister into a hug. "You run and you keep fucking running all the way back to Draco, and then you keep going. We'll catch up."

Something inside me breaks at hearing the lie on Scythe's lips. We both know we're not walking away from this.

"I love you," I tell Ravyn. "You've always been the light of my world."

"I love you too." My sister's voice cracks as tears stream down her cheeks.

"The two of you just need to make it to Draco." I drop my hand from Ravyn's face, turn her away from where the necromantic monster is still tearing through the roots, and guide her to the other side of Scythe's protective barrier. Where there is a gap just big enough for her and Astria's slender forms to crawl through. "Promise me you won't stop, Ravyn."

"We won't," she whispers in a broken voice.

Scythe and Astria murmur their own goodbyes, and I nudge Ravyn towards the opening before whirling around to where the beast has been ripping through the roots. Bits of flesh cling to its face, but most of it is exposed skeleton. A deep, rumbling growl fills our temporary safe spot as it shoves its head and one arm through. Half of its body now dangles inside, and the roots snap as its back feet claw into them.

"*Go!*" Scythe shoves her sister forward, and the two sobbing girls scramble out of the hole. I hear them flat-out running as they get to their feet on the other side.

A pissed-off screech fills the air as the monster sees two of its prey getting away. It's too far inside now to back out though. We just need to make sure it remains focused on us, so I dart beneath it and leap straight up. My dagger slices into the underside of its jaw, where it actually has some flesh, and black ichor pours from the wound, splashing across my hand and part of my arm.

Instantly, my arm feels numb and just wrong, but I keep my grip on the dagger as I drop to the ground and back away. The beast snarls, and I bare my teeth up at it. Dead it might be, but the fucker still feels pain.

I hear some of the mage hunters taking off into the woods, no doubt after the girls, and I have to control the panic that flares inside my chest. There's nothing more Scythe or I can do for them. We have to keep this monstrosity distracted and have faith that Astria and Ravyn can handle themselves. Once they're on Draco's back, they'll be fine. That fae horse can outrun anything.

Magic pulses through the air as Scythe merges her two blades back into one and slashes it across the beast's face. It roars, but a chunk of roots break, allowing more of its body to slip through. It's only a matter of seconds before it falls the whole way in.

The tree groans behind us, and suddenly, the roots tighten around the monster's hindquarters, causing it to let out another shriek of rage as it's pulled a little farther back.

Scythe seizes the distraction and darts underneath it to stand by my side again. "The forest is trying to help us, but its magic is waning and will continue to weaken as long as that thing is here." She looks at me with those silver eyes that I once thought were a curse; now, they're my everything. "Thanks for coming back for me."

"I'll never leave your side again, love." I dismiss my blades back into my palms so I can gently pull her against myself, still aware of her injuries. Her scythe vanishes into her ring as I kiss her deeply, savoring her taste. Scythe's tongue slips into my mouth as she does the same. When we break apart, I know the wolf is looking out through my eyes too, and it's both of us who speak. "Don't even think about trying to make us run again."

"Even if I did have the magic to do such a thing, I wouldn't," she promises and leans her head against my chest, directly over where the mating mark used to be. "I choose you, Talon. For however long we have left."

"I'll find you in the next life." I kiss the top of her head. "Try to be a little more grateful though. I'm sure I'll be equally stunning."

Scythe lets out a raspy chuckle as she raises her head to kiss me, nipping my lip hard enough to draw blood. "Perhaps you'll speak less. That'll be a nice change."

"You adore my clever tongue." I give her a roguish smile, and she rolls her eyes.

"Whatever you need to tell yourself, wolf."

Overhead, roots snap, ending our sweet moment, and I curse the fates for making it so short while also being grateful I at least got something. We look up at the snarling nightmare that will be the end of us, then I try to turn us so I stand between the beast and Scythe—anything to buy her a few more seconds—but she just gives me a wicked grin as she slips out from my arms to stand at my side once more.

Her scythe flashes into existence, and she twirls it fast enough that the silver blades blur. "Let's make the beast work for it."

The monster is only supposed to kill me, but I have no doubt that Scythe will not allow herself to be taken alive. My chest burns, but I force myself to return her smile with a feral grin of my own. At least we'll go out on our own terms and we'll be together. I open my mouth to say what will likely be the last thing I ever say to my mate, but then fall to my knees, gasping.

Scythe screams, her scythe slipping from her fingers as she crashes down next to me, clutching at her chest. It feels like my heart is being burned to cinders. Is this Stelian's work? Did he get tired of waiting for his pet monster to claw its way through our temporary shelter?

I stretch my hand out, and Scythe finds it, even as her body contorts in pain, her fingers tightening around mine. This is not exactly the blaze of glory I was hoping for, but at least I get to touch her. Above us, pieces of the roots fall as the beast thrashes wildly, as if the sound of our pain is kicking it into a frenzy.

Just as suddenly as the pain started, it stops, leaving a tingling sensation over my skin. I feel . . . good. All the injuries that were slowly wearing me down are healed, and my mind is clear and alert. It's like I've just woken up from the best nap of my life.

I yank my shirt down and stare at the bright silver tree tattoo. It starts over my heart just like the previous mating mark, but this one is much larger. The branches extend across my body, and I can tell they reach up my neck. The lunar tattoos that race down my arms have also turned silver, and there are now vines weaving between the different moon phases, linking them all together.

Scythe's fingers tighten around mine once more before releasing, then she rises to kneel on the ground, facing me, and tugs her tunic down. A lunar design, similar to the ones on my arms, arcs across her chest, and her silver eyes glow with magic as tears stream down her cheeks.

"Always and forever," I rasp. "Azdall said wolf mating bonds are wild magic. They cannot truly be broken."

"Wild magic . . . I can feel it winding its way around my soul." She gives me a savage grin. "It likes me."

I smile back at her because I can feel the strange magic coursing through my body too.

The last of the roots holding the undead monster finally break, and it tumbles into the small space. Despite some of its feline characteristics, it doesn't land gracefully but instead slams into the earth in a twisted heap.

A low, deep melody fills the air, and more roots spring from the earth, pinning the beast down. Black ichor oozes out wherever they touch, and the dark wood instantly starts to shrivel up.

"That won't hold it for long," Scythe says urgently as we leap to our feet. "How do you feel about playing tag with an undead abomination?"

"Sounds fun." The wolf chuffs happily in my soul at the newfound power and energy coursing through us. I don't know if this is a temporary boost from the mating bond or what, but I'm not going to question it. It's a chance for us to survive, and that's all that matters. I shed my clothes to make shifting easier. The wolf is faster, and I'll need every ounce of speed and agility I can get. "And what will you be doing while I play with our friend, Princess?"

"Ripping the beast's heart from Stelian's hand and shoving it down his throat." She shrugs. "Probably disemboweling him while I'm at it."

"Gods." My voice turns rough as the shift begins. "It's like you want me to fuck you right here."

My beautiful and vicious mate grins at me as she swipes her scythe from the ground. "We can do that after our enemies lie dead and broken around us."

The beast roars as the roots holding it down weaken. I drop to my hands and knees. This change feels different from the ones before. It's just as fast as when Scythe forced me to shift, but there is none of the pain. Just a slightly uncomfortable pressure as bones snap, muscle rearranges, and skin gives way to fur.

Once it's done, I shake my large canine body, and the wolf surges forward a little more until it feels like our thoughts are one. They understand my plan and let out a low growl of approval. Scythe steps back until she stands flat against the tree.

I move farther away, and the beast's red eyes bounce between me and Scythe. That won't do. I need its full attention. When its gaze falls on Scythe again, I lunge forward, delivering a quick but hard bite to the leg closest to me. The monster lets out a deep snarl, its attention fully locked on me now.

"Ready?" Scythe asks, a hum already on her lips.

It's the wolf that answers her as they let out one sharp bark.

Scythe's hum bursts into a song that reverberates through the air like a bell tolling, and the wall made of roots bursts outward, twisting and sharpening midair while they fly towards the mages like spears. Most of the hunters manage to duck behind trees or bring up shields in time to block the assault, but a few are too slow. Their pained screams are like music to my ears.

Chaos erupts as the beast finally frees itself of the roots and tears after me. To the mages' credit, the ones who avoided Scythe's wrathful outburst have recovered quickly and spread out across the clearing in clusters. Some start chanting, and others have their swords ready to go. I only have a few seconds to take this all in because, while the beast might be lacking in the grace department, it's a fast fucker.

Jaws snap behind me, and I'm pretty sure I lose a few tail hairs. I put on a burst of speed and leap towards the nearest group of mages, who opted for magic over weapons. Bad choice. It leaves them wide open.

For a fraction of a second, I slow down, muscles coiling in my hindquarters before I launch myself at the mage in the middle. His eyes widen in surprise, and he throws his arms up just in time to prevent me from tearing out his throat.

It would have been nice, but that wasn't actually my plan. As soon as my paws hit his chest, my claws dig in, piercing flesh, and I leap over him. I hit the ground running, a raspy laugh that's a blend of me and the wolf rumbling through my mind as the beast barrels into the mages behind us.

I might be its current target, but that just means anything between us is going down. The mages scream as it tears them apart in its rage.

A flash of lilac catches my attention. Scythe is slicing her way through the hunters that have formed lines in front of Stelian, who still holds the beast's heart. I have nothing but faith in my mate— she'll get to him, but I need to continue buying her time.

And, oh look, so many mages left to kill.

Chanting starts from my left. This group is a little smarter than the last. Two mages are at the front with their swords out, and another three are behind them, working on another spell. I wait until the beast is almost on me again, and then I turn abruptly. It stumbles as it tries to make the same move and goes down in a pile of twisted limbs.

The sword-wielding mage on the right mutters something, and his blade erupts into bright red flames that I instantly recognize. My gaze zeroes in on him. This is the asshole who burned Scythe's back earlier.

A roar comes from behind me, and I feel the ground tremble. No. The beast doesn't get this one.

This asshole is *mine.*

Everything shrinks to the closing distance between me and the mage. This is going to hurt, but I'll taste his blood on my tongue. The monster will have to make do with sloppy seconds.

A wall of green fire springs to existence in front of me, and I barely manage to change my direction. I growl at being denied my enemy's blood as I race down the fiery wall. The scent of burnt fur reaches my nostrils as my left side gets a little too close.

Before I can double back, the beast is on me, and I have to race across the clearing, weaving between groups of mages as I try to slow it down. The mage hunters try and fail to put up a deterrent against the nightmarish creature their leader called forth.

I glance over my shoulder just in time to see it crush two of them before swatting a pissed-off paw at another, his head exploding into bits of gore and bone. It must have encountered that green wall of fire too because patches of its fur are now charred black.

Apparently, creatures born of necromancy are nigh inde-structible.

One hunter manages to summon a binding made of ice that traps the beast for a few seconds, and when it breaks free, its focus momentarily shifts from me to him. I relish the terrified screams that spill forth before changing my direction and running back towards the mage whose death belongs to me.

I check on Scythe, who has killed half the mages between her and Stelian. Her lips are curved up into a wicked smile on her blood-speckled face. We're in the fight of our lives, and my mate fucking loves it.

This is the real her. I might have met her as Cerelia, but that was a lie. She was holding herself back, still trying to fit the mold the witches had made for her. *Scythe* is who she was always meant to be. Someone loyal and devoted beyond measure to those she loves, and ruthless and cruel to her enemies.

My wondrous violent beauty.

A harsh cackle spills from Scythe's lips before she cuts a hunter straight through from groin to shoulder, then she starts singing a beautiful melody as she dances through the carnage like there's a band playing her favorite song.

For all their power and grace, the gods have nothing on her. The witch is perfection, and she's *mine*.

The monster is still ripping into the hunter who attempted to stop its rampage. At least, I'm pretty sure it's the same hunter. Hard to tell because now he's just a pile of mush with some bone sticking out here and there as the beast slams its enormous paws down over and over again.

Squish.

Not letting the distraction go to waste, I focus on the prick with the fiery red sword. Some of the mages have decided they've had enough of this shit and fled into the woods. Clearly, they were on board when the odds were in their favor, but after watching an undead beast—created by forbidden magic, no less—turn one of their own into something that vaguely resembles chunky stew, their loyalty to Stelian has run out. I don't want my prey to join those making a getaway.

He's not leaving this clearing alive.

Unfortunately, those green flames are not only still there, but now, they're a complete circle instead of just a wall. He and the two mages holding up the defense aren't making any attempts to help their fellow hunters—most of whom are dead or running at this point. They're probably hoping to wait this out, assured that the necromantic monster will eventually take care of me and Scythe before Stelian gets rid of it.

I eye the flames as I close the distance. My guess is a little over six feet. I can clear that. Probably. The hunter shouts something at the mages behind him, and suddenly, the flames jump up several more feet.

Damn it. I let out a frustrated growl but don't change my course. We can make it. The wolf rumbles their support in my mind. Our mind? The lines between where I end and the wolf begins are more blurred in this form, but we're both in agreement. We're going to taste this hunter's blood.

My focus shrinks to the path in front of us and that fiery wall. If I'm going to clear it, my timing has to be perfect. A few feet before I plan to jump, Scythe's presence brushes across my mind. Her song changes, and without any words between us, I somehow know what she's saying.

The wolf understands even before I do, and they're the ones controlling our body as we jump, not at the wall, but to the open air just to the right. Roots erupt out of the earth, forming a platform, and our paws hit it before we leap again, this time directly over the green wall of fire to the thick tree trunk behind the two mages keeping the fire going.

The wolf perfectly executes each jump and only gives me back control after they've ripped out the throats of both mages. I shake my head a little to clear my thoughts. We'll definitely have to practice passing control because it's a little disorienting. Without the two mages keeping it going, the defensive wall of fire collapses, not that it really matters since I'm on the other side of it. Red flames still coat the mage hunter's sword, which he holds in front of himself as he eyes me warily.

"I have no quarrel with you, wolf," he says evenly.

A chuffing sound spills from my throat—the wolf version of a laugh. He hurt my mate, and he was bringing her to a kingdom where she would have been tortured and brutalized.

Across the clearing, I see the beast rise, finally done pummeling the mage into the earth. It briefly looks at Scythe, who is almost done cutting her way to Stelian, and I tense. If it makes a move towards her, I'll have to abandon my quarry. Fortunately, it turns away from her and starts lumbering towards me, picking up speed as it comes.

The mage before me glances at the monster running towards us and grins as he steps back. I'm the beast's target; all he has to do is stay out of the way and it will leave him alone.

Not a bad plan. I'm clearly on borrowed time, and he does have that fancy sword.

I've never been afraid of a little pain though.

His eyes widen as I leap forward, aiming not for his throat but for his arm—the one holding the sword. My jaws snap closed around his wrist and I shake my head viciously. Blood squirts through my teeth, and the sword goes flying. I clamp down harder until bones snap. The mage screams and falls to his knees.

Knowing the beast will be on us at any second, I drop to the ground and sink my teeth into his thigh, aiming for his femoral artery. I'm not sure if I'm successful, but either way, I got him good. Between his arm dangling at his side, bits of bone protruding through the bloody, mangled flesh, and the wound on his thigh, he's not going anywhere fast.

I hate leaving him alive, but I'd hate being munched on by an undead beast even more, so it's time to go.

Just as I begin to sprint away, the beast lets out a roar and lunges right at me. Instead of trying to dodge, I dart forward, diving underneath its massive form and out the other side. One of its rear paws catches my back, eliciting a pained yelp as it tears away some burnt fur and flesh, then wood snaps as the beast collides with a tree.

I whirl around to face it, staggering slightly—all the wounds I've collected are starting to take their toll. The monster snarls as it gets back to its feet, bloody drool dripping from its jaw, and pieces of flesh stuck between its teeth. My mind rejects the sight of it. Few things give me nightmares, but this will probably do it.

I prepare myself for another attack and hope the pain in my back won't slow me down. Most of the mage hunters are dead or gone. My time of leading the monster on a merry chase around the clearing has come to an end, and there is nothing else to distract it with now.

It lifts one large paw and steps forward, lowering its head as it prepares to charge. My best bet will be to get around it and weave through the trees. It's fast in the open, but it can't turn for shit. Suddenly, the beast rears back like it's been struck and lets out an eardrum-piercing shriek. The hunter whose arm I mutilated stops his attempt to crawl away and clamps a hand over one of his ears.

My head feels like it's splitting in two as I hunker down flat on the ground. Just as quickly as it started, the screaming ends.

Parts of the beast start to slide off, and it's morbidly fascinating. Until the smell hits. I wrinkle my nose in disgust and get to my feet so I can back up. It takes one staggering step towards me before its body completely falls apart. The scent of decomposition fills the air, and that's when I learn that I *can* gag in my wolf form.

Giving the rotting corpse as much room as possible, I skirt around it, to where the maimed hunter leans against a tree. He sees me coming and pushes off it. I allow him to take a few staggering steps before I slam my shoulder into his left leg and he collapses with a scream. As much as I'd love to extend his death, I don't have the time.

My jaws are around the back of his neck, and with one quick twist, he goes limp. I stare at his right hand. It's only hanging on by a few tendons . . . and I do owe my mate a gift to celebrate our bond.

A minute later, I trot up to Scythe and lay the hand down at her feet. Silver eyes glance down at it, taking in the rings on all the fingers, and she grins. "You're so sweet, Tal. Thank you."

I let my tongue hang out of the side of my mouth as I preen at the praise. Fine clothing and jewelry are still my preferred presents, but if the bloody remains of her enemies are what makes my mate happy, then that is what she shall have.

Her gaze goes back to the last mage standing. I can hear the labored breathing of a few others, but those breaths sound pretty numbered. If they're still alive in ten minutes, I'll be impressed. My attention goes to the reason we're in this clearing-turned-graveyard to begin with. Stelian's chest is soaked in blood, thanks to the bloody stump of his arm he's cradling. The rest of his appendage lies at his feet beside a shriveled black heart that's been cleaved in two.

The arrogance is long gone from his expression as his gaze bounces between me and Scythe. Exhaustion and pain are etched onto his features, and I suspect he's fighting to remain conscious right now. I lean against Scythe's leg, and she hums a melody under her breath as her fingers hover over the wound on my back. It itches as the skin stitches itself back together, but once it's done, she runs her fingers through the fur soothingly.

"Wait," Stelian rasps.

A growl rumbles from my chest as I step away from my mate and stalk towards Stelian. Scythe moves to his other side, forcing the mage to split his attention. He tries to back up so he can keep us both in his sight but trips over a fallen hunter's body.

"Is this where you offer us a deal?" Scythe cocks her head as she watches her prey scramble on the ground. It's such a wolf-like move, it sends my heart racing. *Mate*, the wolf grumbles in my head. *Pack.*

Ours.

"I can stop the raids on your forest." Stelian nods frantically. "The king will listen to me. He's already starting to set his sights elsewhere."

Scythe laughs. "What do I care about the men you send to die? My forest is *hungry*."

The mage's eyes fall on me. "I can ensure that the Tolvenian troupes are left alone by city guards."

I snort. No, he can't. The city guards are corrupt assholes notorious for disobeying rules. Plus, in some cities, there is a vendetta between the guards and mage hunters, so those guards would defy Stelian's orders simply out of spite.

Scythe looks at me, a question in her eyes, and I shake my head, trying to convey everything I'm feeling down the bond. She smiles widely, and I know she understands perfectly.

"My mate and I know that neither your words nor your life hold any value to us." Scythe moves closer to him, swirling her blade in a slow and taunting manner. "But your death will."

"The king will retaliate," Stelian argues before shifting his hand a little closer to his chest, but not before I catch one of his rings starting to glow. "If you kill me, he'll send every mage hunter in Eleoyn into your woods. They'll burn it all down."

"You've tried fire before—didn't work." Scythe smirks. "And within a week, everyone is going to be talking about the massacre that occurred today. How you led all these mages to their deaths. The mages in Eleoyn are cowards and bullies. I don't think many are going to be signing up to invade my forest after today, and you said it yourself, the Eleoyn king is turning his attention elsewhere."

Stelian's face twists into an ugly expression before his hand jerks forward and he points the glowing ring at Scythe. Before a single word falls from his lips, my jaws crunch down on his fingers. His scream is abruptly cut off, and I release his hand, dropping back to the ground. Scythe's blade protrudes through his neck, and Stelian jerks like a fish on a line.

Blood dribbles out from the corners of his mouth before his gaze turns glossy and unseeing, then she yanks her scythe out, and the mage hunter topples to the ground. I stare at his body for a long moment, a little annoyed that I wasn't the one to deal the killing blow, but he's dead, and that's all that matters. Now we just need to catch up to the girls and—

Branches snap to the south of us. I jerk my head and let out a low growl.

Scythe spins to face the oncoming threat before relaxing, as if she knows something I don't. Then the wind changes, and I catch their scent. I call on the shift, and a minute later, I'm standing in my human form, glaring at the two people making their way through the trees towards us.

A cloak lands on my head, and I turn to glare at Scythe, who just saunters over to me. She dismisses her scythe between one blink and the next and kisses me. I toss the cloak aside and clutch her to me, tangling my tongue with hers as one hand wraps around her hair and the other grips her ass.

She tastes of blood and wickedness. I growl in frustration, and she just pulls back with a husky laugh. "Put the cloak on. They're almost here."

I grumble about cock-blocking sisters and swipe the cloak off the ground. Surprisingly, there isn't much blood on it, but it still smells like someone else. I grimace and wrap it around my waist just as the girls break the tree line and burst into the clearing.

"Didn't we tell you to run?" Scythe gives her sister a look that would make seasoned warriors quiver.

A familiar, defiant light flares in Astria's eyes. She might not be a true witch like Scythe, but there is no doubt they are sisters. The slender blonde woman plants her hands on her hips and glares. "I told you what you wanted to hear. Obviously I wasn't going to abandon my sister to a cruel and likely prolonged death."

"And I'd never leave you, Tal." Ravyn nods. "It took us longer than we thought it would to eliminate the hunters who chased us. We saw *this* through the trees"—she looks around wide-eyed at the bodies—"and knew the two of you were okay as soon as we got to the clearing, but we were worried you were hurt."

"Clearly, neither of you are *that* hurt though, considering the lip smacking we just witnessed." Astria smirks even as she blushes harder.

"We need to figure out a system for your shifting, my favorite sib." Ravyn frowns at the cloak I've twisted into a makeshift skirt. "I have no interest in seeing your naked ass all the time."

"I'm your only sibling," I point out. "And don't change the subject. You were told to get the fuck away from here." As happy as I am to see them again, they came back thinking we would need their help—knowing there was a good chance they'd die trying to free us. After everything we sacrificed to get them out of the fire, they willingly walked back into the flames.

Seeing my scowl, Ravyn closes the distance between us, her eyes softening. "You don't get to tell us how we choose to protect those we love." She flicks my nose and glances at Scythe. "Either of you."

Before we can reprimand our sisters further, Ravyn practically flounces back over to Astria and grabs her hand. "Come on. We've got a lot of corpses to search. I bet they have some good shit we can sell for a pretty coin."

I stare helplessly at Scythe. "I'm so pissed and yet so proud right now."

"Same, wolf," she grunts and then lets out a surprised exhale when I pull her towards me, wrapping my arms around her waist.

My mouth slants over hers, and I kiss her deeply before whispering across her lips, "Let's go home, witch."

"I'm not sure where that is these days," she whispers back.

"My home is wherever you are." I brush another kiss against her lips. "But right now . . . I'm thinking your woods need a wolf."

Scythe smiles against my mouth before gazing up at me. "Then let's go home, wolf."

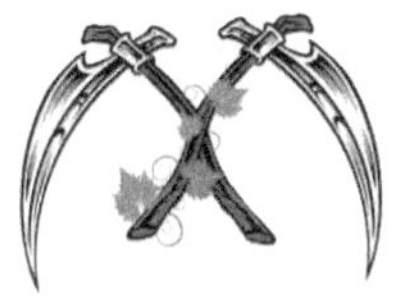

CHAPTER TWENTY-NINE

~

Scythe

"WHAT THE FUCK IS THAT?" Talon points to a pile of . . . something.

I squint at the slender items. They're not just stacked in front of any tree—this is the one with my home at the top. Are they—I step a little closer. Yep. Those are definitely fingers.

"Necos." I sigh. "Get your furry little butt out here."

Silence reigns in the small clearing. Not even a bird chirps. When we stepped into my forest hours ago, I nearly cried. I hadn't realized how much I'd missed it. Branches bent to brush against me as I passed, and flowers bloomed. It missed me too.

The devil cats were suspiciously absent though.

Now I know why. They knew I was back, and they all raced here to see how I would react to my welcome home gift.

"What's going on?" Astria asks, her fingers intertwined with Ravyn's as they step into the clearing. Both Talon and I were pleasantly surprised and relieved when the girls said they were coming back to the forest with us. It's only for a while. When the troupe comes back this way and camps outside Shalewood, they'll join up with them again, but at least that gives us a couple of months to come to terms with them going off on their own.

It still frightens me, especially after everything that has happened, but I need to let my sister live her life. Besides, if they get into any trouble, I have Talon now. Between the two of us, we'll slaughter anything that stands in our way.

"Can someone explain why I'm staring at a pile of fingers?" Ravyn's tone is calm and even, but her eyes widen suddenly. "Did one of them just move?"

We all ponder the pile of fingers that is definitely twitching.

"Sweetheart—" Astria starts.

"*Oh my gods*!" Ravyn screams as a centipede crawls out from underneath some fingers. "Why did I convince you to let me come here? We could be soaking in a hot bath right now!"

Shadows move in the trees above us. I think about calling out a warning, but . . . my sister has it coming.

"This is just a minor thing. Don't let it—" My little sister shrieks as a sixty-pound cat slams against her chest and knocks her to the ground. "Necos!" Astria bats at the devil cat, who is licking her face. "Get off! Cece! Help!"

"Do you hear something?" I arch an eyebrow at Talon.

Talon's lips quirk up into a lopsided grin, and they glance around dramatically. "No. Not a thing."

"Hmm. Must be the wind." I sing a brief note, and a stairway with a railing unravels around one of the nearby trees. "Ravyn, feel free to settle in. We don't have bathtubs here, but there is a hot spring less than a five-minute walk that way." I point to the northeast.

"Okay," she says slowly. "But can you explain the fingers? And what am I supposed to do about this?"

The three of us look at Astria, who is alternating between laughing hysterically and shrieking. Necos has been joined by a dozen other devil cats, all of whom are helping hold her down. A few kittens tumble forward—they must have been born while I was away because they're still tiny balls of grey fluff and lack the grace of the adults.

I scoop one up and hand it to Ravyn, who hesitantly takes it from me and peers down at the kitten. Then she instantly cuddles it to her chest when bright blue eyes look at her and it mewls pathetically.

Sucker. That's how the devil cats get you.

It's all cute little meows one day. Piles of random body parts the next.

"They're cats." I shrug. "From their point of view, we're shitty hunters, and they feel obligated to provide for us. I did ask them to guard the forest while I was gone." I mentally count the fingers. There have to be at least forty. "Assuming those each belong to a different person, I'd say they did an excellent job."

"And the centipede?" Ravyn shudders.

"It just wanted a snack." I try to give her my best reassuring smile. "I'm sure there won't be any in your house. They prefer the forest floor."

Ravyn bolts for the stairs, taking the devil kitten with her.

"She's probably never going to come down." Talon sighs before narrowing their eyes at me. "It also doesn't escape my attention that the stairs going to Astria's home have a railing."

"Are you asking me to add a railing to the one going to my house?"

"*Our* house," they correct me. "And yes. Also one around that death trap you call a porch."

"Aww," I croon. "Is the mighty werewolf scared of heights?"

"I have a healthy respect for them. I'm not scared."

"Mm-hmm."

"Stop flirting and get these vermin off me!" Astria yells.

Necos just bats her across the face, being careful to keep her claws sheathed.

"They're just expressing how much they missed you." I grab

Talon's hand, and we skirt around my sister as we walk towards the tree behind her. A quick little song from me has the stairs appearing—this time with a railing for my delicate princess of a werewolf. "You could try making a run for it to the hot springs. They won't follow you into the water."

My sister shoves Necos and the other devil cats aside and lunges to her feet. Her blonde hair streams behind her as she runs across the clearing, towards the smaller hot springs.

The devil cats give her a ten-second head start before they melt into the forest, chasing after her. All except Necos, who trots over to me and bumps her leg against my thigh.

"Missed you too, friend." I scratch her head. "These yours?" I gesture towards the two kittens, who are now climbing up Talon's pants.

Necos lets out a yowl that I take for a yes.

"You could have let me know you were expecting a litter before I left you, hussy." I still would have gone, but I could have created some more useful shelters for them before leaving. Necos just gives me a look that clearly says she thinks I'm the idiot here.

Gods, I missed the devil cats.

I smile. "We'll watch over them while you torment my sister."

Another yowl, then the devil cat bounds off after the others.

The two kittens leap off Talon—not quite sticking the landing—and start to follow.

"Nope." I scoop them up and pass one off to Talon while tucking the other against my chest. "You're snack-sized for a lot of the things out there, my furry little friends."

"Have I ever mentioned that I'm not really a cat person?" Talon frowns at the kitten, and it lets out a small hiss before sinking its teeth into the hand holding it. Talon's eyes light up. "Okay, that's kind of adorable. Who's a vicious little predator?" They boop the kitten on the nose. "You are!"

Murder shines in the kitten's eyes, and Talon just grins.

"Come on." I laugh. "You can torment the kitten, who is definitely going to try to kill you in a few years, up there." I start up the stairs, and Talon follows. "Once Necos comes back to watch over her spawn, I have a surprise for you."

"Another surprise? After a pile of decomposing fingers and devil kittens?" Talon chuckles. "How you spoil me, mate."

"You *do* spoil me." Talon lets out a contented sigh as they sink deeper into the hot spring.

These ones are different from the springs Astria and Ravyn are off exploring. When Astria left me, I needed a way to distract myself—in between hunting down trespassers of course. This area previously contained a naturally forming pool, courtesy of a creek that runs into it.

It took me several weeks of work—both physical and magical—but gradually, I widened the pool and decreased the depth so I could walk across it. Several smooth boulders line the sides to provide places to sit. Heating it was a bit of a challenge, but I was able to coax several heated vents that ran far beneath the earth closer to the surface.

After I put all the work in, I barely even tried it out. Something felt wrong about using the beautiful oasis by myself. It was more depressing than relaxing.

As I watch Talon duck beneath the water and then shake their dark hair as they rise, I smile.

"Enjoying the view?" A gold sheen rolls over their eyes as they catch me watching them.

"Yes," I admit without a hint of shame. "And I'm glad I finally figured out what was missing from this place."

"Oh?" They lazily swim towards me. "Do tell. What has been missing? I'm guessing it's something that is utter perfection in every way possible? Something that is truly stunning?"

For a moment, I think about telling them exactly what I'm

thinking. That they're what I've been searching for my entire life. That I love them beyond measure.

But where would the fun be in that? Besides, if Talon's ego gets any bigger, they might not be able to fit in our bed.

"Truly stunning," I muse before holding my hand up and gazing lovingly at the silver ring around my finger. "That's exactly it. This ring *is* absolutely the most glorious thing in existence. I can't believe I went my whole life without it.

"That so?" Talon stops halfway to me. "Nothing else comes to mind?"

"Not a single thing," I answer solemnly.

A yelp erupts from me when I'm suddenly pulled underwater. Then something pinches my sides, and I wildly kick to the surface, sputtering and shoving my hair out of my face. I glare at Talon, who is now leaning next to the smooth, rocky side of the springs and grinning at me.

It's been a month since I broke their curse, and I'm still not used to how fucking fast they are. I swear, sometimes it feels like, between one blink and the next, they clear impossible distances. Of course, Talon finds it endlessly entertaining to fuck with me, and the more I threaten them with violence, the more turned on they get.

My mate is depraved.

I fucking adore that about them.

"Don't be rude and I won't try to drown you." Talon sniffs, then starts scratching at the fae brand on their wrist.

"You can't scratch it off," I remind them dryly.

Talon gives it one more distasteful look before dropping their wrist below the water. It's the same look I give the brand every time I see it, so I can't exactly blame them for resenting it. I was . . . less than pleased when I learned of the bargain they had struck with Caspian. Even if it is the only reason Talon found me in time.

Actually, I'm still quite pissy about the whole thing now that I think about it. Next time I see the prince, his blood is going to decorate my new blade.

"Quit thinking about gutting the prince." Talon gives me a knowing look. "Ryllae gets first claim. I get second. You get sloppy thirds."

I curl my lip but don't argue. They can make whatever *claims* they want. All that matters is who reaches the prince first—and I'll ensure it's me. Ryllae and Talon will just have to deal.

"Given how many piercings and tattoos you have, I don't know why that one bothers you so much." I float towards the center of the pool. Maybe I should add a waterfall?

"It feels wrong." Talon holds up their hand again and glares at the mark. "Like I'm always aware of its existence. It's hard to explain, but it gets a little worse each day."

"This is exactly why you shouldn't make bargains with the fae," I chide even as worry blossoms inside my chest.

We looked for Ryllae before coming home to my forest. First, we went back to Albadrid so Talon could collect their things and explain to the troupe what was going on. To my surprise, everyone was supportive of them leaving. Talon would be missed—especially by Mattias and Vesi—but everyone was happy for them.

It was a very eye-opening experience for me to witness that—to see what a family could be. Everyone was thrilled Talon's curse had been broken, and they were even happier to learn we were mates. Our trip home was delayed because of the two-day celebration their troupe threw in our honor. They even cancelled all the public performances and then helped us pack, although most of Talon's clothing and possessions are traveling with the troupe; we'll pick them up when they make it back to Shalewood. My mate has a ridiculous amount of clothing and jewelry. I teased them about it mercilessly most of the way here and only stopped when they threatened to never fuck me while wearing that silver crown of theirs again.

I shut up.

After we left Albadrid with Astria and Ravyn in tow, we went to Ryllae's cottage, only to find it completely empty. All of their personal possessions were gone, and they left the door unlocked, as if they didn't care about protecting the place they'd called home for the better part of a century.

The only message they'd left behind was pinned to the tree in the backyard. *See you around, friend. If any gods are reading this, get fucked.*

Ryllae. Truly an eloquent and gifted linguist.

Worry forms in the pit of my stomach as I think about the note. Ryllae *is* my friend. Whatever they're up to, I would help if I could, which is probably why they vanished without a trace.

There is zero chance of us finding Ryllae if they don't want to be found. What that means for the bargain between Talon and Caspian . . . I don't know.

I scowl harder.

"Come now, my sweet," Talon chides as they swim closer. "Stop stressing about Ryllae and the soon-to-be-dead prince for today."

"It's not like I can just turn my mind off," I huff. "Maybe once the girls are settled, we should go ba—" My words die a swift death in my throat as Talon casually brushes their cuff earring and the silver crown glimmers into existence.

I manage to maintain a semblance of self-control by swallowing the whimper that tries to break free. Talon already knows about my crown fetish; I don't need to feed into their ego any more.

The distance between us shrinks, and I swim backwards until I hit the rocky wall. A cocky grin spreads across Talon's face as they plant their hands on either side of me against the rocks, boxing me in. "I bet I can distract you for days, witch."

My mind instantly empties of all the worries I've been carrying. Still . . . I can't make it too easy for them. I am the Witch of the Woods after all. Reputations are important.

"Unlikely. New wolves aren't known for their stamina." I was going for a witty riposte, but it came out a little too breathy.

"Is that so?" Talon leans forward and nuzzles my neck while their hands slip around my waist. I can feel their hard length against me, the silver piercing warm from the water.

"Yes," I say in a strained voice as their hand sinks a little lower to my thigh. "Well-known fact. I bet you can't last five minutes."

"Hmm." Teeth graze my neck, and I shiver as clawed fingertips sink into soft flesh. Talon is proving quite adept at partial shifting. In addition to my crown fetish, I apparently have a pain kink too. Or maybe it's just that Tal and everything about them turns me on. "So you're saying that delicious cunt of yours isn't hot and wet right now? Aching for my cock?"

This time, I do whimper. "Why don't you find out?" I challenge as I run my hands up their back, enjoying the way their muscles flex beneath my touch.

Warm breath tickles my neck as they let out a wolfish laugh, then Talon's hands slip over my ass and lift me up, notching their broad head at my entrance. My legs instantly wrap around Talon's waist, and I scream as they fill me with one thrust.

"Look at that," they drawl as they pull back before sinking into me again, this time excruciatingly slowly as a golden sheen rolls over their dark eyes. "Hot. Wet."

"If you spend the next five minutes talking"—I gasp when one of their hands drifts around to play with my clit—"then that will prove my point about your lack of stamina."

Talon laughs darkly. "I'm going to fuck you hard enough that you feel me for days, and then I'm going to fuck that wicked mouth of yours for doubting my abilities."

I bare my teeth at them. "More fucking, less talking, mate."

There are no more taunts after that. Just Talon slamming into me as their claws hold me tight against themself. I scream so much, my voice turns ragged. Then Talon roughly plays with my clit as they fuck me exactly the way I want—hard and fast.

At one point, they duck their head to suck on one of my nipples, and I squirm as the sensation becomes too much. Talon holds me firmly in place as they draw out every last bit of pleasure from me.

Finally, after I come for the fourth time, their mouth crashes against mine as they start to piston their hips, getting faster with every thrust. I swallow their groan as they come, filling me with their seed, and my tongue catches against a fang before tasting coppery blood.

Talon breaks our kiss and gives me a feral and bloody smile. "I fucking love you, Scythe."

Once, I would have flinched at the idea of hearing that name from the lips of my mate. Now, I realize *Cerelia* may have been the name given to me, but *Scythe* is who I am.

I'm the Last Witch of the Woods, and my mate is a wicked and cruel wolf.

A content smile graces my lips. "I love you, Tal. You are mine, and I won't ever let you go."

Their forehead touches mine. "Good, because I don't ever plan on leaving your side."

Hours later, we float in the middle of the hot spring and gaze up at the starlit sky. Someday, we'll have to find Ryllae and fulfill the bond. The mage hunters have been dealt a blow, but I have no doubt I'll still need to defend my forest against them and others.

It's Malovias. There are always enemies to kill—both old and new.

I'm no longer alone though. My fingers briefly squeeze Talon's, where our intertwined hands float between us. I'll never be alone again, and if anyone comes for us . . . well . . . perhaps the legend will expand to the Last Witch of the Woods and Her Wolf.

Of Melodies and Maledictions

A Lingering Fates Novella

Be gay. Do crime.
Also maybe eat the rich while you're at it.
And not in a fun way.

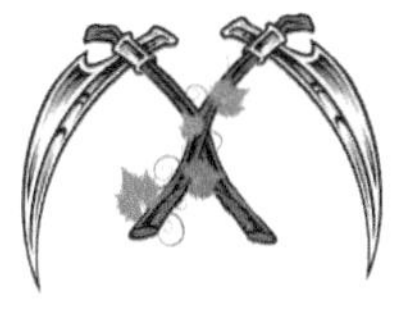

CHAPTER ONE

~

Scythe

SOME PEOPLE ARE JUST ASKING to get punched in the face.

Or killed. Often both.

"What the fuck are you gonna do about it, whore?" the tall, broad-shouldered man with dirty blond hair sneers.

"You don't own this forest," one of his companions adds.

The arrogance and absolute stupidity of humans is truly astounding sometimes. And these men have to be some of the dumbest ones to enter my forest in a very long time. Possibly ever. If only my parents could see me now.

"*This is why you chose to stay behind in this horrendous land?*" my father would ask in that annoying, even tone of his. The one that always sounded like he was bored of the conversation before it even started. "*You could have returned with us and the rest of the witches to Arandia. Lived a life without a human in sight in a land with magic overflowing everywhere. But, no, you chose to remain in this cesspit.*"

"*Always the disappointment,*" my mother would add.

Probably for the best that we cut off all forms of communication when they sailed halfway across the world.

"You shouldn't have come here," I repeat.

My lip curls as I scrutinize the six men in front of me. I've been watching these fools for the past twenty minutes as they boldly scurried half a mile into my forest and hid some stolen loot in a hollowed-out tree. All while boasting about how smart they were for thinking of hiding their stolen goods in a forest that everyone was too scared to enter.

Not them though. They thought they were so clever for just barely stepping inside the witch's domain.

But the witch is the forest and the forest is the witch.

No one crosses onto my land without me knowing.

These men know a witch protects these woods. They are banking on her terrifying reputation to protect whatever they stole. And yet, here I stand—the Witch of the Woods—right in front of them . . . and they don't recognize me for what I am.

Exactly how many women do they think are wandering around this forest with fucking purple hair, silver eyes, and covered in tattoos? Not to mention the pride of devil cats sitting at my feet.

Granted, the devil cats don't look particularly intimidating right now. These ones are mostly juveniles and barely pushing sixty pounds. There are far larger, nastier predators roaming these lands, but what the devil cats lack in size, they make up for with cleverness, tenacity, and sheer numbers.

Sometimes. When they feel like it.

Which the ones lounging around me do not. Instead, the dozen or so felines are lying on their backs and lazily pawing at each other. Thank fuck my sister isn't here. She would be cooing over all of them and telling them what mighty predators they are.

It's honestly kind of a miracle my reputation is as terrifying as it is, considering how much some of the denizens of my forest try to undermine my efforts.

"I asked you a question, bitch!" The blond man pulls out a

long, curved dagger. It's sort of impressive looking. Unfortunately, he's holding it wrong, so it kind of undermines the intimidation factor.

Plus . . . mine's bigger.

"I know." I sigh. "I was just curious to see if you would get smarter after a minute or so. You clearly haven't, so I suppose I can give you another clue as to who I am." I extend my right arm to the side and summon my scythe.

Several men inhale sharply at the sight of the weapon. With its long wood handle and the silver blade stretching out almost two feet from the top, it's rather recognizable. What the people of this land have forgotten is that it was a common weapon used amongst all witches, not just me.

But I'm the last one. So all of the legacy falls on my shoulders.

"You're her. *Scythe*." A man with stringy black hair pales. "The Last Witch of the Woods."

"In the flesh." I bare my teeth at him.

One by one, the leering expressions slip from the men's faces. I relish the fear that takes its place. No one who enters my woods uninvited lives to tell the tale. The only reason my reputation has grown is because I patrol the boundary of my forest where it meets the Eleoyn Kingdom, and the local townsfolk see me.

They always scurry away when they spot me. Something I find very amusing, because I do visit their towns—disguised with magic of course. I love my forest, but it can be lonely sometimes. I can only imagine the panic it would cause if they learned that the witch they all fear sometimes graces their taverns—and takes the locals to bed. If only for a night.

Two of them men take off running, including the one who recognized me first. I glance down at the devil cats. "Wanna do something about that?" The one currently lying across my feet playfully paws at my ankle. Damn it.

This is why I should've made Necos come with me. She's the alpha female and in charge of the pride. But she was taking a nap in the late morning sun and didn't even acknowledge my presence when I told her we had uninvited guests. And since she didn't get up, none of the other adults did either. Which left me with the lazy-ass teenagers.

I stare after the running men in annoyance. They're clearly panicked, because instead of running south to the border, they've run east. Soon, they're going to hit the river and realize their mistake. Despite being well into autumn, we're still getting thunderstorms, resulting in the river being full and raging. If they're foolish enough to try to cross it, they'll drown within minutes. Assuming they're not as dumb as I think they are, they'll double back.

Either way, I have time to deal with the remaining four.

A light breeze causes the branches to sway, and some warm afternoon sunrays dance across my skin. Maybe Necos had the right idea about this being a nap day . . .

"So, who wants to go first?" I ask, suddenly eager to have this over and done with. As much as I enjoy hunting down trespassers and making them scream, it's more fun when it's at least a bit of a challenge. These aren't well-trained mage hunters from the Eleoyn Kingdom or the often cruel but still skilled raiders from the far southern kingdom of Riritha. No, these are just opportunistic low-level criminals who think they can use my reputation for their own gain.

I lazily twirl the scythe in my hand, its silver blade making a whooshing sound as it cuts through the air.

Two of the men shift uneasily. They want to run—I can see it in their faces. Apparently, the blond man, clearly the leader, also senses where they're leaning because he grabs one of them by the shirt and growls in his face, "There are four of us and one of her!"

And about half a dozen devil cats if they decide to get involved. Although, based on the way two of them are snoring, that seems unlikely.

"There's got to be a nice reward for her too." The stocky

ginger-haired man who was contemplating fleeing a second ago eyes me. "And she don't look too tough."

"I kind of like 'em feisty," says the man standing next to the leader. Out of all of them, he's the one I peg as most likely to put up a decent fight. He's holding a sword like he actually knows how to use it, while the rest of them only have daggers.

"Let's try to take her alive so we can have some fun first." The leader smirks. "But dead works too."

"She'll still be warm for a bit." The sword fighter's bright blue eyes linger on my breasts and then between my thighs. "That's good enough for me."

I stop spinning my blade and rest the staff on my shoulder.

The men close in on me until they have me completely surrounded. They pause roughly six feet from me, eying the devil cats warily, but when the felines continue to laze about as if nothing is happening, they take another step forward, only to halt when a cruel laugh pours from my lips.

"What the fuck you laughing about?" the blond man growls. "Think it's funny what we're about to do to you?" He points his dagger at the blue-eyed sword fighter, who apparently has a thing for necrophilia. "This one's a city guard. They do all kinds of fucked-up shit to pretty little things like you."

"Last week, thirteen mage hunters walked into this forest." I jerk my head to the right. "You're correct that there is quite the bounty on my head. I'm all that stands between the Eleoyn King and riches of the Wilds to the north of the Obsidian Mountains."

Of course, their odds of getting over the mountains aren't great—all kinds of nasty things there. And the werewolves of the Wilds aren't particularly kind to outsiders. But none of that matters, because nobody ever makes it past me.

"What happened to the mage hunters?" one of the squirrelier men asks, only to flinch when the leader glares at him.

I smile. "If you walked two miles to the northwest, you'd find out. I'm fairly certain at least some of their bodies are still there—

the devil cats have been hungry though." One of the felines yawns, showing off two-inch-long fangs. "But you're not going to make it two feet from where you're standing, let alone two miles."

"I'm going to enjoy making you scr—"

"Thanks by the way," I cut off the swordsman.

He frowns and glances at the other three men, all of whom are standing almost the exact same distance from me. "For what?"

"Moving closer." Silver streaks through the air at the same moment a low melody spills from my lips. Four heads hit the ground as I finish my spin with my scythe still extended. The bodies slump to the forest floor a moment after the heads, causing some of the devil cats to jump out of the way and then glare at me.

I roll my eyes. Ungrateful lazy shits.

I tap the pinky ring on my right hand three times, and the scythe vanishes. Yet another thing my parents would have been disappointed by—a witch using mage magic.

But not all mages are bad, and I happen to be on friendly terms with one of the good ones. Well . . . good-ish. And while I love my witch magic, it can't do nifty things like stash a six foot weapon into a tiny little ring.

The magic even *cleans* it.

One of the devil cats starts snacking on the swordsman. "He'll *still be warm for a bit.*" I snicker, deepening my voice to imitate his.

Too bad my sister, Astria, isn't here. She would have laughed at my dumb joke. I worry my bottom lip. Astria has been gone a lot the last few weeks. She's always spent more time in Shalewood, an Eleoyn town that sits very close to the boundary of my forest, than I have. Astria genuinely likes humans, whereas I just tolerate them for short amounts of time.

Usually to get laid. Actually . . . only to get laid. I'm two hundred years old and have needs.

It has been a while. Maybe once I finish up here, I'll go into town and see if I can figure out what Astria's up to. A small part of me still worries about her. Astria might be my sister, but she's witchkin—a full-blooded witch with no magic.

Thankfully, she looks human. I have to use magic to disguise my appearance when I go into town, but Astria, with her cornflower blue eyes and blond hair, looks just like any other human girl. Which doesn't do a lot to assuage my concerns, because while I haven't spent much time in the Eleoyn Kingdom, I have met plenty of Eleoyn men in my forest.

My silver eyes fall to the now-dead swordsman. The world is a dangerous place—especially for sweet and pretty young women like my little sister.

"Time to track down the other two. Any of you lot coming?" I glance around at the devil cats, some of whom are still sleeping while the others tear chunks from the bodies. "So glad you all decided to tag along. Super helpful."

They continue to ignore me. I should have befriended wolves. They're probably more useful.

I take off at a fast jog towards the river. The forest whispers to me that the men are still there. Not in words, more of a feeling than anything. My woods don't like trespassers any more than I do. As I go, I take note of the changing landscape. The last of the flowers bloomed weeks ago. Now, most of the plans are entering their dormant stage.

Small critters race along the branches, building up their nests in preparation for winter. Everything in nature requires a balance, and I respect what winter contributes to that . . . but I still don't like it.

The changes here aren't as intense as further north at the base of the mountains, where snow is a regular occurrence, but the colder months are when I spend the most time in Shalewood, finding warm bodies to keep me entertained. Usually it's something I look forward to, but for some reason, this year, I just can't summon any excitement about it.

Maybe because last year everyone I took to bed was . . . mediocre. Not just at the sex part—everything. Not a single person did anything to intrigue me in the slightest.

Hopefully this year will be different. Otherwise, winter is going to be really boring.

An enraged snarl echoes through the trees. My jog becomes a flat-out sprint as I weave my way through the trees to cover the final quarter mile between me and the river. I skid to a halt at the bank, instantly summoning my scythe again.

"Don't come any closer," the man with dark brown hair and pale blue eyes warns. He and the other man are standing on a rocky outcropping that juts out into the river. He had to shout so I could hear him over the rushing current, but even if he hadn't, I would have understood.

Because he has one arm outstretched over the raging water, and struggling in his grasp is a devil cub that can't be more than a couple of days old.

A very pissed-off adult devil cat is pacing the river bank. Shylo. I squeeze my eyes shut for a second. My sister named her that because she's one of the more standoffish of the devil cats. She belongs to the pride that more or less lives with me, but she prefers to give birth in secret. Half the time, I don't even see her offspring until they're a month old.

Three furry heads pop up from a nest of dried-out leaves behind her. I don't know how the men managed to nab one, but I do know that if she had remained with the rest of the pride, this wouldn't have happened. My annoyance at the devil cats increases. First the lazy yearlings, and now the stubbornly reticent Shylo.

Definitely should have lured the wolves down from the mountains.

Magic from the forest pours into me until my bare feet are tingling and my skin feels a little too tight as it pushes me to fix this. Shylo sends me a baleful glare, as if this is my fault.

"The witch is the forest," the man shouts, "and the forest is the witch, right?" He jerks the cub a little bit, causing it to yowl louder and eliciting a very pissed-off snarl from Shylo. "Get that thing away from us"—he points to where Shylo is cutting off their retreat—"and let us leave. Or this one's going for a swim."

"Fine," I grind out and stalk over to Shylo, dismissing my scythe on the way. The devil cat growls at me but backs up as I urge her to move closer to the rest of her cubs. "There you go." I wave at the opening I've created for them.

"Back up more." He narrows his eyes at me, and I oblige him.

I've never been particularly good at hiding my emotions, so I don't bother trying, even though I'm sure my expression is nothing short of murderous. As soon as that damn cub is safe, I'm going to tear these men apart, limb from limb.

The men slowly inch forward on the rocks, back towards the riverbank. The one who hasn't spoken yet leans in to whisper in the other man's ear. Something tells me I'm not going to like whatever he just said.

I'm proven right a few seconds later when the men get about twenty feet down the river bank and hurl the cub into the river.

Unlike these men, I'm not an idiot. I figured that's what they were planning to do, which is why a song immediately pours from my lips. Roots grow and burst up from the water, catching the cub before it's lost to the current.

Unfortunately, what I didn't count on was Shylo darting around me, scrambling onto the rocks—trying to get closer to her lost cub—and falling into the river.

Fucking. Cats.

The men don't waste any time, and they hightail it through the woods in the right direction this time. They'll reach the boundary in no time.

No one has *ever* escaped my forest before.

But I'm not going to orphan these cubs, no matter how pissed off I am at their mother. I wade into the water, bracing myself against the current until it reaches the middle of my thighs. Closing my eyes, I sing a wordless song with low and deep melodies. Shylo has already been swept away, so I can't see her, which makes this harder. I have to let the forest guide me.

Seconds tick by. I ignore the mewling sounds of the kittens still on land and the more frantic ones of the cub caught in a nest of roots a foot above the raging river.

There.

Downriver, more roots spring up to temporarily hold Shylo in place. Then, I sharpen my song, and I hear the distant sounds of a tree collapsing. It died years ago, and its trunk is dry and rotting, so it snaps easily and falls halfway into the river, close enough for the devil cat to scurry onto.

Ten minutes later, a very wet and bedraggled-looking Shylo returns to find me sitting next to her three cubs with the fourth one purring in my lap. "You and I are returning to the rest of your pride, where you are going to fucking remain while I hunt down those two assholes."

Red eyes flash at me.

"Don't fucking sass me right now, or I swear to the gods, I will throw your furry ass back into that river."

I gather up two more cubs and get to my feet, leaving the last one for her to carry. The men made it to the boundary already, but they're likely staying in Shalewood. Even if they plan to hit the road, they'll still need to gather their belongings and pay for any lodging, which means they won't have that much of a headstart on me.

And they might not even be in much of a hurry because all the legends that surround my existence say the same thing—the witch never leaves her woods.

A grin cuts across my face. Little do the humans know . . . I walk amongst them frequently. This hunt isn't over yet.

CHAPTER TWO

~

Talon

Some people are just begging to get punched in the face.

Or robbed. Often both.

"I don't want to hear your excuses, girl," the man who rousted me from my slumber says loudly. I haven't bothered to open my eyes yet, so I can't see him, but he's definitely upper class. The distinctive way he pronounces his vowels while clipping some of his words is a dead giveaway. All the rich assholes in Eleoyn talk in that same posh tone.

"It's not an excuse, sir," the girl—Rosalie—answers politely. "Our last scheduled performance was yesterday. We're actually breaking down the tents today in preparation for winter. I'm afraid you've caught us at the beginning of the offseason."

This is why Rosalie serves as one of the ushers for our troupe. For a sixteen-year-old, she is remarkably composed, even while dealing with drunks. Or in this case, an entitled prick.

What time is it anyway? I crack my eyes open and instantly regret it. Even filtered through the leaves of the tree, the sunlight is too bright. Wait . . . tree?

Fuck. I rub my face, being careful not to dislodge myself from the thick tree limb. A large red-and-white-striped tent looms to my right, which means I'm in the large oak tree towards the front of our camp. I knew I shouldn't have taken that final shot of whiskey last night. For some reason, whenever I get drunk, I climb into trees to sleep it off. Always on the lower branches because I'm not a fan of heights—even when I'm pissed out of my mind, I still remember that.

My head feels a little fuzzy, and my tongue keeps sticking to the roof of my mouth. I want some greasy food and spiced tea to help wake me up. What I *don't* want is to get involved in the argument happening nearby.

Rosalie is telling the truth. Our performance troupe is officially done for the season. Something I was reveling in last night with my friends, Mattias and Vessi. Well, it started as a celebration. Then Mattias got into a fight with Eliza—his on-again, off-again lover—and then it turned into me and Vessi trying to cheer him up.

Which is why I wasn't able to turn down one more shot of whiskey . . . which is why I currently have a tree branch jamming into my spine.

Just walk away, I mentally encourage the pompous twit who is *still* arguing with Rosalie.

She says something so quietly that even I can't make it out with my exceptional hearing, but I do recognize the tone. It's the same one she uses on her six-year-old sister when the child is being an absolute demon. Which, to be fair . . . we aren't exactly sure who the kid's father is. And we do have several not-quite-humans in our troupe—including myself—so it's not that far of a stretch.

Maria, the girls' mother, tended to party on the wild side in her youth. And one night seven years ago, she went to an event that, in her words, was *the best fucking orgy of her life.*

Six months later, Desiree was born. A very healthy baby girl despite arriving quite a bit early.

Aside from a wicked temper, Desiree hasn't demonstrated any magical abilities, so we all just roll with it. Tovenian culture is very tight-knit. If you're a part of our troupe, you're family. No questions asked. Even if you are potentially the spawn of a demon.

A rich, savory scent teases my nostrils, and I inhale deeply. *Bacon*. That's exactly what I need right now. Maybe I can sweet-talk whoever is cooking into giving me a few piec—

Slap.

Rosalie lets out a startled cry, and I instantly roll off the branch. My knees bend at the impact of hitting the ground after dropping ten feet, but werewolves—even cursed ones like myself—are considerably sturdier than humans.

The tree I was sleeping in is twenty or so feet behind the man. I don't run, but I quicken my steps as I close the distance between us, all while trying to calm my wolf down. They consider the members of the troupe their packmates and are intensely protective over them—especially the younglings.

The man continues to berate a quietly sobbing Rosalie, and I have to bite back the growl that almost slips from my lips.

Don't worry, I assure the wolf. *His blood will coat our blades soon enough.*

Looks like robbery and murder are now on the agenda for today.

With his back to me, the man doesn't see me approach, but Rosalie does. Her kind, honey brown eyes widen for a second, and I wink at her before morphing my expression into one of annoyance. It's time to put on a performance.

Every adult in our troupe pulls their weight. Mostly, that means performing in one of our many acts or supporting them like Rosalie. But some of us have . . . other skills.

Part of being a successful traveling performance troupe means people need to feel safe coming to our shows. Absolutely no violence is tolerated. If guests get out of hand, we quickly but firmly escort them out. Sometimes they're just chucked out with a stern warning not to come back; sometimes that warning comes with a bit of roughing up to make sure they get the message.

And sometimes—if they're rich—they get a visit from me and my crew. Always far away from our camp, and we're careful to not leave any evidence or witnesses that would place the blame on our troupe.

I didn't plan on pulling a heist today, but if one is going to fall into my lap, I'm hardly going to say no.

"Rosalie, what are you doing?" I add a hint of reproach to my tone, even as I eye the red mark on her cheek that is already turning into an ugly bruise.

To her credit, the girl doesn't even miss a beat at my harsh tone. Instead, I see a hint of glee because she, like everyone in the troupe, knows exactly what Vesi, Mattias, and I get up to when we disappear for hours or often days at a time.

As if she is performing on stage, the young girl bursts into tears again while muttering apologies. It's a little over the top, and inside, I'm laughing, even as I deepen my frown. We'll have to work on her acting skills later.

"Enough," I bark as I come to a stop so I'm standing slightly between the two of them. Rosalie takes a step back, her head bowed as if she's worried about getting reprimanded, but her shoulders sag a little in relief. "You have chores to attend to," I say coldly. "See that they're done, and don't fuck around or I'll see that your pay is docked."

"Of course," she murmurs and darts away—but not before I see her lips curl into a smile.

She might be one of the worst actors here.

Thankfully, the man is arrogant enough that he doesn't even notice. Instead, he's practically gloating watching Rosalie pretend to flee.

"My apologies." I give him a shallow bow. "Rosalie is still

young and in training. Clearly, she needs more, as she must have done a poor job of answering your questions."

The man straightens, drinking down my honeyed words like a fine brandy. *There's a sucker born every minute.* I internally smirk.

And this man is a very, *very* rich sucker. There's no mistaking the fabric of the shirt he wears, with its slight sheen and wrinkle-free appearance. It's from a type of silk that can only be imported from the southwestern kingdom of Aestelas. The cost of it alone could keep a family of four fed for an entire month. The gold rings sparkling with gems adorning several of his fingers would keep them fed for an entire year.

It's unfortunate that Rosalie had to deal with him, but I'll make sure to get her something nice to make up for it. The rest of the money will go to the troupe. There's a very good chance all of the troupe's expenses are going to be covered this winter. Because he almost certainly has more fancy clothing and jewelry wherever his belongings are. Now I just need to encourage him to leave town so I can divulge him of his riches—and his life.

The asshole hit a sixteen-year-old girl who was causing him no harm. He signed his death warrant with that slap. But we have an unspoken rule with the locals of Shalewood. They let us camp here every winter, and we don't cause them any hassle.

Our troupe has had this arrangement with the northern town for as long as I can remember. Not everyone in Eleoyn is tolerant of Tovenians. We're a nomadic people and don't really consider ourselves citizens of any kingdom. The Shalewood folks are laid back and enjoy the entertainment we bring every winter, since most of them were born here and will likely die around here too. We bring them a taste of what else is out there without them having to leave the safety of their homes.

Eleoyn isn't a safe place despite how rich many of the cities look. Greed and cruelty are far more common than compassion and tolerance. So Shalewood gives us a place to spend winter, and while we mostly stick to our camp, we do make a point to visit the taverns and other shops a few times a week, always tipping handsomely. And we provide entertainment in local establishments with our bards, musicians, and other performers.

"My carriage is being repaired; otherwise, I wouldn't have stopped in this waste of a town," the man says haughtily. "As I was telling that useless girl, I require entertainment while I wait."

With every word he speaks, my wolf grows more agitated, and I can feel them push against my skin. They've been a little on edge lately, and seeing Rosalie's bruise is pushing them to a tipping point. If I were a normal werewolf, I'd shift and burn off some steam running through the woods. But long ago, my ancestors were kicked out of their werewolf pack in the Wilds and exiled here. As if that wasn't bad enough, the witches placed a curse on my bloodline.

I was born a werewolf, but I will never be able to shift. Something my body still hasn't accepted after thirty-two years.

Settle down, I warn the wolf. If they get worked up enough, it will trigger a shift. Which just results in agonizing pain while my body tries and fails to shift before I eventually pass out. The wolf lets out a low growl that rumbles through my mind before going quiet.

I change my charming smile to something apologetic. "I'm afraid that while Rosalie might have been doing a poor job of explaining things, she was correct—we are no longer offering performances, I'm afraid."

"Unacceptable." He points at the main tent with its bright red-and-white stripes. "You still look set up for entertaining to me. The only reason you people are tolerated is to provide a source of entertainment for Eleoyn citizens."

My polite expression stays on my face even as I imagine summoning my daggers and slicing open his throat. "May I let you in on a secret, my friend?" I tilt my head and let a hint of slyness into my eyes. "You look like a well-cultured and traveled man."

For a moment, he's taken aback at my lack of reaction to his insult. His eyes flit to the silver rings dangling off my right ear, a subtle way to clue folks in to my nonbinary nature. It's common to use jewelry to denote our gender in Tovenian culture. It's something we actually picked up from the fae, but few remember any of the fae customs, so they just associate it with us now.

"I am," he says almost hesitantly before saying a bit more confidently, "I am."

"Well"—I step a little closer to him, as if I don't want to be overheard, even though we're standing on the outskirts of camp and no one is around—"I only recently joined this troupe," the lie easily glides off my tongue. "Minor disagreement with my previous one led to me seek another. This troupe is fine and all, but I will say that the performers here aren't quite up to my standards— which means you would surely be disappointed by our humble efforts."

I can see the moment he relaxes and his annoyance fades. A few well-timed compliments and the hint that he's getting exclusive information is all it takes. This might be the easiest money we ever make.

"That may very well be," he concedes and gives me a condescending smile like I'm a pet that's done a neat trick, "but anything is better than nothing. I can't be expected to just sit around all day."

"Oh of course not." I clap him on the back several times before gently pushing him forward in the direction of town. "But I'm on good terms with one of the local tavern owners, and they rent a carriage between here and Renswood. Now, I'm sure the carriage isn't as fancy as what you're used to, but it's not even an hour ride down the road, and I promise you, it's worth it. You see, I'm familiar with the troupe that's currently there. Usually, they stick to the cities on the western border, but they wanted to expand a bit."

"And what exactly makes them worth the hour ride?" he asks curiously.

"Their most popular act is two young women who perform all kinds of . . . tantalizing feats." Once again, I lean a little towards him like we're good friends sharing an inside joke. "They're very flexible."

He lets out a knowing chuckle. "That does sound like a fine way to spend the afternoon."

"Indeed it does." I grin. "By the time you return, I'm sure your own carriage will be repaired and you'll be able to be on your way." We walk past the large performance tent and gaze at the town of Shalewood just across the meadow. "Simply tell Josephine at The Barlow that I sent you. The carriage ride to Renswood is on me on account of the rude hospitality you received."

"Ah, that is very courteous of you . . ." He trails off. "I never did get your name."

"Talon." My smile sharpens ever so slightly. "The name's Talon."

I WAIT until the man is halfway down the path that winds through the meadow before whistling sharply. As if by magic, a boy with blond hair so light, it's almost silver appears in front of me.

"How'd youse know I was there?" He wrinkles his nose as consternation fills his bright green eyes. Jules is an unusual-looking kid. He was left in front of our performance tent when he was a babe with no indication of where he came from. It was Vesi who named him on account of how his eyes resembled emeralds. She used to refer to him as "our troupe's little jewel."

Jules is hardly the only child to be left in our care. Usually, it means they have something besides human running in their veins, but we've never been able to figure out what Jules is exactly—other than quiet. At eight years old, he is too young to join my crew, but he is already vying for it. If he is still interested in six or so years, I'll probably take him up on it.

I tap my nose.

"That's cheating," he complains.

"That's using my resources." I playfully cuff him on the head. "I'm assuming you heard all that?"

He nods, sending his silvery blond hair flying. In addition to its unusual color, it also grows wickedly fast. We cut it to his shoulders at the beginning of every month, and it'll be down to his waist by the end.

"Good. Run to town and tell Josephine to lend that man the carriage when he asks for it but stall him for an hour. Then watch from a distance and tell me how many guards he brings."

"How's youse know he's got guards? Maybe he's traveling alone."

I snort. "Upper class can't be bothered to wipe their own asses —he ain't driving a carriage. He's got at least a driver and likely two or three guards for the road."

"What if—"

"Jules." I point towards town. "Go."

"Fine, fine," he grumbles. "You're so grouchy when you're hungover."

He's not wrong. Although, the prospect of making a good chunk of money and snuffing out the life of a useless rich asshole has helped me ignore how shitty I feel. Now, I just need to track down that bacon to banish it altogether.

I might not be able to shift into my wolf form, but my senses are still far sharper than any human's. Plus, I'm quicker, stronger, and I heal faster. Sometimes, I wonder how much all of that would improve if I wasn't hindered by the curse, but I try to not let myself dwell on that because there's no point. If there was a way to undo the curse, surely my parents or any of the other cursed were-wolves would have done it already.

The only bit I allow myself to dwell on is my rage at the

witches. They were the ones who laid the curse on my bloodline. And they could have undone it before leaving the damn continent.

Well . . . all but one. The Last Witch of the Woods.

Personally, I doubt there is still a witch in that forest. The locals claim to see her walking around the edge sometimes, but those could just be drunk ramblings.

Seems more likely that there are just some nasty beasties prowling around in the forest that make snacks out of any idiot who wanders in there. And the woman people see is just that—a human woman. Maybe she wanted to be left alone, so she built herself a little cottage in the forest everyone is too scared to enter.

Everyone knows the witches left these shores well over a decade ago. Why would one stay behind?

I glance briefly to the forest that looms on the other side of the meadow before letting out a derisive snort and heading farther into camp. The performance tents are on the outskirts, closer to Shalewood. Tents are great for entertaining, but not so great for sleeping in. At least not during winter. We've set up all our personal wagons in clusters, mostly families or close friends, and those are what I'm wandering through now.

"Mornin', Talon!" Two women wave at me from where they sit on the steps of their wagon.

"Surprised to see you both awake." I smirk at the newly married couple. "Pretty sure the two of you drank enough wine to get Mattias drunk three times over."

They dissolve into giggles. Still drunk then.

I continue weaving my way through the wagons, half of which still have snoring owners inside them. Last night turned into an unofficial celebration for the end of the season, and I'm pretty sure at least half the troupe got blind drunk.

A lithe form falls into step beside me, her red hair looking particularly bright in the sunlight.

"So we're gonna kill that rich asshole, right?"

"Murder?" I give the newcomer a shocked look. She glares

at me, but since Vesi is five foot nothing and has freckles sprinkled across her nose and cheeks, it's not all that intimidating. We've been best friends for almost two decades though, so I recognize the wicked glint in her green eyes and drop the act before she smacks me and aggravates my slowly fading hangover. "Of course we're going to kill him. He hit Rosalie."

"Prick," she mutters. "Can't get blood on that shirt though. Kayla and Nicolai can probably help us sell it, or they can reuse the fabric for something else."

I give her a sly look. "Still trying to court them, huh?"

"Shut up, Tal." She scowls.

I let out a wolfish laugh. The two designers live in one of the coastal cities, and while they're not Talvonian, they're friends with our troupe and regularly help us fence stolen goods. Vesi's had a crush on them for some time now, but she refuses to admit it because my best friend is hilariously bad at talking about her feelings.

She much prefers to discuss murder.

The scent of bacon gets stronger, and we both walk a little faster. "Any idea where Mattias is?"

"I left an hour after you stumbled home." She grins. "He was still arguing with his lady friend when I left."

We break through the last row of wagons to where a cookout area has been set up beneath an open air tent. One of our elders, Elaine, is cooking, and both of us slow down slightly. My nostrils flare as I scent the air, trying to determine if this is going to be sad bacon.

Elaine is a decent cook when she's in a good mood. But if she's feeling angry or frustrated about anything . . . things tend to come out burnt or massively overseasoned. Given that Rosalie is sitting next to her and sporting a bruised face, I'm wary of the food situation.

It doesn't smell burnt though . . .

"Oh, stop your worrying, Talon." Elaine does a passable impersonation of a wolf growl. "The food is fine."

"There was never a doubt in my mind." I shoot her a flirty grin as I take a seat next to Rosalie.

Elaine snorts before handing Vesi two plates. "Don't bullshit a bullshitter, kid."

I laugh and take one of the plates Vesi holds out to me before she settles onto the empty bench and tucks into her food. Elaine is one of my favorite people. She's well into her seventies now and is just as sharp as ever. She has this sweet grandmotherly appearance that she uses to her advantage the same way I use my charming masks and good looks.

Elaine was the one who taught me that if you play into people's expectations of you—show them what they expect or want to see—it's so much easier to manipulate them. I never underestimate Elaine. Because I've seen her shoot a crossbow from two hundred paces away and hit dead center bull's-eye. Every. Single. Time. Her hand-eye coordination is scary.

Not as scary as her cooking can be though.

"How's the cheek?" I give Rosalie's face a critical look. My wolf growls as we notice the swelling and the red already giving way to a deep purple.

"Hurts. Not as bad as that time I fell out of the tree and hit two branches on the way down though." She steals a piece of bacon off my plate, and I let her. "Gonna see the twins after this. I stopped at their wagon on the way, but they were barely capable of stringing words together to form a sentence, so I figured I'd give 'em a bit to wake up." She squints at me. "Exactly how much did y'all drink last night?"

"There's probably not a drop of ale left in this town thanks to these degenerates," Elaine mutters.

"Really?" Vesi says around a mouthful of toast before pointing a strip of bacon at the older woman. "Pretty sure I saw you dancing on a table last night while singing a song so lewd, it had *me* blushing."

"Don't talk with your mouth full, Vesilia." Elaine glares at her. "We wouldn't want you to choke."

I let out a raspy chuckle before passing another piece of bacon to Rosalie. "Go see Aditi and Priya before it gets worse." Rosalie rolls her eyes but bounces to her feet and walks back towards the tents.

The twins will get her fixed up in no time. We have a few healers; some gifted with magic, others just have the proper training. Aditi and Priya are the only mages in our troupe currently, and while they're not particularly powerful, they're good at healing small injuries.

Aditi and Priya joined us a few years back, and the twin sisters fit right in, although it took them a while to open up. They've seen some shit in their two decades of existence, and it's clearly left some scars.

Technically, mages are still human, but they can do magic, while most humans can't. That simple difference is part of what led to the Great War centuries ago that resulted in the fae leaving the continent for good—most of them anyway—and the birth of the four kingdoms: one mage kingdom and three human kingdoms—the latter of which have varying degrees of toleration for mages and magic in general.

In the Eleoyn Kingdom, mages are welcome as long as they swear fealty to the king. They're called mage hunters, and the Eleoyn king uses them to hunt down rebel mages as well as any other magical beings.

You join or you die. Those are your only options as a mage in Eleoyn. Which is more than the fae and other nonhumans get. Their only option is death.

"Do we have your blessing?" I turn my attention back to Elaine as I shove the last of the eggs and bacon into my mouth. The heists I pull off with Vesi and Mattias are what allow our troupe to take time off like this. Otherwise, we would have to continue performing through winter, which gets rough when the bitter cold and rain set in. But there is a risk to what we do, not only for ourselves, but the troupe as a whole. So before we set off on any job, we check with the elders. Most of the time, they support whatever we have planned, but occasionally, they deem the risk of backlash to the troupe too high—in which case, we drop it. The troupe is our family, and no amount of riches is worth bringing harm to them.

The sweet grandmotherly woman vanishes, and Elaine looks after Rosalie's retreating form before giving me a hard stare. "I don't like the short notice around this. We don't know who's traveling with that man—you know someone that rich has protection."

I nod but don't say anything, even as the wolf paces in their cage. If she says no, my wolf is going to lose it. Taking out our frustrations on that piece of shit who hit Rosalie will help ease the wolf —and me. We're only buying time. Something is going to push us over the edge and the shift will start. And then we'll be in a world of pain as our body tries to tear itself apart in a vain attempt to fight the curse.

Vesi pauses eating for a moment to give me an appraising look. My friends know me well enough to spot the signs of an impending doomed shift. Which is helpful, considering I always pass out for several hours afterwards, making myself vulnerable.

"You may proceed"—she holds up a warning finger—"but I'm trusting you lot to use your best judgment. If it's too dangerous, back off. You hear me?"

"Loud and clear." I nod.

Elaine's gaze falls on Vesi. "Loud and clear," she mumbles through her full mouth.

The grandmotherly mask snaps back into place, and Elaine rolls her eyes as she wraps up a sandwich in a cloth napkin and hands it to me. "For Mattias."

I take a bite out of the sandwich and quickly duck when Elaine tries to smack me. "It's the delivery tax." I grin at her before rising to my feet. "Ready, Vesi?"

"Yep." She shoves the last of her food into her mouth, causing her cheeks to bulge a bit.

I kiss Elaine on the cheek. "We'll be back in time for the festivities."

She snorts. "I have no doubt. You're never one to miss a good party." A devilish glint shines in the old woman's eyes. "Good hunting, wolf."

CHAPTER THREE

~

Scythe

I STAND at the boundary of my forest. This is where my domain ends and the Eleoyn Kingdom begins. Most forests sprawl a bit, thinning out before they end. Not mine. There is a straight line of forest that cuts across the entire continent of Malovias. When the witches came to these lands almost a thousand years ago, they intertwined their magic with these woods. Even though the witches are gone—except for myself—this forest is forever changed, and the trees will never grow beyond this point.

Long stocks of sun-bleached grass reach towards the sky. The meadow has long since spent its seeds for the season.

With a sigh, I step across the boundary that, aside from the abrupt ending of the tree line, is invisible. The boundary itself cannot be seen, but I can *feel* it. My magic isn't dependent on the forest; I have my own well of magic, and at two hundred years old, that well is vast. But witch magic is nature based. We interact with the world around us and ask it to do our bidding—never force.

The forest here is forever linked to me. Which means when I

ask it for something, it responds instantly like an overeager wolf pup. Outside of my domain, nature is more like the devil cats—responses vary.

Which means I have to be more specific about what I request and not push for too much. It's more than that though. Every time I step past this boundary, it's like I'm leaving a part of myself behind.

I'll be back soon, I reassure my forest as its magic reaches for me.

I'm not surprised that my parents were able to leave *me* behind. Our relationship became strained after Astria was born and I refused to allow them to send her away. They were ashamed of having a child who was witchkin. But all I saw was a little sister. Regardless of how easily they left us, I don't understand how they were able to leave the forest—how all of the witches were able to leave it.

We may not have been from these lands originally, but the witches poured so much of ourselves into these woods . . . and they just walked away from it all.

True, the four kingdoms to the south are slowly falling apart, but that's never been our problem. We stayed in our forest and periodically went through the Obsidian Mountains to visit the Wilds above them. The rest of Malovias never mattered to us.

Instead of staying and protecting the land we had called home for so long, the witches chose to go back to a continent none of them had ever seen with their own eyes. Our ancestors might have come from Arandia, but even with our long lives, there was no witch alive who didn't have at least two generations between them and that place. All we had were the stories of a continent overflowing with magic and no humans in sight.

That's what they decided to go back to—a fairytale.

I pull my hood up as I start the twenty-minute walk to Shalewood. The simple silver chain that adorns my neck was created by the same mage who made the ring on my finger. Instead of hiding a weapon, the necklace changes my appearance to allow me to blend in. My distinctive lilac hair is now a strawberry blond, and my silver eyes are the same bright blue as my sister's. The necklace even hides the tattoos that cover a good amount of my body.

It's not foolproof though, so I have to be careful. The mage warned me that if my magic flares, then my true appearance will flash through the glamour. It hasn't been a problem so far, but my temper is running hot, and with it, my magic is practically vibrating in my very soul. I'll need to be careful when I find the men, and if they're still in town, I'll have to wait until they leave.

Shalewood is convenient, and I'd hate to burn my reputation here. The locals are used to my sister and me visiting. We told them we live in a cottage a ways outside town, and they've never questioned it. The people here mind their own business, and they're more than happy to let you keep your secrets—as long as you don't bring trouble.

Laughter draws my attention across the meadow. The Tovenian troupe. Apprehension flickers through me, and I pull my hood up, even though they're too far away to see me clearly. The first time they set up camp outside Shalewood for winter, I was annoyed but assumed it was a onetime thing. While my knowledge of things outside my forest was limited, I was familiar enough with the Tovenians to know they made a living by selling tickets to their performances—something they couldn't exactly do in Shalewood with it's small population. It might be on a main road but most travelers passed, preferring to stay in a larger town with more going on.

But for the last decade, they've returned every winter. Usually arriving just in time for the late fall celebrations and leaving as soon as the frost melts. I watch from beneath my hood as they break down the large red-and-white-striped tent.

A boy with silvery blond hair races through the tall grass and waves happily at the people taking the tent down. That kid and others like him are the reason I'm wary of the Tovenians. I've seen the boy around; he's not human, at least not entirely. Most likely elvish blood with that hair color.

The elves left with the fae, but some of their progeny remain—and they often end up in Tovenian troupes. Depending on how true the blood runs in that kid's veins, he could possibly see through the glamour that disguises me. The Tovenians might keep the secrets of those within their troupe, but I have no reason to believe that courtesy would extend to me.

And that is why I am annoyed that the Tovenians have started spending winters here. The first few years, I avoided Shalewood altogether and traveled to some of the other towns that are close to my forest but nowhere near as convenient as Shalewood. When it became clear this was going to be an annual thing, I learned how to skirt around them.

Luckily, the Tovenians mostly stay within their camp and they favor one tavern in particular. I simply avoid that one, and if I happen to step into one of the other taverns and there are Tovenians there, I leave.

A thought occurs to me, and I swear under my breath. "Astria, you better not have befriended the fucking Tovenians." My sister knows why I avoid them and never pushes me on it, even though she is of the opinion that they wouldn't tell anyone that the pretty strawberry blond woman introducing herself as Lia is really Scythe, the Witch of the Woods.

Several townspeople wave at me as they drive wagons full of wood towards the Tovenian camp. Fuck. The blood moon festival is tonight. Astria mentioned it a few days ago, and I forgot. There go my plans of finding a warm body to keep me company. The Tovenians will be everywhere, so I have no chance of avoiding them.

I hasten my steps as I head towards one of the town's inns. There are only two of them, and my plan is to check them first before searching taverns and shops. I need to track down these men and take care of them quickly because I still want to find

Astria so I can see what—or who—has been keeping my sister busy these past weeks. And I need to do it before the celebrations start.

At almost twenty years old, it's not like my sister is helpless or incapable of making her own decisions. But I know Astria. She has all these ridiculous ideas of what love can be. Which is impressive, considering she had a front-row seat to my massive failure of a relationship.

My little sister might not have learned anything from that, but I certainly did. Love is fleeting and not worth the inevitable heartache.

Shouts draw my attention ahead. Two black horses pull a carriage up to the inn I was planning on searching first. I step to the side to get out of the flow of traffic and lean against the wall of the butcher's shop. As I watch, a man storms out of the inn. He's definitely not from around here. His clothes look too clean and perfect, and his russet brown hair is perfectly styled. Must be nobility passing through.

"I don't care what happened to the others!" he snaps at the two men who follow him out. "I only hired them based on your recommendations. Clearly that was a mistake. Get your shit together and drive this carriage to Renswood."

My mouth quirks up into a small smile. Not only have I found my quarry, but they're going to be conveniently on the road outside of town shortly. I already know of the perfect spot to ambush them.

It'll be easy enough and then I'll get to spend the afternoon sunning myself. I push off the wall, and I quickly make my way out of town and back to my woods. As soon as I cross the boundary, I break into a flat-out run.

THE BRISK AUTUMN breeze feels good against the light sheen of sweat that coats my skin. My cloak hangs on a nearby branch as I try to figure out the scene before me. I ran as fast as I could, but even then, I shouldn't have been able to outrun the carriage. I'm fast, but not faster than a galloping horse.

Something must have delayed the carriage because there is no sign of them yet. I raced to this very spot because there is a bend in the road, which brings it very close to the border of my forest. Normally, I try not to use my magic outside my woods, but dead men tell no tales. And I can take care of business and dive back into my forest with no one being the wiser.

Only two of the men are my quarry, but I'll hardly lose any sleep at night by offing their boss. He seems like an asshole, so really I'm doing the world a favor.

Unfortunately, when I arrived here, the road wasn't empty. Less than twenty feet from me are three people on horseback. They haven't spoken; instead, all three are focused as they stare down the road, clearly waiting for someone from Shalewood to arrive. Given how they're positioned to block anyone from passing —and that two of them are wielding crossbows—I'm assuming they're up to no good.

Normally, I wouldn't care, but their nefarious plans seem likely to conflict with *my* nefarious plan, and that just doesn't work for me. The added complication is that they're definitely Tovenian. I've seen the big one around—he's kind of hard to miss—and the rider closest to me has turned their head a few times to look in my direction.

Them, I definitely don't recognize—because I would absolutely remember that face. After two centuries, I thought I was past being dumbstruck by a pretty face. But here I am, gawking at the dark-haired hotness in front of me. But I'm grateful for the distance and the tree that mostly hides me from sight; otherwise, I probably would make a fool of myself.

Silver earrings decorate most of their right ear, occasionally catching the rays of the late morning sun. Thick, dark hair frames their chiseled cheekbones and perfectly cut jawline. They're absolutely stunning—and they're absolutely *not* for me.

Not only are Tovenians trouble, but I always keep my trysts simple. One night of fun, and then they go on with their lives and I return to my forest. Whoever this person is, I know in my bones that sleeping with them would be anything but simple. Their gorgeousness isn't worth the inevitable heartache.

Best if I avoid them altogether. Shalewood is off-limits until the Tovenians are gone. I'll just have to go to one of the other nearby towns if I want to find someone to play with for a night.

In the meantime, I need to figure out how to deal with my current problem. This is my preferred spot to launch my attack, but I can just move farther up the road. It'll require me to be out in the open instead of lying in wait in the trees, but I'll manage. It's not like my targets are mage hunters. They're just some assholes who got lucky. I can use my magic to disrupt the road, create a blockade of sorts to get the carriage to stop, kill everyone who needs killing, then erase all signs of my magic. If the Tovenians get impatient and wander farther down the road, they can pick the pockets of the corpses. I care little about money.

I start to pull back, tearing my gaze away from the dark-haired stranger, when I hear the telltale sounds of hooves pounding into dirt and the creak of carriage wheels turning rapidly.

Shit. Out of time.

The familiar carriage driven by my quarry comes to a stop. Chances are the Tovenians are going to kill them. I could just let it play out, confirm their deaths, and go back. There is no reason for me to get involved.

"Get the fuck off the road!" the man who held the devil cat cub over the river demands.

For a second, it's like my vision turns red as my rage surges back. Their deaths are mine to claim. I need them.

Besides, for all I know, the Tovenians are simply going to

demand a price for letting them pass and then I'll have to chase the carriage farther up the road.

Fuck this.

I'm still wearing my necklace, so my glamour is in place, disguising my appearance. Just in case, I snatch my cloak off the branch and put it back on, pulling the hood up so my face is cast in shadow. Despite the different eye and hair color, there is a good chance the men will recognize me, and if they out me to the Tovenians, I'll have to kill them too.

And that will definitely raise questions. The Tovenians are protective of their own, and they won't overlook the disappearance of these three. I don't particularly care about never going back to Shalewood, but Astria will be pissed at me if I tell her she can't either, just in case they recognize her as witchkin.

I'll keep the cloak in place, but I can't use my scythe—it's too recognizable. Luckily, it's got all kinds of tricks. I call it forth, and as soon as the weapon appears in my hand, I push two fingers onto a straight line etched into the hard wood and feed a little of my magic into it. The long silver curved blade protruding from the top vanishes, leaving me with only the staff.

Perfect. Bash in a couple of skulls. Return to my woods. And never set eyes on the captivating Tovenian again.

Simple and easy.

CHAPTER FOUR

~

Talon

"You fucking deaf?" the man with brown hair a few shades lighter than mine angrily shouts. "Get off the damn road!"

The man sitting next to him starts to reach for the crossbow resting on the bench next to him.

"I wouldn't." Vesi snaps up her own crossbow and aims it at the man. Unlike him, she had hers ready to go. These two are clearly not professionals. Sloppy to not have weapons at the ready when traveling the main roads in Eleoyn.

Bad for them. Good for us.

The blond man, who'd been reaching for the crossbow, holds up his hands and gives a nervous look to his friend. "Told you this day was cursed," he mutters.

My brows raise a bit, not sure what he means by that. Doesn't matter. They'll both be dead soon enough.

"The two of you accepted the wrong job," I say coolly. "And I'm afraid it's going to be the last mistake you ever make."

"Let's make a deal," the man who originally spoke rushes out. "I'm sure we can come to an agreemen—"

"Those two are mine," a feminine voice calmly announces.

Vesi swears but keeps her attention on the men. My head whips around as I twist in the saddle and spot the woman standing just to the side of the road, ten feet behind us. Where in the fuck did she come from and how did I not hear her?

Mattias steers his large horse around so he can keep an eye on the carriage and the newcomer. The *pretty* newcomer.

Granted, I can't see much of her face thanks to the cloak, but what I can see . . . I like. Soft strawberry blond curls tumble out of her cloak. Most of her face is hidden beneath the hood, but on display are full lips and sharp cheekbones set against lightly tanned skin.

"Forgive me . . . my lady?" I pause to give her a chance to correct my assumptions on her gender or give me a name. A small smirk plays across her lips as she simply nods. My gaze latches on to that luscious mouth for a moment before I shake my head. *Focus. You can get laid later. Maybe by this tasty little morsel—once you get her out of here.* "Our apologies, but we have some business with these men and their cargo." I glance at Mattias, and he dismounts, already knowing what I want him to do.

"Little miss," he says in a friendly tone that always has people settling down, "I'd be more than happy to escort you to town. Perhaps you can tell me how these two have wronged you and we can see about setting it right."

"If you ever call me *little miss* again"—she points her walking stick at Mattias—"I will shove this so far up your ass, the local farmers can use you as a scarecrow."

And just like that, I'm instantly hard.

Vesi snorts while Mattias just holds up his hands and backs slowly away from the woman before looking up at me. "Yeah, this one's all yours, Tal."

Fuck yes, she is.

"Secure our friend in the carriage," I tell him before dismounting and taking a moment to adjust my pants before moving out from behind my horse, Draco. I hook the reins on the saddle so he won't trip on them, and the bay stallion joins Mattias' mount on the side of the road, where they both munch on grass. I walk towards the cloaked beauty. As amusing as this is, I'm too old to be distracted by a pretty face. We need to get her out of here so we can do what we came here for. Because if she witnesses anything, then I'll have to kill her, and that'd be a shame.

It's been a long time since someone has intrigued me. Even my wolf is curious about this bold creature before us.

"As my friend was saying"—I give her a smile that usually has women tearing off their panties and throwing themselves at me— "we're just taking care of a small disagreement that I'm afraid involves the two men you have an issue with. Please allow Mattias to escort you to Shalewood. It's not safe for a young woman such as yourself to be traveling alone. I realize you feel you have a claim on these men, but I promise to make it up to you later if you allow us to have them."

I come to a stop a few feet in front of her, and she has to tilt her head back a bit to look at me. Piercing blue eyes meet mine.

They're a lovely shade that goes well with her hair. But I can't shake the feeling that there's something off about them.

"Trust me, I'm well aware of the dangerous things that prowl this area." She twirls the staff in what is clearly practiced motion. "Perhaps a *pretty young thing* such as yourself should be worried about walking along these roads." Her lips curl up into a leering grin. "I'm sure your friends can help you get back to town safely— leave these men to me."

"You think I'm pretty?" I step a little closer.

She snorts. "I think you know you're gorgeous and it's a weapon you wield quite well." Something dark and dangerous flutters through her eyes. She uses her staff to point at the blabbering man Mattias is pulling out of the carriage. "You lot can have him and whatever riches you want. It's only those two I'm after." She swings her staff to point at the other two men. "I have no interest in the rich asshole, and I have no interest in you."

Liar. I bite my tongue. I can smell her arousal. She wants me as bad as I want her. What a fun chase this will be. The wolf perks up even more.

We could do as she wishes and then just track down the men later. They can't be left alive, and I see no weapons on her, so I don't think she means to kill them. Although, I'm curious as to why she's so determined to take them from us.

"Why do you want them?"

"Not your business."

"It seems it is." I shrug. "Perhaps we can offer you something in exchange. Did they steal from you? I'm sure one of the rings on that prick's fingers will cover the loss. I'll even wipe away the blood after I cut the finger from his body."

She grins, and it has a wicked edge to it. "What if I want the finger too?"

"Anything you want." I move closer and slowly reach out to play with a lock of her hair. Her eyes drop to my hand, but she doesn't stop me from winding some of the strawberry blond strands around my finger. So soft. I can't wait to wrap my hand around it later when I have her writhing beneath me.

Because I'm absolutely bedding this woman tonight.

"Anything?" She arches an eyebrow, and I nod, still toying with her hair. The woman tilts her head, and for just a moment, I swear I see her eyes flash silver out of the corner of my eye. But when I focus on them, all I see is blue. "I want their deaths—by my hand."

A wolfish laugh spills from my lips. Maybe the fae gods are still around and have blessed me with this divine creature. I'll be sure to make a good offering tonight at the blood moon celebration to show my thanks.

"And why is that, my vicious little friend?" I ask, the strangeness of her eyes forgotten as my desire builds.

"They hurt a friend of mine—threatened her life. Nobody fucks with what's mine and lives." Again, I see that predatory glean in her eyes. Perhaps she's part fae? Doesn't matter to me, but that could explain some of the strangeness of her appearance.

"I don't know what weird kind of flirting the two of you are doing, but can someone just tell me who I'm killing?" Vesi drawls.

I let the soft curls fall through my fingers and take a step back. "It seems our lovely lady has a prior claim on the two men—they're hers. Rich assholes is ours."

"What?" the blond man squeaks. "What do you mean we're hers?"

"Down you go." Vesi uses her crossbow to point at the ground. "Josephine will be pissed if we get blood on her carriage."

"You can't do this!" the man Mattias currently has shoved against the carriage argues. He tries to shove back against Mattias, but it's like a fly trying to move a mountain. "I'm Davon Amato! Do you know who my family is!"

"Amato?" I give him a startled look. "As in Amato Vineyards? The family that own the rights to all wine flowing in and out of Tenresan?"

There are quite a few cities in Eleoyn, but the largest and most grand is the capital, Tenresan. It's known for its fine dining, exclusive brothels, and upscale bars. And only Amato wine is served in the city walls.

"Yes!" Davon glares at Mattias. "Now call your brute off, and I'll consider forgetting this ever happened."

"Of course." I turn back towards the woman whose name I still don't know and smirk at the confused look she's giving me. Her brows furrow together, but I'm already striding towards Davon. "Release him, Mattias."

My friend grunts before stepping back. I smooth out the creases in Davon's shirt—would it have killed Mattias to go easier on the fabric? This shit is worth a fortune.

"Now, unhand my men and—"

My fist connects with Davon's jaw hard enough to send him spinning into the carriage. He lets out a startled yelp, but I've already grabbed a handful of his hair and proceed to bash his face into the door several times before hurling him back.

He skids several feet across the ground before coming to a stop and clutching his bloodied face. I crouch down in front of him. "That was for Rosalie, the girl you slapped." My thumb brushes against the symbol tattooed on my right palm, and a curved blade springs to existence in my hand. "The only family we care about is ours—and you hurt one of 'em."

"It was just a slap," he wheezes.

Mattias lumbers over to us, a thunderous expression on his face. "How many other girls have you hit?" He delivers a solid kick to the man's torso, and I hear the snap of several ribs. Davon screams and tries to scramble away, but Mattias slams his foot down on the rich asshole's spine. "You expect us to believe that the worst you've ever done is backhand a sixteen-year-old girl?"

"To be fair," Vesi calls out, not taking her eyes or her crossbow off the two men kneeling on the ground, "we would have killed you for that alone. Honestly, I would've killed you for just looking at her funny."

I watch the cloaked woman stalk towards her quarry. *We sure she's not one of us?* I ask the wolf. She moves like a predator.

My wolf rarely speaks, and when they do, it's usually one-word responses. But I can feel how focused they are on this woman. Like she's the only thing in the world that exists to them.

A blood-curdling scream sets my ears ringing, and I turn to find Davon's arm bent in a way it's very much not supposed to be. Mattias might be the calmest of the three of us, but he has zero tolerance for men who beat women. It's one of the only things that gets him to lose his temper.

Still, if Davon lets out another shriek like that, it might burst my eardrums. A strong breeze picks up around us as I take a step towards the bloodied noble begging for his life, intending to slit his throat and be done with it, until someone shouts urgently behind me. I stop mid-step before twisting around to see what the commotion is about.

The woman is now standing a few feet in front of the men. The wind has torn her cloak back. Her strawberry blond hair falls in soft curls to her waist, and her face is even more striking now that I can see all of it. But it's the men's expressions that snag my attention.

They're terrified. As if they're looking at a monster and not a beautiful woman.

"You're—you can't—not here," the man who panicked at the beginning of this encounter sputters, his pale blue eyes wide with fear. He scrambles back from his kneeling position to land on his ass and raises one hand. "She's the—"

Crack.

Almost faster than I can track, the woman slams her staff onto his head with enough force that one would expect the wood staff to shatter. It doesn't. The man's head sure does though.

"Great," Vesi mutters. "Now I'll never be able to crack an egg again."

The man who mouthed off to us stares at the blood and gore of his friend's skull and lets out a stream of curses as the body slumps to the ground close to him. He whips his head back to the woman, teeth bared. "It was just a fucking cat, you insane cun—"

Another crack.

This time, I'm not watching the staff break open the man's skull. My gaze is locked on the woman's face and the way her eyes light up at his death. Her bloodlust rivals my own. She's got to be part fae. Maybe even full fae. There are still quite a few of them hiding in these lands.

That could explain why she was so determined to track down these men and kill them. They must have somehow figured out her secret. Being fae is a dangerous thing in any of the kingdoms in Malovias, including Eleoyn. The mage hunters will happily kill any fae they find, and raiders from the southern kingdom frequently cross the border just to hunt down fae trying to escape them.

I'll have to be careful about how I hint that I know what she truly is—and that I'm more than fine with it. It's not like cursed werewolves are any more welcome. We're just so few in number that most people think we've died out entirely.

Still at least one left though.

My wolf growls, and the sound rumbles through my mind. They're running out of patience. The fair-haired beauty with a vicious streak calls to us both, and if I don't act on it soon, the damn pushy wolf is going to trigger a shift.

Unless you want us rolling around on the ground and screaming —not in a fun way—then settle the fuck down, I warn them.

I flinch slightly when it feels like claws rake down my insides. I stalk back towards Davon, who is sitting on the ground, clutching his ribs while blood drips from his smashed nose.

"Wait." He holds up a hand. "Everything I have on me—take it!"

"Oh, don't worry—we will," I growl, and I know at that moment, my eyes are wolf yellow. Davon's desperate plea is cut off as I lash out and my dagger slices through his throat, spilling bright red blood down his chest.

"Shirt's definitely ruined now," Mattias mutters.

I dismiss my blade back into the tattoo before I turn around. "He'll have more back in his room. We'll clear it out. Josephine has already marked him as checking out this morning in case anyone comes looking for him."

The woman stands off to the side with an amused expression as she watches Vesi quickly and efficiently search the other two bodies for anything of value.

Mattias glances at the woman, whose name we still don't know, before hesitantly asking, "What should we do with the bodies?"

Good question. In the cities, people barely bat an eye at

murder. Even amongst the upper class, it's not uncommon. But Elaine will have my hide if there is any blowback on our troupe. And Mattias will be pissed if Josephine catches any flak for this, because she's the sister of the woman he's in love with.

"Toss them into the forest."

The three of us look at the cloaked woman.

"The . . . witch's forest, you mean?" Mattias purses his lips as he looks into the woods.

"Scared?" The woman gives him a wild smile that is more like a baring of teeth.

"Aren't you?" Mattias challenges.

She shrugs. "My sister and I grew up around here. We're used to the rumors."

Something about that statement is . . . off. I don't know what exactly, but it's setting my instincts on edge.

"Have you ever gone into them?" I crouch down and start pulling Davon's rings off.

"Only a fool would go into those woods." She laughs. "Don't you know the witch kills trespassers? No questions asked."

"She kills humans," I hedge as I continue relieving the dead man of all his worldly possessions while surreptitiously watching the woman's reactions. "Maybe she'd welcome fae or any of the other nonhumans that still survive in this godsforsaken land."

"Perhaps." A hint of wariness enters her expression. My pretty little liar. If she really is fae, it's a miracle she's survived this long without giving herself away. Then again—my gaze drops to the bodies—maybe she's just been killing anyone who realizes it and tossing their bodies into the witch's woods.

Ha. There probably isn't even a witch. Just a murderous fae using the legend of the witch to her advantage.

Still. Sooner or later, her luck will run out. Our troupe will be here for at least a few more months. Plenty of time to get to know her better. If I'm still this intrigued by her in the spring, I'll convince her to come with us when we leave. She can bring her sister too if she wants.

I snicker under my breath. *My* sister is going to laugh herself hoarse when she finds out about this. Ravyn is the one who believes in all those romantic stories about love at first sight. I'm not willing to say what I feel is love, but it's . . . intense. And I've never felt anything like it before.

Fuck. Is this love? Is it even possible to fall for someone this hard and fast after knowing them for less than an hour? Without even knowing their name?

A cold lump of dread settles into the pit of my stomach. Love is a dangerous thing in Eleoyn. It gives you that much more to lose. Which is why it's something I've never wanted. Having my sister and friends is already bad enough, plus the general responsibility I feel for the troupe.

For a moment, I feel the overwhelming grief that still lingers from my parents' death. How their unfaltering love for each other was their downfall. Then I look up, and my gaze connects with hers. Those bright blue eyes have a hint of trepidation in them too.

I see the flash of desire when she looks at me. It seems we're both a bit caught off guard by this intense attraction. All I know is I'm not ready to let go of it yet.

"Do you live far from here?" I drop all the jewelry and money I collected into a pouch tied to my belt and rise, brushing my hands together.

"Why?" Her grip on the staff tightens.

"Because you can't come to the festival tonight looking like that." I gesture at the blood splattered on her clothing before grinning. "I know it's a blood moon and all, but I think bits of brain matter are a bit over the top."

"I have no interest in the festival." She takes a step back.

"Actually, you do." I close the distance between us. She doesn't retreat any farther. Instead, she straightens her spine and doesn't budge when I stop so that barely an inch separates us. "Because I'll be there."

"You are not who I came here for," she tries to say evenly, but it comes out a little breathy.

"But I'm who you found." My grin widens. "Name's Talon. Come to the festival tonight."

She stares at me for a long moment before shaking her head. "No."

"Scared?" I tuck some of her hair behind her ear, and she goes perfectly still, as if she's fighting with herself to not react. The question is—would she push me away? Or lean further into my touch?

"There isn't much that frightens me."

For someone who wears all her emotions on her face, she's good at giving nonanswers to my questions. If she's trying to dissuade me, it's not working. Now, I only want to know her secrets more.

"Then prove it." I lean down so I can whisper in her ear. "I dare you to come. Dance with me once around the bonfires, then you can leave if you wish."

I pull back, and she studies me intently, worrying her bottom lip with her teeth. "I'll think about it." She steps several paces away, as if she needs the distance between us. "As long as you don't set foot in the forest, the witch won't care. Don't go past the tree line. Throw the bodies over it." She points the staff at me. "And do not follow me."

"Only if you tell me your name." It's hard to watch her walk away. I need something; otherwise, I'm not sure if I'll be able to stop myself from tracking her.

"Cerelia." Something like surprise flashes across her face before she says a little shakily, "My name is Cerelia."

CHAPTER FIVE

~

Scythe

"STOP FIDDLING WITH THEM," Astria scolds.

I drop my hand from the soft white flowers she intertwined with my hair. They're oddities amongst the local fauna and bloom late in the year. One last burst of life before the dormancy of winter.

After I parted ways with Talon and their friends, I walked up the road a bit before ducking into my woods. Once there, I raced back and watched as Talon did exactly as I'd suggested and tossed the bodies into the forest.

None of the Tolvenians set so much as a toe across the tree line, but Talon stared into the trees for a long moment. There was almost a wistful expression on their face. Something was different about them, but I didn't know what exactly. I kept a tight control on my magic while interacting with them, which left me a little blind to the world.

Maybe they have fae blood running through their veins. If that's true, then it's either a small amount or large enough to put a glamour on themself. I wouldn't know unless I let my magic out to play—and I absolutely will not be doing that.

A group of drunk and very loud humans stumble past us. I think they're singing . . . or trying to. The sun set hours ago, and the locals clearly wasted no time in starting the festivities.

"Regretting coming with me?" My sister grins.

Like me, she has flowers woven into her hair. But on her, they look more natural. They just feel like a lie in mine. Maybe because almost everything about how I look tonight is a lie. It's more than just the color of my hair and eyes being different and my tattoos hidden. I look . . . soft.

To my surprise, Astria was waiting for me when I got home. She'd prepared an entire speech about why I should come to the celebration tonight.

The look on her face when I instantly agreed had almost been comical.

I still don't know exactly why I did. Just like I don't know what the fuck possessed me to give Talon my real name.

Astria chatted away while she helped me get ready. It's been a long time, well over a decade, since I dressed up. Not that the simple white dress I'm wearing tonight is all that fancy, but most days, I just wear loose-fitting pants and a tunic. During hot summer months, I trade the tunic for a band around my breasts and I wrap my hair up in a messy bun.

When I make my periodic visits to town to find a bedmate, I don't bother wearing anything different. Just pants and a clean tunic. So the question is—why am I dressing up for Talon?

And why the fuck am I so nervous about seeing them again? We interacted for not even an hour. But I haven't been able to stop thinking about them all afternoon.

Not once in my life has anyone made me feel this way. Not even the witch I was mated to for a century. A familiar sharp pain stabs at me just as it does every time I think of Vaeril. The man who swore his life to me . . . and then left like it was nothing.

Like I was nothing.

"You okay, Cece?" My sister's big blue eyes peer at me in concern.

"I'm fine." I shove all thoughts of my failed mating bond away.

Astria loops her arm through mine and leans into me. "We can leave if you want," she says quietly.

She would too. I gave up everything for my sister, but she's given up a lot for me as well. I won't ever leave my forest—which means she can't ever leave. Not for long, anyway. Because I won't ever let her go. The world—especially this kingdom—is a cruel place. I won't let my sister fall prey to it.

I plaster a fake smile onto my face. "Everything's fine. Let's have fun tonight."

"Okay . . ." She draws out the word as doubt shows clearly on her face. "There's someone I want you to meet. Why don't you dance for a bit, and I'll find you later?"

My smile turns genuine. I love to dance. Always have.

My sister kisses me on the cheek before striding away. Several locals call out greetings to her, which she happily returns . . . and so do a number of Tolvenians. Multiple large bonfires have been set up between Shalewood and the Tolvenian camp.

Just like earlier, I'm keeping my magic tightly contained. That won't help if some of them can see through the mage's magic, but if there is ever a night for someone to look the other way at the Witch of the Woods dancing around a bonfire—it's tonight. We're here celebrating the blood moon—an event that is closely connected to the fae gods. It's illegal to hold such worship in the Eleoyn Kingdom, but Shalewood gets away with it because of how remote it is.

Slowly, I make my way over to the hordes of people gathered around the bonfires. The band is playing a fast and wild beat. It calls to me, but I remain on the outskirts of the whirling and rhythmic bodies.

"I think I like you more with a little blood on your face." A person wearing a silver mask stylized to resemble a jackal stalks towards me.

My heart beats faster.

Even if I didn't spot the silver earrings nestled against their dark hair, I would know it was Talon. They move with this languid grace that draws my attention and keeps it. And part of me instantly goes hot and tight at the low raspiness that underlines their voice. I want to lie to myself and say this is just a bad case of lust, but I can't, because this feels like so much more.

It's both terrifying and exhilarating. The rational part of my mind knows this is a bad idea, but I can't stop myself from closing the distance between us any more than I could have restrained myself from coming out tonight.

Maybe I just need to channel some of Astria's constant optimism? Surely something will work out for me? Haven't I sacrificed enough? I want to be selfish this one time and get something just for myself.

I eye the silver crown that adorns their head. It should be ridiculous, but somehow, it fits them perfectly.

"Funny." I barely recognize the throaty purr of my voice. "I was just thinking that you wearing the mask associated with the god of thieves was a bit on the nose." My fingers glide across the cool silver before I keep going and do what I wanted to do earlier. My fingers run through their silky dark hair. "I think you wear this mask better than Azdall themself."

Talon laughs, and I swear I think I see a golden sheen roll over their eyes for a second, but it has to be a trick of the light thanks to the bonfires burning around us. Or the way lust and desperate need are fogging my brain right now.

Whatever this is between us won't last. It can't. I'm the Witch of the Woods. But at least for tonight, I don't have to be Scythe—I can just be Cerelia. And I'll let myself enjoy what my heart desires for one godsdamn night.

For several bated breaths, we just stand there, looking at each other, only a few inches apart. Neither of us moves, as if we're not ready to break this moment.

Then Talon holds out their hand. "You owe me a dance."

"What if I came to dance with another?" I arch a brow at them, not taking their hand just yet.

They lean forward, one hand brushing my hip while the other grabs my hand, intertwining our fingers. "Then the witch's forest will get another body tonight, because nobody is touching you but me."

A wicked heat rolls through my body at the possessiveness of their words. Talon pulls back and gives me a feral smile that has my heart hammering in my chest before they tug me into the crowd of dancers. Some wear masks like Talon, others have little trinkets pinned to their clothes as dedications to whichever fae god they prefer.

Technically, tonight should be a celebration for Lunos, the god of fates. But the fae have been gone for a long time, far longer than the witches, and humans have forgotten which celestial events belong to which gods.

It's not like the gods of the fae care anymore. They've left these lands too . . . mostly.

Talon pulls me flush against themself, our bodies molding together before Talon whirls me away. A laugh spills from my lips as we swirl and dance around the bonfire. The beat becomes wilder, faster. And we move with it, losing ourselves to the music. I wish I could let my magic out to play right now, but it's safely locked away.

The other dancers fade away too. Talon and music are all that exist to me at this moment.

"To think I was worried you wouldn't come tonight." Talon spins me before dropping their hands low on my waist and pulling me back against their hard chest. One hand flattens on my stomach while the other slinks a little lower on my hip.

"I still haven't come tonight." I let out a low chuckle when

Talon's grip on me tightens and they tug me harder against themself until I can feel the outline of their erection pressing against my ass.

We've been dancing for a while now, and the party is getting wild. People are in various states of undress, and more than a few have their hands beneath clothing.

"You clearly love to dance, and I want you to revel in everything this night has to offer." They dip their head and nip my neck as the hand on my hip slides forward a little more until it's right above where I desperately want it to be. "So, tell me, are you enjoying yourself?"

"It's tolerable," I say evenly before gasping when Talon bites my neck again, a little harder than before.

"So your pussy isn't dripping wet right now?" they rasp in my ear as their hand slides between my thighs, only the thin fabric of the dress separating us.

Their fingers push against it, and I'm so turned on that the fabric is instantly soaked with the evidence of my desire. I don't know how they do it, but without even being able to see it, Talon's nimble fingers find and circle my clit. I let out a strangled moan as they teasingly graze it.

Warm breath tickles my skin as they laugh. "You can't lie to me, love. You're as desperate for me to fuck you as I am to sink my cock into this cunt and claim it as mine."

"Not yours," I pant as they continue to rub their fingers against the damp fabric, creating a delicious friction. Suddenly, their hand vanishes and I'm spinning again, my dress whirling around me.

Talon stops me so I'm facing them, and their hands land on my hips as we move to the fast beat without missing a step. The other dancers glide around the bonfires, lost in their own revelry. Above us, a bloodred moon peeks out between the clouds.

Their silver mask is gone; somehow between one spin rotation and the next, they lost it. The memory of that wicked dagger of theirs vanishing without a trace earlier tickles the back of my mind. I assumed they just had a hidden sheath they stashed it in . . . but where did the crown go? Surely they didn't toss it on the ground. It was so pretty . . .

"I think you are." Talon bares their teeth at me. "*Mine.*"

Fae. They have to be fae. Only a fae could be this wildly possessive. And it would explain how they're making things disappear.

Hope unfurls in my chest. If they're fae, then perhaps they won't care about me being a witch. Not just *a* witch—but *the* witch.

Maybe Lunos is going to bless me this night and things between us won't have to end before they truly begin.

"I'm *not* yours." I close the distance between us until my chest presses against theirs. My fingers delve into their dark hair, and I pull them down, claiming their lips with my own. Talon's hands slide to my back, yanking me closer to themself as their tongue plunders my mouth. I drink in the taste of them before breaking the kiss and staring into their dark eyes. "I'm not yours," I repeat. "You are *mine*."

A low, raspy laugh spills from their lips. It reminds me of . . . something.

Before I can dwell on it, Talon is kissing me again. One hand remains on my back, but the other moves around the dress to the slit on the side. There's no teasing this time. They slide through the hot slickness they find waiting for them and thrust two fingers inside me while their thumb pushes down on my throbbing clit.

Talon swallows my scream as their arm clamps around my back, holding me up when my knees threaten to give out, thanks to the orgasm tearing through me. My pussy clenches around their fingers as they continue to fuck me through it while skillfully teasing the sensitive bundle of nerves until I'm trembling.

Only when I sag a little in their embrace do they pull their fingers from under my dress. I watch with rapt attention as Talon raises two glistening fingers to their lips and licks them clean.

"You taste like you're mine." They grin.

Fuck me. They have to be fae. No human I've ever been with has been like this. And I need them to be something other than human so I can keep them.

"You were right earlier," I say in a low, rough voice. "I do love to dance. What is it you enjoy, Talon?"

The light from the bonfires catches their eyes, giving them an eerie glow.

"To chase—and hunt."

A thrill runs up my spine, and I take a step back. Talon's hand on my back slowly glides over my hip before letting me go, and a predatory focus sparks in their gaze.

"Then let's see who's faster." I wink before darting through two dancing couples and sprinting into the night.

CHAPTER SIX

~

Talon

CERELIA DASHES away from the crowd and into the orchard that sits just outside of town but well away from the bonfires. The wolf wants to chase her down, but I give her a head start. Because when I catch her, I'm going to make her scream—and I don't want an audience for that.

A few of the local men gave her appreciative looks after she came all over my fingers and swayed in my arms. The look I gave them had the men holding up their hands and backing off. It wasn't like me. Normally, I don't mind people watching, but if Cerelia didn't initiate this chase, I'd have been seconds away from dragging her somewhere dark and secluded.

I couldn't keep my hands off her while we were dancing, and as soon as my fingers slipped into that tight little pussy of hers, it was fucking over for me. The need I have for her is all-consuming, and I hope she's ready when I catch her.

Because I absolutely will be catching her. And then she'll be coming on my cock instead of my fingers.

Deciding she's had enough time, I take a step forward—

"Tal!"

Fuck.

I turn towards the young woman with red hair so dark, it's almost black and light brown skin. Her pretty, bold features are flushed, and she has a silly, happy grin on her face.

"Kind of in the middle of something now, Ravyn." My eyes flick back to where Cerelia disappeared before returning to my little sister. "Catch up with you later?"

I'm already moving as she calls after me, "There's someone I want you to meet!"

"Later!" I yell over my shoulder as I weave my way through the crowd. As soon as I'm through, I break out into a flat run. Cerelia has disappeared from sight, but I can still smell her. She smells like the forest just before a thunderstorm. There's a chaotic and wild energy to her that calls to me—and to my wolf.

There's no way we're letting her get away tonight—maybe not ever.

I follow her scent as I race through the bare apple trees. Reddish beams of the moon occasionally pass overhead before the clouds cover it once more.

Cerelia is surprisingly fast, which only furthers my suspicion—and hope—that she's part fae. If she's fae, I doubt she'll care about me being a werewolf. We can hide in this fucked-up world together. And considering how things played out earlier today, I think she'll fit in nicely with our heists.

The memory of her beautiful face, flecked in blood with a feral smile surfaces, and I run a little faster.

Just as I'm about to break through the tree line, I catch a flash of light-colored hair before it disappears behind the enormous oak tree that borders the orchard.

I alter my course slightly and dart around the other side of the tree. Cerelia is a few feet off the ground, reaching for the lowest branch, when I snatch her by the waist.

"Gotcha." A low growl punctuates my words as I push her against the tree facing me, her hands pinned above her head."

"For now." She bares her teeth in a wicked grin that has the last of my control snapping.

"Keep your hands above your head," I order and release my grip. We're both wearing far too much clothing, and I need my hands to solve that problem.

"Or what?" She lowers them an inch.

"Or"—I slide my hand between the slit of her dress again and drag my fingers through her arousal while avoiding her clit—"I will keep you on the edge for *hours*, love."

"Not your love," she pants while thrusting her hips.

I move my fingers away and snap my teeth at her. "Behave, and you get rewarded." I brush my thumb over her clit, and she groans. "Misbehave"—I pull my hand away—"and you get nothing."

Those pretty blue eyes narrow at me, but she moves her hands back up the tree. I let out a raspy chuckle and start to swing my right hand behind my back but pause and hold it out to the side instead so she can see my palm. This one has the fae symbol for life tattooed onto it, and I see the recognition flicker in her eyes. She doesn't look the least bit surprised when I trail my thumb across the tattoo and a curved dagger appears in my hand a second later.

Her gaze flicks to the silver cuffs attached to the top of my right ear. "Mask?"

"You catch on quick." I grin and wait to see if she'll admit to being fae, but she just leans her head back against the tree.

"Going to do something with that dagger? Or did you just want to show off your toys?"

Her eyes light up when I hold the dagger against her throat before trailing it across her collarbone. There isn't a hint of fear in her scent or on her face—just desire. I don't know if my cock has ever been this hard in my life. As much as I want to tease her a little more, I think I might lose it if I'm not buried inside her in the next minute.

I grab the front of her dress and yank it away from her smooth, unblemished skin as I slide the silver blade down. It easily cuts through the fabric, and I duck my head to lick and suck at her bare breasts. She moans as I swirl my tongue around her pebbled nipple, and I give it a playful nip before dropping to my knees.

Tilting my head back, I meet Cerelia's stare as I continue dragging the blade through the remainder of her dress. It falls all the way open, revealing all of her to me. I dismiss the blade and cup her ass with both of my hands as I shove my face into her glistening pussy, licking her straight up the center.

The sweet taste of her fills my mouth, and I groan.

"Fuck." Her hands fall to my hair and urge me on.

I pull back and arch a brow before pointedly looking at the trunk above her head.

She lets out an adorably frustrated growl before releasing my hair and putting her arms back in place against the tree. "Happy?"

"Good girl." I let go of her ass with one hand and dive forward again, sucking on her clit while thrusting two fingers into her cunt. She lets out a strangled scream as I continue to roughly play, lick, and suck, bringing her closer to the edge. Her pussy clenches around my fingers, and I add a third one, stretching her out a little more.

Her breathing quickens, and I can hear the rapid beat of her heart as the climax builds. As delicious as she tastes, I want her coming on my cock. I swirl my tongue around the tense bundle of nerves one more time before pulling back and springing to my feet.

I unbutton my pants, freeing my cock. Cerelia licks her lips and takes a small step away from the tree as she hungrily looks at it. But before she can drop to her knees, I muscle her back against the tree.

"You can choke on it later," I grunt.

Cerelia barely has time to hiss her complaints before my hands grip her ass and lift her up. She instantly wraps her legs around my waist, and I don't hesitate before slamming my cock all the way in.

"Hands around my neck," I demand. This time, she does as she's told without a hint of snark. Her fingers dig into my flesh painfully as her legs tighten around me, urging me on.

I fucking lose it.

There is no teasing or letting her body adapt to me. I rut into her, my thrusts hard and brutal as I force her to take my thick, hard cock over and over again. The night is filled with wet sounds as skin slaps against skin. My fingers press harder into her soft flesh, and I know she's going to have bruises tomorrow—and that just makes me fuck her harder.

Mine. This wild and wicked creature is mine.

Ours, my wolf corrects in a throaty growl.

Ours, I agree. *We're not letting her go.*

"Talon," she moans. "More."

Fuck.

I step back from the tree, taking her with me. "Drop your legs," I order in a low, guttural tone.

Once again, Cerelia does as I tell her—but then keeps going until she's kneeling in front of me and tugging my pants farther down.

"Ah." Her tongue darts out to lick the tip of my cock. "I was wondering what felt so good."

She admires the silver bar running straight through the top of my head and out the bottom, both sides ending in a silver ball. As much as I love the idea of fucking that gorgeous mouth, I want to come in her pussy first.

"Cerelia," I growl, reaching down to pull her back up. "Get your ass up—fuck!" I ground out as she swallows my cock with zero hesitation. A chuckle rumbles in her throat, making my balls tighten, and she slides me out with a pop.

"You had your fun," she purrs. "My turn now."

I groan as she flattens her tongue and slowly drags it up the underside of my shaft before swirling it around my head and licking off the bead of precum.

"Not in the mood to be gentle, love." I grunt as my fingers get a good grip on her hair.

"Not in the mood to be coddled, *love*." She grins before taking me in her mouth once more and sliding up and down my cock. My entire body feels like a tightly coiled spring as I try not to lose it. She's taken everything I've thrown at her so far, but the night is young, and I have so many plans—I don't want to scare her off now.

Just as I feel like I'm getting back in control, Cerelia lets out a huff of annoyance, and then teeth lightly graze me as her eyes flash in warning.

"Fine." My fingers tighten around her hair. "You want to play like that, my wild little beauty? Then let's fucking play."

I slam my hips forward, hitting the back of her throat. Fingers tighten on my hips as she gags but doesn't try to pull away as I fuck her mouth unrelentingly.

Her lips stretch around my thick girth, and her tongue flattens, letting me glide over it easily. A low hum builds in her throat, and the pleasure I feel is unlike anything I've experienced before. Something flashes in her eyes, but she quickly slams them shut, and I'm too far gone to think about it.

"I was planning on spilling myself in that tight cunt of yours." My hips snap forward as I push her head down further. "We'll do that next—we have a long night ahead of us. For now, I'm going to come down this lovely throat of yours, and you're going to swallow every fucking drop."

She moans, and her throat flutters around my cock as I spill myself into her. Only when she's swallowed it all do I ease up before slowly pulling my cock from her mouth.

Cerelia takes a deep breath, her pink tongue darting out to lick her lips. I ease my grip on her hair and soothe her scalp with my fingers. She leans into my touch, and for a few moments, we stay just like that, her kneeling in front of me while I gently play with her hair.

Then I drop to my knees in front of her, slam a brutal kiss against those amazing lips, enjoying the taste of myself on them, before flipping her over onto all fours.

"Fuck, Tal," she moans as push my rigid length back inside her.

"Told you." I pull back and tease her entrance, letting the silver piercing rub against her clit a few times. "We have a long night ahead of us—and I want to hear you scream my name louder."

I slam into her slick heat, and Cerelia throws back her head and screams.

CERELIA'S EYES stay locked on mine as she rises up and down on my cock. She's absolutely insatiable. Which is good because I can't seem to stop burying myself in her.

Five minutes ago I was fucking that wicked mouth of hers until I myself spilled down her throat again. As soon as I was done, she practically pushed me onto the ground and sank onto my still hard length.

I've always had impressive stamina, but this is a lot, even for me. Maybe the gods have come out to play with the blood moon and their magic is saturating the air tonight. I have no idea and don't care as long as we don't stop until we both pass out.

What's left of my clothes lie on the ground around us. She ripped them off me somewhere between rounds three and four. Her own torn dress is over by the tree.

The blood moon is still high in the sky, filtered through the clouds. I have no idea how far away dawn is, but at some point, I should move us back to my wagon. The bed in it is far more comfortable than the ground. Plus, I don't want anyone else to see Cerelia's naked flesh.

"How do you feel this good?" Cerelia asks in a breathy tone. A trickle of blood drips down her chin from the part of her lip I nipped a little too hard. Based on how she moaned when I did it, I don't think she minded.

"Maybe we were made for each other." I groan when she rolls her hips forward, and my nails dig in harder to her hips.

She tilts her head back, causing her long hair to cascade around her in a soft wave. A reddish light falls on her, the blood moon finally breaking free of the clouds, giving her hair an almost eerie glow.

"Gods, Tal," she pants. Something glimmers on her throat, a faint marking I can't make out.

My cock tightens as her pace increases. I buck my hips up to meet hers even as more faint markings flicker in and out of existence on her flesh. I try to focus on them, but then she reaches down and starts to play with her clit, and my gaze is locked on that.

"Come for me again, Cerelia." I pull her harder onto me. "I want my seed dripping down your thighs."

She lets out a low laugh. "I think I'm going to be feeling you for days."

"Oh, love." I thrust my hips up, eliciting a sharp inhale from her. "You're going to be feeling me for weeks. Because I'm dragging you back to my bed after this and keeping you there until dawn—maybe all day tomorrow, actually."

"Can't," she argues huskily. "Have to go home."

"Stay," I growl.

Her pussy clenches around me, and Cerelia throws her head back farther as a scream erupts from her throat. I follow a second later, feeling our mixed pleasure gush out of her and soak my hot skin.

Her movements become languid, and I relax my hold on her hips, resting my hands on the tops of her thighs instead.

"We need to wash up and get dressed for a bit," she says while trying to catch her breath.

I frown, not liking the idea of her washing away my scent. My wolf *really* doesn't like that.

As if she can read my mind, Cerelia chuckles. "I'm sure we'll get dirty again, but I need to find my sister before she finds us and sees a lot more than she ever bargained for." Again, she lets out that breathy laugh that already has me hardening again inside her. She leans forward, pressing her chest against mine as she begins trailing kisses up my neck and over my jawline. "Once I check in with her, we can go to your bed and you can do your best to convince me to sta—"

Cerelia's words end abruptly as she straightens and stares down at me.

"Your eyes," she breathes, her own wide with surprise and dread.

Oh fuck. I didn't notice how close the wolf was to the surface, and I'm guessing my eyes have a luminescent golden sheen to them right now.

"I can explain," I say quickly, trying to shove the wolf back down, but they fight me, not wanting to go. *You're going to trigger a fucking shift,* I scream at them. That gets them to back off—a little.

"There are no werewolves south of the Obsidian Mountains," she whispers, "except the cursed."

Suddenly, magic fills the air, charged and wild. Between one blink and the next, the fair-haired beauty who stole my heart vanishes, and I find myself staring at a silver-eyed devil.

"Witch," I growl.

Lilac hair falls around her naked form, and her previously unblemished skin now has glowing silver tattoos. A serpent on her right arm and an antlered buck on the other. Vines with thorns wind up the thighs my hands are currently touching, and a pair of crossed scythes on her neck confirms who she is. Scythe—the Last Witch of the Woods. Looks like I was wrong about her not existing after all. And I'm all the fool for it.

All this time, there has been a witch left in these lands after all. One who could have ended my curse. Could have ended it for my parents, who might still be alive if they'd accessed their full abilities. But what the fuck did Scythe care? Hiding away in her forest while we suffered.

Is this a fucking joke to her? She's a witch. How could she not know I'm a wolf? Isn't she able to sense the curse her ancestors put on me? Fuck. For all I know, she was part of those who laid the curse. Witches live for a long time after all.

My fingers dig into her soft flesh, and for the first time tonight, Cerelia flinches.

Not Cerelia. *Scythe.*

CHAPTER SEVEN

~

Scythe

"Talon—" I start in a strained tone, but they cut me off.

"Is there anything in your nature other than deceit and cruelty?" Talon sneers before shoving me off them.

Cold hatred shines in their golden eyes. A wolf. Not fae. Talon is a cursed werewolf.

I didn't even consider that as a possibility. The uprising amongst the werewolves of the Wilds happened before my time. I wasn't involved in the cursing of the bloodlines that revolted against the alpha packs and then were exiled to live below the Obsidian Mountains.

It's been decades since I've seen one . . . I assumed they all died out.

"What did you do to me?" Talon rises to their feet and angrily swipes their pants from the ground and yanks them on. They pick up their shirt, but I ripped it in multiple places in my haste to get my hands on their smooth, muscled chest, and they drop it to the ground in disgust. "Did you use magic on me? Is that why I feel this way?"

"Hate to disappoint you, but I didn't use any magic tonight. Not intentionally anyway." I stalk over to the tree and grab my dress off the ground, grimacing as I pull it on. It's cut straight down the front, but I manage to tie it together in a way that has me mostly covered.

"What does that mean?" Curved daggers appear in both of their hands, making me stiffen slightly.

"It leaks sometimes, and when it's brimming close to the surface like this, it's noticeable." I gesture at my hair and tattoos. "Wild magic likes to come out and play during a blood moon," I mutter, not wanting to admit I didn't fully think about how the damn moon would affect my magic tonight.

"So, what," Talon pushes. "You were just going to disappear in the morning? Or were you going to keep lying to me!"

They're looking at me the same way they did at that Eleoyn man earlier in the day. No. Not the same. This is so much worse. This isn't some cool, detached hatred. It's intense. Personal. Talon *loathes* me.

A sharp agony tears through my chest as hot tears trail down my face.

No. They don't get to make me feel this way.

"I didn't want this," I hiss as fury overtakes the pain. My scythe flashes into existence in my hand. "*You* asked *me* to come here. I was perfectly happy in my forest!"

Lie, a voice whispers in my mind. But that voice can go to all the hells.

Talon takes a step forward, their daggers glinting in the light of the blood moon. "I thought you were fae." They point a dagger at me. "Not a witch." Their mouth twists in disgust.

"And I thought *you* were fae." I spin my scythe as I step closer to them. "Not a pathetic dog."

"Pathetic, huh?" In a blink, they close the distance between us. I feel the kiss of their dagger at my throat—and I'm sure they feel my scythe against theirs. Talon leans forward, not even wincing as a thin bead of blood forms where my blade is pushed against their skin. "You were *begging* for my cock not that long ago. So who's the pathetic one here."

"I was just trying to motivate you." I bare my teeth. "Thought maybe with enough encouragement, you'd do something interesting, but you were nothing but a disappointment. A forgettable waste of time."

The dagger at my throat presses a little harder, and I feel the prick of the other one against my soft belly.

Am I fast enough to slit their throat before they cut me open? More importantly . . . could I do that? I can still feel the evidence of what we did coating my thighs. And I remember vividly what it feels like to have their hands on my body, coaxing more and more pleasure out of me.

The scythe trembles slightly in my grasp. I can't die here. My sister needs me. Which means I'll do what I must to survive—even if it destroys whatever is left of my soul.

For what feels like an eternity, Talon and I stand there. Our blades at each other's throats and neither of us dropping our gaze.

Crack. We both snap our heads in the direction of a branch breaking.

"Cece?" my sister calls out, and my blood runs cold. What if Talon hurts her to get to me? My grip on the scythe tightens as I prepare to slice open their throat, knowing it'll likely mean my death too.

"Tal?" another voice calls out, this one a little deeper than my sister's but with a feminine lilt to it. "You out here?

"Fuck it all," Talon curses. Suddenly several feet separate us, and their blades are gone. "Over here, Ravyn." They shoot me a death glare and then look pointedly at my scythe before skimming my hair and tattoos. If they want me to hide who I am, they can fuck all the way off. I'm not getting rid of my weapon, and I'll use my magic if I have to. I already have no intention of ever coming back to this town, and Astria can hate me all she wants, but she's not returning here either.

"Oh! There you are!" My sister rushes out of the orchards. "I've been looking all over for you. What have you been up to . . ." She trails off, and her mouth hangs open as she looks at Talon, who is frowning at her.

"Wait," Talon says slowly. "I've seen you around town." They glance back and forth between me and Astria before their heavy gaze settles on me. "She's your sister?"

All I can do is nod because the beautiful dark-haired woman stepping up to stand beside my sister draws my attention—especially the way they're holding hands.

"Fuck. It. All," I repeat Talon's words from earlier before glaring up at the blood moon. *Think this is funny, Lunos? You can take your fate and shove it up your ass, god.*

I swear I feel a pulse in the magic around us for a moment, but I chalk it up to my imagination. Surely the gods have better things to do than mess with me.

"You really are her," the woman—Ravyn, apparently—says, a little awed.

"Told you," my sister whispers.

I narrow my eyes at her. "What exactly did you tell her?"

Astria glares back at me, raising her chin high. "She knows who and what you are. Ravyn and I are in love—you don't keep things from those you love."

"Hmm." Talon lets out a low, raspy laugh. That's why that laugh felt familiar; it's the way a wolf laughs. "Your sister is considerably more honest than you."

"My sister is none of your concern." I slash my scythe through the air, pointing it at them. "And you will never see either of us again."

"What the fuck are you talking about?" Astria snaps. "Did you not hear what I just said?"

I tear my gaze away from Talon and stalk towards my sister, grabbing her hand and yanking her away from Ravyn—or at least, I try to. The other woman stubbornly holds on until Astria is caught between us.

"You can't stay here, Astria!" I growl. "It's not safe. Talon will hurt y—"

"No harm will come to her," Talon interjects and strides towards us, only stopping when I press the edge of my scythe's blade to their throat. They stand perfectly still and raise a dark eyebrow at me. "Is your sister a witch?"

"I'm witchkin," Astria answers, and a muscle under my eye ticks. Great. She all but announced that she has no magic and is basically defenseless. Sure, she could pick up a weapon, but she's absolutely shit with a blade and barely passable with a bow and arrow. My sister's naivety is going to be the death of her someday.

"Then I have no quarrel with her," Talon says evenly, their gaze not leaving mine. "My sister's happiness is everything to me. It's not Astria's fault whose family she was born into."

Sister. Ravyn is their sister.

No. This can't be happening. I need Talon out of my life.

I stumble back, letting go of Astria's hand and dismissing my scythe.

"Cece?" my sister asks, her voice full of concern. "What's going on?"

The endless pit that has been growing in my soul ever since the witches left—since my mate left—widens.

"No harm will come to your sister," Talon says cooly. "I would never harm her to get to you." Slowly, they walk towards me. I know I should call my scythe forth, but all I do is stand there as they stare down at me with bright golden brown eyes. "You are nothing to me."

I square my shoulders and stare back at them. Magic brims

beneath my skin, making my silver tattoos glow faintly. "And you're nothing to me, wolf. But know that if anything ever happens to my sister, I'll burn down your fucking world."

A growl ripples up their throat at the threat, but I'm already striding back towards my forest—and I'm never leaving it again.

CHAPTER EIGHT

~

Talon

"I NEED TO CHECK ON HER," the young woman holding my sister's hand says worriedly.

Astria. The witch's sister.

Of all the people for my sister to fall in love with, she had to pick the little sister of my enemy. I recognized the protectiveness of Cer—Scythe's stare. She's definitely the older sister.

I meant what I said though. Astria didn't choose to be born witchkin. And it's not like she had any say in being related to Scythe.

My sister deserves to be happy, and if Astria gives her that, then I'm in full support of it—as long as neither of them expect me to play nice with the fucking witch.

"Go," Ravyn says. "Make sure she's okay."

The two of them murmur back and forth, but I can't make out what they're saying thanks to the sharp pain erupting in my chest. *No. I beg.* To my wolf. To the gods. To fucking anyone who will listen. *Not now.*

I'm vaguely aware of Astria racing off after her sister. Ravyn's face fills my field of vision as I grasp at my chest. But there's no physical wound. Nothing to heal. My wolf is letting out a low keening sound that rattles around in my head. *Stop.* I gasp.

They don't listen.

It feels like my body is on fire, and I drop to my knees. Ravyn falls with me, her hands on my face. "Talon," she says frantically. "Stay with me."

"Can't. Stop. It." I arch my back painfully as muscles twist and tighten, trying to shift into a form they can never take.

Because of the witches. Because of her.

"Shit." Ravyn's pretty features pinch together. "I'm not going to be able to carry you. Hang on. I'll find Mattias and Vesi." She kisses my forehead. "I'll be right back."

"Not going"—I collapse onto my side, panting—"anywhere."

"Fuck, fuck, fuck," Ravyn chants, springing to her feet and running back through the orchard.

I curl into myself as the wolf claws desperately at the cage they'll never break out of.

She's not for us, I groan. *This pain. She did this.*

The wolf growls, and I growl back.

Thoughts become difficult after that as my body tries over and over again to shift. Darkness encroaches on my vision, and I welcome it. Glad for the pain to finally be over, even though I know the memory of it will linger for days.

But as the darkness claims me, one last memory surfaces . . . of wild silver eyes that still call to me.

Acknowledgments

Thank you so much for reading Of Silver and Curses!

When Talon and Scythe rudely burst into my head last year, I knew I had to write their story. Unfortunately, my writing schedule tends to be... intense. I'm in the middle of two very long series and I typically release 3-4 books a year. So fitting in ANOTHER book seemed crazy.

Hi. It's me. I'm crazy.

So I went into my writing cave and didn't come out for almost nine months. Which is basically how long New England winter lasts.

Yes. I know that's not accurate. BUT THAT'S WHAT IT FEELS LIKE.

Sorry for yelling. I really hate winter.

Writing this book was more than a little daunting. I've written multi-pov before in my why choose romantasy series, Lunaria Realms, that I publish under the Alex Frost pen name. But dual-pov just has a different feel to it.

This was also my first time writing in first-person present tense. Which is why I need to take a moment and thank my amazing editing team, PollyAnné (Proofs by Polly) and Rachel (Rachel Tops Editing) for doing an amazing job and not driving to Massachusetts and smothering me with a pillow.

Thanks for not murdering me in my sleep.

I'm so proud of how this book turned out and I can't wait to tell more stories in this world. If you've read any of my other series, you know that I tend to have a lot of queer characters in my books.

But I've never had a nonbinary main character and that was something that I really wanted.

As a queer nonbinary person, I'm thirsty for that rep in books. So I figured I could contribute. The Lingering Fates series will always feature a nonbinary main character. Sometimes they'll be masc leaning like Talon. Sometimes femme. Sometimes androgynous or gender fluid.

There is no right or wrong way to be nonbinary.

Okay, one more quick shout out. This gorgeous cover was designed by Catrin from Subtle Touch Creations and not only is it gorgeous but she helped me during somewhat of a cover crisis when things feel through (at the last minute) with the original cover.

Thank you to everyone who made this book possible! It made my queer little heart so freaking happy.

If you enjoyed reading this book, it would be amazing if you could leave an honest review on Goodreads or whichever platform you prefer. Reviews are super important for authors and we really appreciate it when y'all take the time to leave one!

Need more fantasy romance in your life?

Lost Legacies

A fast-paced fantasy romance featuring a morally grey FMC with a slow burn romance, banter, and all the found family vibes. Perfect for elder millennials who grew up watching Buffy and Supernatural.

Learn more here - https://greymalkinpress.com/pages/maddoxgrey-lostlegacies

---

Lunaria Realms

If you love vampires, court intrigue, and love interests who don't mind sharing, dive into the first trilogy of the why choose romantasy series, Lunaria Realms!

Learn more here - https://greymalkinpress.com/pages/alexfrost-lunariarealms

Greymalkin Press Shop

Visit the author's shop - Greymalkin Press - to browse signed paperbacks, exclusive special editions, and bundle deals!

About the Author

Maddox Grey is a queer nonbinary elder millennial who still remembers vividly what it was like to be emotionally damaged by the season two finale of Buffy the Vampire Slayer.

They write morally grey characters who fall for equally unhinged morally grey love interests. And the banter flows as fast as the action in the stories they craft.

When they're not putting their characters through hell, Maddox is playing video games, reading smut, burying their nose in comic books, or hiding behind a pillow while they watch horror movies.

To get regular email updates about new releases and other announcements, be sure to sign up for the newsletter on maddox greyauthor.com

facebook.com/maddoxgrey.author

instagram.com/maddoxgrey.author

tiktok.com/@greymalkinpress